HE WHO IS A FRIEND

SADIK
BOOK 1

LOVE BELVIN

MKT Publishing, LLC

HE WHO IS A Friend

THE Sadik SERIES 1

CONTENTS

ISBN: *978-1-950014-01-9 (Paperback)*
ISBN: *978-1-950014-46-0 (eBook)*

MKT Publishing, LLC
First print edition 2018 in U.S.A.

Cover design by **Visual Luxe**

March

Sadik

"Oh, she's lovely!" The dark-haired woman glanced above her shoulder to her beaming husband. "Isn't she lovely, Matteo?" His smile deepened and he nodded, eyes low to the topic at hand. The woman's hand moved to Lia's belly. "Oh, my! You're small, but tight in there. When are you due?"

"This July." Lia smiled, elated.

The woman's chestnut eyes rose to mine. "Do we know what's in here?"

Lia's glossy blonde mane rolled back as she lifted her head to peer at me behind her. She couldn't hide her excitement as she turned back toward her parents' guests. "It's a secret for now. I want to do a reveal party. I'm sure Mamma will be inviting you."

The woman leaned in, the silk strands of her dark hair fanning over thin shoulders. "As in gender reveal party?" Lia nodded with enthusiasm. This was news to me. "Is that something—" Her eyes roved up to me towering over Lia. "—something they do in Sicilia?" Her expression was aghast.

Lia chuckled nervously. "No. That's just something that's been done here lately..."

The woman's face folded tightly. Her husband, Matteo, who I'd seen in a meeting or two with Salvatore over recent years, recognized her expression of displeasure. For a minute, his smile faded, but hers recovered with another, wider than before.

"It was nice catching up with you, Rose." Lia wrapped up the chat in passing. "Give my love to Nikki."

Rose nodded, lashes batting as she turned and sauntered into the crowd aside her husband. Lia turned to me, taking a deep breath as she rolled her eyes.

"Such a fucking bitch," she grated, thin lips gripping her teeth. "Racist cunt. And could he be a bigger dick?"

I shrugged with my brows, then caught the oncoming server approaching with a silver tray in the air.

"It's your father's birthday party. Play nice, Lia," I partially joked.

I didn't want to be here at all. This was an obligatory appearance in the name of my family.

"Mauve and room temperature green tea," the server called, lowering his tray to hand us the drinks.

Lia took a sip, then inhaled deeply. My eyes circled the large and celebratory ballroom of the banquet hall. A live band was arranged on the stage, playing beautifully. The lighting was mild and energy spirited as I downed half my brandy, taking it all in.

"Fuck..." A soft hand at my chest had me glancing down, so unaccustomed to such an intimate touch. "My cousin, Teresa, is on her way over," Lia whispered conspiratorially. "I'm going to make up an excuse to go to the bathroom. When I'm done there, I'll be ready to go. I want that pie Iban promised we'd stop for." I peered down on her long and wide nose as her lashes fanned her cheeks.

"Lia! There you are," a woman chirped. "I've been looking all over for you."

Lia's eyes rolled up to me, and a faux smile spread on her face as she turned around. "Teresa! Papá told me you were coming. And here you are... just as I need to hit the ladies' room." Lia began to move, lifting her gown to do so. "Be a dear and give me a minute, will you?"

And she was off. As I swallowed back the last bit of Mauve, I caught Teresa's eyes crawl over to me. They melted as she took me in from head to toe. After a soft snort, I raised my empty tumbler to an oncoming server. Once my glass was collected, I offered a nod and strolled off in search of the men's room. A text from my brother had me opting for a stall instead of a urinal. It was business as usual, but the nature of that topic was always private.

Iban: *Warehouse at eleven.*

Me: Copy. About the boat?

Stowing the cell in my jacket pocket, I handled my business. While assembling my pants, I heard a set of hushed voices.

"Salvatore wants everybody down at the seaport on Thursday."

"Why?"

I couldn't make out the voices right away, and it didn't help that they went suspiciously silent. A few footsteps sounded in search of intruders. I didn't move. The wooden doors reached to the floor, leaving total privacy in the stalls.

"Anybody in here?" A voice barked, now more familiar but still unidentifiable.

I didn't speak. My interest was now piqued.

After a few more seconds of silence, the shoes clacked away.

"I think he's got a plan," was delivered in more of a secretive murmur.

"About the hit the other week?" Silence. "Shiiiit," the same voice continued. I was now believing it to be Luigi, a worker from old man Salvatore Rizzo's crew.

"He's not letting that shit go." That was definitely Marco, Lia's brother and Salvatore's son.

"How did he miss that?" Luigi asked. "He was working that night. Right?"

There was a pause for the answer. "He missed it..." Marco hesitated. "You swear on your lives to keeping this shit between us?" He tried his best to whisper.

"Yeah."

"Yeah, man!" Luigi whispered.

"He was in the back of the lot...way back there, between two of the three big ass Hanjin containers. He has a small trailer he uses for..." Marco coughed, revealing the missing details. "He was entertaining that night, and no one was watching the cameras in the front office when the hit happened."

"It could be any fucking body," Luigi argued. "The Russian fuck, Lopez—shit, somebody from out of town. These are the ports; prime real estate!"

"He's right," was one I couldn't quite grasp...yet. "We're doing business with every fucking body now. Clean...even dirty, like that fucking Haitian, Pierro."

"I don't think it was him," Marco murmured lowly as though his thoughts were traveling.

"But we don't fucking know. Shit! It's like a goddamn backyard barbecue now with Salvatore's new way of doing business."

"What the fuck are you saying, Matteo?" Marco's tone was now agitated.

Matteo...

The smiling, nodding fuck with the racist wife whom Lia had just talked to minutes ago.

"I'm saying, I just spent two hundred-forty seconds in the Ellis kid's face, indirectly talking about how he knocked up sweet Lia. The son of the same Ellis that Salvatore has been in business with like we're all on the fucking rainbow!" He groaned.

A smile spread on my face as I faced the toilet, wondering what my piss would look like draining from his face.

"Shit, Matteo." Marco laughed. "You and my father are racist fucks. One thing this new generation like me and Sadik, out there, knows is in business, there's only one color: green. As long as we understand that and respect each other, we're good."

"Bullshit! No, I am not. My kids have friends from decent families, but what about when they taint our good Sicilian bloodline like he did with our precious little Lia out there?" Matteo wasn't backing down.

"Ahhhh..." Marco dismissed the argument with a sigh. "Like my father says, 'if Lia likes to fuck niggers and is stupid enough to get

8

pregnant by one, let it be one from a solid standing family. That's what the Ellises are. And if she's gonna do it with any of the Ellis boys, better it be that educated nigger than the crazy one!"

A shower of laughter boomed through the room, raining over my stall even. Then it passed in the distance, telling me they were leaving. I gave it two seconds to really know before I stepped out of the stall. Slowly, I went about washing my hands, observing myself in the mirror. As fine, rich, and superiorly astute to those remedial Sicilians as I was, I was still a nigger.

Chuckling, I grabbed a paper towel and dried my hands. My phone vibrated against my chest in my inner jacket pocket.

Iban: We'll cover it at the meet tonite. Hows it going?

I chuckled.

Don't you wanna know...

Me: Easy. Still being a nigger.

My mirth followed me outside, where the party was still flowing. Lia wasn't too far off the hallway when I spotted her waiting on me.

"Ready to blow this bullshit ass gig?"

Biting her lip, she nodded with a giggle. I took her at the small of her back, and we began toward the doors.

"Lia! Sadik!" boomed from my left as we weaved through bodies. It was Salvatore Rizzo. He looked stately in a black tuxedo and gloss oxfords. "I'm glad to catch you before you kids skid out of here." He greeted me with a firm handshake. "Lia said she was tired and you two are leaving. Thanks for helping an old man bring in sixty in a grand old way, huhn!" He grabbed me into a hug, one I wasn't too keen of.

I was sure to keep it brief.

Pulling back quickly with a cool smile, I offered, "Grazie per l'invito. Mi dispiace mio padre non ha potuto partecipare. Molti ritorni, Salvatore."

"Ah!" He beamed. "You're teaching him, Siculo!" He slapped my shoulder boisterously.

After my eyes trailed his grasp, they swept over to his daughter, whom I threatened through my eyes not to lie. I could participate in the shits, but to a fucking degree.

9

"Papá, you know Sadik is a Blakewood man." Lia snickered, but with tact. "His teachings are above my head."

You better fucking believe it...

"Well, I'm sure mia principessa has taught him lots about our culture." Salvatore kissed her temple dotingly as she gushed. He turned to me. "Grazie, Sadik. Give your father my best."

I offered a nod as I patted my chest as a gesture of gratitude. Then I swung my arm out, prompting his daughter. Lia moved into me, backing up to my palm. She smiled at her father before we turned away to leave.

I could feel Salvatore's derisive gaze on my back as I led his daughter away.

With concentrated rapt focus at the bottom of the cheesecake sitting on top of the cooling rack, I poured warm ganache with measured movements. From my peripheral, I could see two figures arriving at my worktable. I couldn't tend to them just yet. If the presentation was going to be flawless, I had to stay here and observe my technique.

When done, I spun the tray carefully to be sure the casing was smooth and blemish-free. Across from me was an imposing stature, perched on a barstool, observing my work, too; my boss, Nicky. My chest swelled with pride as my lip twitched, fighting a boastful smirk. Then I turned and found Pedro and Maria standing just behind me quietly, but with impatience, holding small metal bowls.

I started with Maria first, taking the bowl. My finger dipped inside the burnt-orangey mush, and I dabbed my tongue with it. A hum pushed from my nostrils as my eyes danced against the ceiling.

"No nutmeg."

"No, Bee-lon!" she argued passionately. "I put the nutmeg."

I shook my head. "You OD'd on cinnamon. Remember, there are dos brown spices."

Maria's face fell, likely realizing the error in her sweet potato pie batter. She took her bowl and backed away on a bow.

"You'll get it, Maria. Just try again." I tossed my chin to Pedro. "Let's see what you're working with."

He approached me with his bowl. I dipped a fresh index finger and tasted it. This mixture was better, but not as I instructed them for the past two days when teaching the new bakers how to make my sweet potato pie recipe. It was actually my mother's, one of many that got me the job at this diner years ago as an assistant baker to one of the two owners.

"Good, but you forgot the pinch of salt."

Pedro slapped his forehead, telling me I was right. I handed him back the bowl, snickering with him. Then my attention went to my boss.

"What do you think?" I used my forehead to point to the chocolate-covered cheesecake.

Nicky snorted, face its usual expressionless state as he gazed my way. He was rather large and round. His face and body were heavily wrinkled, like a Neapolitan Mastiff.

I nodded with hiked brows. "I nailed it, and you know it." My attention went back to my gorgeous creation. "I think last time, it was just as you said; I didn't chop the chocolate up small enough. I was impatient." I shrugged, then peered over to him again.

"When you get married?"

I froze, quickly sifting through his thick Italian accent.

11

A smile bloomed on my face. "I need a man first—or woman."

He grunted, motionless on the stool. A displeased sound of his tongue suctioning the roof of his mouth had me chuckling hard.

"No. Man only. You need to get married. A pretty girl like you…smart, can cook, still a budding rose."

"Awwwww…" I smiled charmingly, shoulders lifting. "Thanks, Nicky, but it takes two people to get married and so far, I'm the only subject in the equation."

"What you do after the graduation?"

"It's a month from now. Hard to say."

"You leaving me?" His demeanor was as it always was; droopy and without expression.

His Santa Claus belly moved more than the muscles in his face did.

My arms stretched into the air before dropping to my hips on a slap. "Gotta have somebody to go with before I leave you, Nicky."

"You get another job?"

"Not yet." He grunted again, belly vibrating in response. "I'm sure something'll come through."

"What about the other job?"

"My teacher's assistant gig?" I had the coveted role at my school for two consecutive years. "It expires when I get my degree."

"Then you need more money," he guessed.

"You going to pay more?" He snorted, rolling his eyes. Nicky knew I was showing sass. Michelle's Diner, named after the brothers' deceased mother, had been generous to me over the years. My job here came with its share of annoying elements, but I couldn't say they didn't compensate me better than anyone else here who wasn't a relative of theirs or Italian like them. "Nicky," I sang, wanting him to drop it. "I'll be fine."

I knew what he wanted. The man who hardly spoke past giving me instructions, I'd now been giving two new and cheap hires like Pedro and Maria, didn't want me to quit the diner when I graduated in less than two months. He also didn't want me to go broke by working here. It was a bag of contradictions with this guy.

12

Gino, Nicky's nephew, came bustling through the swinging doors into the kitchen. "Bilan, they need you up front for a few minutes!"

"Ugh!" I groaned, closing my eyes. "I have to get out of here. I'm already running late."

"You should hurry." That was Nicky's humor...no smile attached, though.

I rolled my eyes and pushed from the table, shooting Nicky a wry smirk. Quickly, I washed my hands and grabbed my assigned apron by the double swinging doors. Inside the front kangaroo pocket were a pencil and pad for orders.

Here at Michelle's Diner, I was a baker, cooking up a specific menu of items for customers of a particular culture—skin hue, too. Only on a few occasions was I called up front. To act as a waitress when unruly Blacks were patronizing the place, or when there was a severe shortage of help on a shift. Each time I was called to the floor, it was met with anxiety because they used little me as a bulletproof vest from time to time.

"Down at the end of the counter," the girl at the register informed me in a rush as I took off onto the floor.

I backed up, rerouting my steps. My eyes shot to my left, and all the way at the end of the counter was a familiar face, causing me to push a puff of relief from my lungs.

"He's so fucking hot, B," Marta, a Polish waitress holding a tray of drinks, muttered as I passed by her.

I rolled my eyes, fighting a serious beam. Then the usual wistful anxiousness kicked in as I neared him.

"Hey, there," I greeted with a soft smile, then pulled out my pencil and pad.

"Hey, Bilan," his voice was soft, kind...deceptive, considering his reputation.

But everything about Damien's appearance contrasted with who he was known to be in the streets of Paterson. His warm umber skin tone dazzled with his thick, wavy jet black hair that was as dense as a carpet, and as sheen as the moon. Damien's hairline and cut brought Denzel Washington to mind. He swung his arm out from his lap to place his elbow on the countertop as he peered into my eyes with unknown intent.

"Haven't seen you in what…two weeks?" I could hardly meet his eyes.

I never knew how to take Damien. He was inarguably handsome and charming, quiet spoken, and dressed to the nines. But he was also known to be dangerous and because of that fact, I couldn't decide which persona to rest safely in.

"I've been out of town, visiting family." His cheeks lifted warmly, eyes brightened with appreciation. "You been good, though. Right? I haven't heard about my guys needing to run up in here."

I nodded, hands lifting into position. "What can I get for you tonight?"

"You got any more of that pecan pie back there? I know it be racing outta here."

No need to write that down…

I dropped the pad and pencil into my pocket and took off for the display counter's fridge where they were usually stored. There were two slices left. I slipped on gloves and began to box and bag one. By the time I made it back to the counter, Damien had a ten-dollar bill in front of him.

"How's ya brother?"

"Oh…" I thought for a second. "He's good. I spoke with him a couple of days ago. He's counting down the days, you know?"

"Yeah. He'll be a'ight."

I grabbed the ten. "I'll get you change."

Damien was pushing up from his stool. "You know I'm good. Enjoy your night, beautiful."

"Thanks, Damien," I murmured, giving him the obligatory smile when I wanted to do much more.

I wanted to ask a gazillion questions about why he came in here the way he did and never ordered food, just desserts. I'd been dying to know why he acted as a superhero for me at the diner and in the neighborhood. Was he only "Clark Kent" when around me? Or did he make another lucky girl feel as special as I did each time he came in here?

But that was Damien. Even the owners knew what he did for me which, in turn, helped them. That was why whenever he came through those doors, all the staff would find me to wait on him. It was weird, but was my life over the past six years.

"One of these days, you'll grow the cojones to tell him he's good looking. I bet then, he'll sweep you off your feet." Carina, my other boss' wife, rolled her eyes as she hissed.

When I turned to face her, all I caught was her jaw chomping on gum, as she always did. Carina was tough, but sweet. She didn't take crap off any of the staff, customers, or owners and was respected for that.

I gained on her near the register.

"Why do you always say that?"

Carina's head whipped to face me so fast, her blonde tresses cascaded in the air. "Because it's true. Life ain't about a fairy tale, Bilan." Her Italian accent was faint. "In the real world, not every man has it in him to kick shit off. You probably think cheating is a reason to divorce." She shook her head.

I didn't want to go there. That could have opened a can of worms I didn't want to eat. It was known around the diner how Vincent, her husband, flirted heavily with the young girls on staff. He'd even slept with one or six over the years. That type of behavior wasn't what I'd ever agree to accept.

"Do me a favor," she proposed over her shoulder while counting cash. "Take this one for me so I can finish this."

I glanced around and found all the girls who worked the floor and counter busy with customers. Instead of rolling my eyes, I held my breath as I turned to the incoming customer. My posture stiffened, muscles all over went rigid. The air holding in my lungs jostled through my nostrils, some sputtering through my lips. I blinked a few times and tried to manage the choking happening from my attempt to swallow and breathe at the same time.

His distinctive golden eyes swept the long counter, clearly in search of something. Dessert. It had to be something in the display counter fridge. The black tuxedo he wore had to be cut with specificity of each inch of his frame. The skin of his russet head glistened under the ceiling lights. He stood with one hand in his pants pocket, revealing the details of the crisp white dress shirt beneath the jacket. The man wasn't particularly tall, but his presence was vast and commanding, introducing him without words.

He began his stride toward the counter, and what a graceful one it was. His confidence was clear to me already. I watched fixedly when his regard swung up and landed on me. There was a slight stumble in his smooth gait. His expression was flat, but eyes alive when they fastened onto me. His skin was roasted almond—you know…the outside of the nut. No. Tan—maybe the color of a paper bag. I couldn't decide. He was definitely light-skinned, but with rich olive undertone.

He arrived at the counter, and I had to tell myself to snap out of it. I needed to get out of here and not melt in my shoes at the sight of a stranger. Possibly a lost stranger. An incredibly, impossibly good-looking lost stranger.

"Ha—" My pitch was too high. I cleared my throat and attempted again, so caught up in trying to count the colors in his irises when I breathed. "How can I help you?"

Under those dense, unruly brows, I finally counted four: a dark brown perimeter enclosing a hue of green, then yellow and an impossible orange before a speck of black at the mecca of the iris. I'd never seen such exoticism in my life. Tangerine hair sprouted from his face, trimmed into a meticulous five o'clock shadow. Friggin' orange facial hair—that wasn't dyed. That tangerine against russet skin made his beauty otherworldly.

When his eyes settled on me at a closer proximity, I watched his full lips part as his tongue swiped the inner lining of his bottom lip, back and forth. He wasn't hurried with his response. He just…gaped at me.

Seconds felt like extended minutes, and I quickly grew self-conscious. Around me, I could feel bodies briskly move, but couldn't shift my eyes away from him.

"I'm looking for sweet potato pie." His words fell effortlessly and with self-possessed pacing.

Before I could find the words to reply, quick clacking steps our way stole my attention. My regard shifted to a tiny woman wearing a red, *flowing ball gown as she ambled to his side. Her creamy bountiful breasts spilling over the bustier. Her sky-blue eyes peered over to him timidly, then shot over to me. She didn't speak, and he didn't regard her. His eyes were stapled to me, lips still ajar, tongue still brushing the inside of his bottom lip.*

Oh…

I got it. Both dressed like extras for "Gone with the Wind." They were together; making it abundantly clear was her hand rubbing her bulged belly. She was pregnant. The woman was White. Swathed in a gorgeous ball gown. And very pregnant.

That jolted my brain into the here and now.

I cleared my throat. "Sweet potato." I scribbled onto my order tab. "Will that be all?" My eyes brushed back up to him.

I caught her hand going to his arm… The one with the hand in his pants pocket. "And banana pudding." Her soprano was soft, timid.

The guy's sights never left me. "And your banana pudding." Again, his words were unhurried.

Unlike my initial reaction to her presence, he was unaffected. His eyes narrowed and he chewed on the inside of his mouth before he uttered, "Sweet potato pie and banana pudding for the lady."

With an internal flutter, I scribbled and nodded before taking off. I pushed the order slip into the hand of the first waiter I passed.

"Fill this, please," I grumbled, not stopping on my way back into the kitchen.

I was annoyed. Why? I didn't know. Since when did seeing an incredibly good-looking guy get to me? Why did seeing him with his…wife make me react that way?

Quickly, Pedro and Maria were at my feet with new mixture samples to taste. I really needed to go, but couldn't be rude to them. After tasting them and giving feedback, I grabbed my things.

"Nicky," I shouted over to the other side of the kitchen. "I'm out. Be back in a few hours to get started on my cakes for tomorrow!"

I was out the back door, knowing a response or acknowledgement wouldn't come.

It was close to eight by the time I walked into the church. I stopped in the vestibule I imagined was just outside of the auditorium. I could hear a man speaking in there. It was confirmed when a woman with an all-white nurse's uniform strolled out of one of the auditorium's doors. That's when I caught a glimpse of the vast audience inside as I pulled my phone from my bag.

Me: I'm here.

I waited, looking into the packed auditorium now that the door had been left ajar. I hadn't been near this place in years. It was one of the biggest churches in Paterson, one that invited celebrities into the city; that was the impression I got from an old friend who was a member. I hadn't heard from her in years, which made my invitation from a new friend ironic.

Tasche: *Bitch you all late and shit I'm coming back for you*

I knew she was angry. My arrival time was crazy, later than the six-thirty start time she gave me. This wasn't Tasche's church, and she wasn't exactly happy to be here. Tasche was from Harlem. She moved to Paterson two years ago to work at a strip club out here. I met her at the diner after her shift one morning. She came in complaining about how the city was mini-Puerto Rico. She said they would never let Hispanics take over Harlem the way Patersonians clearly had with their city. I laughed my ass off because I was sure Vinny, the second owner of the diner who was listening in, may have felt that way about Blacks coming into Paterson when Italians pretty much ran it.

Almost done with my baking in the back, I waited on her that morning and we caught conversation, going from one topic to the next. Since then, almost every morning Tasche worked, she stopped in to eat before going home to crash. She'd turned into a friend, something I hadn't always been open to. But the girl had one of those personalities that was as though you never met her for a first time. If she was comfortable around you, she'd talk your head off. If she didn't pick up the best vibes from you, she'd close up.

"I straight up thought you flaked on me, yo?" The fire in her tone as I turned to find her approaching me had my head swinging back and eyes blinking. "Don't look at me like that," Tasche tried to whisper. "I fuckin' begged you to come with me for over a week now."

"I know, T. I swear." I tried pleading with her despite her unusual nasty agitation. "I told you I had to train two people in the kitchen this afternoon and get my usual orders done. I'm not even finished. I have to go back in tonight."

Tasche rolled her eyes, and I was able to catch her ensemble. She wore...flat shoes. They were black leather ballerina shoes, paired with a fitted green dress stopping above her knees and a yellow, waist-length cardigan sweater. It didn't cover her bountiful rump, but the look was hella modest for my girl.

"You look...wholesome." I coughed into my hand, ignoring her flash of ugliness.

Tasche's eyes rolled down to her feet before closing tightly. "It's too tight, I know."

My eyes ballooned. "Nooooo!" I breathed under the sounds of the speaker inside preaching. The dress was rather short, but nothing illicit, I thought. "You look fine, T," I whispered.

"Nah." She shook her head. "I already know. Look at my ass, yo." As she turned a three-sixty angle, I flinched. Tasche's panty line was not only screaming through the cotton, but the cotton itself hugged her like shiny polyvinyl. When she heard me squeak, Tasche turned to face me.

"See!"

"It's okay." I searched through the tote bag on my shoulder and pulled out a denim jacket. "Here. Wrap this around your waist. It'll cover your rump."

Tasche quickly pulled the arms of the jacket around her tiny waist, tying it before reaching back to be sure it covered her voluptuousness.

"See. That worked out."

"Easy for you to say," she hissed, eyes sweeping my clothes. "You know how to dress for shit like this."

She cussed again. "We're in church, Tasche," I whispered even lower.

"I know! That's what the fuck I'm saying, yo!"

And again…

My eyes circled the small foyer. Not many had passed through here, I'd guessed because the program had begun.

"What I mean is…" I decided to go a different route. "I got dressed for a meeting on campus this morning. Besides, this isn't a regular place for you or me. No one should judge you because of that."

"It ain't about judgment, yo. It's my home girl from Harlem, man. Her and her old man is doing this here tonight. That's him speaking in there now." She pointed toward the door she came out of. "He a big time preacher, travel around the globe…the nigga is a big damn deal in their network. This dude got mad school degrees—one from Oxford, wherever the fuck that joint is overseas—done traveled to places a bitch can't name, speak a bunch of different languages and is so damn smart, it makes him weird as fuck!" she whispered as though shouting in my face. "And you know the crazy part of all that shit?" Her dark, drawn-on brows lifted. "The fact that he scooped up my girl from Harlem World."

With a wrinkled forehead, I shrugged. "So what? That's great."

"Nah, it ain't, 'cause it means if he checking for her regular ass—nah, Lex-Dawg something kind of special, but she got that fuckin' Harlem Pride—it means he can judge me."

"And if he does, that's his problem as a minister…reverend or whatever. Not yours. And why are you here if you think he's like that?"

20

"I 'on't know if he like that, like that. Ezra always been a cool cat with me, and he a real one. A real stiff nigga. Dude don't drink, smoke, cuss, and I ain't get word 'bout him cheating on her, and they been married for like three years, or some shit." There she went again with her language. I was not religious in the least, but my mother taught me to respect faiths. And I was quite sure cursing was sacrilegious around here. "She the one who invited me here."

"Okay. So, you're here to support her! Never mind him."

"It's weird, is all I'm saying."

"I don't get it."

"When I told her I was quitting my old spot, Rusty's, and moving to Jersey, she got crazy souped, and shit. Then when I hit her with the fact I was coming out this way to dance at a new club, I could tell she was disappointed."

"Real friends don't judge," I protested firmly.

"Lex never judge, but that don't mean she ain't grow the hell up and change for the better. We used to work at the same spot. She was a bar girl and I danced. She left for...whatever reasons and kept improving her situation. She went back to school, like you doing, and got her degrees. And then turned around and married this rich ass preacher dude. I 'on't see shit they got in common, but the nigga is crazy about my dun, yo!"

I shook my head again. "Okay. So what's the problem, Tasche?"

"When she said they was coming around the way and invited me, I wanted to show some love." Her eyes swept around as she adjusted the jacket at her waist. "I told her I was bringing a new friend, somebody in school and shit..."

That's when I finally understood. My being here, by her side, was a big part of Tasche's plan tonight.

I took a deep breath. "You want to show her you're evolving, too." Her eyes fell, confirming my theory. I turned to be shoulder to shoulder with her, then wrapped my arm around hers. "Let's go support your friend. My hooya—"

"Your what?" Her face strained, confused.

I cracked a smile. "My mom used to say your heart speaks a language louder than your tongue. It's sweet you want to support

21

your friend and do it her way." I urged her to the door of the auditorium, hoping her friend appreciated it, too. "Let's show her that love by not missing all of the show."

Tasche didn't speak, but she did let me guide her into the sanctuary, where I was struck with anxiety the moment we crossed into it. It was quiet inside, other than the raspy speaker with most eyes fixed on him. Walking toward the row where Tasche was seated, I noticed the man on stage running rosary beads through his fingers as he calmly paced the stage.

"But against principalities, against powers, against the rulers of the darkness of this world—when you think it's your job, it's not. When you think it's your husband, it usually is not. When you think it's your wayward child, tabernacle, it likely is not. It is your assigned spiritual warfare. It is your destiny breaking through." He stopped pacing as he gazed intently into the crowd, which was now stirring with claps, outbursts, and jumping to their feet. "It is that battle you take on with one or more of those gifts He left behind before ascending to heaven to complete the will of the Father."

He gave a moment for the crowd to get out their hoots and hollers. More were standing at this point, tossing their fists into the air, spiritedly shouting.

"Against spiritual wickedness in high places," he murmured contemplatively before returning to his normal octave. "And in the seventeenth verse of First Thessalonians, chapter five, the Bible tells us to pray without ceasing. Tabernacle, if you can't see or understand your opponent, you have to stay connected to your covering. Instead of you fighting in the flesh—fighting on your job, threatening divorce to your spouse, or losing hope for the child He entrusted to your care—you need to apply the same fervor of your fear and frustration to supplication."

The bearded preacher traveled down one step of the podium, engaging the crowd. As he continued rousing them, a tall woman with dark skin and thick, long, and coarse hair bouncing in the air behind her traveled to the lectern on a subtle, but feminine strut. She was dressed in an A-line cut, black denim dress with a wide leather belt tied at her narrowed waist. Her three/fourth quarters sleeves were

22

rolled up on her arms with what I knew to be silver Cartier LOVE bracelets on each. The soles of her high-heeled booties matched her red belt. Quietly, she collected what I assumed to be the preacher's things with a bowed head, then made a beeline to leave the stage.

"You must combat your unseen enemy by encasing yourself in His promises, putting that breastplate of righteousness in place, taking up the shield of faith, and taking the helmet of salvation and the sword of the Spirit!" he shouted, but not before nearly the entire room was on its feet, slapping palms and screaming their approval.

My neck whipped over to Tasche to find she'd done the same, our expressionless faces communicating the same thing to each other. The organ sounded, then drums. Then we heard what I could only describe as an Indian war cry. A running woman sped down the main aisle. The next thing snatching our attention was a man jumping to his feet and stomping the floor rhythmically.

After a few minutes more, it was clear to me he was done with his speech, but the people weren't. They were all over, screaming and dancing. It was alarming to see this behavior I'd heard joked about regarding church people, but never seen live and in color. It was somewhat frightening to experience.

I'd never been to a church service. My family was of Islamic faith, though my father hadn't been the best steward of it due to his addiction. My mother's practice of it had been mild and almost neglectful as she tried keeping up with my father. I had faint memories of being in a mosque as a child, but I was certain there was no display of emotion of this kind there. These people were going crazy in here. The music matched their zest, if not incited it.

I glanced to my right at Tasche again, where she mouthed, "See. I told you!"

So this was her friend's husband. I couldn't lie; he was a particularly handsome man. The raspy voice and composed demeanor in an animated and lively environment didn't hurt either. Even now, I was able to see him in between two dancing bodies and his intense gazing out into the room, his eyes were thin to the point of touching lashes, his mouth between the wiry hairs of his face moving rapidly as though he were speaking Spanish or something.

23

A short guy took the mic and began singing a slow song, somehow not breaking the energy of the room. In between belting out impressive notes, he encouraged everyone to praise God as if He was in the room with us in that moment. The minister began pointing people out in the audience and inviting them up to the stage. I didn't understand why. From what I could see, he spoke to them, clearly using words that struck them emotionally because most cried, some shouted in praise, and two actually passed out. I shook my head, unable to believe people were fainting when this man laid hands on them. One guy was bigger in build than the preacher!

As fascinating as this all was, it came to an end at some point. Another man, this one wearing a priest collar, took over the podium and began giving final words. He thanked the preacher, whose name apparently was Pastor Carmichael, for his service here tonight. He also thanked his minister of music. As this new guy spoke, I felt my eyes instinctively shift to the right of him, my gaze slamming into the preacher. His regard was blank but he was definitely staring, and so hard I began to feel uneasy. I shifted in my seat, clearing my throat before going back to the reverend on the mic.

Two minutes later, the same thing happened. My gaze found the preacher man gaping at me. He swiped down his full beard this time as he gawked. That's when panic struck in my chest. Was he checking me out?

Not when his wife is here, where he's supposed to be sharing the word of God!

That thought annoyed me to the point that I decided not to look his way again, no matter the pull into that direction. If that didn't work, Tasche tapping and motioning for me to go did. I turned to my left where the aisle was and saw a different woman in an all-white nurse's uniform wave us on. Once out into the aisle, I let Tasche get in front of me because I had no idea where we were going. I followed the pair to a side door off the stage and down a hall. We traveled to a room where the dark-skinned woman with a wild mane I'd seen in the auditorium was with a toddler, feeding her crackers.

"Hey, Tasch!" Her smile was luminous, and her eyes danced at the sight of Tasche.

24

"Whaddup, Lex Dawg." Tasche was lower in volume, but just as familiar. She crossed the room for the little girl at the table, chomping away, watching the screen above on the wall of the auditorium we'd just left. "Hey, Lisa-Mare! I miss you, lil' buggy," she singsonged.

The little girl giggled, turning toward Tasche.

"Hi." Her voice tore my attention from witnessing the softest side of Tasche I'd ever seen. The woman neared me with her hand extended. "I'm Lex. You're Tasche's friend?"

"Oh, hey!" I took her hand. "Yes." I smiled to match hers. "My name is Bilan."

"Yeah. This my baker-student friend I told you about, Lex. She came through tonight."

"I appreciate that." I caught the New York accent in Lex's voice.

"That was your husband. Right?" I asked.

"Yeah. That was my Ezra. I hope he didn't go too hard for you."

Too hard, as in strange? Pretty much...

"Oh, here he go," Tasche murmured, and both ladies' attention went behind me.

Lex moved in the same direction. By the time I turned, the bearded pastor was in her arms and I could hear her mumble something in his ear. His eyes were closed as he listened.

"Amen," he rasped. "Thank you, beloved."

When his eyes flashed open directly on me, my heart plummeted to the floor. Lex released him, backing away as his gaze was on me. My neck whipped over to Tasche, who was now holding the little girl's hand next to her.

"Hey, Ez. You did good out there, as usual," Tasche complimented. "I keep telling you, you gone have to teach me a few of them fancy words." Her chuckle was nervously delivered.

The guy wouldn't stop staring at me! Thank goodness his wife noticed. But Lex didn't appear alarmed, as I would have thought.

"Carmichael, this is Bilan, Tasche's friend over here." Lex made the introduction.

For a while, he didn't speak; only his eyes bore into me. My skin began to feel like it was crawling, forcing me to look away.

"I hate to be outré with my presentation to you, and I assure you it isn't indecent." That got my attention, returning my gaze to him. I could see Tasche and his wife's regards were on him, too. "It's just, strangely enough, while in the sanctuary, the Holy Spirit began to speak to me concerning you. Do you have siblings—a brother, perhaps?"

My eyes whipped to Tasche, Lex, then back to him before I bit my lip nervously and nodded.

"Your parents deceased?" I nodded again, mouth secreting excessively. That's when Pastor Carmichael nodded, too, his eyes sweeping the floor. "As my regard was on you, my attention was on the story of Joseph. Are you familiar with that biblical account?" I shook my head, insecure in the moment.

Ezra's eyes narrowed and he switched weight on his hips as his gaze deepened. "Where are you from?"

"Here—"

"No." The speed of his retort was record-breaking. "Your bloodline…heritage. Where are you from?"

I sucked in my lips again, eyes falling. "Somalia. My parents were brought over as young babies—one still in the womb."

Again, he nodded as though I'd confirmed something. "Other relatives around?"

"Kinda. Not really."

"Yes. Lorn."

"I wouldn't say all that." I hated the defense in my voice.

"You wouldn't say you're afraid each day, at a specific part of it either. You also wouldn't share your deepest yearning with those closest to you," he rasped, thick curly beard lifting in the air as he challenged me.

My eyes shot over to Tasche again, who looked just as spooked as I felt.

"I'm not afraid of anything. I've been on my own for so long now, I know how to protect and look out for myself." If that didn't come out just as weak and uncompelling as the worst acting attempt, I wouldn't be ready to cry. "I don't know what you think you know about me, but I'm just fine."

Scoffed. He actually pushed the air from his nostrils that screamed, "Bullshit!" But why?

"You're not," he rasped. "But you will be. You do, however, have a turbulent voyage ahead of you, similar to Joseph. You see, people focus on the betrayal, then the ultimate overdog nature of his story, when I'm always reminded of the journey of his faith. Yes, Joseph was deceived by his siblings, and sold into slavery. He was lied on by his boss' wife, accused of attacking her with sexual intent. But Genesis, chapter thirty-nine, verse two tells us, 'The Lord was with Joseph.' Joseph was then imprisoned for, some say, thirteen years.

"It was those years of despair, confusion, and imprisonment that impress me the most about Joseph. He was alone and in captivity. And once again, in verse twenty-one, we're reminded, 'But the Lord was with Joseph.'" His smile was handsome, unexpected, and alarming. "We learn in chapter forty-eight how Joseph may have appeared to have been removed from his birthright, but his birthright remained in him each moment of what turned out to be twenty years of separation from his family. In the end, God not only released him from that prison, but He made him ruler of Egypt under the pharaoh of the time: the second most powerful man of Egypt," he made clear.

"Joseph became what's called a vizier and decided..." He considered his thoughts for a few moments. "What you millennials refer to as 'who got to eat, and eat well.' He went from a slave to a prisoner to a high-ranking official, ruling over the brothers who betrayed him."

My eyes blinked and I shook my head. "I don't get what you're saying. Why are you telling me all of this?"

His face lifted again, and in a disarming and cheeky grin. "The Holy Spirit revealed to me a similar path you're about to take. You've been in a valley and have more time in it, but the amazing thing about God is no matter your Islamic roots, He covers you. Your upbringing, culture, current lack of knowledge of Him is inconsequential to His covering and will for your life. He still wants to be in a relationship with you."

"Why?" Another defensive clap of my lungs.

Why would a stranger want to be in relationship with me? How would anybody's god know me?

"Pastor?" a woman stepping into the room called out. Pastor Carmichael peered over his shoulder at her. "Bishop Peterson wants to take pictures with you and your daughters." He nodded in answer before turning back to me.

After a long and decided period of quiet, Pastor Carmichael spoke again.

"In the vision, some of your nights were long. You witnessed things only seen in cinema or between the pages of a novel and/or pamphlet. You were thrust into a world never known to you. You will feel pain, joy, betrayal, bliss, deeper loneliness, and contentment like no other period in your life. There will come a time where you will flee—run in fear." That made absolutely no sense to me. "But the Lord will be with you." My heart thundered in my chest at the grave dipping of his voice. "The Stranger you've never known knows each strand of hair on your body, has covered you since your conception, and will continue to during this next phase of your life."

"What phase?"

"The one you would do better in if you remembered He's protecting you every step of the way." His gaze shifted behind me. "Ms. Remah, can I have her?" I didn't know there was not just another woman in the room—an older one—but a baby, too. "Now, I need to go, but before I do, would you mind if my wife and I prayed for you? I'd like to speak protection over you before we part ways."

I sucked in a breath, eyes sweeping below while my brain whirred with confusion. I shrugged, not knowing what he was asking or what my response should have been. Before I knew it, Lex was in front of me with her soft hands clasped over mine. Her tall and thick husband stood behind her with his hands on her shoulders as he rasped words of praise to his god. Then, I realized he moved on to commands for my health, safety, journey, birthright, purpose, and family.

"I declare right now, Satan, you may tempt, but cannot destroy. You may come near, but cannot touch. You may plot, but you will not conquer. In case you did not know, this soul belongs to The God Who Sees. El Roi has already seen into her future, has already lain the trap

28

of her faith…" As he spoke powerfully about events unknown to me, in between uttering words of another language, Lex mumbled words I could not make out.

His pitch rose and fell depending on his words, and Lex's right hand slipped from my left and pressed into my chest, over my heart. It then pushed into my belly, then swiped over my forehead as she muttered words I couldn't hear coherently.

When Pastor Carmichael's theatrical prayer came to a close, Lex's long arms immediately encased me, pulling me into her warm bosom. When my eyes opened, I could see Pastor Carmichael's frame brushing past us as he held a baby in his one arm and the tiny hand of the toddler in the other hand. The older woman followed them with a car seat in one hand and a mountain of their family's coats in her other arm.

"Damn! That nigga stay on 'I' for intense as fuck," Tasche breathed.

"Are you okay?" Lex asked as gentle as her New York accent would allow.

My mind was utterly blown. I had so many questions. My brain wanted to believe he was insane or fanatical with religion, but standing here with these two women, who hadn't been shouting those accusations, caused my disinclination on that call. And the way he'd just left… It was as though he hadn't just dropped a bomb in my already stressful world before skipping out with his children for a photoshoot. For a while, I couldn't breathe; forget speaking.

"This…vision," I hesitated. "Does he have more details?"

There was a decided pause before Lex spoke. "He usually knows more than he reveals. He only shares what he's told to part with."

Panic struck my chest. "What does he know?"

Her head shook softly as she peered deeply into my eyes with what looked like concern. "I don't know. I may never know until you do and decide to share it with me. My husband is rigid about his gift. But in the event you need me…" She went into her pocket and pulled out a business card. "Here's all of my information. We have a safe house where women in need can come and…disappear."

I sucked in a wop of air and my eyes ballooned. "Disappear to where?"

"From the sight of trouble. I can't give more details than that, but I can say since we've opened, no one has been located until they're out of hiding. Call and give them your name. We'll take it from there."

"Beloved," a deep rasp sounded from behind me. "The call has been placed to DiFillippo's. Time is of the essence at this point."

I turned to find Pastor Carmichael waiting with pinched brows, holding their baby. He was ready to go.

My head swung back to Lex "I—"

"I have to go." She cupped my hand and squeezed. "Call anytime you need," she whispered, taking off.

Lex quickly hugged Tasche and exchanged a few words of mumble before gaiting off to her waiting husband. Tasche then turned to me, standing nearly as stiff as I was with shifting eyes.

"C'mon, baker girl." She took me at the arm. "Let's get you back to work."

Hard yelps of a grown ass man met me the moment I sauntered toward one of the back rooms of the warehouse. It was no surprise they were in this particular room. The space was small, and easy for the men to clean after slaughter.

Jim, one of our guys, opened the door when I approached. I nodded as I crossed the threshold, taking in the room.

"He's finally here," my father announced, sarcasm lined in his voice. "We thought you had better things to do."

I approached him first for a respectful handshake and hug.

"Sorry about that. Had to make a stop before dropping Lia off," I explained so generously.

Moving along to my brother, I hit him with blank eyes as I repeated the physical greeting.

"Thanks, Deek," he whispered in my ear.

There were four others from my father's crew in the room, to whom I offered a nod of acknowledgment. They were all returned, along with a few mumbles as my attention went to the corner where the kid sat, tied to a chair. A large, plastic tarp stretched out several feet around his leaking body. His eye was swollen shut, shirt ripped and bloodied, and jeans soiled with urine. Big John stood over him with a power drill at his kneecap. I could see blood staining his jeans there, too.

"What do we have?" I asked.

"He says he doesn't know," my father muttered.

I turned to him. "Doesn't know?"

My father shook his head, his lips pouted. "Our crew found him at his baby mother's house on Governor Street. Ran up in there at four in the morning. He snuck back into town last night."

Widening my legs, I switched stances, clasping my hands behind my back while gazing at the kid again, noticing a broken nose. "On the run for six years," I murmured "and he doesn't know anything?"

"This muthafucka know something!" my brother, Iban, shouted. "Fuck that!"

"I don't! I swear!" the kid cried. "It wasn't my idea. They told me where to meet up at, and that we was gonna get..." His teeth rattled vociferously from fear and pain. "...like five apiece if we hit the warehouse. I told them I was down!"

"Who set it up?" Iban demanded.

"Dis— this dude, Ab—"

"Who the fuck is Ab?" my brother shouted in the kid's face with his usual impatience.

31

"The nigga that set everything up. We did time in the county together a few years back. He— ahhhhhhhh!" he cried as Big John pushed the tip of the drill into his knee as an incentive to keep talking.

"Keep talking, muthafucka, or I'mma have him on your left one!" Iban warned.

"Ab did it! He pulled everybody together," he mumbled in a cry.

"Who did he say he got the drop from?" I asked.

"He ain't say. He was the only one that knew!"

"And that's the kid that's locked up?" my father asked us. I nodded. "He should be coming home soon. Correct?"

"Yup." Iban approached the kid, snatching the drill gun from Big John. "Too bad you ain't ask questions. At least you'd know who was responsible for your death." He revved the drill engine. "You can ask ya boy, Jamal, about it when you get to hell. You know we got him right after y'all robbed us. Right? His dumb ass ain't run." He snickered.

At this point, I knew what was coming. Nothing excited my brother more than violence and pussy. He'd been dying to exact this type of revenge on these dudes since they broke into my father's old warehouse six years ago, killing three of his men in pure luck.

I backed up, ready to leave the butcher room. "You ain't gone suit up before you handle that?" I asked, considering the suit and shoes he wore.

I felt a tap on my shoulder. "Let me rap with you for a minute, son," my father requested.

He recognized what I should have right away. Iban was so far gone at this point, he didn't hear me. Very few things could change the fate of the kid screaming for his life in that chair. I turned to leave and heard the beginnings of a man screaming from seeing the last seconds of his life.

"Which body part's ya favorite? I'll leave it intact and that'll be the one dropped off on ya granny's porch in the morning," Iban taunted what I believed were his plans.

The door was closed behind us as we strolled down the hall, away from the sounds of the room.

"This is joker number three," my father began to muse. "This shit is almost six years old now. You said to wait, and here we are, all these years later, and no closer to the man who robbed me. What are your thoughts?"

I stretched my forehead, then let out a cooling breath. "Let's see. Joker number one, we just learned, is the Ab kid who's about to be released. Joker number two, we killed without talking to—thanks to my capricious brother in there—which was a lost opportunity. Joker number three is in there, probably shitting on himself as he's inching toward his last breath. Joker number four ran, and hasn't been located yet."

He stepped in front of me, ending our stroll. "And joker number five?"

"Damien." I nodded, catching his drift. "We wait him out, too. It'll all come together, I swear."

"Son, this wait and see method ain't my groove, man," he bit out.

"I understand, sir." I gave him a nod of respect. "I really do. Considering all the moving pieces, this isn't a matter to address in haste. If it was Damien who stole from you, it will be Damien who will pay for it dearly. Remember, we're dealing with low-level block huggers; not skilled and reputed killers. They got lucky killing your men at the old warehouse."

"Our men," he corrected, grounding out. "Sadik, I don't give a shit how much of your own man you are, you're still my son. You're still an heir to my fuckin' throne."

I nodded amicably, but gave no verbal acquiesces or confirmations. Only patience. Simple patience.

When the potential storm had rolled over, I continued. "Damien will pay. Okay? Of that, you have my word."

"When, Sadik? How?"

"For starters, not allowing any body part of that kid in there being chopped up to appear anywhere. We don't need anyone to know we snatched him up within hours of him coming back into town. We need to lay low. For all we know, the Derrick kid is behind him."

"And if he's not?"

"Then we always have the Ab kid. He's still alive. We have eyes and hands on him in State Prison."

"And what about insurance?"

I began nodding before he could finish his predictable question. "We've had intel on all of their families, which is how we knew this kid, Lenny, was back in town. The Ab kid has a sister working at a diner in Paterson—at least she was when the robbery happened. I'll have my guys check on her status."

"Let's get on it right away, son. I can't have any of these niggas around here thinking there're no repercussions to robbing me. The old Double E Bags would have had all their heads cut off and lined up on the corner of Broadway by White Castle so everybody could see the fools who tried me."

"I know. I swear, I understand."

"No, you don't. This time, I left it to my sons, believing they were old enough to take over infractions like this. But now, I'm wondering who the real fool is." His eyes narrowed.

I snorted. "I'll have someone on Michelle's first thing tomorrow."

I felt my face fold, remembering her.

"What is it?"

"I was just there tonight."

A flash memory of the Halle Berry cut, high cheek bones, and cinnamon freckles zipped before my eyes.

"Michelle's and not Energy." His lashes fluttered, eyes sweeping away.

His gibe didn't go unnoticed.

"Yeah. Anyway..." I took a deep breath, ready to go. It had been a long ass day. "I'm on it. We'll have Damien's involvement in this in a few short months."

I offered my palm to end the conversation. My father obliged, pulling me into a hug.

"You know I'm proud of you. Right?" he grumbled in my ear, holding me tightly. "You're my last son, but my first and last hope."

I understood his feelings on that, too. My father had made clear his wishes for my future long ago. He hadn't been happy with my take on them and actions against them. However, there was still a mutual respect between us we couldn't deny. He was formidable, feared, respected, and proven. I was smart, driven, promising, calculating, and—to his frustration—independent and unpredictable.

In his embrace, though shorter than him by mere inches, I whispered, "I'm working to make good on that hope every day, sir."

"Try harder," he retorted as we pulled away.

Trying to manage my smug grin, I dropped my eyes to my feet. "How am I not, Pops?"

"You know how!" he growled. "You know what I want of you— need of you!" His hands opened and he turned, gesturing to the grim walls of his warehouse. "This, son. I want you to take over everything."

"We've discussed this."

"And we'll continue to until I get through that thick skull of yours that I adore and loathe at the same damn time. I mean…" He switched stances, widening his arms in the air. "You're breaking my heart here, youngin'. It was one thing, you telling me just before leaving for college you didn't want to be a part of my business. But then…in your late-thirties you surprise me with a baby by a damn Rizzo?"

Inhaling deeply through my nostrils, that shit hurt. My lids fluttered just a bit before I rebounded. There was no way in hell I'd let him see me affected by any deliberate decision I may or may not have made.

I snorted and smiled softly. "Good night, old man." I gripped and squeezed his shoulder. "Kiss my queen goodnight for me." I winked before taking off.

A few feet into my journey, I heard him. "Sadik!"

I turned to face him. "What were you doing in Paterson? The diner?"

I snorted, eyes averting as I swiped my nose. "Lia wanted sweet potato pie."

When I was just about to continue my exit, I caught his grimace, then he grumbled incoherent words. I didn't have to know what they were to know what he felt. Finally, I left for good.

∞ 3 ∞

The door swung open to her glowing caramel skin, voluptuous figure swathed in a red silk robe tied at her waist. Her natural hair coiled in big loose curls, stopping at the neckline, exposing a distinct tattoo of butterfly wings on her soft flesh.

I twisted the small cupcake box in the air. "Happy third anniversary, Energy," I murmured with my face toward the floor, wearing a cheesy ass smirk.

"I said I could come to your place." Her eyes were deadpan. Full, red satin lips slightly pouted.

I knew the underscoring message in that reminder.

Snorting, my eyes fell below to her coral-painted toes before roving back to her pretty face. "No need. I was in the area."

She turned to rest her back on the doorjamb, her arms crossed. "Your father showed up to Energy last night."

I went to rub my tight eyes. "Oh, yeah?"

"Yup. Him and his women. He's traveling with both now, I see."

Tired as a motherfucker, I didn't want to travel down that road of discussion.

I cocked my head to the side and stretched my brows. "You want this cake or not?"

Tiffany's smoky eyes brushed down my frame. My dick twitched to life when she wet her bottom lip. Then when her sultry gaze met mine again, she informed huskily, "I'll have that cake for breakfast. Right now, you'll have mine."

Her compelling strut into her dark apartment was my command.

36

Bilan

A cold shiver coursed my spine as I turned down the dark alley on the side of my house. Up until this point, the streets in my neighborhood were well lit. I whistled in the bleak cool air as I approached the opening of the gate leading into my backyard.

"Dog," I called out at a moderate volume, considering the hour.

Unhinging the metal latch, I took gingerly steps inside the yard. I'd have to walk a couple of yards before the sensor light clicked on.

Another whistle trickled from my chords. "Dog!"

Then I caught his fierce growl. My head whipped to the left. Good. He was in his kennel. At least he wouldn't attack me as he nearly did in the past, not realizing who I was coming back here. I continued to whistle as I toed to the back of the house. I just needed the light to catch, so I could see. My heart beat fiercely against the wall of my chest, and my frame vibrated with familiar fear.

The light appeared, shining narrowly into my haggard yard. When I turned, I saw the dog shoot off in my direction.

"Whoa!" I yelped, panicking.

He stopped inches away and began to growl again. That's when my shaky hands went to my tote and pulled out a plastic bag.

"I've brought you dinner." I swallowed hard and unexpectedly; so scared. After opening the Styrofoam container, the pit bull began to whimper. "Yeah. You know what this is."

I tossed out scraps of chicken and beef I'd been having the waiters pack up for me each night to feed him. The dog went to town on the meat right away. That gave me time to grab the hose and fill his bowl with water. Having a dog these past few months had been challenging. Sometimes, it was worth the peace of mind it brought and other times, it wasn't. I hadn't even named him; just called him Dog.

One of the cooks at the diner recommended I get one when I'd mentioned feeling like I was being watched a year ago. It took months of heavy consideration, but after feeling so vulnerable living in this house alone, I conceded. Unless there was extreme weather, I kept him outside. When I felt extra afraid, I'd bring Dog inside and put him in a metal cage that cost more than him.

As he chowed down, I let myself inside the house by way of the back door. The alarm system was disarmed with the punch of four numbers. The irony in this daily action was, while the system was functional in terms of scaring off an intruder, it wasn't connected to a service that could call for help. It hadn't been in over ten years.

I dropped my bag in a kitchen chair and succumbed to an unforeseen yawn. It had been a long day, and I was actually tired. I should have been; it was close to three in the morning. Such was the life of a baker in a diner opened twenty-three hours a day. Retrieving my phone from my bag, I shuffled to the back of the house, clicking on light switches along the way. I tried fighting the fear of being alone and possibly attacked tonight. That was the benefit of being exhausted.

After a hot shower, I tossed on an old t-shirt and a pair of my father's old boxers. My stomach growled, leading me back to the kitchen, where I left my small container of sweet potato pie. I'd taken a slice of Maria's last attempt. Pedro couldn't do another. He got stuck on garbage duty. I forked a piece as I swept across the corridor floor in my slippers.

"Mmmmmm…" It was pretty tasty.

She'd nailed it. I dropped onto my bed, thinking how I'd tell her tomorrow when my phone rang. My forehead wrinkled. Not that I didn't get calls at this hour, because anyone in touch with me knew I'd likely be up, but I'd grown to be aflutter in my own childhood home.

I saw the name flashing across the screen and answered quickly to get back to the pie.

"Hey, Jason." I chewed away.

"Hi, my Somali sister."

"So, you're Somali today?" I cracked.

"You know what I mean. I'm just leaving campus and wanted to know what time you'll be making it in today."

I dropped the phone from my ear to put him on speaker and check my calendar.

"Looks like I'll be checking in no later than one. I have to finish those calls for surveys." I rolled my eyes. "That'll take me well into the evening."

"I'll meet you there around that time. I need your help with the fall's course scheduling. I told Langston that's a faculty role, and his response was to work with you and it'll get done."

I rolled my eyes again, sighing. I placed the container on my nightstand and lay back on my pillows.

"Yeah..."

"Question."

"Yeah?"

"Are you dating anyone?"

And there was the eye roll thing happening again.

My eyes flew open when I realized the phone buzzing wasn't a part of my dream. I turned to the nightstand and lifted the wrong one at first. When I made it to the second, I felt her warm body shift underneath me.

"Yeah…" A hand reached up and stroked the bare skin of my head.

"Damn," she droned. "You still sleep?" My assistant was a sharp four-foot-eleven alpha, but annoying as fuck first thing in the morning.

"The hell is it, Rory?" I rubbed my eyes.

"Deek, Palmer just called. Apparently, the Lopezes wanna meet at two o'clock."

Lopezes?

I pulled the phone from my ear for the time.

"That's an hour and a half from now. What that got to do with me?"

"He wants you to lead it."

My face turned to stone. I could tell her to call back and decline. I could actually call my father, myself, and ask why the fuck was he trying me. But I knew none of those actions would address the reason he was demanding my participation. It was his leash. This game we'd been playing for months now had to end. I couldn't live my life this way.

I took a deep breath, mentally resigning to awakening and beginning my day. It was just fucked up my agenda was made for me. I had other shit to do. Legit shit to conquer. But as he knew, I would acquiesce to this. There was no need to ask where. I knew the location.

"A'ight." I swiped my nose.

Sitting up, I swung my feet onto the floor. My eyes strained against the morning light. That's when I realized Tiff never closed the curtains last night. I rubbed my eyes, taking in a deep breath.

Her hand was at my back. "Mmmmmm..." She hummed. "I thought we could catch brunch at that restaurant on the water."

"Duty calls." I stood to my feet, stretching my arms out.

Padding into the bathroom where I relieved myself, I began to get upset all over again. Even while washing my face and brushing my damn teeth, I battled with defiance over loyalty. When I returned to her bedroom, Tiff was still in bed, engaged in her cell phone.

"Did I hear correctly that Earl's calling you to duty?"

"Yup." I strained pushing into my shirt.

"Is it family business or family business?"

"I don't know." I lied. "Won't know until I get there."

"Have you changed your mind about taking over?"

I didn't answer. It wasn't a discussion I'd take on with Tiffany right now. I took to the task of attaching the invisible buttons on my shirt as I gazed blindly out the window. I had a meeting with my trucking staff that would have to be pushed back now. The thought to hit up Rory with that request came to mind, though she likely handled it the moment we hung up. I'd have just enough time to shoot to my place, shower, dress, eat, and head over to my father's warehouse for this meeting.

Should I reschedule the walkthrough at the port until next—

"Sadik..."

"Hmm?" My head didn't come up from the task in front of me.

"Last night, at Energy, Earl asked if I could live with you having a baby with someone else."

Finally, I turned to her. Tiffany rested on one elbow tensely, her right breast half covered and the left fully exposed, peaking at its apex. Facing forward again, I snorted, reminded of just how much my father had been struggling with Lia's pregnancy. I could never admit the guilt I carried from it. At this point, my hands were tied. I gaited over to the chair to grab my socks and shoes.

"Aren't you going to ask what my answer was?"

41

I gazed over my shoulder again to her bare face. Rarely did I see the young Tiffany I grew up with. The little girl, who was known to mostly rock the two big ponytails on either side because that was the only hairstyle her widower father knew how to do, and she would never let his women lay a finger in her thick mane. Tiff had always been a force to be reckoned with.

The hardened, self-contained, super-confident millennial woman was nowhere to be found in this moment. Right here was the presence of your typical wistful girl with dreams of being swept off her feet by Prince Charming and promised to be protected, loved, and cherished forever. All the things every woman who desired them should have. The only problem with it was I wasn't that guy.

Tiffany was gorgeous as hell, bordering plus size, shapely, confident, one of the smartest women I knew, and an astute entrepreneur.

I may not have known the exact words she used to answer my father, but damn sure didn't have to ask her. I knew. It was why I didn't fuck her at my place, and rarely here at hers. It was why I waited until she was thirty-years-old to lay a hand on her, believing it to be a safer time for her mentally. It was why I never formally labeled what we had between us. It was why people could only speculate. It was precisely why her voice was an octave and a half above its normal pitch as she approached this topic.

Impatient with the delay in my response, Tiffany rolled over and licked her swollen lips as she sat up in the bed.

"I told him having children with someone, for a man like you, isn't the same as a partner." She dipped her chin. "Partners know the game. They understand the sacrifice. Know the lifestyle." Her eyes rolled away. "I get it. All of it. I was built for it."

She'd never say what "it" was, but I knew that, too. Once my socks and shoes were on, I grabbed my jacket and took to her in the bed. My lips of respect brushed her forehead.

While taking in a cooling breath, I lifted my head to the side. "He mention Larry in that equation, Tiff?"

She visibly stiffened, curling her legs under her ass. Her bottom lip hung and she pulled the sheet over her chest. I waited, but nothing came.

"Have a good day, Tiff."

I stood, paying her a final acknowledgment.

"You came and celebrated the third anniversary of my latest club and managed to make me feel like shit after." She bit her bottom lip, squinting her eyes my way. "But I still have cake to help me recover."

I snorted a dry chuckle. "Can I send my peoples to you to plan my staff party?"

Tiff rolled her eyes. "Sure."

I wiggled her toes hidden beneath the thin blanket before taking off.

"The fuckin' three hundred level seats?" Tasche agonized.

Randi shrugged. "It's either that or the four hundred. Look." She sighed. "At the last damn minute, we better be lucky we can even find tickets. Pixie's show is gonna be lit like a muthfucka."

Tasche's head dropped toward the countertop.

"Nicky's calling you, Bilan!" one of the cooks peered out of the double swinging doors and shouted. "He said he needs the pastry bag or some shit."

I nodded my acknowledgment over my shoulder before going back to the conversation.

"I wonder how much these cost." I pointed to the seating chart of Madison Square Garden on Randi's tablet.

"Shit. Prolly like five hun'ned." Tasche grunted. "We still paying a buck fiddy for fuckin' nosebleeds seats."

"Look," Randi cut in, clearly losing her patience. "We gotta order these shits tonight. My girl, Brenda, gonna put them on her card. I'm meeting up with her at the bar before we run over to Energy."

"That new club?" I asked, impressed. "You've been there before?"

Randi's neck jerked back, sounding her hoop earrings as they swung into her cornrows. "That place ain't new. It's been open for about two—three years—"

"What I wanna know is why these tickets going on somebody else's card?" Tasche's tight face was set with confusion. "Who the fuck she is, yo?"

"Why is because she's coming," Randi made clear. "She's my girl, been knowing her for mad years now. Besides, you got a card we can charge these to?" Her eyes shot toward Tasche's hips to make a point.

Tasche mumbled, going into her waist bag. "The fuck ever." She peeled off a few crisp bills, then pushed them over to Randi. "Bitch, I got green: fuck plastic."

Randi shook her head. I had my wallet handy and counted out one hundred-sixty dollars and handed it over to Randi. It was strange she didn't ask me to use my card, but I wouldn't make it a point of mention. As long as her friend could be trusted, I didn't care who purchased them. Also, Tasche had no business being on her "no new friends" tip, knowing I'd brought her to Randi to chill with us. However, I understood Tasche didn't trust Randi. She'd been clear about that since the day they met. She claimed Randi was shallow and couldn't be trusted. I'd never argued with her, nor did I provide assurance of her beliefs.

"Shit. Let my ass get outta here and go meet her. Ricky been bitchin' about me being out late and I know I'mma hear it again." Randi stood to go.

"Oh," I chirped. "Don't forget I need to borrow your Fendi shirt and black Pigalle Follies."

"Damn, bitch. You need panties and a bra, too?"

My chin collapsed, but my eyes stapled into hers. Randi had often said snappish stuff to me, but she kept it to a minimum in front of others, which made me believe it was light-hearted. This didn't feel good at all.

As I was caught up in my feelings about that outburst, I barely recognized when Tasche croaked, "Who the fuck is that sitting over there?"

"Oh, my…" Randi grumbled under her breath as a waiter tapped me on my shoulder and pointed behind her. It was Maria, holding a mixing bowl, and I knew what that was about. "Fine ass fuckin' Sadik."

I winked and nodded to Maria so she could go back into the kitchen.

"I'm 'bout to bounce outta this bitch," Tasche mumbled, returning my attention ahead. Randi was already off when Tasche gave me a manly dap. She'd dealt these every once in a while. I reciprocated and released her to go. "I'll hit you later, mama."

After taking a deep breath, I headed back to the kitchen to get my mixtures in the pie crusts, then into the oven.

I closed the door to ten pies baking in the commercial oven. After setting the timer, I went over to one of the refrigerators and stirred a spoon in the bowl of fresh cream cheese frosting I'd made for the carrot and red velvet cakes I needed to finish before I clocked out for the night. When I determined it was almost at the right consistency, I checked the time on my cell. It was after one in the morning and instead of being tired, I was annoyed about not being tired.

I grabbed the book I'd been reading from my bag on the coat rack.

"I'll be out on the floor," I yelled to Nicky, and anyone on the baking side who could hear me.

Especially Nicky, who peered up from feeding the pasta machine cannoli dough. He didn't respond, but his eyes on me meant he acknowledged my announcement. Out on the floor, I rounded the counter, hoping my favorite booth for this time of the night was vacant. Michelle's was a twenty-three-hour diner, and constantly had a flood of people, but this hour on a Monday night it could be slow, too.

Thankfully, the last window booth near the counter was available and I slid onto a bench, opening my book. Then I stopped to check the timer on my phone, forgetting that quickly my agenda. Once that was done, I opened the book again, picking up from last night.

Movement in the corner of my eye had my head shooting up. Dimensional eyes under thick messy brows met mine. A russet, radiant bald head glimmered. The tangerine five o'clock shadow was cut with precision, just as it was the first night I'd laid eyes on him. His striking leather jacket was a shade of gray, and the V-neck sweater underneath was bone. A far cry from the black tux of last week, but it was crystal clear the man exuded elegant style. He carried a small plate topped with sweet potato pie in one hand, and in the other was a mug. Smoothly and uninvited, he slid onto the bench across from me.

"Love in Warm Hues. So, you're a romance junkie?"

Man, was he good looking...devilishly so, and I believed he knew it. A flame of knavery danced in his slightly slanted kaleidoscopic-hued eyes, reacting to what he saw.

I closed the book, wedging my thumb between the pages and gazing at the cover. There was nothing about it that said romance or chick lit. I didn't read romance novels.

Expressionless, I returned, "I hardly indulge in fiction."

He used his palm to swipe down his jaw. "So, what about love?"

His face relaxed into impassive articulation, eyes were communicative and stapled to me. He spooned a piece of pie, then dabbed it on the dollop of whip cream before feeding himself. His teeth. They were big, aligned, and alabaster, which was how I knew they were real.

My eyes shot down to the book as I reopened it. "That it's perfectly fine in Black hues."

He sat back, unresponsive for seconds long. One arm reached over the back of the booth, and his head angled as though he was considering something.

"But it's not of the romance genre?"

"No."

"Who's the author?"

I flipped back to the cover.

"Christina C. Jones," he murmured. "So, what does she write?"

"According to her bio in the back, she pens romance."

"But this particular book isn't romance? Have they created a parallel fictional genre and are calling it love?"

His voice… I didn't recall it being so velvety alto. His pitch was slightly scratchy, but still thick and commanding.

"No. This is…" I had to consider that for a moment. "Reference."

"Reference?" His tenor was deeper.

I shrugged. "That's what it was listed under on Amazon. It's different."

"Is that why you're reading it?"

My eyes cut to glance out the window. I wondered why he was talking to me. He was hysterically gorgeous, dressed stylishly, and here at an odd hour during the week.

"No. I'm reading it for—" I wouldn't explain. I didn't know him. "It was recommended."

He nodded, eyes still penetrating me. "What's it about?"

"How Black love is misrepresented and under-exposed in American culture."

His brows lifted as he scooped more pie. "Interesting. Also a mouthful. What's her argument?"

I decided to let the author speak for herself and read a passage I'd highlighted earlier on. "We should be all for seeing Black women get their happily ever after, no matter the shade. But if I pull ten pairings from the most popular shows, movies, and TV, and only two of those put a Black man and woman together, that's a problem. It doesn't reflect reality, and it pushes a narrative that 'we' can't be happy together."

He nodded, chewing. And my stupid eyes stapled to his mouth, entranced.

"I agree and can take her argument even further. There has been a deficit of Black love and commitment presentation in America."

"Really?" My tone was doubtful.

Did my book really appeal to his senses? I doubted it. Hard.

"Absolutely." He pushed his plate aside and lifted his mug that I could now see was filled with coffee. "Yes. And it's one of the reasons why in the twenty-first century—four centuries after African slaves were brought here—Blacks are still the minority. This is after the Census Bureau announced Hispanics edged past Blacks as residents in this country. Do you know why?"

A faint smirk warmed his face as he waited.

"I'm waiting for the correlation."

He pulled his mug to his center on the table and casually answered, "It's because our reproduction as a race here in America has declined." My brows lifted in question. His head was angled to face the table, but those yellowish eyes rolled up from his mug to me. "Black men and women aren't making babies at the rate of our forefathers."

I was now intrigued. "Please elaborate."

"Less than one hundred years ago, your great-great—hell, great—grandparents were reproducing more than I'm willing to bet you desire to."

"I don't understand."

"My great-grandparents down in Warren County, North Carolina bore eighteen children."

My face drew up. "That woman was pregnant eighteen times?"

He took a swig of his coffee, managing a chuckle. God, he was good looking. Deceptively so. I had a strong inclination to believe he was using this opportunity to show me he was not only handsome but informed, too—or at least capable of informed conversation.

"I honestly don't know how many times she was impregnated. Women of that time held their mouths on topics concerning their bodies. But I do know she was pregnant at least fourteen times. She had four sets of twins. My point was to the amount of reproduction happening at that time for Black families versus today."

"No way I'm having all those babies," I grated lowly, rolling my eyes.

He chuckled again, and boy, was it musical. Captivating. "Predictably. So..." He sat up. "...my great-grandmother bore eighteen children, one of her twins was my grandmother, who bore four children. My father stopped at three. And here I am, in front of a gorgeous millennial woman, who swears to..." He was leaving room for me to answer.

My eyes fluttered and I cleared my throat, uncomfortable by the turn of the conversation. I found myself sitting up, too.

I was unable to look at him when I answered, "Well, that'll be a decision I make with the man I decide to take that step with. But it won't be as many as your great-grandmother."

His eyes glimmered with humor. "Not your husband?"

"Huhn?"

"You referenced the father of your future offspring as a man and didn't give him a title," he reminded me, expression starkly sober.

My eyes fell again. This time, I was a little embarrassed in front of a stranger.

"It's not easy for women...like me to find companionship." That's when I decided to look at him again. I had nothing to be ashamed of.

"Like you?" His eyes brushed down all of what he could see of me from inside a booth.

Taking in and releasing a heap of air, I breathed, "Yup. Men who look like me, for some strange reason, don't show much interest. And once you add degreed to my characteristics, well..."

His dancing feline irises were still light; I could even decipher a perceptible grin in his cheeks. He tossed his chin to my book.

"Where are you up to now?" The faint grin was gone when he shared, "I'd like to hear more."

Instinctively, I opened the book to where my finger was wedged.

"Historically, there has been a push for the breakup of the Black family. The purposeful separation of families during slavery, mass incarceration, police brutality, hiring bias, the purposeful injection of

49

drugs into our communities, welfare rules that encourage the exclusion of Black men from their homes, and the false narrative of the absent Black father. All of these are consistent and, unfortunately, effective tools of white supremacy, pushing an altered reality that we shouldn't buy into. Your family can and should look however you want it to, as long as it's built on love. But there is power and promise and real joy in seeing that, despite hatred's best attempts, we can overcome those barriers and still find forever with each other."

My eyes rolled up to him.

His brows lifted and he gave a cursory nod. "I have to say again, I agree."

"I don't."

He sat back, arm stretching over the back of the booth again. "Why not?"

"I don't believe white supremacy in America has as much power as we conspiracists like to promote it does. I don't believe this mythical body of evil-doers to Black people control our decisions. We do. Black men decide who they want to romanticize, marry, and impregnate. Yeah, maybe there is or was a propaganda to architect the standard of beauty here in the West, but some things are instinctual. When you're born of a Black woman, you should naturally feel a visceral connection and draw to her. So, when you're finding yourself attracted to the opposite sex, your first stop should be what you share DNA with."

His brows narrowed. "I don't see a conflict in views there. I agree with you as well."

I continued. "So, why then is a woman of my age, education, and lack of baggage, as in kids, left with little to no options when it comes to her male counterparts? Why am I overlooked by a man who looks like me, struggles against white supremacy like me and who, despite being the most targeted and disenfranchised civilian in this great country I still love, honor, and support, prefers other than me?"

My phone vibrated, alerting me of the end of the baking time for the pies.

"I can't answer that."

"Yes, you can." I scooted to leave the booth.

"How do you suppose?"

I stood over the table, glaring down at him. It didn't matter how fine he was or how incredibly delicious he was scented, I knew what I knew.

"Was that not you in here last week buying pie for your..."I glanced down at his bare ring finger again,"...pregnant lover?"

It was slight, but realization washed over his handsome face and his eyes rolled down to the table before returning to me. I also caught the twitching of his lips.

I nodded. "Yeah. White supremacy has its remote control over your eyes and dick, too, huhn?"

"I'd like to explore that accusation," he pushed, eyes on his coffee cup.

His arms were bent, flexing his palms into the edge of the table.

"And I'd like to get back to work." I took off for the kitchen.

"Is that a TBA?" His scratchy alto carried across booths.

As I turned back to him, my face tightened. Why would he assume I'd want more face time with him? "I don't even know your name."

His pupils dazzled again, even from the short distance. Then a smile seizing my breath spread on his face. "Sadik. Sadik Ellis."

When that information should have meant he was an open man, eager to want to engage, it instead felt like charm. Charm was always accompanied by manipulation. And his presence... It was heavy. He was alone, but had an aura of authority and power. He was too clean, too confident, too well spoken to be in a Paterson diner at this hour. The hour that now seemed familiar to him.

My head shook faintly. "I don't know what you want from me." I swallowed hard. "But it sure ain't to discuss Christina C. Jones."

His head twisted slightly, and his brows lifted. "To be a friend. I just want to be a friend."

That ridiculous claim had me taking off to the kitchen for real.

∞ **4** ∞

"I want a Corona and…" Randi's white lined eyes perused the menu over the counter of the concession stand. "…I guess those chicken fingers. Damn, I'm hungrier than a muthafucka!" she swore beneath her breath.

"Who that singing?" Tasche inclined her head toward the nearest door of the arena's auditorium.

Brenda, Randi's friend hanging with us tonight, tugged at the hem of her black leather skirt as she click-clacked in her heels toward Tasche.

"I hear something, but the voice doesn't sound like hers," I answered.

We were in the hall of Madison Square Garden, and just in time for the Pixie concert. Everybody was talking about this show. We'd been stressing over the details of getting seats for tonight and finally, here we were. Randi insisted we got food first. My eyes swept the dozens upon dozens of anxious bodies taking flight to their respective seating doors.

"Shit!" My head snapped to the register in front of me, where Randi's hand frantically scoured her oversized Louis Vuitton bag. "I didn't throw my wallet in here when I switched bags. Dammit!" she barked.

I went inside my fanny pack for my wallet. "I got it."

"Good looking." That was it. That's how she said thanks, for some reason.

"Nah! That ain't her," Tasche shouted from near the auditorium door.

I nodded my acknowledgment as I handed over cash to the guy at the register.

"Whaddup, Randi," a deep, gruff voice called out. "My boss want you and ya people to watch the show from his suite."

As the whopping figure of a guy neared us by the counter, Randi's head swung back with full-on insolence. "What damn suite?"

His nub of a chunky thumb pointed behind him, and that's when I saw he was followed by another tall man wearing an all-black suit, just as he was. "The Lexus Suite, or some shit," his voice waned, but not his confidence or authority.

This was extra weird. Randi's man, Ricky, was in the dark world, dealing guns. God only knew who would be requesting her by name.

And summoning her to a suite at The Garden?

"We just paid for our food," she argued, and I got what she really meant.

That's when a tiny woman—especially petite—wearing the same uniform of an all-black pantsuit approached us, counting out dollar bills. Her skin was the shade of peanut butter, big eyes bulged to caricature proportions, hawk nose swollen at the beak, and her body—posture, too—resembled a young boy.

She licked her fingers and peeled off at least two hundred-dollar bills and damn near shoved them into Randi's hand. "What it do, though, Randi?" she emitted nasally, void of warmth.

The small woman's empty smile read more like a leer. Her hair was braided down her back in cornrows and she wore no makeup. Randi looked spooked as the woman peered into her eyes.

"Who the fuck is your boss?" Randi croaked, affected.

"C'mon, man." The big guy sniffled as he swiped his nose, then locked his palms at his waist and rolled back his broad shoulders. "You know who Rory boss be, Randi."

From just at her shoulder, I could see Randi's eyes fall to the floor as she rolled her tongue between her teeth and upper lip contemplatively. Her eyes rolled beyond me to cue Tasche and Brenda, who were now closer to us.

"Come on, y'all. At least we got a better view." Her voice was dramatically deflated.

When the guy at the concession stand placed our tray on the counter, the big guy held out his hand. "Nah, homie. Y'all can keep that."

I wasn't offered a refund by Randi, likely because she was caught off guard by our invitation.

The tiny woman, Rory, strolled off with mild speed and one hand tucked into her pants pocket, displaying her confidence of us following. She was right. Randi began slowly, taking off on Rory's heels. Brenda started right behind them. Seemingly at the same time, Tasche and I followed.

When we caught up with Randi, Tasche's pebbly voice was able to murmur, "The fuck is this about, yo?"

Slowly, Randi answered, "I don't know. Could be something shady because this guy knows I fuck with Ricky. But I don't think they're beefing."

My brows met. "What does that mean?"

Randi's eyes rolled. "He ain't tryna' hurt me. Probably sniffin' around my ass."

Oh...

"Mmmmhmmm!" Brenda agreed.

I was anxious. In fact, my heart began to beat against the wall of my chest. We walked to an elevator guarded by the arena's staff. Our group of seven was let on, and the car descended as my mouth secreted with unease. Once again, we were following these people, passing more security, and to an unknown destination. Finally, we reached a door being held open by another black suited man, into a lounge area settled with dark leather sofas and candlelit coffee tables. The walls of the next area we passed into were lined with closed chafing dishes and a colorfully stocked bar. We stopped there, where I couldn't help but waft in the delicious aroma of food.

"They here," the Rory girl announced ahead, where I had the most incredible view of two women performing on stage from the lower bowl.

A man stood from the theater seats, suspended out into the general arena. Slowly, he turned with a tumbler in his hand. At first, I could only make out the contour of his shape. His fit, yet medium frame was capped in a dark fleece shirt and matching sweatpants. The jazzy lighting of the suite made the color indistinct. But what wasn't was the radiance of the jewelry he donned around his neck. Three modest-sized pieces, but pure diamonds made up each link. His sleeves were rolled up three-quarters of the way as he placed the tumbler on the small peninsula countertop to the left of him en route to us.

"Fuck," Randi swore lowly.

That's when I recognized him.

The guy from the diner, whose name I couldn't recall.

"Now, I'm believing me seeing you last week at Michelle's wasn't random." Randi applied all the sauce she had bottled to express that.

But when did she see him at Michelle's?

He cracked a grin that beckoned a squeeze in my groin. Then he ended his gait and faintly bounced back on his heels with spread legs. His hands slipped into the pockets of his fleece sweats, and his chin dipped slightly.

"Purely random, and this is coincidental." His thick brows lifted. "Give my regards to Ricky, by the way."

"How you figure this is coincidental? I don't wanna be in the middle of a damn war between you two beasts."

His snort was mild, too, but certainly effective. "I've got no beef with Ricky." His eyes swept against my face, causing a shiver to course my spine. It had to be anxiousness. This was all unnerving. "Bilan's making this coincidental tonight."

Randi's head whipped back to me, incomprehensible betrayal in her eyes. "What the fuck she have to do with this?"

Tasche shifted closer to me, protectively. Brenda mutedly observed the awkward exchange.

"I wanted the pleasure of enjoying Pixie with her, too." The croak in his voice was dangerously illusory and powerfully seductive.

How was it that this guy was getting to me in ways patently effectual, compared to the first two times I'd encountered him? And, at this point, I believed him. Randi was not his target. It had to be me. Him sitting down at the booth last week with food already never struck me as suspicious. However, summoning us up to a luxury suite at a Pixie concert was starkly clear. The guy now had my attention.

As he gazed into me intensely, his eyes sparkled again with an agenda I still couldn't determine. And when he traversed the small space, nearing me, my entire frame heated.

"There's another act after this, then Pixie hits the stage. Can I offer you something to eat?" his voice...that commanding alto brushed velvety against my ear. I shook my head, biting on the inside of my lips. "Perhaps a drink?"

Perhaps? He used the word perhaps. I wasn't used to hearing those types of adverbs off campus. And boy, did a drink sound like a perfect balm to my edginess now!

Without looking at him—because I couldn't—I nodded.

He ambled over to the bar. "Anything in particular?"

"She don't know how to drink," Randi hissed. "A shot of anything'll do, but just one. Me, Bren, and Tasche'll take Hennessy."

His eyes were on me when I found my regard shifting to him. There was shock-humor there in his golden irises. "You drink Hennessy?"

My God, did he smell magnificent! Why? Why was I so affected? Could it have been because I wasn't in a familiar environment? Had to be. He was fine when I met him close to two weeks ago. He was even devilishly handsome last week. But tonight, he was dangerously tempting with his gorgeous features. Those full lips with the drop in the center of the top one, they did tricky things to my panties. And the orange in his five o'clock shadow was a mix of dark brown and honey blonde. All natural on this very black man. How was this possible?

I shook my head because I didn't drink Hennessy. It made me a performer. I couldn't be that tonight.

"I didn't think so," he remarked. "Let's try Ace of Spades to celebrate. Then if you're interested, we'll start making you a Mauve woman tonight." His eyes were still sparkling with an inspiring emotion I couldn't identify.

Mauve?

Yeah. He was definitely Randi's speed. She was the only person in my basic world who got close enough to Mauve.

"They'll take Hennessy," the ruthlessly handsome fellow murmured to a short man who'd just sauntered into the suite, dressed in all-black but for his burgundy vest, like a bartender. He poured two flutes of bubbly in a practiced manner. Then his gaze met mine. "You mind if we talk a little before Pixie hits the stage?"

I didn't know what to say. Would that mean leaving my friends? That wasn't going to happen. Besides, I was officially intimidated by him at this point. What Black people watched concerts from a suite?

Clearly noticing my hesitance, he clarified, "Just right here." He pointed to the small lounge area behind me. "I'd like to continue the Christina C. Jones-inspired conversation."

"What's there to continue?" I finally found my voice.

He grabbed the flutes and sauntered over to the small lounge area. I watched as he quickly reached into a leather satchel on the floor aside the sofa. He pulled out a book I didn't recognize. My eyes squinted as I tried to see the print on it.

"You'd see clearer if you were over here," he teased with one cheek lifted.

That had me straightening. I glanced around to find Randi and Tasche's eyes on me. Brenda was being handed a tumbler. Tasche mouthed to me with a hard regard, "go."

Her dark eyes bulleted from me to the guy whose name I needed to be reminded of. "Y'all good, love. Enjoy." Tasche then accepted the drink as she nodded and smiled. "We gone be right here watching the show. Holla if you need me."

She turned to go claim a seat facing the stage. Tasche was sure to take Randi at the arm en route, forcibly breaking her deep gaping of me. Brenda followed them.

I turned back to face him, almost blinded by the jewels on his neck, and those of his eyes. I almost always had an aversion to guys with flashy jewelry. It was so immature to me, especially in my late twenties. But this guy's was tasteful and a statement maker. It spoke wealth with a dash of pomposity.

"Seth?"

His brows lifted, exposing another gorgeous expression of his face. Then his muscles relaxed into a boyish grin. "Seth? I'm insulted."

"Don't be." I shook my head, blinking excessively as I moseyed over to the lounge area. "I've met, I'm sure, at least a dozen guys whose names began with an S." I took a seat, safely across from him.

The muscles around his eyes tightened, lips broadened, but his cheeks never rose. He was examining me, maybe?

"But I'm confident..." His delivery was velvety, tone cool, "...you've not encountered another Sadik."

Sadik!

That was his name. It was unique, maybe ethnic? I didn't know. It would make an interesting Google search.

I scratched the back of my neck as I nodded, eyes averted to the moving bodies in the suite. Sadik brought the book cover into my peripheral, reminding me of his topic of conversation. I turned for a better view.

"Haunted," I murmured the title. "I haven't read this one."

He placed the book down on the coffee table between us. "I didn't think you had. You said Love in Warm Hues was recommended. I can tell you she's pretty good, even from the romance prose."

I grabbed my champagne while fighting a smirk, suddenly roused by the conversation. "Oh, really? Do you read romance?"

With a soft smile, he shook his head. "I'm sorry to say I do not. It's something you and I have in common."

He remembered.

"So, what makes this book, Haunted, good?"

"I said she's good. The woman seems to be entirely about the Black experience as it relates to the romance literary industry. Did you know she writes in two subgenres of romance?"

I cleared my throat nervously, raising the flute to my lips as I watched Sadik follow my every move. "What do you mean?"

"She writes paranormal and suspense. This one..." He pointed to the book between us. "...is paranormal. It's some deep shit."

I swallowed faintly sweet bubbly. "What makes it deep?"

"Several things, one being her illustrating a love...bond between a man and a woman that transcends time." He dipped his chin for emphasis. "And I don't mean ten to sixty years." Sadik shook his head with tempting, pouty lips. "Nah. Centuries."

"Centuries?" I parroted like an idiot, struck by that detail.

"Try four." His tongue swept his lips as he sat up on the sofa. "This dude, Aram, loved this woman for the better part of one hundred years."

I scoffed. "People don't live that long!"

Sadik didn't respond so quickly. In fact, he took a swig of his champagne, maintaining his gaze on my every movement. I found myself gaping in the area of his mouth when his tongue traced his top lip, chasing away the sparkling wine.

"Nah, but love does." His fixated regard on me penetrated. "It's a paranormal, Bilan." The sound of my name falling from his lips was lenitive. "Stories of that genre defy time and physics. They're metaphysical...supernatural, transcendental. Jones is so smart and...passionate about her campaign for Black love, she made it preternatural."

My lungs shuddered as I exhaled, frustratingly affected by his vocabulary. No. I didn't know all the words he used, but I understood them. However, it was him I didn't get. Who in the world was Sadik?

"Why do you care?"

His forehead stretched, clearly bludgeoned by that untimed question. But smoothly, he recovered. "Why would I not?" Sadik sat back, stretching his arms across the back of the chair. "We're talking about a novelist who dedicates her work to uplifting, illustrating, and promoting Black love. A man my age should be able to appreciate passionate cultural art."

"How old are you?"

Again, Sadik didn't answer right away. His regard was still intense on me, but for the first time, his confidence shillyshallied. His tongue ran against the inside of his bottom lip as he stalled.

"Thirty-eight." He reached over for his champagne.

I sipped mine and swallowed, suddenly feeling emboldened by his sheer interest in me...and the bubbly, encouraging my glib energy.

"How old are you?" he countered.

"Twenty-eight."

"And with no kids." He remembered that, too.

"Unlike you." I ducked my head for another sip, the flute nearly empty now.

"I don't have any kids, Bilan." His tone was resolute, body language unrattled.

"Yet." My eyes swung over to the bodies moving about the suite. Behind me, Randi had just finished toppling her plate with food. The big security guy who shadowed us down here guarded the small hall leading to the door. For what? I swallowed back the remainder of the champagne. Then I realized I'd walked down a dead-end road. Why did I care he had a baby on the way? I'd had dozens of guys in the same position trying to approach me. Plus, I didn't want to lead him to believe I cared. "So," I let out a string of air. "You read?"

"I read a lot. Books, minds...bodies..."

"And I guess this is where I'm supposed to ask what mine are saying," I murmured, unable to look at him.

He smelled so frigging good again.

"Your mind is saying shut me out. Your body is reminding you that you find me attractive."

My eyes bulleted his way. I found Sadik licking the inside of that bottom lip again.

"It's all good, Bilan." His brows lifted, extended fingers drummed the arms of the leather chair. "I find you distractingly attractive myself," he rattled off casually.

I found my head twisting, eyes averting to my friends behind me as I fingered my neck. That's when it dawned on me.

"You sure you understand who I am?"

"What do you mean?" He pulled out a ringing phone before discovering it wasn't the device sounding, then pulled out another.

I watched as he observed the screen, then tapped to ignore it. Sadik's eyes had only left my face for a split second.

"I mean, I'm not that girl. I know I'm friends with Randi, but we don't run in the same circles."

"Bilan, I may not know much about you, but give me credit for knowing you're an unknown in the whole state of New Jersey."

My neck jerked, head popped back. "And you would know?" Sarcasm lined my words.

"More than I care to admit," he murmured so quickly while retrieving his champagne glass, I had no faith in my ears. He quickly gulped down the last of it.

"I don't know what that means, but my point is I'm not looking for a man, and especially not drama."

His head shifted slightly to the right as his eyes narrowed on me. Sadik's dangerous smirk lifted on his face. "I'm drama?"

A blast of applause rang out in the arena behind me. My head swung around as Tasche called over to us.

The dark-skinned stripper yelled back into the suite just as Bilan whipped her head around. That gave me a view of her tapered cut in the back and her long neck. As nice as the view was, I was missing those brown splatters dotting her sculpted cheekbones. "Pixie 'bout to hit the muthafuckin' stage, yo!"

That's when I heard the crying horns announcing an introduction. The show was about to begin. It felt like we'd began our brief exchange just two words ago. Bilan turned back toward me. Her eyes bounced around after their initial brush against me. And again, she was stumped. She'd found herself in that bewildered state often in this short stretch of time.

Bilan stood, eyes tightened and lips pursed. "You may not think you are, but your incoming baby spells it out."

I sat back when she turned toward the theater and made her way to a seat. I watched the crusade of her ass and hips in painted on yellow pants as she retreated. Her girls, who continuously turned back to check on her while we'd been speaking, waved her on.

"Can I offer you another glass of champagne, sir?" the bartender asked.

"Nah." I didn't look at him when answering. "You can take two thumbs of Mauve out to the young lady who just left. See if her friends need refills."

"Yes, sir." He bowed before turning for the bar.

A tiny body plopped down in front of me, purposely killing my view. "That ain't the plan."

Finally, I swung my attention from the back of Bilan's head to Rory's splayed nostrils.

"What's not?"

"Her pussy."

"Plans change."

She sighed, tossing her miniature torso back against the sofa. "So, we changing up the plan?"

Disinterested in the conversation, I shrugged with my forehead. "Maybe. Maybe not. Either way, the agenda never does."

"What—" She lowered her voice, shifting forward. "What the fuck that mean?" she whispered.

I reached over to my bag and grabbed my laptop. "It means..." I grunted, arched over, "...I've got a few reports to get through for work and a damn strategy plan to conjure for my damn father and brother to lay low on this Damien shit, all before I meet with them tonight."

As I opened the flap of the computer and began typing in my login credentials, I could see her standing in my peripheral.

"Shit. Good!" Rory grumbled. "Long as your mind ain't on nothing close to Ricky's hoe-ass girl." I chuckled, pulling up my email. "Be nice, Bean."

"What the fuck ever," she hissed, strolling toward the fridge for a bottle of water.

Bilan

"You lied…
You cheated…
Abused…
Misused.
Abandoned…
Defeated…
I've got nothing to lose," I sang along with Pixie, hating we were nearing the end of the show._

She'd been at it for close to an hour and a half, and I'd been right there with her, jamming. Tasche and Randi were to the right of me, shouting the lyrics, too. This track, "Our Last Goodbye," was almost two years old, but one of her bigger records. It had a hip-hop/rock feel to it and had been written and produced by Young Lord back when people didn't know he'd been writing a string of R&B hits. Pixie was smart and got in on it quickly. But as a blog wisely stated, she helped put Young's writing and producing skills on the map.

"Thank you, guys!" Pixie offered the audience as the band continued to rock out. We responded with our spirited cheers and hoots. "Can we give it up for the sickest band on the planet?" She swung her arm behind her, giving attention to the musicians.

As Pixie began to name them one by one, Tasche turned to me. "I gotta pee like a muthafucka, yo!" She added a little shimmy. "I hope it ain't far from here."

Randi sucked her teeth. "Bitch, we're in a fuckin' suite. There's one right there!" she didn't shout, but offered nastily. Something was eating at her. "Let's hurry the fuck up so we can get out of here. I ain't tryna get no shit spilled out in the streets and back to Ricky's crazy ass." She rolled her eyes and shuffled out of the _auditorium-style seats_.

There were two sets of two rows and a total of twelves seats: two rows of two on one side of the short stairs, and two rows of four on the other.

After Brenda let her out into the aisle, Randi led the way with Tasche on her heels and me trailing last. As soon as I turn toward the suite, I saw his powerful figure coming our way. Did he watch the show? I made sure I didn't turn back to look for him the entire performance. Sadik made me nervous...and tingle.

"The bathroom this way. Right?" Randi asked briskly.

Sadik's security pointed and nodded. Randi and Brenda walked Tasche near there when Sadik stepped in front of me, breaking the trail.

"Can we continue our conversation?" There was a nonnegotiable utterance to his tone—it wasn't forceful, but certainly beseeching.

"I didn't know we had more to discuss." In a span of seconds, my brain whirred with the details of our previous one. "You read one of Jones' books in the past and you brought it to show me. I get that. Okay, we've talked about—" My jaw fell and eyes bounced all around the room before slamming into him. "How did you know you'd see me here?"

Sadik smiled coolly at first. Calm and unperturbed. Then his chin dropped to his chest. "I've been carrying the book around since I bought it...the day after our chat at the diner last week. Not only have I read Haunted, I've also finished Love in Warm Hues."

My eyes averted again and I took a deep breath. This guy wasn't fond of ambiguity. He'd been making his pursuit of me clear. From just at his shoulder, I could see Randi peering over to us intently and her girl, Brenda, next to her doing the same. I didn't like that. I may have been a novice at men, unlike Randi, but I could handle my own.

With one step, I shifted from her line of view.

"What do you want from me?" I heard the crack in my voice.

"What I told you last week. To be a friend."

"And what does that entail?"

"Only getting to know you." His tone was just as quieted as mine.

"I won't sleep with you."

"I haven't asked you to."

My tone disclosed my impatience with this. "Then what are you asking?"

"Let's go somewhere and talk. Just a friendly, informative conversation."

"About what?"

"You haven't heard my thoughts on Jones."

"They don't matter. I'm not a fan of her work. I told you I'd heard about that particular title and gave it a try."

"Then while I'm trying to be a friend, let me attempt to argue her very valid and poignant views."

My face fell. "Who are you? Where are you from? And do you dye your face?"

His cheek lifted first, mouth expanded just slightly. "Hell no, I don't dye anything on my body. And you'd find out that and more if you gave me the time."

"When?"

"Tonight. Now."

"Where?"

"Some place quiet." I tossed a gaze over his shoulder at a gaping and scowling Randi. Then he shifted even more to turn his back toward her. "Alone."

I considered it for a moment. Like...actually began sending my acquiesce down to my throat. "I'm not going anywhere with you."

"Why not, Bilan?"

"I don't entertain guys in a relationship."

His head lurched back, brows met in indignation. "I'm not in a relationship."

I scoffed. "But you're expecting a baby. Guys fresh out of relationships get voted off the boat, too. Does she know you're not in a relationship?"

He took a deep breath, pushing his hands into the pockets of his sweatpants. Sadik turned away, mouth twisted. Then almost like lightning, he recovered. His hand pulled from his pocket, holding a cell phone.

"If she told you we're in no relationship, would you feel comfortable coming with me to have a private conversation? I can drop you off anywhere you need to go when you're ready."

Before I could respond, his phone was lighting up in service. My tight face swung left to right as I tried to figure out what he was doing.

I heard a fuzzy sound before a woman's voice broke through.

"Hi, Sadik," a feminine voice greeted warily. "Everything okay?" There was a soft panic to her voice.

"What up, Lia? Nah. Everything's good. I just need a favor from you."

There was a slight pause before she uttered, "Okay…"

"I'm trying to take a friend of mine out. She's a little hesitant because of the pregnancy. Would you mind telling her I'm a free agent? I have you on speaker."

There was another pause of hesitance on her part again. My pulse raced. This was so unnecessary. I didn't think going out with him was a good idea anyway—no matter how cute I found him.

"Awwwww…" vibrated off the device he held in the air. "I can totally understand her position. Thank god for real fucking women still left on the planet. But yes, it's totally fine. Sadik and I are not in a relationship. He's totally free to date whomever he pleases."

I didn't have a response for that, other than staring at him like he was extraterrestrial.

"Thanks, Lia," he spoke into the phone. "Talk soon."

"Okay, Sadik! Hope it works out."

He scoffed, gazing into my eyes. "No doubt." Sadik tapped to end the call. "The moment you're ready to go, I'll take you wherever you say."

I sucked in unexpected air as my eyes swept around him, where I felt Tasche, now out of the bathroom, gaping at us no different than Randi and Brenda.

∞ 5 ∞

Bilan

"This way, sir." A doorman directed Sadik the moment we walked into what looked like a brick residential building in Midtown Manhattan.

I trailed behind him as we were led to an elevator. The doorman pressed the call button and, within seconds, the bell tolled. The lift was small, as was every other space in New York City, which was why I didn't understand why so many people I grew up with fantasized about moving here.

Awkwardly, I stood in the center with Sadik behind me since he stepped on before me. Mentally, I counted down until the moment we'd arrive. A soft touch of his pinky finger sending prickles of electricity had my eyes bulging when I didn't know they were closed, my head swinging up. Slowly, I peered over my shoulder and found Sadik's face toward the floor. His eyes rolled up, expression blank until he winked at me. My neck whipped hard away from him, immediately rendering me embarrassed.

The car tolled, and the doorman led me out with Sadik's heated presence on my back. So unnerved, I stepped aside so he could proceed ahead of me. We passed apartment doors, and I wondered which was his at each one. I didn't want to go to his place. That wasn't what I had in mind when he proposed this. Just when I was nearing a panic break, the doorman walked toward a metal door and pushed it out into the night air.

I followed Sadik onto the rooftop of the building, lit with strings of small, white globe lights hanging from post to post. Tealight candles lined the enclosure wall. Mild music played, the artist I was unfamiliar with. To our left was a bar where a handful of people were. Seating was sparse throughout the lounge area, though there weren't many present. Soon, my attention was drawn to the segregation of the space when we were being escorted to the opposite side of the bar to a fireplace with seating for no more than four. Two loveseats faced each other, adjacent to the blazing hearth with a coffee table in the center. Heat from the crackling flames thankfully warmed my chilled bones. Late March temperatures at night could be brutal.

"Just a bottle of Mauve—Platinum—and two glasses, please."

Hearing Sadik's commanding voice woke me from my stupor. I hadn't realized someone from the bar had come over. Both the doorman and bartender broke from our private fireside lounge. I caught the inviting smile on Sadik's face as he invited me to sit with a nod of his forehead.

As I did, he took to the loveseat across from me. "Is this place okay?"

My forehead lifted and eyes blossomed in shocked-stupor. I didn't know what to say.

"I guess," was all my brain could produce.

He grinned, eyes sparkling again. "Thought it would be nice to have a quiet and private place to chat."

My eyes brushed against the backdrop of the city. I could see the highlights of New York City; the Empire State Building, Madison Square Garden, and Times Square.

"The view isn't bad either." I shrugged.

"And there are people around to expel the assumption of my agenda tonight being sexual."

I rolled my eyes—more at myself for assuming that—and fought a sheepish grin.

"I was just looking out for myself. The only person checking for me is me." My shoulders lifted again before I rearranged myself on the sofa, trying to relax.

"You're the only person looking out for you? That's a morose claim for a human being to make, much less a young woman."

"Well," I began as a man and woman arrived with tumblers and glasses of ice water. One carefully placed the bottle of Mauve on the table. Brandy was poured for the both of us, and Sadik dismissed the pair once we were served. He pushed my glass toward me, inviting me to it and then with another nod, he encouraged me to continue. Blinking as I shook my head, trying to recall the conversation we were in, I continued. "I was only going to say it's my reality."

"What is?"

"Having to look out for myself."

"You don't have family to help with that monstrous task?"

"Family? Some. Help? No."

"Where are your parents?"

I held the cool glass in my misted palms over my lap. "They're gone. My father passed about a year after I graduated high school. My mother died five years ago."

Sadik stretched his neck, head circling over his shoulders, expressing discomfort. "I'm sorry to hear that."

"It's okay." I shrugged and nodded coolly. "It happens."

"What does?"

"Parents dying. It happens every day."

For a moment, he didn't speak. It was clear Sadik was measuring my words. Did he not agree?

"Brothers and sisters?"

I nodded. "One brother." I rubbed what was left of my lipstick together with my lips, eyes dropping to the table. "He's..." I cleared my throat. "Incarcerated."

Sadik nodded mutedly, again delaying his response. That's when it hit me. I found him intimidating, and I didn't like it. Just like earlier, and even the last conversation I'd had with him last week at the diner, he'd been the raider, probing for conversation. Yeah, he'd shared his family history with that story of his great-grandparents having a shipload of kids in North Carolina, but other than that, the only other piece of information he'd offered up was his name.

"Where are you from?" My eyes rolled from the tumbler twisting in my palms to his handsome face.

"Mostly Oakland—Bergen County," he offered right away. "Then we moved to Hunterdon County when I got to high school."

"We?"

69

His cheek lifted into a grin before he sat up, raising his glass. "Before we go any further, can I get a toast?"

My forehead wrinkled. "For what?"

"For finally having you to myself for real dialogue. Not on borrowed time from your job or muscled time from your friends at a damn Pixie concert. But a consensual conversation where we can talk."

I took a deep breath, not completely understanding his accomplishment. However, I appreciated the endearment. I pushed my arm into the air, over the table until my glass clinked with his. Then I gestured with my forehead for him to continue exactly how he did me earlier.

A guttural chirp cut the air and he tossed his head back, chuckling. "Okay!" His face opened, beam illuminating. "I uhhh..." With a curled index finger, he scratched his nose, trying to lose the laughter in his voice. "...have two siblings—"

"Two?" I was struck by my sharp interest.

He nodded. "Two. I'm the middle child. My brother is forty-two. He's married with two unearthly gorgeous girls. And I have a younger sister, who's twenty-six."

I didn't breathe when I asked, "Is she married?"

"No. Far from it." He pushed out a small chuckle from his belly, causing his head to jerk back. "Far from it, to my family's consternation."

"Why? She's not old?"

Sadik's brows met, and an expression of confusion set on his face. "Well, I imagine it's because of what Christina C. Jones is trying to convey to the world. Black love. My family is small, but steeped in core values, standards, traditions, and family norms, one of which is marriage. We believe in marrying with the purpose of extending the family, strengthening it. By the time our mother was twenty-six, she was married, a mother of two, and armed with two degrees. She holds a doctorate."

"All of that with two degrees?" My jaw went slack. "How?"

"She was smart. Got skipped in school a couple of times. She went to college in the middle of her high school years. By eighteen, she was married and had her first baby."

"Which came first?" I took my first sip of fancy-shmancy Mauve.

"The baby. Only because legally, the only thing that could come first was a baby. They'd been together since her freshman year."

"Just hers?" That quickly, I was enraptured. Smiling, I noted, "High school sweethearts. How much older is he than her?"

Sadik's eyes narrowed with dangerous amusement, and his lips spread. "When my parents met, my mother was deciding on which college would give her the most scholarships for a degree her mother couldn't afford. My father was twenty-six and had just acquired his first half a million dollars."

My eyes ballooned as I nearly spit out the sip I'd just taken. After a quick gulp, I struggled to breathe and coughed up a lung. It took a minute to quiet myself.

"Your mother was a sixteen-year-old child and pursued by a man with a fully developed brain?" Sadik's demeanor didn't shift an inch. "He's ten years older than her!"

"And still married to her. Still committed to her. And still protects her fiercely." His piercing gaze bulleted into me, only his mouth moving. "Forty-two years solid, this year."

With that, my eyes swept to the fire and I gulped down more brandy.

"Your mother sounds like an accomplished woman." I tried stepping back into the conversation. Before sipping from his tumbler, Sadik nodded. "What does she do?"

"She's been an educator for over thirty years. She has a few charter schools in the state."

"What about your sister? What does she do?"

"At the moment, photography." He shifted, bringing his torso forward to rest his elbows on his knees. "A year ago, it was teaching yoga. Next year, it could be a dog surfing instructor." He shrugged crossly and even rolled his eyes adorably.

I snorted a laugh. My palm flew to my face and leg suspended in the air as I tried to control my amusement. What made him less intimidating was his obvious concern and possible annoyance about his sister's life choices.

"At least someone finds humor in it. She has a master's in economics."

"No wonder she doesn't know what to do." I knew a few people in that program at my school. It was one of those degrees you had to be super focused and strategic about career goals in order to be successful. "She's twenty-six; she has time."

I took another sip of my drink. It burned my esophagus even less. When I happened a glance his way, his eyes were locked on me, mouth slightly parted and tongue running the lining of his bottom lip. Sadik seemed to be in a trance. He didn't stay there long. Catching himself, his gaze roved up to my eyes, then rolled away.

"How long have you been at the diner?" His aplomb expression communicated so much, my heart literally leaped; all humor washed away.

I took a deep breath. "Too long." Sitting up, I placed the nearly empty glass down on the table to remove my jacket. I was sure it was more than the fireside flames heating me. This Sadik guy and his Mauve assisted. It also didn't help that his eyes surveilled my every movement as that tongue discretely caressed the inside of his bottom lip. "When my father died, we needed all hands on deck like never before. My mother's income was good for health benefits, at best. My brother was too busy in the streets." I shrugged. "I'd had experience in restaurants, so I was able to get the job at Michelle's."

"What experience does a nineteen-year-old have in restaurants? Washing dishes?"

This was the part I hated sharing. Hated reflecting back on the years when my family was normal...together. We'd never been rich, but my parents were entrepreneurs and earned enough to take care of us.

"My parents owned a restaurant—two, actually. I kind of grew up in them."

"Oh, yeah?" His interest appeared genuine. "What kind?"

"African and soul food. We're Somali. My grandparents on both sides came to America for work. My paternal grandmother had the opportunity to move her husband and small children here for a job as a rare chemist with the Food and Drug Administration. I think my Dad may have been two or so years old. Ironically, my maternal grandfather, who didn't know my paternal grandparents, migrated over months later when my grandfather was granted an engineering role at one of the largest pharmaceutical companies at the time."

Sadik's face morphed into one of shock, impressed.

"Yup," I nodded, going for the last of my Mauve. "They settled in New York. My mother was born here eight months later. They had a mutual friend who linked them through a mosque in Jersey. My mother's family ended up moving to New Jersey when she was about eleven. They bought a house in my father's family's neighborhood. My father was just a couple of years older and said by high school, he couldn't take it anymore." I sputtered a laugh at the memory of him telling this story a gazillion times. "My father said just before taking her to his junior prom, he told their parents he wanted to marry her."

"And?"

I couldn't explain my bashful nature, regard whipping to the angry fire. The music had turned jazzy. Conducive to comfort.

My face wrinkled, brows met. "Are you really into this story?"

Sadik reached over and poured us both fresh glasses of Mauve. "Embarrassing transparency?" I caught a waft of his cologne as I nodded. "It's the most interesting conversation I've had all damn year. You want something to eat? They have sandwiches, salads, and things like that back there." I shook my head. "Now tell me, what did your mother's parents say about that declaration?"

I accepted the glass from him. "Well, my mother said her mother was concerned. They were so young. But my grandfather claimed his wife had become too westernized and had experienced a cultural shift since being here." I swung my hand, dotting that story. "When my father told the story, he said her parents were so happy, they cried. In fact, there wasn't a dry eye in the room. My mother said she was somewhat grossed out by the prospect." I fake whispered, "I think I'll go with my mother's rendition."

Sadik smiled. "But they finally married, had two kids, businesses..." He shrugged before sipping. "I'm sure they were married when your father passed."

Miserably so. "Yes."

"Okay. So, why do you look so spooked? That's a successful Black love story. Your grandparents stayed together, too. Right?"

"Yeah. They did."

"So, that's three fruitful unions. This is what Jones argues hasn't been shown in America. She believes the only successful love stories exposed to us via pop culture are those of White people. You and I are two healthy and balanced individuals who know differently—and can follow the legacy of 'family' passed down from our examples."

"Family." I rolled my eyes.

"What's wrong with that?"

I shrugged, suddenly wanting to disappear from this conversation...this place...his company. "I don't have family. My brother's away. My aunts and uncles live completely separate lives in nearby towns. They haven't been in our lives since..." Before trouble hit. "Since I was a kid. I mean, I see them a couple of times a year, but it was clear my parents, brother, and I were on our own. My mother was an only child. My father's sisters cut him off when I was a kid. My household felt the effects of the severance."

"I'm sorry to hear that."

My neck jerked back. "Why?"

"Because family is everything to me. My brother, his family, my sister, and I have dinner at my parents' at least once a week. We even take family vacations a couple of times a year. We're really tight."

"What about cousins?" My mood turned dreamy.

"I have lots. We see them often. My family hosts cookouts, and shit. Thanksgivings and Christmases can be overwhelming when my father extends the invitation outside of our unit. My family is my identity. That's why I can't wait to grow it. Have my own legacy to add to the tree."

"You only have a few months, from what I gather." When Sadik's eyes met mine, my pulse sprinted from the darkness coating his expression.

74

His face turned stony, and I returned the gape as my right leg bounced while crossed over my left.

He used the arch of his index finger and thumb to comb the lower half of his face. "Let's get this out of the way now." He leaned over his knees again, heated gaze piercing me. "I know what you think about Lia and her being pregnant. I understand why you think you know what you know. While I can't speak about it in detail, what I can say is I am not bound to her or any woman. I am a single man, free to pursue my life with anyone I choose. You have every right to have your questions, but no reason to be concerned. She's not a topic of discussion to be had between us." There was authoritative irrevocability in his tone.

The once fairy tale smitten chat partner was now an authoritarian? Because clearly, he was practiced in his firm tone. He'd done this before: called the shots, made demands, decided fates.

"Then why are you going out of your way to talk to me? What do you want with me?"

"I told you. To be a friend."

"What kind?"

Sadik sat back, stretching his arms aside his shoulders on the back of the loveseat. "That's to be determined." He was unsmiling.

I should have bolted out of there, but couldn't. The murkiness in his aura pulled at something vulnerable inside. Helplessly, I was attracted to his dark energy like a magnet to an underbelly of the unknown. The nefarious enigma didn't spook me like it should have. Instead, it pulled at my core, beckoning me not to run to the clear heavens away from this guy.

"She's having a baby," I tried to reason with him.

"And I'm sorry about that. I really am, Bilan. Nonetheless, that's unlikely to change until she gives birth. Even still, I see nothing standing in the way of us getting to know each other unless you put it there. The baby is not between us. At all."

His gaze stapled me to the loveseat. It was the brandy. It had loosened my defenses and possibly good senses. He'd disarmed me and now, I was without my usual vim. His phone ringing bought me some time to recharge, or at least attempt to. Sadik pulled it out, read the alert, then opened an app.

"Shit…" he grumbled. His eyes lifted to me. "We've spent the last of our time together discussing futile matters." Did he really put that on me? "I've got to go. I'll drop you off. I need your number first."

"For what?"

He was clearly annoyed.

"To keep in touch."

"And what if I don't want to?"

His head fell to the side as his gaze narrowed and shot into me. "You don't want to keep in touch with me, Bilan?"

This guy! Ugh! His handsomeness was distracting. Those curled lashes. The enticing five o'clock shadow. The swag he exuded in a simple sweat suit and sneakers. It all worked against my usual resolve.

I went to my fanny pack for my phone. "I'm only doing this because I can easily block you when I get home and process the end of this conversation. Because, I hope you don't think I'm going to be okay with—"

I tapped in my password, and Sadik reached over to grab it before I could finish speaking.

"Before you decide to hit the block button, remember my intention here."

"And what's that?"

Without hesitation, he made clear, "To be a friend. And you're telling me I can't because of a pregnancy. Don't be unreasonable, Bilan."

My forehead stretched in response.

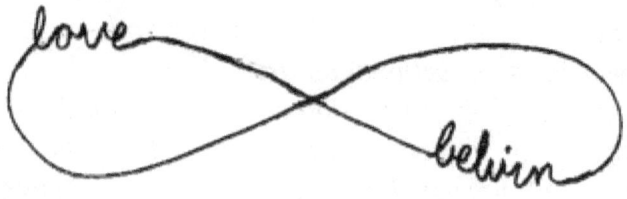

It was close to three in the morning when I sauntered into the diner. Just when I thought the place was empty, I saw a small crowd congregated in a booth near the end of the long counter.

"There she is!" Tasche croaked, her eyes pink and lips dry, reminding me of the late—or early—hour.

I made my way over to them. Randi and her girl, Brenda, were seated across from Tasche.

"Why y'all here this late?"

"Waiting on your ass, to make sure you was good," Randi bit out.

My eyes narrowed and lips pushed out. "Since when do you wait up when I have a date?"

"Since when did you date?" she challenged me.

"Gooood," Tasche groaned, rolling her eyes. "Can I please go home now? Some bitches gotta work tonight."

"I didn't mean to hold anybody up." My palms went into the air. "I don't remember telling you I needed this—"

"You do," Randi asserted with tight lips and a crook in her neck. "You ain't got a flying fuckin' clue about who that nigga is, do you?"

My gaze brushed around the table and saw Brenda and Tasche's eyes wide and expectant.

My head shook faintly, suddenly curious myself. "No."

"I ain't think you did. That's Sadik fuckin' Ellis. You never heard of his family?" My brows tightened and I shook my head again. "He's the second son of Double E Bags. That nigga is the biggest drug lord in the state—Black, at least. He used to have the whole fucking state on lock. Back in the day, he was like Nicky Barnes, Frank Lucas, Rich Porter and them cats, but in New Jersey. From the top of the state to the bottom, back in the eighties, nineties, and early two-thousands, if you was making money slinging in the Garden State, you had some connection to Double E Bags and his crew. His fuckin' sons."

She pointed behind her. "That Sadik nigga is his youngest son. His oldest one..." She tapped the table. "I can't remember his name right now, but he's a fuckin' crazy ass hothead, they say. He did a bid recently for murder."

"Murder?" Tasche's head snapped back. "You ain't say all that!"

I glanced around, hoping no one heard us.

"'Cause I just remembered. Ricky went to his welcome home party." Randi turned to me again. "He did a four-year bid or something like that, because he actually got off. Murder charges'll get you way more time than that, but his daddy, Double E Bags, hired the best fuckin' lawyers in the country and they got that shit reduced to something small, and he only got a few years."

"Damn," Tasche breathed.

That was how I felt. Randi was a beautiful, worldly thirty-year-old from Irvington. She'd been around the block a few times, so to speak. So, I believed every word she cautioned me with. She'd been with several known ballers in her day, was even with one now. Ricky Ricardo, as he was nicknamed, was a Haitian guy from East Orange who was heavily into guns. He had a reputation of selling and using them when needed. He pretty much kept to himself and had been transient over the years for his safety, though not many wanted to meet him in a dark alley. He was feared…dark and dangerous.

Over the past ten years or so, Ricky had been sought after by the cops for questioning in two murders—that I knew of. He'd been so elusive, they'd never been able to find him to bring him in. Some say it was because he had committed the murders; others have said it was because his Visa had expired and he knew he'd be deported. I didn't know much other than what Randi and a few others from around the way had told me over the years.

Randi had been with Ricky for three years now. They weren't living together, and probably didn't consider themselves a legit couple, but the streets did. On occasion, Randi would hear of him cheating with another girl and there would be hell to pay. I never understood why she'd go to the extent of fighting women for her fidelity. That was Ricky's responsibility. But then again, they weren't an official couple. Right?

"Yeah. That's how deep their pockets run," Randi continued, obviously reading my shocked reaction to her information. "This Sadik guy, they say, is different. He wasn't raised in the streets, like his brother. He went away to school. Matter of fact, Double E Bags supposedly lives out in PA, somewhere so he can't be touched."

"I think he retired, though," her friend, Brenda, suggested. "My uncle, who used to run with Double E Bags' people, said he retired and left the game to his son. But I 'on't know how true that is because right after, his son got locked the fuck up."

"Maybe his drug empire is defunct." I shrugged.

The girls snickered at my expense.

"Bullshit!" Randi laughed. "Don't show ya age, Bilan, and don't be naïve. Double E Bags was in that drug world so hard and for so long, he could only leave it with a bullet or a lifetime prison bid. That nigga ain't in a grave, and he ain't locked the fuck up either. He the type of man that breeds drug lords. That's what we saw tonight at the concert."

"Shiiiiiit!" Tasche breathed, not hiding the goofy smile breaking from her face. "That damn suite was fuckin' life, yo! Yooooo, you see all them drinks they had in there?"

"Ohhh! Girl, and the food and view to the stage!" Brenda hi-fived Tasche. "That shit was life!" she screamed, causing me to look behind myself in the nearly empty space. "And them damn bodyguards. I saw the quiet one had a gat in his waist." Her palms shot into the air. "But if he want that pussy, Bilan, just give it to him and see what he gone give in return," Brenda advised.

"Sleep with him?" My chin dipped and voice dropped deep. "To see what I get?"

"It'll be worth it." Randi nodded while shrugging with her lips. "I 'on't know who the nigga, Sadik, fucked with around here, but he paid out the ass. He should know how to trick a bitch."

"He betta," Tasche hissed. "My girl worth more than a pair of Loubs, too. He betta fuck his way to a Chanel bag!" She sucked her teeth and rolled her eyes before yawning.

Randi's eyes were on me. "Niggas like that don't ask for much with the pussy. Don't expect to be romanced too much. Shit, he probably got a lil' ass dick. They be happy for you to suck that shit and swallow!" Laughing, she slapped palms with Brenda, who was the oldest at the table.

"Well, thanks for the advice, but I ain't sucking nobody's nothing or spreading my legs. If he's giving out designer clothes for good conversation, I may be available for that. But thanks for the heads up." I pivoted to leave. "I gotta get started back there. Y'all want anything, let me know."

"Shiiiiit!" Tasche yawned out. "A bitch want a fat ass blunt and her bed right now. Fuck what you heard." She moved to stand.

"It was fun, y'all!" I smiled, remembering the night we'd planned for weeks.

"Damn sure was!" Brenda agreed, standing too.

"Next up is ya graduation joint. We gone bless you, B!" Tasche offered a dap I reciprocated.

She was so…Harlem.

"Y'all really don't have to. We can do something simple. Hit up the LQ and throw some stuff on the grill at my place."

"That sounds G, but let us call it," Tasche argued. She chucked the deuces, drawing away from me. "Fuck niggas, get money."

By this time, Randi was on her feet, too. There was something in her eyes, something concerning. That bothered me. Was anything about this Sadik guy worth trouble between us?

Tasche began her trek toward the door with Brenda on her heels. When I thought Randi would follow them, I turned myself for the bathroom.

"B," I heard behind me and turned. Randi was there alone. "Be careful, girl. Niggas like that will wine, dine, and fuck the sanity out your ass. Then you're left behind, looking for your wig when he move on. And I don't mean your hair. It's your mind that go when he do."

I wanted to ask if that was her situation with Ricky. Had that been Randi's experience at all. I'd known her for years and she ran in life at the same pace: dangerous men, fast living, easy money, and then on to the next adventure.

But I didn't utter a word. I nodded before continuing to the bathroom.

I was let into the large meeting room in the basement of one of my father's laundromats in Haledon. Sporadic sounds of radio interference zipped across the room. To the untrained ear and unknowing party, the swishes and zaps could be perceived as disturbing noise. Clouds of smoke filled the room, and the tension was so thick, it was difficult to move. My entire frame coated with resentment at the sight of the crowd present.

Seeing these men gathered here, absorbing information from my father at the head of the room only meant one thing: there was a problem. Hearing the bug interceptors was a major telling of the nature of the meeting. That and voice scramblers were technology I purchased for my father's empire to ensure the FBI or any other law enforcement agency's surveillance equipment couldn't get a clear recording of the room if listening in. Anger bolted from my belly. He knew I didn't like being in meetings like this. Didn't want to be in the same room as these cats, making me complicit in any business they had. Couldn't be. Quietly, I gaited toward the back of the room, out of the congregation.

"So, this federal grant money. I know you said Paterson got awarded and shit, and Bridgeton," Crew, a long standing soldier on my father's team, spoke up at the table, waving his index finger in the air as he spoke. "But what about our other major cities, like Newark, Jersey City, Passaic, Trenton and them?"

"You know Newark been had a special drug unit. They been doing strategic investigations for a minute now," my father began his answer.

"You right." Crew nodded.

"Yeah," my father continued at the head of the table, standing over the chair. "But so far, no federal money's been given to them. I don't even know if them fuckas even applied—or qualify—for this type of bread."

"But we gotta be smart, is all this mean," Iban interjected. "What I mean is hit up ya connects in ya city, and telling them to be smarter...keep they eyes open. The state got investigations and you know they work up, 'cause they can't start at the top. It only take one weak ass muthafucka getting popped, bitchin' up, and giving away crumbs that'll lead them pigs to this table." His index finger stabbed into the table on a hard thud.

His yellowish eyes circled around, hard-balling the eight men who made up the core of my father's network of distributors.

After a few seconds of silence, my father moved to close the meeting. "Anything else? My son's here, and I need to meet with him."

Most of the men around the table mumbled their noes.

"Other than that fuckin' dough boy ass Rizzo, sending subliminal threats about a damn robbery at the port." Millie, the Newark distributor, complained. He pointed my father's way. "I know about your alliance and shit, but I'll put a bullet in the head of that wop and any one of 'em that come in his name. My crew don't fuck with them, but we got all the fuckin' smoke if he want it!" Millie's eyes rolled toward me in the back, I was sure with Lia in mind.

"Easy." My father pumped his hand in the air. "Easy, Million. I spoke to Rizzo about the robbery. He don't know who hit him, so he's reaching right now. Nah, he can't be threatening our street soldiers, but we can't be going to war without permission from me. So chill. Fuck 'im. Let him figure out where the fuck his security was when they fucked him in the ass."

Anger flared my father's nostrils. The Rizzos were a sore topic for him in more than one way, the first being he was expecting a grandchild by them. My father would never express his disdain for that family publicly. He was too wise and prideful to. It would make him appear feeble, and we Ellises didn't do feeble.

"Now, if that's all," were his final words before the men—some of the wealthiest in the state of New Jersey—began moving, understanding their meeting was adjourned.

As my father promenaded my way, his eyes were locked on me. My brother, Iban, gave a few words of murmur to D-Rock of Camden before he was on our father's heels. His embrace was ceremonial, fully encapsulating me into his fold, then holding me at arm's length for seconds long before releasing me. I was sure he could perceive the annoyance in my aura, one I would never speak out of respect. But Double E Bags' ego would never let him cave to negative energy shooting his way. Even if it was from his beloved son.

"Let's meet over in here," he murmured.

I pivoted to follow him out of the room and into a smaller one stacked with boxes of individual use packets of laundry detergent. The doors were closed behind us by armed security.

"I'm glad you were able to come right away, Sadik." He turned to me, stroking his goatee while his eyes were to the floor ruminatively. "I need you to look into something." When I didn't respond, he continued. "Paterson and Bridgeton just got federal funds to bring on top detectives to form special drug investigation units. You know that puts us in dangerous waters. I'm hearing more cities are applying for this grant—my cities. I can't afford to get caught with my pants down. I need to let my distributors know what's coming down the pike so we can prepare. Your boy, Edwin, down at the FEDy's field office; I need to know which of my territories they're targeting next. Can you get him to find out?"

Holding his gaze, I took a deep breath. "Dad, Iban has a high school friend working for Paterson PD. Why can't you ask him? Your godson is a tenured detective for Trenton PD. Why not ask him?"

"Because they're known connects, Sadik. I need someone they wouldn't expect."

Edwin and I have been friends since college. Who doesn't know that?

And here we were. The battling of the two ultra-alpha wills. The better part of me was what my father created. I was all the good that made him, and some would say even better. One trait carried from Earl Ellis' DNA was the ability to rule and generate fear without raising a voice. It was the quieted danger brewing from the belly, and warning from the eyes. Only his tactic didn't work on me.

"Sadik," was his warning shot, though it sounded like a plea.

My fear of my father was not of his wrath. No, it was far deeper. It was of disappointing him. It had been my honor being the underling of one Earl Ellis. A privilege only a certain caliber of leader—a boss—would understand and appreciate. I honed my skills of power and leadership under his tutelage. It was still my desire to be worthy of carrying his hat. Yet still, I was my own man. I'd created and was building a legacy in my own lane. A lane he believed I'd abandoned his inheritance for.

"I'll look into it," I assured without blinking.

With a firm nod and grip to my shoulder, my father accepted what he knew was a lie. He accepted it because he knew, though I wouldn't approach the task the way he asked, he'd have the information he needed, and in a timely manner. It was a drill of ours he'd grown accustomed to and had come to accept. The work—though not in my preferred line of business—would get done. Because that's who I was.

"Thank you, Sadik." He offered a head bow before proceeding to the door.

My jaw tightened in mounting irritation. "The Lopez meeting, sir..." I called after him.

The one he'd called me out of a woman's bed for. It was an inappropriate ask, nonetheless, I took on the task.

My father turned back to me with an expression of satisfaction. He asked with lifted brows.

"The purpose of calling me in on that?"

I knew the answer, but had to present resistance to his strong will every now and then.

"Because it involved your mother and I knew you'd handle it with...the delicate blow needed."

Manipulation at its finest. Even Iban sensed it, seeing how he scoffed, bringing his back to us. That was an act of defiance I'd never dared to make when it came to Earl Ellis. Ever. It was one of the many dissimilarities between my older brother and me.

"Lopez assured his men will never be on a corner of Ellis Academy again. A three-corner radius, in fact."

"You never disappoint, Sadik. One of the many reasons why I value your service, son." That shit nipped at me, sending bolts of fury through my heated veins.

He waited, peering at me speculatively, waiting for an ill-reaction. It had been building between us for some time now, bubbling since Lia's pregnancy announcement. Reeling in my anger, I silently breathed through it. Controlling my emotions, I allowed my pupils to dilate, a means of mental retreat. Earl taught me to never express emotion in front of a known opponent. I taught myself, years ago, how to implement it.

When he was satisfied I wouldn't challenge him, my father turned toward the door and tapped. It opened for his departure and closed right behind him.

"You a better nigga than me, G." Iban cackled.

My eyes were still to the door, breathing still purposed and controlled.

Iban continued, "You told him you didn't want no parts of this, and he still calling you in on shit he can get me to do. When you gone just say no?"

That's when my neck flicked over to him. "When you finally tell him about Lia."

The haughty, provocative smirk drained from his face. "What that shit got to do with this?"

"It's his punishment. You don't get it? Until he gets over Lia, he'll continue to press me. He's going to keep fuckin' with my business."

Iban hung his head. "Okay." He held his palms to me. "A'ight. I told you I just needed some time to break this shit to Monica. Then I'll tell Pops."

"The girl is fuckin' six months, Iban," I reminded him, measuring my tone or I'd explode on his ass.

"I know, man! Don't you know I fuckin' get that?" He yanked his body away from me by the shoulder, turning into a corner.

So fucking childish...

The small storage room went silent. I focused in on my temper and gave him time to think about his next move.

"You just don't know how hard this shit is. You ain't married, bruh," Iban tried with his weak ass argument.

"And I'll never be if you don't man the fuck up and handle this shit like a G."

"I am—I will!" he shouted. Then his eyes squeezed closed, reigning in his tantrum. When they opened again, he took a deep breath. "I ain't never have to deal with no shit like this. I just need for you to hold me down on this."

I began my gait toward the door. "I always do. Always will. Just don't forget about the cross it's causing me to bear."

I tapped on the door and waited either for his rebuttal or for it to open.

The door came first. His voice never did.

∞ 6 ∞

April

Bilan

"Okay, you two." Professor Langston closed his portfolio over his desk. "The fall class schedule looks good. And Dr. Jefferson has the results of the survey calls. Great work on that, Bilan." He stood from his desk and ambled over to Jason and me seated in front. "I have to say, you two have been a wonderful asset to the department. Bilan, you've held the coveted position of student administrator two years in a row—an anomaly here."

I nodded, agreeing. Being a student administrator was hashtag goals in the College of Arts and Science. The role stretched across over fifty programs. It was an unpaid role you had to apply for amongst, at least, one hundred other classmates. I was given three student assistants of my choosing to carry out my workload; the role was that significant. Grades, reputation, experience, and competency were all factors. My role at the department increased my confidence and gave me a taste of professionalism before becoming a graduate.

"And Jason, your contributions to our IT matters have held strong against other departments, thanks to your fresh ideas and dedication,"

Professor Langston complimented. "I understand it's only April, but there are only a few weeks left in the semester. What are you guys' post-graduation plans?"

Anxiety. It struck the way it always did when thinking about the next step. My eyes averted to the corner of the room. I honestly had no idea what my plans were after graduation, other than preparing for grad school this fall. The big question was, which program I'd choose among my acceptance letters. What I'd do between now and the fall was still unknown for me.

"I've applied to a few places. No one's really biting but one, who say they have an opening more suitable for my area of study. I'm actually going south a week after graduation. My uncle called me with two small companies needing help with website work...design and program installation for clients and personnel," Jason shared proudly. "A new, private nursing home and a veterinarian office looking to upgrade its system."

"That's great, Jason!" Professor Langston's veiny hand patted him on the shoulder. "You'd do great at that level." Then he peered over to me. "Bilan, let me know if I can be more than a reference letter for grad school for you."

"I will," I returned, less spiritedly than Jason. "Thank you."

"Well, I need to get on to this disciplinary meeting over in the science wing." Professor Langston grabbed a stack of folders and writing pads from his desk, then headed for the door.

"Have a good one, sir," Jason bode as we stood.

I checked my phone for the hour. The meeting ended at the perfect time; otherwise, I would have had to excuse myself.

"Hey!" Jason called out as I traveled toward the door myself. "Where're you going?" His eyes lit with inspired interest. The freckles on his almond-cased face dotted intermittently. His teeth were a little yellowish, but all present and healthy. And his hair was short with tight coils. "You look like a woman on a mission today." He smiled.

Jason was a twenty-two-year-old computer science major from Maplewood. Although I was six years older, we'd met our freshman year here in college. We shared many of the same general education courses. He had been the College of Arts and Science school's information and technology student assistant, causing us to work together often over the past two years. It wasn't until recently that he'd began taking interest in me. I honestly didn't mind the subtle flirting, even used it to pass the time. God knew I had no real prospects. But there was a disconnect in our chemistry, something I couldn't put my finger on.

I took in a long breath, forging a smile at the door. "I have a call I need to take in the study room."

"Okay. I'll wait up for you."

When I thought to decline the proposal, I recalled how short these calls could be.

"Cool. My treat for lunch?"

"I would say yes if you ate anything. My treat." He winked.

With a nod of "touché," I scurried out of Professor Langston's office.

The moment I hit the hall, on my way to the private study room, my phone rang with a call from a New Jersey State Prison inmate. Once inside the small room, I waited out the automated message.

I closed the door behind myself and took a seat at the small table when, "Yo. Whaddup," pierced through the wire.

"He—" I sat up in my seat. "Hey, Ab! How are you?"

"Goodie. I need you to do something."

"Okay."

It wasn't that I heard from him regularly. When he wanted to call me, he'd have one of his girlfriends stop at the diner with the date and time of the call. Since his arrest and long stay at the county jail before his trial and sentencing, I had calls forwarded from the house phone to my cell just for him. Inmates couldn't call mobile numbers, and I was hardly home for that to be a possibility. Abshir didn't reach out often, and made it clear he didn't want me visiting him. Hearing him shoot off orders didn't help me forget our estranged rapport. Abshir and I hadn't had anything resembling a healthy sibling relationship since he was in seventh grade and hadn't yet been seduced by the streets. Fighting or completely ignoring each other were common dynamics between us before his incarceration.

"I need you to get a word to Damien. Tell him I said Lenny been missing for like three weeks."

"Lenny who?" My face folded.

"None of ya fuckin' business," he croaked, already annoyed when asking me for a favor. "Just tell him that next time you see him, he'll know what I mean."

Spirit now deflated, I went silent, not knowing what to say. Abshir and I fought all the time as teens. He'd been physically rough with me and even betrayed me deeply just after our father passed. It was a pain still palpable whenever I allowed my mind to travel back to our childhood. When he was pulled over and found without a driver's license, which prompted a search of his vehicle—where he was in possession of heroin, cocaine, and a handgun—he was arrested and jailed.

I had to comfort our agonized mother through the entire process alone—while she battled pancreatic cancer. He was charged with possession and intent to distribute, because it wasn't his first charge of that nature. After a grueling two and a half year-wait for trial, my brother was sentenced to seventy-one months with thirty-one of that time served. That meant he had three and half years to serve out in prison.

Instead of continuing down the typical galling road of fighting, I tried to change the tempo of our conversation.

"You're nearing the end." I bit the inside of my cheek, anxiously awaiting what he'd throw back over the wall to me.

"What you mean?" His tone hadn't improved much.

"Your time." I cleared my throat. "You're almost done. This summer. Right?"

My eyes bounced around blindly in the room so hard they hurt.

He grumbled, "Something like that."

"When?" My pitch hiked. "Have they given you a specific date?"

"Why?"

I shrugged, though he couldn't see me. "The house is crazy quiet. I could use your presence around there."

"It's what you wanted. Right?"

I rolled my eyes shut. "I've never wanted to lose my entire family in the span of six years. That's messed up for you to say!"

"Look, man." He groaned like an angry bear. While battling him face-to-face, I showed no fear of him. After being separated from him for six years, I knew not to dismiss his new playground of temperament. Abshir likely had new defense mechanisms, and less of a filter when using them. My brother seemed to have hated me for years; I was sure prison intensified the sentiment. "All you need to know is this summer. I'll hit you when the time come. Don't be going around telling people I'm coming home, either—"

"Not even your family?" I pushed back.

"Hell no! Fuck them. They 'on't give a shit about me." He scoffed. "Truth be told, they 'on't give a shit about you either, but you keep kissing they ass, wanting to be down. Fuck them." The line went silent. Again, I didn't know what to say. Abshir was right: the only known family we had in the States was on my father's side, and they didn't exactly extend themselves often. "Look, just do what the fuck I said. I'll let you know when I get out."

"If you need me for anything when you get out, don't you think you should show just a little respect, Abshir?"

He snorted. "Respect?" His tone was punctuated with a level of resentment I didn't understand. "Fuck you mean?"

"Ab..." My face collapsed into my palm. "I don't want to fight. I'm honestly asking because I thought we could go to Mommy and Daddy's gravesite when you get home. Maybe sit down and talk about..." I took a trying breath. "...I don't know...us being better to each other now that we're all we've got."

There was a slight pause on the line before I heard him release another breath. "Yeah. I 'on't know about all that, but make sure you get that message to that nigga. I got another call to make, so I gotta go."

And after a few hard thuds in my ear, I realized he was gone. I tossed the phone on the table, and pushed my face into my palms. Without notice, my shoulders trembled violently and my belly constricted, releasing a bucket of tears. It was getting to me again. I realized two years ago it wasn't loneliness encroaching on my sanity, because I had a busy life between school and work, and was around a constant stream of people all day. I'd come to realize I was alone.

Working at Michelle's gave me unbelievable flexibility. I could avoid going home to an empty house until the break of dawn, if I wanted. Some days, I'd go home and sleep just two hours, only to shower and be on campus, tackling one of many of my assigned tasks. There was no one to account for my time at the place I called home, but Dog. Professor Langston's question about my future was a depressing reminder of me losing a huge piece of pastime. And I couldn't forget my boss, Nicky's, string of questions about my plans after graduation.

I had none.

That had me spit out an unexpected snicker. Was I really here crying about a bright future? What was wrong with me? I'd be fine. I'd figure it out. As long as I had good health and kept my head on straight, I'd be fine. I wiped my face, feeling silly. My chest collapsed and head rolled back over my shoulders. Stretching my neck, I needed to relax so I could leave this room without a trace of tears or sour emotions.

My phone chirped on the table. I glanced down and saw the alert of a text.

Your Friend: *Three questions.*

My friend? Who was my friend, and when did I program a contact under that—

Sadik…

Me: What?

I hadn't heard from him since he dropped me off at the diner after the rooftop fire excursion in the City a few days ago.

Your Friend: *I want to reach a middle ground. Tell me when I can see you again so you can ask me three questions and I'll answer all three honestly.*

The phone pinged again before I finished reading the previous text.

Your Friend: *Oh, and you have to reciprocate.*

My eyes bounced from wall to wall, processing this.

Me: How? When?

Why were my limbs softly trembling, the heels of my feet bouncing in the air?

Your Friend: *By you answering my questions honestly and fully. What about today?*

As I bit my bottom lip, inexplicably intrigued by his proposal, I sniffed back the tears of pain experienced just moments ago.

Me: Today doesn't work.

I brushed the top of my index finger under the tip of my nose as I waited pensively. Here I was again, feeling…aswoon over this guy.

Your Friend: *Tomorrow. I'll pick you up wherever. Five pm sharp.*

How many ways could I delay an answer? It wasn't that I wasn't intrigued. God, I was intrigued. Too intrigued. It was because I knew, after learning about this guy and his family, I had no business going out on a date with him—if it would be considered a date.

Wait…

My fingers busied, typing my response.

Me: Like a date?

I drummed my fingers over the circular tabletop.

Your Friend: *Call it whatever you want. Just tell me where to pick you up.*

Sadik

"You ain't hearing me, Deek," he asserted.

"I am, Iban, but you gotta chill," I tried.

"Chill? Chill!" he shouted, blasting into the Bluetooth of my car. "Fuck you mean chill? You ain't hear what the fuck I just said? That fat ass Rizzo don't wanna give the baby the Ellis name. Type of bullshit is that? So what, she ain't fuckin' married! That's a fuckin' Ellis in there. Ain't no damn Rizzo put that baby there!"

Rory's big ass eyes rocketed into me from the rearview mirror. I closed my eyes, pushing myself into the backseat of my car.

"Man, fuck him," Iban continued his meltdown. "Fuck 'em all! I keep telling y'all, fuck the waiting shit, and let's snipe Damien's ass! We need to remind everybody who the fuck we is!"

"We can't do that, and you know it," I droned fruitlessly. "It goes against protocol."

"Man, fuck protocol!"

"We can't fuck off the commission."

"Yes the fuck we can. That weak ass agreement with them weak ass rules is what the mafia did. We ain't the muthafuckin' mafia. Rizzo came up with that shit, wanting shit to be run like it was when his father and grandfather ran shit. Them bitches weak as hell now. They can't even take out the Lopezes—they that fuckin' weak now. Fuck 'em all!"

"You spoke to Pops about this?"

"He ready to clip Damien's snake ass, too. Everybody ready but you." Rory rounded her index finger in the air, telling me to wrap it up. "And we all know how the story go with Double E Bags and his favorite son—"

"Aye," I spoke over him. "Incoming. I gotta go."

"Wait. I ain't get to ask about the Ab kid or his boy, Derrick. We ain't got eyes on him yet?"

Briskly, I answered, "Not yet. I'll hit you later. Love."

"Love," he puled predictably before Rory disconnected the call.

As I sat up in my seat, the door was being opened and Jefferson was sliding in with a manila envelope.

"Hey." He nodded to me, then acknowledged Rory, who didn't return it. "Here you go." I accepted the envelope. "I looked into the calls from Lenny Jenkins' family. The police department is looking into it because it's been over two weeks. They only have one man on the search, though. As of this morning, they have nothing."

I nodded, relieved. Iban wanted to cut up the Lenny kid's body and send a part to his family. This confirmed my father ordered Iban to chill on his menacing inclinations. That gratified me. I pulled out documents with familiar names on them.

"And as you can see, on one of the reports in there, Vero Amato filed for divorce from Marcu Amato in 2001. It was..." He seesawed his head from side-to-side while flashing his clenched teeth. "...ugly and sooo not Sicilian, completely going against their Catholic beliefs. He fucked around on her so much over the years, she fucked his cousin. The cousin..."

I pulled up a distorted image of a corpse hanging from a noose. His head hung to the side, bloodied face darker than his hands. Blood stained the crotch of his pants and ran down his pants.

"What's hanging from his mouth?" I asked, squinting into the shoddy copy of an already faded original.

"That's Raphael Amato, Marcu's first cousin, and his detached cock and sacs," Jefferson explained, sans audible dramatics.

He didn't need any. I'd seen pestilent shit coming up in my father's line of work. I'd even carried out vicious penalties myself. However, most of the work I'd seen was delivered swiftly and abridged for legal reason.

"Shiiiit." I breathed. Needing to progress from that grim state, I moved on. "And Derrick Little? He's still laying low in Greenville?"

"Yup." Jefferson sighed. "He's not made a peep in South Carolina in all the six years he's been down there. My guys did pull over a car

95

with his friend driving. He had to cough up ID, but was let off when they realized he's tagged." I nodded.

I closed and stretched my eyes, exhaling.

All goodie…

I needed time. Time to link these independently working parts.

"And the girl?"

"Oh!" Jefferson scratched his eyebrows, recalling. "Bilan…" He snapped his fingers. "Asad—"

We finished it at the same time. "Yasin."

"Yes," I made clear. "Asad-Yasin."

Damn…

Even hearing her name set butterflies loose in my damn belly.

"I didn't get anything about her other than what I told you. College student. No real debt—oh!" He snapped his fingers again. "Her house is in foreclosure."

My head jolted back a bit, and Jefferson caught the mild reaction.

"Yeah. It's in there. It's been in that status for over two years now. But other than that, there isn't much on her. No arrests, nothing suspicious."

Continuing to nod, I knew it was time to bring this conversation in.

"Thanks, man. One other thing."

"Sure," he acknowledged.

"There's a grant opportunity being awarded to qualified police districts in the state to fund new drug task forces. Paterson and Bridgeton just jump-started theirs. I need to know which other towns are coming down the pike."

Jefferson nodded. "Sure thing."

"Thanks, man. How's Mandy's pregnancy coming along?" I tried transitioning my state of mind and posture to close this meeting. "Last days can be brutal."

Jefferson relaxed into the seat himself and sighed. "Yeah, man. She's becoming more sentimental, but I'm taking it day by day. I get it. There's a whole damn human being growing inside your body. I just take all the shit she throws my way, man." I nodded, expressing understanding. It was their first child. "And she's loving the scalp

96

massages, man. She keeps talking about how relaxing they are for her."

"Good. Glad she's enjoying them. A few more weeks to go?"

"Four. And it's like I get more and more paranoid the closer I get. It's like when your wife is pregnant, her safety is more stressful and more task-heavy than ever. That's two lives at stake. You know?"

I didn't. Having a family was so far off my radar.

I lifted my hand into the air. "Thanks for this."

After slapping palms, he expressed, "No doubt. Hey, you heard about Edwin's father being in the hospital?"

Edwin Johnson was a good friend of mine from Blakewood University. We were college roommates for a few semesters. After graduating with a degree in criminal justice, he joined the police department, then quickly worked his way to investigations. He was now a commanding officer in Newark. Our relationship had been too noted for him to be my inside eyes in law enforcement. Mike Jefferson here had been an independent recruit by way of means no one knew.

I bowed. "I was just there this morning. He's going to pull through. We're sure of it."

"Cool, man. Be good," he bade before letting himself out.

"Jefferson," I called behind him, causing him to peer over his shoulder. "Look a little deeper into the Bilan chick."

"Asad-Yasin? Anything in particular I should be searching into?"

Brushing my chin with my thumb, several thoughts shot through my head, like where I'd take her tomorrow, what she'd smell like, and what topic I'd use to engage her.

"Anything that doesn't line up with a twenty-eight-year old college student." As though those were typical characteristics. "Anything like a druggie husband or a carpet-munching girlfriend or some shit. I don't know." I scoffed. "Anything odd."

"You got it, man." Jefferson stood from the car, closing the door behind him.

My eyes swept the front of the car, catching big round eye balls with black dots shooting into me from the rearview mirror. I crooked my neck, raising my brows in question.

Her face dropped to her lap and she shook her head. "Fuck you doin', sire?" She joked often with that title.

"Doing?"

Rory's head lifted, and I caught her smirk as she rolled her eyes. "You know what I mean. Why the fuck you wanna know about the Bilan girl? You know about her. She ain't the target, Deek. Her brother ain't even the target. Ain't he 'posed to help us get to the target?"

Ignoring her unspoken questions, I pointed to her in the mirror. "Your target is getting some food together for a picnic, Bean."

"What food you get for a picnic?"

I smiled. "Picnic food."

Her eyes rolled again at my wink.

"Fuck is picnic food?"

I shrugged, my gaze moving outside of the car as we pulled off. "Cheese, fruits, nuts…vino. Some shit."

"For who?"

I scoffed. "Me and a…" I felt my forehead wrinkling. "…a friend. A good friend." My stretched lips twitched at that prospect.

Rory's tiny shoulders dropped, and her neck rolled. "The whole fuck?"

I stepped out of the car he sent to the diner to pick me up and glanced around. Trees, grass, people, and...

"Mic check. One, two. One, two," a woman voiced a distance away. "Mic check. One, two. One, two." Then a horn blew.

I turned a complete three-hundred-sixty degree angle in search of the source as a keyboard sounded. A car pulled up behind us. A ruby black-colored Mercedes-Maybach. The one I had the privilege of riding in the night of the Pixie concert last week. The one with the nut brown quilted leather interior that felt like a pillow beneath me. The very one whose owner was stepping out with full-on confidence, wearing a heather gray suit with a stark white shirt opened at the neck and no tie. The owner whose kaleidoscopic eyes that appeared green today scowled the parameter before roving over to me.

And God, he looked delectable sauntering toward me, honeyed eyes searing through me and the lining of his full lips looking more pronounced inside of his stark five o'clock shadow. He acknowledged the guy, Lamont, who drove me here with a nod but no eyes, because Sadik's eyes were always stapled to me when we were together. His heavy gaze made me feel self-conscious and I found myself wiping down my skirt and on their own accord, my legs extended, lifting in my heels. It was a reaction to my spiked anxiety.

∞ 7 ∞

Bilan

"Hi, Bilan." My name spilled like champagne from his lips.

"Hey." I bounced on my toes, swiping the back of my neck as I gazed away.

"Glad you were able to make it." His scrutiny was still on me.

"I said I would, Sadik."

"Well, thank you." His friendly grin was dangerous.

"Where are we?"

"You mean Montclair?"

"No. Here."

He pivoted, throwing his regard around. "Looks like a park to me."

I scoffed, rolling my eyes. "I know. I mean why are we here? I hear music."

"Yes. It's jazz in the park. I thought it would be a good opportunity to talk more."

I muffled my question of "talk more about what" with a smile.

"Okay, even though I don't get why you're so pressed to talk to me." I hoped that would lead to something close to an answer.

"I think I've explained that more than once. You see the name I'm programmed under in your phone. Right?"

Sarcastically, I snapped my finger while nodding. "Right!" I sighed. "To be my friend."

"Ahhhh…" He smiled beautifully. "She's finally getting it."

From the corner of my eye, I could see body movements. It was his "people." Lamont, the big guy who drove me, was carrying a picnic basket from the trunk, and Rory had a bag in one arm and a blanket in the other as they walked further down the green.

"Ready?" Sadik asked, reaching for my hand.

Without thought, I met his warm palm and my breath hitched. That small, but significant reaction annoyed me. Though he still affected me viscerally, this man wasn't the same one I'd encountered in the diner or at the concert. Since that night, I'd learned so much about him. Things that should frighten me.

Hand-in-hand, Sadik guided me down the walkway and gingerly onto the grass, where his team had quickly assembled a legit picnic setting. It was complete with food, wine, and a traditional red gingham blanket.

"What's this?" I cracked on half a laugh.

Sadik's lips lifted as he observed the last of the set. "A picnic. Hope you eat cheese."

"That looks like more than cheese." My gaze was a few feet away, on the blanket.

"Let's go see what else is there."

I turned to him with my lips pouted suspiciously. "Because, of course, you forgot all you packed in there before driving here to the park."

Running his index finger against the patch of hair just beneath his bottom lip, he chuckled quietly. "Right. You're a quick learner."

As we approached the spread, Lamont was taking off for the car. Awkwardly, I lowered myself onto the blanket, trying to keep my skirt at a decent length as I arranged my legs beneath me. Then I tossed my phone inside my purse and pushed it to the top of the blanket, where I could see it. When I chanced a glance up, my attention turned rapt at the sight of Sadik peeling out of his suit jacket. He folded it symmetrically and handed it over to a waiting Rory. I couldn't pull my eyes from him as he spoke in a hushed tone to her while handing her his two cell phones. She nodded before taking off.

I pretended to push back my cuticles as Sadik descended to the blanket, across from me. He went straight to the basket and lifted a bottle of wine, scanning the label.

"You prefer red, white? Sweet or dry?"

My shoulders lifted in indecision. "I'll let you choose."

"A man—and especially one my age—shouldn't be caught sipping sweet wines," he mumbled, searching the humongous basket for his preference.

Once selected, I watched him deftly open the bottle of white with an opener. He poured my glass before his. He then pulled out a tray that didn't resemble one picked out of a grocery store, which made me wonder who packed the basket.

"Oooh," I breathed. "Grapes, strawberries, cheese, crackers..." My eyes ran the length of the platter. "Nuts and spread. I'm impressed. There are four types of cheeses here."

With playfully narrowed eyes, he joked, "I'll tip my assistant." Sadik pulled out real plates and cloth napkins. "Help yourself."

As he searched through the basket, I lifted my glass, but didn't drink from it.

"So?" He inhaled, a glint of inspiration in his eyes.

"So?"

He shifted to face me. "Time for our questions." My face fell. When he was able to perceive my bemusement, he reminded me, "The three questions of truth we agreed to."

My mouth formed an "O" as my regard slipped over to the band on stage.

The show had begun, though we were at a distance to other attendees. I was sure that was by design. We could still hear each other and had privacy.

"You ready?" he asked.

I rolled my eyes while grinning. "I guess. The question is, are you ready?"

Broadening his chest perceptively, he gave the posture of transparency. "I'm always ready. Would you like to go first?"

I shrugged, lips pouted to mask my smile. Though prepared, suddenly I felt embarrassed. "I would let you do the honors, but the one I'm leading with may bring all of this to an end." I eyed him closely.

"I would hope not, unless you're going to pull out your dick."

I snorted, stupidly finding that hilarious.

"No. I've heard about your family." Again, I watched him carefully.

His chin dipped and eyes pinned to me. "What have you heard?"

"That you're Google'able." I jerked my head to the side, feeling smug. "So, I Googled you all. There are a fair number of articles about your father, dating back to the nineties. After reading the context of them, I'm sure there are even more, but they were published before the big Internet era and aren't as easy to find. But if I were to ask my IT friend to search, he'd come back with more charges, arrests, and other legal factors that paint your father as a drug lord, I'm sure."

Sadik didn't react other than to lift his glass for a nip of wine, but I was confident I had his attention.

"In fact, some argue he was the biggest Black kingpin in New Jersey. Earl Ellis is estimated to have been worth forty-million dollars at the height of his reign. His drugs fueled the state, from High Point State Park to the surfers in Cape May from the early eighties until—" I felt my face harden when I couldn't recall the end of his supremacy. "I guess...until. But from before I was born until...I don't know..." I shrugged. "...maybe a few years ago, there are documented arrests, convictions, and affiliations. Your father did prison time in the mid-seventies."

According to one article, Earl Ellis, aka Double E Bags, had been convicted of drug possession before he became the reigning king of the state. What he'd been convicted of was severely light, compared to the business he grew after his release.

Sadik's expression remained implacable as he listened in silence.

"Another Ellis faced a conviction," I continued. "Your brother, Iban. He was sent to prison for murder."

The only reason that fact didn't freak me out to the point of me declining seeing Sadik again was, foolishly, because the pictures I saw of him online weren't of your typical hardened criminal. Eighty percent of the images I was able to gather of Iban Ellis had him dressed in impressive formal wear. Suits, shoes, and sometimes even ties were staples of his ensemble. According to an article on his arrest and booking, Iban was six foot two and one hundred-eighty pounds. That meant he had to be a tad bit taller than his younger brother, Sadik, here, who I estimated to be just under six feet and possibly weighed just as much. And although Iban was convicted of murder, his countenance was much like his brother's here: nondescript, debonair, unassuming.

Safe...

After a spell, a single muscle on Sadik's body finally moved. His brow line lifted, and he licked his lips before reaching for the food tray.

"Well." He swiped cream onto a cracker with a knife. "I'm glad we got that out in the open. You don't have to hide all the gory details you've heard—"

"Learned," I countered.

"Heard," he clarified. "Not everything Google told you is one hundred percent factual." He tossed the cracker into his mouth.

The entire cracker.

And I couldn't help my fixed gaze on his mouth as he chewed and swallowed it in record time with complete insouciance of how enrapt I was.

So...male...

"Really?" I challenged, snapping out of that torpor. "I doubt much of what I read is false."

"Two-hundred, fifty-eight million."

"Huhn?" I hummed.

"According to the federal prosecutors, my father's operation netted two-hundred, fifty-eight million dollars annually at its height." My mouth fell to my lap. "And I can tell you categorically, that isn't true." He popped a grape into his mouth. As my brain whirred with the figures, I couldn't rip my eyes away from his full churning lips as he chewed. His jaw flexed like a machine and eyes darkened. "Like I said, it's good you have an idea of my history. You would've become aware, at some point. Now, I don't have to worry about you running or crying later down the line when it becomes clear."

"Later down what line?"

Sadik didn't respond right away. He cast his attention to the stage, where the band had transitioned into a new song. It gave my roiling belly a moment to settle.

"You should eat something."

Mechanically, I grabbed a block of cheese and bit off just a small corner of it. Sadik's usual intense gaze, for once, wasn't on me.

"Okay." He brushed the palms of his hands together. "My turn."

"Wait! You're not going to address what I just shared?"

"You never asked a question."

My head drew back. "Do I need to?"

"To adhere to the agreement, yes."

Was he serious?

"Okay. How much of that drug empire were you involved in?"

"None," his answer came swiftly. "While my father is an integral part of my life and the man I am, I have my own business."

"Which is?"

"For starters, I have a third-party logistics firm. Any and all physical articles coming into or leaving the country must be documented and approved by the government. It's a multifarious process to implement, hence my role. I employ two customs brokers, licensed with CBP—Custom Border Protection, that is—and a support team. Together, they prepare and submit documentation to notify or obtain clearance from government agencies for international goods trafficking. We transfer and store goods at my warehouse and arrange for dispensing them, according to my customers' preferences. And that's completely legal and non-drug related."

Customs...

"I didn't know that..." My voice faltered.

"Not many do. It isn't the most understood and popular industry, such as teaching or law, although just about everyone in the country benefits from my service in some way or another. I'm sure you don't quite get it either, and I can understand why. It's rather complex, but I work hard and have been successful at it."

"How long have you been in business?"

"Since about a year out of school, so over fifteen years."

"School?"

He flashed a faux smile, disturbingly alluring considering he was being sarcastic.

"Yes. The son of a reputed 'drug lord'—" He used air quotations. "—was afforded a college education. Twice, actually. After I got my bachelor's, I dabbled in real estate—investment purchases—before starting my customs business. It was supposed to serve as a small project, mild income while I worked on other pursuits."

"How were you able to dabble in investment real estate without earnings from a real job?"

"My grandmother I mentioned to you. When she was tired of living alone as she got older, she gifted me her house in West Orange. Not having a need for it, I sold it in college. Used a little of that money to invest in projects a couple of my friends, who were recent BU alums had going on. That paid off, doubling my outlay." He smoothed down the front of his shirt, gazing across the park. "I had a few lucky opportunities, one being an apartment building in one of the most prime neighborhoods in the City." His head bobbed, implying he did well.

My face folded. "The fireplace rooftop spot?"

Sadik gave an affirmative nod this time. "I bought up shit, flipped some of it, and moved on. Real estate doesn't move me."

"And what does?"

His gaze journeyed to me, face blank as he reached for more nuts. "Apparently, Somali women."

With flamed cheeks, I averted my gaze. Hearing that was weird for me. While I was very much aware of my heritage, I identified as American. It was like the Somali piece of my identity was distant. I'd never visited and didn't have much family in my world to keep me attached to the culture.

"Can I go now?" His deep tone resembled a wearied child's.

Winded by the information just uncovered, I didn't have it in me to decline. So, I nodded, rubbing the back of my neck.

"Why don't you have a man in your life—romantically?"

"Who said I didn't?" My rushed words made it clear I was defensive. Sadik grinned sinisterly, popping a grape into his mouth. I reached for my glass, needing a mental blur immediately. "I have..." I lowered my chin, feeling all kinds of defensive. "I have friends."

"Really?" There was that glint of inspiration in his honeyed irises again as he inclined himself to me.

"Really." I nodded, taking the first gulp of my wine. "In fact, you should be lucky I was able to carve out this time for you. I don't see guys during the week."

"Really?" he repeated.

"True story!" I pouted, eyes locked to the stage.

"What type of guys do you…see?"

I shrugged. "There's a range. A short one."

"Be more specific." His entire frame faced me.

"Well, driven men, of course. I mean…there are only two I take seriously."

"Right. Because you told me that night in the diner women of your age and education, who lack baggage like kids, are left with little to no options when it comes to your male counterparts. Remember, you're overlooked by men who look like you?" Sadik pretended to examine the skin on his hands. He even went to the extent of touching his face to prove the point of us being the same race.

I rolled my eyes. "I said little to no options, not no options. I have options."

"Tell me about them," he pushed.

"One is a…" How could I describe Damien, who hadn't asked me out or exactly pursued me? "An entrepreneur. He has a…security firm," I embellished. "We've known each other for about six years now and have just been taking it slow."

"Is that it?"

"No. There's another. He goes to my school…graduates next month, too. We've been…dating," I stretched the truth. "…for about two years now. Again, I see no need to lock in a relationship at this point in my life." I shook my head, hating the inclination to lie. I couldn't remember the last time I told them consecutively. "My turn for question number two."

He reached over to pluck a few grapes off the vine, a stream of his delicious cologne wafting into my nostrils. "Go for it."

"How often do you have security around?" My gaze shot over to Rory, glancing away after trying discretely to gain his attention.

Sadik followed my line of vision to her. Rory looked at me, then her boss before she flashed the face of a cell phone.

Is she telling him he had a call?

"Is she your security?" That question suddenly settled over me.

Rory was a tiny woman. I couldn't imagine her being effective in taking down an attacker.

Sadik shook his head at her, communicating a "no" before turning to face me. "Rory's one of my assistants. She may be tiny, but she's trained to protect." He tried for a smirk.

"Why do you need protecting in your line of work?"

"Because of who my father was. It's an expensive assurance, but a number of us in my family have security most of the time." Then one cheek rose sheepishly. "If you make me number three on the dating circuit, I'm afraid you'll have to get used to them. Believe me, at some point, you will."

My pulse galloped. Looking for a distractor, I plucked the rest of the cube of cheese I'd been holding forever into my mouth. "Your turn."

With a sober expression, Sadik nodded. "If there was one thing in the world you could have that you don't already possess, what would it be?"

My eyes squinted as I thought about that. I found myself twisting, attention going toward the stage. Blindly, I watched the big-bellied guy blow hard into the saxophone. His effort appeared great.

"I didn't know we were going…deep," I murmured.

"Is it deep for you?"

I turned to him again. "Doesn't have to be."

"Apparently, it is. We agreed to honesty. To get it, you have to give it," he delicately warned.

I took a deep breath, slightly annoyed again by his probing questions. When I turned, I found him peering into me with that intensity I'd become accustomed to from him. It was the type a girl could get used to. Get lost in. It was in that penetrating gaze that I found safety, for some strange reason. They were caverns I could escape into.

"Something silly."

"Nothing's too silly."

"It's something money can't buy."

"Try me." His eyes darkened, and his nostrils flared just slightly.

I scraped my bottom lip through my teeth, deciding to just go with it. "Family." My lashes fluttered and head shook to correct myself. "My family."

"Your parents? Brother?"

"Told you it was silly." I rubbed my lips together to smooth over the gloss, curling my legs more beneath me.

Suddenly, his hand palmed my knee and a shiver coursed my spine. "Don't close up on me, Bilan. I find you fuckin' fascinating," I swallowed hard at his elongated pause. "Just because I can't explain why doesn't mean you should put up guards against me."

I scoffed. "It's not that."

"Then what is it?"

"It's just…personal, Sadik. It's something meaningful to me that could come off as silly to someone else."

"Not someone who sincerely wants to know," he argued.

"My family wasn't perfect, but we accounted for each other. We were present every day. Our fights were just as predictable as our meals. Our fears were just as identical as our features. We were a unit. I don't have that anymore. I don't have anyone."

"You're lonely?"

I shook my head, firm on the answer from my recent revelation. "Alone. My schedule is flexible and demanding at the same time. I fill in the hours by staying busy. It would be nice to come home to the people I feel connected to." I swallowed hard, keeping my eyes wide to ward off the heavy emotion encroaching upon me.

There. I shared it with someone and didn't cry…

My attention went out to the solo violin number renting the air softly. When I faced Sadik again, his heavy gaze was to the blanket; ruminating, it appeared. I told him it would be silly to him. Instead of feeling sorry for myself, I decided to be grateful for a listening ear. I could never share something so vulnerable with Randi. And it seemed Sadik's reaction was rude. Maybe he was still processing my crazy.

I didn't realize I'd turned away from Sadik again until, out of nowhere, we locked eyes. And again, there was a glint of inspiration in his honeyed irises.

"Your last question is up," he warned forlornly.

"I'm sure you're happy."

"Your questions have been painless. We should do this again."

"Again?"

His eyes were on the stage when he asserted, "Yeah."

"Why are you so interested in me—and you can't say to be my friend." His eyes rolled toward the sky, and the most adorable grin split Sadik's face. It caused my own unexpected chuckle. "I've researched your name. I get it now. You've probably used that line on a million women."

That sobered his expression, and Sadik's eyes were on me again. His head shook softly, and his eyes softened with passion. "I've never said that to anyone before you."

My face tightened. "Then why me?"

His regard dropped to the wine glass beneath him. "I've been asking myself the same question for days now. To be real, the only answer I could come up with is there's something about you— something you try to hide from the world—that I can sense, and it appeals to me."

"On what level?"

"Is that your final question?"

"No!" My head bobbed on my neck with that one syllable.

He fingered the mouth of his glass as he murmured. "I don't know. There is more than one, but one's definitely...sensual."

"Sensual?" I stabbed my chest with my index finger. "Me?"

That's when he did that thing with his eyes. The muscles around them tightened, and his jaw flexed. It made him appear either angry...or repressed. "Why not you, Bilan?"

Our gazes locked. I couldn't be more attracted to this guy, could I? I mean, this was ridiculous. In that instance, I craved to know how his masculinity felt beneath the pads of my fingers. Again, ridiculous!

"The other night… You stared at me a few times…weird-like."
My eyes faltered before I fortified myself and peered at him directly
again. "Why?"

Sadik's face wrinkled as he re-adjusted himself, bringing his torso
up and resting his arms on his knees as he considered it. His regard
averted, too, peering over to the stage.

"You want the real answer or some cute shit?"

I sat up, nipped by that question. "This was your idea. You said
you'd answer three of my questions honest—"

"You're talking about when you couldn't keep your eyes off my
lips at the concert, making me wonder how yours taste? Or after, on
the rooftop when you peeled out of your jacket and I envisioned you
naked, on top of me, riding my dick hard with nothing on but a long
ass Chanel lariat with layered metal chains, glass pearls, and other
jewelry." His thick brows nearly met in a chilling expression. "Have
you ever seen one of those?"

Sucking in a deep breath, I swung my head to look away. My frame
heated all over, pulse beat frantically in my neck. My misted palms
curled into tight fists. But I couldn't. I couldn't look away from him
this time. Those eyes…inside the honeyed irises was a reflection of me,
and instead of seeing my usual anxiousness, exhaustion, or
insecurities, I saw something unfamiliar. The woman in his eyes
satisfied Sadik. She appealed to him in a way that curled him.

I'd done the search into his family, had been in his presence enough
to know I'd been sharing air with a man of power. His walk was
different…chest more expanded than any man I've met. His chin
remained symmetrical with anyone he gave orders to. And while his
spirit seemed calm, there was a raging fire in his eyes, telling of the
commanding nature of his aura. Who he really was when not
examining me with those eyes.

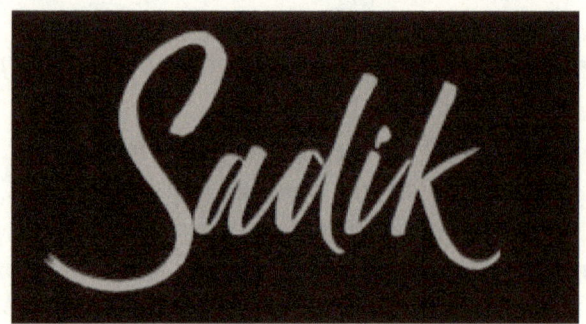

Sadik

"Was that too much honesty for you, Bilan?"

She was doing that thing again. Staring at me with parted lips, breathing visibly as she did it. And with just a foot between us, I could see her pulse beat in her neck. Those speckled dots on her caramel chiseled cheekbones teasing me. I wanted her. It was patently clear to me in this moment. Over the past two weeks, since laying eyes on her, Bilan played in the back of my head. She intrigued me to the point of taking measures to have face time with her, but lately, thoughts of her had been occurring too frequently.

And with her mouth open, I wanted to finally taste it. I wanted to throw her back on this blanket and run my tongue all over her body, starting with her lips. My fingers itched to fuck up her Halle Berry, holding her to me as I drove into her walls. I was also a logical man and knew that wouldn't bode well.

But maybe just a peck...

My body leaned into her, moving slowly so my brain could process the slightest resistance. The only thing moving on Bilan's body were her eyes toward my mouth. She was attracted to me.

I knew it...

I heard someone clear their throat and was convinced it wasn't the woman now just inches away from my lips. It couldn't have been because Bilan was panting, air expelling harshly.

"Sadik," was a voice I'd recognized with earbuds plugging my ears.

Turning over my shoulder, I saw Rory standing there, holding my phone in the air. That could mean just one thing. It was important. I'd given her my phones and told her not to bother me unless it was some shit that couldn't wait.

"Shit!" I muttered, reclining to stand. "Excuse me," I called back to Bilan, who I caught blinking excessively while pulling at the hem of her skirt.

I stood and took a few lunges over to Rory.

"It's the office. The customs didn't clear on a vessel. Rachel forgot to clear it, and it hit the border this afternoon."

I grabbed the phone, pissed the fuck off. "Which account?" It had to be a big one for me to get called in.

"Uhhhh…" I heard my office assistant typing in the background. "Kaiser Laboratories…GHGX348."

Shit!

"What did she say happened?"

"The usual. She's overwhelmed."

Clenching my waist, I turned toward Bilan to find her visibly uncomfortable and trying not to make it clear she was watching me. I glanced over to Rory and circled my index finger, telling her to wrap the picnic up. I had to get to the office to make sure the staff was supported in rectifying this. Human Resources needed to be involved. Rachel's ass would be fired by the end of the day. It was something I needed to deal with right away, before my flight out to Orlando.

"I'll be there within an hour. Call Karen and tell her to initiate the paperwork for separation."

"Got it."

The call disconnected and I tapped to get into my email, ignoring all the text messages waiting on me. I sent a few lines to reach out to one of the top guys at Kaiser Laboratories, Geoffrey Griffin. I'd had a great rapport with him and needed to get ahead of this delay personally instead of deferring it to a staff member.

When that was done, I glanced up to find the blanket and basket packed up. Lamont was leading the way up the pathway to the truck with Bilan involuntarily switching behind him. Rory stayed back, waiting for me. Once at the truck, Bilan stood waiting for me as I texted while making long lunges toward her. Lamont stood at the driver's side waiting as well. I'd just finished the text when I made it to Bilan. I grabbed her hand, continuing to my car.

"I got her from here, L," I shouted without looking back.

My tone was off, I knew it. As much as I wanted to go the fuck off about having my alone time interrupted, I knew I had to make the most of what was left of it. Bilan. She was still here. I'd steal more of her time by dropping her off. Rory hopped behind the wheel and I let Bilan in, opening the door for her.

After slipping inside and closing the door, I asked, "To Michelle's?"

"No," she breathed, gaze lost in my eyes again…that soon. "I'm going home."

Home…

I was surprised to hear that, thinking she didn't want me to see her place.

I played it smooth. "What's your address?"

Subconsciously, my eyes rolled up to the rearview mirror and immediately, I realized why. Rory was shooting me fucking missiles through the mirror as Bilan recited her address. So what I'd already known where she lived? Bilan didn't have to know.

"I hope everything's going to be okay," Bilan softly inquired.

That was progress for her. She'd been giving me a run for my money, and I still had no fucking clue why I'd been chasing her. Pursuing women with effort had never been my thing.

"What are you thinking?" she whispered as we pulled off.

"Why I want you so bad."

Bilan swallowed hard. Her eyes bounced across my eyes and mouth.

"Don't do that," I warned her.

"What?"

"Look at my mouth like that—me like that."

Her forehead stretched in earnest. "Why?"

"Because it makes me wanna kiss you, Bilan."

Her lips parted again, eyes narrowed as though she was intoxicated. There was something so chaste about her, though I couldn't imagine her being inexperienced in any manner. But when she peered into my eyes the way she did, my torso innately inclined toward her. Her eyes continued to bob around my face with a hunger I knew was there.

114

"Can I kiss you, Bilan?" I whispered mere inches from her face.

Her regard shifted toward the front of the car, where Rory's little head peered over the steering wheel to drive as a Johnny Gill number flowed through the car.

It's Your Body. How apropos...

When her soft palm pushed into my chest, I fucking lost my breath. All my will to take it slow, to keep the shy, yet feisty rabbit out of her hiding nest had worn thin. I leaned into her until our lips met, then kissed her, pulling at one side of her bottom lip. The small, yet audible sound of her exhaling fueled something primal in me, and I brushed against her soft lips again, this time running my tongue across them then pulling the bottom one into my mouth. Quickly, I released it, then slowly swiped my tongue inside, tasting her. The faint tang of fermented grapes and her unique flavor danced on my senses, teasing me.

It was delayed, but she responded with her timid licks against my greedy dives. Her frame vibrated against mine as she pushed into me, getting closer. That combination of reticence and helpless need drove me crazy, and I took her at the back of her head, lashing against her emboldened tongue, wanting her to feel my desire for her. Bilan's hands grasped my overgrown facial hair as our mouths smacked against each other.

This was dangerous for me. Enjoying a woman to the point of feeling weak and subdued, uncaring of where we were or how vulnerable I may seem to her was no good for me. This wasn't a part of the deal. But my body said otherwise when my palm grazed down to her hip and slipped beneath her skirt. Bilan moaned, body shivered hard as she expelled air into my mouth.

Fucking delicious...

My hand swept up toward her ass. The feel of her pantyhose made my blood fucking boil. I needed to feel her excitement. Wanted to touch her swollenness and have it beat around my fingers. The moment I reached the waistband of her stockings, Bilan pulled back, heaving out of breath.

Her head shook vehemently as she panted. "I can't. I'm sorry." She could barely whisper.

"My bad." I tossed my eyes to the, barely, five-footer zipping in and out of lanes on the road. "We're not alone."

Bilan continued to shake her head. "No." Her eyes closed as she pressed her fingers into her lips. "I can't—" She rolled her eyes before whispering. "My period is on."

Oh...

I snorted quietly and pulled her skirt back down. Leaning over to kiss her forehead, my head then shifted to her right ear.

"I lost my manners anyway. I'm sorry, Bilan."

I was. I'd never jumped all over a woman in the backseat of my ride. Couldn't say I hadn't had it done to me, though, but that was another story.

"I'm here," Bilan murmured, gathering her purse with one hand and arranging her skirt with the other.

I glanced up to find us on a residential block. I'd been too distracted to know we'd even stopped. My senses kicked in and I moved to leave the car. By the time I made it to the other side, Bilan was stepping out, facing me, but unable to look me directly in the eyes again. Shit... I'd lost her, acting on instinct and not calculated sense. She wanted me, I knew it. There was no reason why I couldn't ration the lust bouncing between us.

I gave her a nod to prompt her to her house as I followed. Quietly, I paced behind her to the stairs leading to her porch. Bilan didn't look back until we made it to her door, where she turned to me. Her mouth smeared with gloss opened, but no words followed. Subconsciously, it dawned on me the reason for the disarray on her lips, and I wiped my own mouth of the greasy balm. When I realized she struggled with what to say, I leaned over and kissed her forehead again.

"I'm going out of town tonight," I shared with my eyes over her head, feeling hers locked on me again. "I'll be gone for a few days, but hope to hear from you before I come back."

Finally glancing down, catching her eyes ghosted, I trekked down the stairs to leave.

8

"Bilan!" Gino shouted into the kitchen, standing inside the double swinging doors. I glanced up from rolling pastry dough. "Damien."

I lifted from the table, regard shifting to the left of me, where Nicky gave a nod of acknowledgment. As I went about washing my hands, I tried to recall the last time I'd seen Damien. It wasn't that he'd come in often, but just the mention of his name brought about the distance between his popups. I pushed through the doors and glanced left and right before Carina, manning the register, jerked her head to the left. After a few steps, Damien came clear into view.

That typical feeling of nervousness danced on my stomach as I approached him. It was also when I realized I hadn't grabbed my order tab or apron.

"Hey, Bilan," his chords trickled with familiarity as he smiled my way.

I couldn't help my flaming cheeks around this man. Thank God for my melanin. But my girlish grin couldn't be masked.

"Hi, Damien. What can I get you this afternoon?"

His smile lingered on his umber face, response delayed, and that added to my anxiousness.

"I think I'll get a slice of sweet potato pie. It's been a minute." He yanked at the neck of his black leather jacket.

His dense, jet black hair shined like the moon, and his shape-up was lined with precision. Damien gazed into my eyes with unknown intent, as he typically did. And once again, my question about his interest in me—or lack thereof—illuminated in my mind.

I rested my hip against the counter. "It has. Still out of town visiting family?" My eyes formed playful slits.

He chuckled. "Nah. But I been away, though. Bought a big ass house down south and tryna get shit situated."

"Oh." I straightened, releasing a sigh of wonder. "How far down south? I'm jealous. Hopefully, somewhere by the beach." My eyes widened. "I hear Georgia has some pretty amazing beaches."

Damien laughed, something I wasn't quite used to. "Nah." My shoulders cowered. "Not that far. My spot is in Cumberland County. You familiar with that?" I shook my head. "It's here in New Jersey."

"Shore area?" I had a true and unapologetic fascination with the ocean.

He shook his head. "Nah. Down past the shore. No water around, just big ass forest and mad White people."

"Oh!" I chirped again.

"How ya brother doin'?"

"The same," I mumbled, mind on the Cumberland County place I'd, embarrassingly, never heard of. One of the things on my to-do list was to rent out a beach house and sleep outside. I'd always wanted the sound of the ocean to put me to sleep— "Oh!" I trilled even louder, remembering Abshir. "He asked me to tell you something." All semblances of friendly pleasantries drained from his chocolate face.

"What?" he practically growled.

My eyes blossomed hard. "Uhhhh…something about Lenny being missing for a few weeks?"

"A few weeks? How many?"

My wide eyes rolled all over, desperately trying to recount the number. I'd honestly forgotten about Abshir. It was easy for me to, to help deal with his nastiness.

My forehead lifted. "Three weeks, I think."

Damien nodded, his eyes to the distance below. Our entire vibe shifted in seconds, and I didn't know him well enough to influence his mood either way. So, defensively, I withdrew internally.

I pointed behind me. "I'll go get that pie wrapped up for you."

Damien hadn't responded by the time I scurried away.

"I'm going out back for a minute!" I shouted over my shoulder on the way to the back door.

The exchange with Damien had been playing in my mind since he left a few hours ago. His reaction to this Lenny guy was strange. And it sounded business-like. What business did Abshir have with Damien? It was another question I'd never ventured to with either guy. It was enough Damien had appointed himself my security since Abshir had been sent to prison. I was over pondering the relationship between those two.

For close to two days, I'd been haunted by other, more compelling thoughts. Those of honeyed eyes with green borders, causing me to shiver as I stepped outside. It was cool out under the pitch black sky. I sat on the crate used by smoking cooks. The days stretched longer now that spring had arrived, but not even that could lift my mood. My body ached of fatigue, but my mind was alive with worry and anxiousness. I took an unexpected deep breath, releasing it with closed eyes. I felt...empty. With the mounting problems I had to sift through, there was still enough space in my mind to realize the emptiness. More bizarre was my time with Sadik the other day making it all the clearer to me.

He wanted to sleep with me, I knew it. The way he swiped his tongue against mine with a hunger I'd never seen. The way he clawed up my thigh and caressed my hips, and the groans he made me swallow. And his conversation...Sadik tried keeping me engaged, wanting to know more about me. When I finally shared something so unexpected and personal, he didn't laugh or clam up at my slip. I still wrestled with how to take that. It was delayed, but I was now intrigued. I wanted to know more about him—from him. I wanted to know his truths, his habits, hobbies, religious beliefs...anything I couldn't find on the internet.

Everything.

And I wouldn't ask Randi, though she'd texted me a few days ago asking if I'd heard from Sadik again. I lied to her, answering no. There was something about her warning of him that I still hadn't settled on in my mind. The more I thought about my time with Sadik, each time he forced his way into conversations with me, he'd been cool— aggressive, but pleasant.

Before I could stop myself, my hands began to move across the screen of my phone.

Me: Hey

My heart thundered in my chest as I bit my bottom lip and rolled my eyes. Why did I just do that? What would I do if he answered? How would I feel if he didn't?

So stupid…

The phone vibrated in my hand, startling me.

Your Friend: *She's obedient. Hey to you.*

A wop of air pushed from my lungs, and my shaky thumbs moved across my screen again. He was being a wise ass.

Me: What's up?

That read stupid…

I tried again.

Me: What are you up to?

I took a deep breath.

Better…

But was that invasive? I groaned, palm to my face.

Your Friend: *Well now I'm conked out on the bed watching my princesses feed a damn giraffe.*

My brows furrowed.

Me: You have kidZ?

Are you flipping kidding me?

A bubble had burst. Ice had been thrown into my face. It was one thing to deal with a pregnancy by a woman he was no longer with; him having more kids would be a deal-breaker for me.

Forget that!

Your Friend: *www.FaceMe.com*

Huhn?

Your Friend: *Click on the link and download the app to your phone.*

I twisted my nose and lips as my eyes went blindly around the back lot. Taking a deep breath, I tapped on the link and went to the site. It led me to Play Store, where I was able to download the app for free with pursed lips. Seconds later, I received a text with a FaceMe six-digit code. I pasted the characters into the app, clicked a few "no thanks," and then I waited.

"Why did I just do that?" I murmured to myself.

The door opened next to me. It was Pedro and Jose, coming out for a smoke break.

My phone began to vibrate in my hands. With a galloping heart, I tapped to receive a call. The screen transitioned to a live image of—

Sadik...

He was goddamn gorgeous. Just...flying fine as he wanted to be. His rainbow-hued irises glimmered with positive appraisal, full lips commanded my regard far too long. His skinned head smooth and glistening. And his facial hair was like a beard now, more unkempt than it was the last time I'd seen him.

"You hear me?" his croaky voice broke my bubble of attention.

His eyes were tightly narrowed and when my regard shifted lower, I noticed his cheeks were hiked and mouth wider. Sadik was smiling. At me. And man, was he fine!

"Huhn?"

"We gotta get you an iPhone."

I cleared my throat, blinking away the fog. "Why?"

"Because you need a downloaded app just for me to see your stunning freckles." His grin was captivating.

Beautiful? I didn't feel that way. Mechanically, I licked my lips and rubbed them together. Dang... I had nothing to say to that.

"Bilan."

"Huhn?"

"I don't have any kids."

"What?"

"You asked if I had kids with a 'Z' in that last text. I don't have kids."

"Oh." That conversation bounced to the front of my mind. "You said princesses and giraffes." I swallowed, feeling uncomfortable about prying. "You said you'd be out of town for a few days and I thought..."

"I was with my wife and kids?" One russet cheek lifted.

"Or kids' mother."

Sadik's grin deepened, and I could make out him sitting up from a bed. He began to walk, and my eyes windswept the background intently. He was in a large bedroom. A hotel suite?

"Ivana...Iesha, come say hi to my friend," he called out.

My heart raced and face went tight. The camera was turned, and I saw the coat prints of an animal. After a few movements, I picked up the tip of a rounding beak and churning mouth to what could indisputably be a giraffe. It was eating from the hands of one of the little girls.

One turned to the camera with a shy smile. "Who is she, Uncle Deek?"

"My friend, Bilan," he answered, out of my view.

The adorable little girl with clear bows and barrettes giggled bashfully. "She's pretty."

"Very," Sadik emphasized firmly. "Are you going to say hello?"

"Hello?" she chirped before falling into another bed of giggles.

The other one, who seemed older by the estimation of her height, turned with a curious expression. "Where she from, Uncle Deek?"

There was no sign of mirth or merriment or bashfulness from this one.

"She's from Paterson, Ivy—well, Woodland Park," he explained.

"Oh." Ivy abruptly swung her head and trunk back to the bigger and better party: giraffe feeding.

"Don't be mean, Ivy," the little one scolded.

"I'm not." I watched the back of her. "She's cute."

Then the camera was shifted back to pure handsomeness, but not before I caught someone in uniform assisting with the feeding of the animal. Sadik sauntered away from what I could now clearly see was a balcony.

"Where are you?"

"Disney."

"With your family?"

"Yeah. My nieces."

"Just the three of you?"

He shrugged his answer with his brows and mouth. "Ivana is averaging all A's and B's on her progress report and Iesha's on her way to Principal's List, it seems."

He lay back down on the bed.

"Oh, wow." I blinked, out of sorts. "Looks like I was born into the wrong family."

"Nah. Your way into the Ellis family shouldn't be through blood. Otherwise, how would I explain the Chanel necklace fantasy coming into fruition?"

An unwelcome smile split my face, and I rolled my eyes away.

"What's that about?" he asked with humor in his voice.

I scratched my chin. "It's the baby thing."

"What about it?" His forehead wrinkled, and even that had my stomach leaping.

"You want to shut down all talks of it unfairly. You tell me to trust you and that you're not with her. She agreed, but..."

"But what, Bilan?" he barked my name like we'd known each other for years.

Then I looked him square in the eyes, needing to be heard. "But I don't feel like I know you well enough to trust you."

"And you won't know me if you don't spend time with me."

I want to. That's the problem!

"I don't want to spend time if I'm wasting it because you're not being straight up with me. Spending time can be risky, and that's unfair."

Have you seen yourself in the mirror lately?

"Life ain't fair, Bilan, but I can damn sure fill yours with spice." I could have sworn he groaned.

My eyes ballooned and, for a while, I was speechless. I swallowed deeply.

"Thursday. Be ready at four." His timber was strong, pitch authoritative.

"I work Thursday."

"Call out."

I could have pushed back just because...I could have. But did I want to? Instead, I swallowed again, knowing I needed to head back inside. "I'll think about it."

"Don't think too hard."

I snorted. "I'll try not to, but what kind of date starts at four in the afternoon? What are we doing? How do I know what to wear?"

"What size are you?"

"Why?"

"You asked about what to wear. What size?"

"In what?"

"Hmmmm..." His orangey golden eyes circled the ceiling. "A dress and shoes—heels."

"Why? Are you going to buy me something to wear?"

He shrugged with a brow. "Maybe."

I got the distinct impression that would be all I'd be getting out of Sadik. Plus, I had to go.

"Nine in shoes. I haven't worn a dress since my mother's funeral. I'd have to try it on to see if I could still fit it."

"Text me the size." His eyes glistened again as they narrowed.

"Whatever. Bye." I smiled.

"Lata, Bilan."

I tapped to end the call, my netherland wet, hot, and fluttery.

"Another date with Sadik," I whispered into the cool air, still not able to get over guys still "dating" nowadays.

Sadik

When the chat disconnected, I peeped out onto the balcony before tapping to make a call.

I needed to do this before starting shower time with the girls. It was almost eleven at night and their mother, Monica, would have my ass if she knew they were up this late and had dessert twice tonight. It was a good thing I knew she'd never find out. The girls would be in just as much trouble as my ass.

After a few rings, he picked up. "Yeah."

I sat up from the bed, rubbing the back of my head. "Anything interesting?"

"'Bout a hour ago, some Fourth Ward niggas ran up in there. Ol' girl served them and shit got outta hand. Even we could see that shit from the fuckin' windows. Then two niggas pushed through the doors and chased them lil' mu'fuckas out."

"Word?" My face went hard. "What two niggas?"

"I got Beats over here with me at the diner today. He recognized one."

"From where?" He was talking too damn slow.

"Damien's crew."

"Damien, Damien?"

"Yeah. Beats said he was locked up with the mu'fucka a few years back."

"That all you know?"

"Nah. After the shit went down, I caught a waitress leaving out and asked her what all the ruckus was for, and she said they tried to grab ol' girl's ass, but her peoples handled it the way they always do."

"That's it?"

"That's it, chief—" There was mumbling in the background. "Ahhhh...yeah..." he breathed. "That's that muthafucka." He spoke into the phone. "You'll never believe who pulled up earlier!" Finally, he was lively.

"Who?"

"Damien. He was in the joint for a few minutes, kicking it with shortie."

Why the fuck would he be there? Michelle's had been around forever and was a hot spot in the city, especially for niggas like him who tried staying under the radar. His crew ran niggas out of there earlier, and he'd shown? Talking to Bilan?

Strange...

"Vincent Ricci and his brother, fat ass Nicky Ricci, still own that jawn?"

"Yeah. Vincent wife... What's her name?" he pondered out loud. "Carina! Yeah. That bitch still bad as hell, bruh." He whistled.

When times got hard for the diner, Vincent used to let my father's Paterson connect run supply through there discreetly. It happened twice, earning him a few grand a day until he got caught up. Then he'd ask my father to suspend the deal because he was out of hot water. My father would let Vincent stop when he wanted to under the agreement, when the favor needed to be returned, Vincent would comply. It may have been time for me to be sure Ricci didn't forget his debt to the Ellis family.

"Uncle Deek, he licked my face!" Iesha came into the bedroom crying-laughing.

I winked at her, knowing I needed to go. "A'ight. Keep me up."

"A hun'ned percent."

I hung up and followed my niece outside.

Bilan

I layered a few more pieces of chicken cutlets in the to-go Styrofoam container. Dog ate anything I brought home, but I noticed he'd go for these first. Thank God I worked for a diner; otherwise, I'd go broke trying to feed my home security. I closed it up and grabbed my bag on my way out back.

"See you, Nicky!" I shouted over my shoulder and waited for his usual grunt of an acknowledgment.

Anxiety peppered my nerves as I hiked from the back of the diner to the car in the small parking lot. I rarely drove, didn't even have a car. When I needed to be somewhere in a timely manner NJ Transit couldn't meet, I'd take my family's Corolla. It was old and had belonged to my father. I drove it a lot once he passed to transport my mother to doctor appointments, court dates, and visitation for my brother. And once she died, I pretty much got comfortable with my feet and the bus system. Living in a city had its benefits.

Today was unusual, and the primary source of my jitters. Today was the appointment Sadik had arranged for me. I couldn't believe I was doing this. Going out with a man—as I learned he was ten years older than me—who had a baby on the way. My mother would have never gone for it.

My phone rang in my pocket. I pulled it out, seeing it was Randi.

"Hey, girl," I answered, now at the car fishing for my keys in my bag.

"Hey. You texted me about my stylist the other day and I forgot to hit you back. I was in the Poconos with Ricky. What you tryna get done?"

My brows lifted, recalling. "Oh. Don't worry about it. I got an appointment tomorrow morning."

Sadik called me three days after we spoke on FaceMe to say he had a hairstylist if I needed one. Of course, I did. It just wasn't something I'd share with him. But I sure did take him up on it. The girl who usually did my hair did it in her house. She'd had a baby two weeks ago and wasn't available.

There was a beat before Randi replied. As I finally found the keys and pulled them out to let myself into the car, I figured she was busy with something herself. "Oh. Who you going to?"

"Some girl named ShawnNicole."

"In New York?"

"She has a new spot here in Jersey, but I think that's her."

"How the fuck you get in ShawnNicole's chair?"

I shrugged with my brows, though she couldn't see me. "I don't know. You heard about her?"

"Bitch, yeah! She be doing the celebrities' hair! You ain't see that video Pixie posted in her chair? That bitch be killin' Brielle's wigs, too!"

My heart dropped to my feet. "Are you serious?"

"Yeah! Where the fuck you been?" She laughed. "I 'on't think you can afford her hands, Bilan," she warned. I knew I couldn't, simply because of who made the appointment. I didn't have to see her price chart to know that. "Shit! Anyway, I gotta go. I'll drop by later…got a taste for a BLT."

Across the small parking lot, on the sidewalk, I saw a familiar physique stapling paper to a wooden pole.

"I'm actually leaving work now. Got an appointment in the city." My words fell nonplussed as I studied the back of the girl. "First, I need to stop by the house and feed Dog."

"In the City where?"

"JAGMisha…" The girl turned to the side and I was sure it was her. "…Boutique."

"Bilan, what the fuck is you doing at that place? You selling bricks I 'on't know about?"

That snapped me out of my stalking. "What?"

"You going to ShawnNicole and JAGMisha! Bitch, that's for the rich and famous! Who the fuck— Sadik?" she deduced. "You fuckin' with Sadik?" she croaked with disbelief.

"I wouldn't say that, but yeah..." I blinked a few times. "I'm going out with him tomorrow."

Again, Randi didn't respond right away, but this time, I had a feeling it wasn't from distraction of anything but my words. Why? Why did she make this thing so awkward? Did she know about his baby? Because then, I'd understand.

"Randi." My attention went back to the sidewalk, where the girl stepped back and studied the paper she stapled before going back and stapling it some more. "I have to go. I see someone I want to talk to." I started ambling out of the parking lot.

"A'ight, with ya fast ass," was all she replied, and I hated it.

"Talk to you later. Use my discount for the BLT if you want," I offered.

When Randi didn't reply, I hung up, feeling even more awkward. However, the distraction from the girl proved to be greater as I approached her.

"Latasha?" I called out to her on the way. "Is that you?"

When she finally turned, I was relieved that I hadn't played myself and was heading to a stranger. But something was off about her. Her eyes were red with glaring bags underneath.

"Oh, Bilan," she tried for a soft soprano, but there was no light in her eyes. I'd known her since we were kids. Our brothers had been friends just as long.

"What's going on?" My eyes brushed toward the fresh paper she'd just posted.

It was a picture of her brother. My whole body went rigid.

"How long has Lenny been missing?" I asked, fighting against panic as the correlation between her brother's face and missing status on the pole, and Abshir's message to Damien a few days ago finally connected.

"Weeks now. The police saying they doin' everything they can, but they still ain't found him." Her eyes welled with tears and suddenly, her disposition made sense.

"I'm so sorry, Latasha. Knowing Lenny, it's possible he's fine. He had been laying low over the past few years. Is this just another one of his slips from the surface?"

I recalled Lenny being incognito during Abshir's trial and sentencing. When my mother asked Abshir about it, he said Lenny had gone into hibernation and not to look for him. That was weird, seeing how cool they were. But just like so much around that time, that brief mention was a blur and insignificant compared to what we were up against with my brother's sentencing.

She shook her head, answering no. "He was back for good for a few days before he left out to go to his baby's mother's, and ain't never came back."

This began to sound too similar to the last time I saw my brother outside of police custody. I needed to go and not go back to that painful place.

"Hey," I tried for an upbeat tone. "You have another one of those? I can put it up on the diner's board to help."

"Nah," she breathed. "That was my last one. I can drop one off to you later, though."

"I won't be there, but tell them I said for you to leave it for me. I'll hang it the next time I'm due in."

"Thanks, B," she droned.

"These brothers we have." I squeezed her upper arm as a mark of connection. "They stay away long enough for us to forget how much they stress us out." I shrugged with my mouth.

Latasha returned a shrug with her brow. She was markedly distraught.

She stretched her lips, exposing her pearly white teeth as she gaped at me. "I think you're going to need help to your car." I glanced down at the large, black matte paper shopping bags with the gold embossed JAGMisha logo bold across the front. There were ten of them. "Where are you parked?" JAG asked.

My eyes roved up to the petite mocha diva standing a yard away in five-inch, multi-strap suede leather sandals, stopping at her chestnut eyes. When I arrived at JAGMisha Boutique, I thought it was just to pick a simple dress and maybe shoes. Apparently, Sadik had other plans I was told while being shown ball gowns in the four-digit price range.

Once that painful task was settled, the shoe selection was easier, thanks to JAG's knowledgeable assistance. The man left a spending limit still unknown to me. He insisted I be "liberal with my pickings," according to JAG. When I sent a text to say no thanks, he briskly warned either I picked the clothing I liked or he'd pick what he'd like and have them sent to me. These clothes were hella-expensive! Yeah, I had ten bags, but not one item inside them cost less than fifty dollars. Some were close to a thousand, but JAG said I needed those to pair with my more modest pickings.

I took a deep breath.

"Or I can go get the car, swing back and pick them up."

"Okay. I can have my guy bring them out to you." She walked behind the counter for the phone. "I'll look out for you from the window."

After a nod, I was off, trekking two blocks to a parking garage for the car. When I drove back around, as promised, JAG was opening the door for a guy dressed in dark dress pants, white dress shirt, and a matching vest. He strode over to the car as I popped the trunk. I got out like an idiot and tried to help.

"It's okay, sweetheart," JAG asserted with a million-dollar beam. "He's got it. Just be prepared to shoot me a text with how those YSLs fit. I love giving Tony Vaccarello my take on their practicality."

"Okay!" I agreed as though I had a clue who Tony was.

From the rearview mirror, I could see her wave me off. Overwhelmed. This had all been nice—fairy tale-like, even—but so overwhelming. Why did I agree to this? Why was it hard to not give into this guy's push to get to know me?

I had less than twenty-four hours to figure it out because that would be the next time those kaleidoscope-colored eyes would be caressing me again.

9

"Please! Please, Double E!" He choked on a cry. "I swear, I don't know what that man's business is. We been cool for fifteen years and he ain't never speak a word to me about what he do!"

"Yeah, but you moving to South Jersey with him, though," Iban snarled at dude.

I looked away. Fucking annoyed, I checked the time. They did this shit for breakfast, lunch and dinner. I had better things to do.

"It ain't just me!" Tank, an affiliate of Damien's, apparently caught stumbling out of a male's review club in Elmwood Park, tried to convince the angry trio standing over him. My father's shooter, Travis, rocked a mean scowl that would make anyone on the other end of it piss their fucking pants. "It's like four of us. We all friends. We all moving down there."

Iban scoffed, rolling a toothpick around in his mouth. "A bunch of fuckin' grown ass men living together sound gay as shit to me, Tank."

Tank's eyes closed in defeat and squeezed in anguish. My father's reputation was solid in the streets, and it was known if you were taken by Double E Bag's crew, you weren't coming back. For him, Iban's eyes weren't glossed over, body wasn't fidgety, which meant he wasn't over the edge at this point. It also meant Tank would live to see another day. My father stood stoic and silent, nostrils flared and jaw twitching.

Tears streamed from the sides of Tank's eyes, and snot dripped from his nostrils. I could tell his toes curled from the form of his shoes. His mouth shivered as he continued to plead. "All I'm saying is, I don't know what beefs Damien got. I don't know his business, man.

You talking about something that happened six years ago. I ain't even know him then..." He sobbed hard.

Smelling the fear of a petrified and anguished man in the air, I'd had enough. Dressed in my favorite tux, I was too clean for this sweaty ass environment of my father's warehouse, where another associate of Damien's was being questioned.

"Move on," I growled, ready to dead this bullshit.

"Just chill for a second." Iban moved to stand in front of me. "He ain't shit hisself yet. We still got more time." His leer game was serious.

I shook my head. "Sir," I called over to my father. "Can I rap with you for a minute?"

"One second, son." He pulled out his favorite gat, a G29, and fired a single shot into Tank's head, leaving his neck to go limp and his body to flop in the chair.

Ears ringing and head fuckin' spinning, I turned to leave.

Fuck this!

By the time I reached the door in the dim storage room of the warehouse, one of the men opened the door for me.

"Wait up, Deek!" I could barely hear behind me. Then my brother grabbed my arm. "Hold the fuck up!" He winced, holding his ear.

"I'm good, man." I yanked away. "I don't need this bullshit."

"You think we could let him go after bringing him here? Fuck no!"

"Then why the fuck am I called in?" I cocked my head to the side, questioning. "Why the hell am I even involved in this? You and Pops can take it from here, shootin' up muthfuckas like it's Call of fuckin' Duty out this bitch!" The ringing in my ears wouldn't relent.

"Nah, young man," my father announced, approaching us. "This Double E Bags Black Ops, and that muthafucka was lying through his fuckin' teeth. You heard him say he was cool with Damien for fifteen years in one cry, but in the next say he ain't even know that nigga six years ago? This the bullshit I can't tolerate. You told me to be patient and wait, but for some reason, you don't think six years is long enough!" He hit his angry soprano. I widened my stance, hands clasping at my pelvis as I gave him my undivided attention. "Fuck

134

that new aged bullshit. These muthafuckas need to remember my name!" he barked loud in my buzzing ears.

Shaking my head, I stretched my lips, reigning in my building anger. "Y'all got this, man. I got better shit to do." I turned to leave, cognizant of the time.

"Sadik!" my father's commanding voice halted my steps.

I didn't turn to them when he uttered what seemed to be low to my beating eardrums.

"I'm sorry my business… My method of making a living that's provided you a fuckin' superior life ain't good enough for you."

That blow had me sucking in a heap of air and expelling it right away. Heated all fucking over, I took off.

"Good, Geoffrey." I nodded with the phone to my ear. "I'm glad we were able to finally bring in the shipment, despite the delay."

"Hey, man," he uttered into the line as I checked my watch and glanced up to the front of her house from inside of the limo. "Shit happens. We understand that here. Carmichael was able to stretch what we needed when you called with the heads up."

Geoffrey Griffin was the assistant to Carmichael, the top engineer at the laboratory my firm had an account with. I appreciated his blithe persona. "I just need you and the big man to understand I value my relationship with Kaiser Laboratories. You could choose a competitor to import your chemicals, but you've solidified this relationship by trusting me for close to ten years."

"Looking forward to more, brother. Take care."

We disconnected the call, and my gaze swung ahead to Rory in the driver's seat. "Jet ready?"

"Fueling now." Her head was down when she answered.

"Food?"

"Taken care of."

Why the fuck was I so nervous? I tried to think of the last time I'd been on a serious "date" with someone I tried pursuing in earnest and couldn't recall.

Having spent enough time procrastinating, I placed my fingers on the door handle. "Send a text to Clifford's office and tell them we're on the way."

As she responded, I stood from the limo, and headed to the steps leading to the porch of her house. Before I reached the top, the door opened slowly and Bilan appeared in the doorway expressionless.

But her goddamn beauty...

Why his exotic features caught me off guard each time I saw him was beyond me. His five o'clock shadow was freshly lined, and the blonde bristles of it glittered in the afternoon sun. Butterflies took flight in my belly, and anxiety danced on my bladder. His honeyed eyes darkened as he stood motionless, paying inspection from my head to the hem of my gown. I followed his line of vision and when my eyes ascended to his face again, I caught his tongue roll, swiping the inside of his bottom lip.

God...

I glanced away. "Stop it," I muttered. "I can still change my mind."

Challenge that statement!

I needed him to say something, killing this awkward moment.

"You're absolutely stunning."

My eyes roved up his black tux, reminding me of the first night we informally met. His regard jumped all over my face.

136

What's wrong?

"Then why the wrinkle in your forehead?"

He stretched his lids, jaw collapsed just slightly. "I just hate I can't see your freckles."

My hand instinctively flew to my face. "Oh. That's because I'm wearing foundation to even my complexion."

"I like your skin tones."

My belly fluttered. "That's not the point."

He extended his palm to me. I accepted it and was gently yanked into his chest. I yelped, being hit with the warmth of his palm, and hardness of his chest; the assault from his delicious cologne had my lashes fluttering.

His mouth was at my ear. "You accept advance apologies?"

My eyes mushroomed. "For what?"

"For not being able to keep my hands off of you. You deserve a gentleman."

I sucked in a breath, taken by his charm.

"And what are you?"

"When you're around: a wolf."

My eyes closed as I felt a dollop in my panties. I swallowed hard. "I need to lock up."

He squeezed my hand. "Hurry."

During the entire ride, Sadik was on his phones. And as rude as it could have been perceived, I was actually relieved for the time to settle my nerves about all of this. After getting settled in last night, I pulled out all the clothes from JAGMisha Boutique, including the gown. The brand was MEEHAR, a designer I'd never heard of. So my Google fingers led me to learn the gown Sadik had picked out for me was from MEEHAR's Spring 2017 line and went for as much as two

thousand-four hundred dollars now! No way I could afford that. And for that reason, I stopped snooping. I refused to look up the other things JAG and I had picked out.

But the gown felt different. It was layered and heavy, certainly nothing cheap. I couldn't move an inch without it taking effort. Sadik, on the other hand, appeared well-versed with formal wear. His medium build owned the black suit he donned. The whole cut, black leather oxfords didn't present not a single scuff. His enticing cologne fragranced the air to a teasing level, shaming my little Bath and Body Works body spray—

What am I doing here?

We pulled into the parking lot of a high-storied business building. When the limo came to a stop in front of the door, my face fell. Was this where we were going?

"I gotta go, Jill," Sadik told his caller—latest caller. There had been four. "I'll hit you tomorrow about the meeting." He cupped my hand with his own, his touch snatching my attention. His chin swung toward the entrance. "One stop before the show."

His door was opened for him and with a gentle yank, I was prompted to shuffle behind him. With a bit of effort on my part and patience on his, I was helped out of the limo. The first set of eyes my regard fell on was buggy ones. Rory never greeted me or smiled to show I was welcomed, but I decided immediately to swallow my concern. There were more important things to tend to, like why we were at the brick building.

Holding his hand while trailing behind him, I followed Sadik inside. Behind me was big Lamont. Once inside, it was clear to me this was an office building. Names and business types were listed on a glass-encased directory board. I didn't have enough time to read before I was urged into a waiting elevator. We ascended two floors before Sadik led us out.

A…nurse greeted us.

"Mr. Ellis, we're all ready for you. This way." She turned to head down a hallway. We passed by a waiting room, where I counted four people and a receptionist desk with just as many people working behind it. All women, and all but one rubbernecking the bald, russet-

skinned man with an orange five o'clock shadow. One even tapped another to call her attention to him. I got it. I really did. Sadik's features were attention-snatching alone, and those mixed with his confident gait and compelling aura could have you hypnotized. But I still didn't like it. "Right in here." She swung an arm into an open waiting room. "Now, I wasn't clear on if we would need two rooms or one—"

"One is fine," Sadik barely let her finish.

I turned behind me for his security and saw he was nowhere to be found. Why were we at a doctor's office? Why was there a need for two rooms? This was freaking me out as he held my hand and we ambled into the room.

"You look very nice, ma'am," the pudgy woman complimented with a smile.

I had nothing for her. The minute I turned to ask Sadik what was going on, a booming voice entered the room.

"Sadik!" I turned to find a silver haired, balding man wearing tiny glasses enter the room. One of the women from the front desk—the tapper—followed behind him, fighting for covertness of her ogling. "You're oh so prompt. I have my girls ready for the screenings. There's just some paperwork I need this beauty to fill out." He acknowledged me. "Well, lovely lady, your arms are out, so you're good there. However, we're going to need a urine sample for a full screening."

I jumped in my shoes to Sadik as he removed his suit jacket. "Doctor Clifford." The two men shook hands. "Glad you were able to fit me in."

"Oh..." the doctor droned as he waved him off. "Anytime. Anytime." He grabbed papers from the ogling nurse with heat creeping up her neck. "Here's the questionnaire and registration papers. We offer gynecological services, though..." He skimmed down my gown. "...I don't think this afternoon would be an ideal time to offer a full vaginal exam with pap smear, but you can always schedule a time to come back with the girls up front."

I shot hard eyes to Sadik. "What am I doing here?" My tone was helplessly uncompromised.

"What are we doing here," he corrected, undoing the cufflinks on his right wrist. "We're doing the responsible thing. I almost lost it on you in the backseat of my car last week."

My neck whipped to the doctor turning beet red behind us. The sight of him being visibly uncomfortable over the topic had my pulse racing. The crushing nurse blushed scarlet with her mouth open.

When I faced Sadik again, his forehead was creased as though he was confused. "It was just a kiss," I grumbled through gritted teeth.

"A kiss that had me ready to tear your skirt," he argued. "Look..." Sadik shook his head. "...I'm a very forward man. I want you, and I'm going to have you. I've already convinced myself to be patient, but it's inevitable, Bilan."

"Are you serious?" I croaked as a new skittish nurse rounded me on her way to Sadik. She carried a small plastic basket with syringes and other things my mind couldn't process, thanks to the conundrum I found myself in.

His head shook faintly as he rolled up his sleeve. "About wanting you? Hell, yeah."

"About dragging me to a doctor's office for testing without asking for my consent first."

The room stiffened, bodies steeling in place. Sadik's head leaned to the side, and a disarming grin formed on his face as he stepped toward me. "Sweetheart, consent is for the actual sex. These are just measurements for the uniform. We're going to play the field, I'm sure of that. And if you could get honest with yourself, you do, too. Now, they'll be drawing blood today, but nothing harmful. There's no need to make this awkward." He shifted even closer, licked his lips and lifted one cheek—a sharply lined cheek from the barber. "Now, we have to hurry this along to catch a show, so if you need help lifting that gown, I'm volunteering."

One of the nurses sputtered a giggle she struggled to contain. Another muttered something I could have sworn was shit. And the doctor, the only other male in the room, cleared his throat.

My face fell. "You're serious!" I breathed as his phone rang.

"Deathly," he affirmed before taking the call.

The nurse began to rub an alcohol swatch on his extended arm while another quickly swiped his mouth with a swab. He didn't flinch when pricked by a needle.

"That oral swab is for rapid HIV testing," the doctor discretely shared over my shoulder. "We can have the test results back in less than twenty minutes. The blood draw is for other diseases like herpes, hepatitis, and syphilis. Meredith, over there, has a cup for a urine sample. That'll give us the status on gonorrhea and chlamydia…"

As he rambled on low in my ear to not be heard over Sadik's call, I watched the nurse taking his blood. She couldn't stop shifting her weight from hip to hip. Her eyes careening between an occupied Sadik and the window they stood next to. The woman was behaving like a horny teen.

I was effectively embarrassed, and strangely jealous. I turned toward the doctor, snatching the paperwork from his hands. "Where's the bathroom?"

After throwing myself onto the leather bench in the backseat of the limo, I adjusted my dress, completely ignoring Sadik sliding in across from me. I could feel those feline eyes burn into me, but refused to acknowledge him.

How embarrassing!

I was all dressed up for STD testing. Unbelievable!

His security got into the front of the cab, and we were off. My heavy gaze was out the tinted windows as I second-guessed myself. Was Sadik really into me? Or was I over my head as Randi tried to warn? I didn't date. Had never been on a real one, so I had no point of reference.

A white box being pushed into my range of vision appeared, breaking my thoughts. Sadik wanted my attention.

"What's this for?" I finally looked at him.

"So I can see your face when we chat. I can't count those freckles."

It was an iPhone, reminding me of the conversation we had over the weekend.

"Is this how we're going to handle what just happened?"

With lifted brows and a faint smile, Sadik shook his head softly. He was gorgeous, making this unfair. It hit me again, how unusual this all was for me. I'd never been so attracted to a man in my life. It actually scared me.

"What happened wasn't a grave matter, Bilan. It was just precautionary."

"It was presumptuous. We've never discussed that. I don't even know you."

"Yet. You don't know me yet. But we're getting to know each other with the time we spend together."

"Time that will end if you pull another stunt like that again, Sadik." My eyes were hard on him. "I'll admit, the dating stuff is new to me, but having my feelings dismissed isn't. I won't have it."

I had to take a stand. As I'd sensed of him before, there was something uncompromising about his aura. I couldn't get rolled over by it. He'd never respect me, and I'd lose it for myself. We battled with stubborn glares for countless seconds, and while he quit first by tipping the box onto my lap, Sadik didn't forfeit at all.

"And I have ample experience?" He sat back in his seat, tossing his arm over the back of the bench, and gazed out the window. "Being accommodating is outside of my element. Time is a comfort only I provide in each relationship I engage, including business. I write the rules of engagement and break them if it suits my agenda. I set goals and pace. I create the parameters and regulate the boundaries." He then turned to me, honeyed eyes darkened. "I choose, I pursue, I conquer, and I cancel. Sorry to have to tell you, you're my current pursuit."

His ringing phone effectively broke the moment. Yet once again, it was a timely distraction. His words were weighty, the conviction behind them palpable. With a galloping heart, I stewed on them as he took the call. So many thoughts zapped through my mind under the sound of his commanding, scratchy alto conducting another business call. So lost in my head, I hardly realized when the limo pulled to a stop.

The front of the car's doors slammed closed, and my gaze went to the surroundings outside of the window.

"Phil, I have to go. I've been rude to my date." My head whipped over to Sadik's smirk as he scooted up the bench. "Yeah. Just have Bryant email the paperwork to my office. They'll know what to do with it." There was a brief pause before he ended with, "Okay," his tone professional.

The door was opened, and he slid out of the limo. Without words, Sadik reached back in with his hand and helped me out. We were in a parking lot, and jet engines could be heard all around. One airplane was landing over us as we took off. Once again, I was trailing behind his confident gait. The big security guard was ahead of us as we began our journey. We traveled through a narrow gate next to a building, where a huge runway lot opened and dozens of planes were all around.

"Where are we?" I tried speaking over the airport's noise pollution.

Sadik answered over his shoulder, "Teterboro."

Trekking behind him in high heels, I turned to see little Rory was on our trail. She sported aviator sunglasses with her black button-up shirt, black slacks, and maroon leather jacket. The big security guy was near two men, one white, one Asian, engaged in conversation. I saw when he handed one of the men wearing a captain's hat a file folder as we approached.

"Mr. Ellis!" one greeted, lifting his hat slightly.

"Evening," the other did the same with an added nod.

"Fellas," Sadik returned, passing them.

We were boarding the plane after Sadik's security. A private friggin' plane. Oh, my God! A private plane! The smell of food invaded my nostrils right away. As we walked into the cabin, his security slammed himself into a leather seat.

"This ain't up to date like yours," he observed out loud to Sadik.

Sadik scoffed, using his free hand to rub the back of his head. "It'll have to do."

We continued past a divider of sorts, moving into another section with oversized leather seats. Sadik led us farther down to another section, where he gave a cursory glance to what I could tell was a dining area.

"We can bunk it over here." He tossed his chin toward the middle section. "You can have any seat you want," he mumbled, grabbing a remote. "Get comfortable. We should be taking off right away."

I turned, my regard on the area around me. I was on a private plane. On a private plane, and Sadik behaved as if this was routine luxury for him.

"Where are we going?" My stomach roiled and pulse quickened, finally finding my voice.

"To Miami," he answered without looking at me, busy flipping through channels.

"Mi—" I blinked, chin dipped as I swallowed hard. "Why are we going to Miami? We don't have clothes."

I don't even know you to stay with you!

Sadik turned to me, his eyelids collapsed. He tapped his forehead with the remote as though distressed. I watched as he took a deep breath, exhaling a gust of his arousing cologne my way. He moved toward me, taking me at the hand to be seated. Then he lowered himself on the leather chair across from me.

"I'm sorry, Bilan. Again, I'm fuckin' up." Dramatically, his head collapsed as he released a perceptible breath. "I set this up over the weekend, and a man with a schedule like mine has a lot of shit happening in the space of a day. The fact that I haven't told you where we're going never dawned on me."

"How long are we supposed to be in Miami?"

"Just a few hours."

"A few hours?"

"Yeah."

"What are we going to do in Miami for just a few hours? How are we getting back?"

"We're going to a show. I'd like to keep that part a secret until we get there. And we'll get home the same way we're getting down there." His eyes rolled toward the roof to gesture the plane.

144

"Mr. Ellis?" A man appeared in uniform, wearing a friendly smile. "I'm Jeremy and will be serving you and your guests this evening. Dinner is set. The captain's been given clearance for takeoff. Can I offer you two a drink while we're taxiing?"

Heavy knocks had all of our attention going to the divider toward the front of the plane. It was Rory craning her neck through.

"Shit," Sadik breathed, going for his pockets.

Rory stepped in and collected both his cell phones. "No calls unless it's death or Code Double E."

"Gotchu," she muttered, sauntering back to the front area.

"Yes, Jeremy," Sadik addressed the flight attendant. "I'll have Mauve, straight up. What about you, Bilan?"

My eyes widened, shifting back and forth. "I...uhhhh... I'll have the same."

"Very well," Jeremy acknowledged before taking off.

Sadik turned to me, and I could feel the plane move. He gathered my hands in his, stroking the back of them. His innocent touch sending volts of stupid sensations shooting up my spine.

"Are you hungry?" His voice too sweet. "I'm starving."

I shook my head. I didn't have an appetite.

Sadik lowered his chin, studying me. "I apologized for earlier—"

"Actually, you haven't."

"Do I need to say the words?"

"Is that too hard for Mr. Demanding Alpha?"

His face cracked in a big smile and he snorted, eyes unmoving from me. I tried chewing the inside of my mouth to keep from mirroring his contagious expression.

"I've rattled you. I'm sorry. For everything," he made clear. "How can I gain your trust back, Bilan?"

Feeling petty, I shrugged, one shoulder higher than the other as I tried looking away from him. Sadik made it hard. Him. His face and being were the compelling attractions.

He yanked at my hands gently. "Tell me." His words poured in with genuine affection.

"Make me forget you're a stranger," I whispered, feeling silly for phrasing it that way.

I should have been more direct, but it was hard to under those feline eyes. The green in them glimmered.

The captain spoke from the overhead system, announcing takeoff and requesting we buckle our seatbelts. Jeremy appeared with drinks and we pulled up the tray tables attached to our seats. I watched Sadik rub the tumbler of brandy in his palms on top of the tray as he peered heatedly into me. It made me squirm ridiculously.

"Do I make you nervous...intimidate you, Bilan?"

Clearing my throat, I squared my shoulders and mimicked his actions with my own glass. "No," I stated emphatically, because telling the truth was harder. "By the way, what are we doing?"

The sides of his eyes crinkled as he smiled. "Warming the brandy."

My mouth formed an "O." When Sadik was done, so was I. When he took his first sip, feline hued eyes locked onto me, I followed suit. When he didn't speak, I held my tongue, too. Ascending was a difficult event to get through when imitating a man who likely took flights—private flights—more times a year than I bought tampons. But I got through it...with Mauve. With the immediate-acting sedative, I got through shooting up above the clouds. My burning chest went completely ignored.

As promised, Jeremy appeared at the door, announcing dinner as soon as the captain advised we were in-flight and could remove our seatbelts.

Sadik reached for my hand, and led me to the room farther to the rear of the plane, where there was a romantic dinner setting for two. A garden salad awaited us as we sat at the table.

"Please tell me you eat chicken," Sadik questioned. "I've never seen you eat, so I didn't know what you liked. If you're vegetarian, I have a backup. Herb-crusted salmon. If you're vegan, there's couscous."

I lifted the fork to pretend to be hungry, but I wasn't. I giggled nervously when I caught him watching closely.

"I eat chicken...and fish, I guess."

"You guess?" He didn't move, waiting for my answer. I shrugged, not knowing what to say. That's when Sadik put down his fork. "Do you want to try the chicken now instead of starting with the salad?"

With a squished nose, I shook my head. "I told you I'm not hungry. To be honest, I'm not a big eater."

His eyes fell to my breasts in the tube top portion of the gown; I was sure he had my body in mind to survey. "You're not all that small, so I doubt if you have much of an eating disorder."

I shook my head again. "I'm just not a big eater." I rolled my eyes, suddenly frustrated by not being able to be completely honest with him. "I lose my appetite easily," I droned, pinching my brows.

For a while, Sadik didn't speak. I peered up at him, catching the wrinkle of skin between his eyes. Then out of nowhere, his shoulders collapsed and he moved to take off his suit jacket.

"Okay," he screeched, peeling out of it. He caped it on the back of the chair next to him before adjusting his tie to begin eating. "This or that."

"What's that?" I watched him chew.

"A game we're gonna use to get to know each other. We'll have two different options to choose from to describe our preference and hopefully gain more knowledge about the other person." He went for his glass.

I didn't exactly follow, but was too embarrassed to say. So, I shrugged. "Okay..."

"Alright." His eyes went to the ceiling as he cleared the contents of his mouth with his sweeping tongue. That rude table behavior increased his sexiness for some stupid reason.

"A cook or housekeeper for your home?"

My mouth stretched and rotated in a circular fashion. "I don't eat much, and I'm never home to clean. So a housekeeper would be a lifesaver."

Sadik nodded, going back for his plate.

My turn...

"Michael Jackson or Prince?"

"Ragee." His answer was delivered without thought.

"Ragee's voice is unparalleled, but he couldn't hold the coats of Michael or Prince."

147

"Ragee is Jersey goods," he stated categorically while stuffing chicken into his mouth. "His voice is stellar: he ain't gotta dance. Just give him time to keep building his catalogue."

Ragee's weird…

The only thing he had comparable to those legends was the level of privacy he chose to live his life with. Oh—and the rumors! Michael and Prince's sexuality were still debatable to some to this very day.

"Love stories or suspense? And don't be predictable," he warned, flashing those honeyed irises.

I pouted. "Suspense—action filled, too!"

Sadik's glass was midair and his forehead dented when he asked, "Why?"

I shrugged. "I've gotten comfortable with the unknown in life. It's been hard when it included death and imprisonment, but it's given me my war scars. I'm afraid to get comfortable with the pattern or routine you find in love stories. That's why I laughed when you assumed I read Christina C. Jones' romance stories. Romance is…corny. It isn't real. They're fantasies and given the drama and suspense I've had in my life over the past few years, love stories are an insult to the human psyche."

"Damn…" His lids stretched closed, blinking deeply before reclining in his seat. His gaze was locked onto me. I gave an affirmative nod. "A blossomed flower without sunshine," he quoted lines from a recent Young Lord record.

I squinted, head shifted to the side as I smirked. "You are Jersey strong, aren't you?"

"Good stuff is bred in Jersey, girl." He went back to his plate.

Mine looked…lonely.

"Alright." He chewed around the word, so rude. So manly. "Cabin life or beach house?"

My eyes ballooned. "Beach. As corny as it sounds, it's a fantasy to spend the night at the beach." That was an easy one.

I'd never dreamed of traveling the world so much as I had being near the water. And any clean water would do. Everyone around me knew. I low key believed that was why Randi would have to name drop when she went out of town. She didn't always go to beach destinations, but that getaway piece was what I lacked in life. I knew it and she did, too.

"You've never stayed at a beach resort or gone down to the shore in Jersey?"

I shook my head, looking away. "Other than my aunt and her family who live by the shore. They've invited us out for the day when I was young, but that would just be a few hours at a time. My parents worked dog hours when the business was going. And after, we had no money for much. My father died, brother got in trouble, then Mommy got sick."

"And since then, you've been a struggling college student?"

The question form was more gentle than a statement. I shrugged with my mouth.

Instead of answering, I took my go. "Are you happy or just content?"

"Content." He reached over and forked salad leaves from my plate, stuffing it into his mouth. "Happiness has come in intervals for me. Not sure if the little I experience is something I'm owed or should expect." He lifted his brows, poked his lips. "But I take whatever I can."

Such a forlorn state of mind about happiness. It was up there with my being alone theory.

"Why can't happiness be an obtainable state like it is for everyone else?"

Sadik gazed at me through his lashes. "Everyone?"

"Yeah. Unless you're dealing with a pre-existing, uncontrollable condition like depression, why can't you, a man with all these resources, be happy?"

"I hate to sound so cliché, but money doesn't bring happiness. It brings headaches from trying to keep and grow it. It brings snakes, liars, actors, and posers. Money can be a source of stress. It's like a repellent for trustworthy people."

Hmmm...

I grabbed my glass and pulled it to my mouth for a sip when he uttered, "Pills or shot?"

149

I almost choked on the water. Sadik sputtered a hearty laugh. His eyes rolled back and hand splayed at his abdomen. Birth control. He wanted to ask about birth control after hauling me off to a gynecologist without a heads up.

Still cracking up, he stood from his chair. "I need to use the little boys' room real quick." He excused himself and sauntered to the back of the plane, amusement still pulling at his lungs.

I shifted in my seat, careful not to make my movements too abrupt or extreme in the dark purple, smoky-like ceiling of the hall. The ambiance was velvety, the artistic sounds were rich and poetic, and the view was Somali exotic. We were past the intermission and over one hour and a half since start time, and I spent much of the show ogling her profile.

This was wrong and I knew it. Having her down here, wanting to be around her, pretending she was fair game. It was all fucked up, and I knew it each time I decided to see her again. I knew it when I set up the romantic, cop-a-spot in the jazz park, too. Bilan fought hard as hell to keep her guard up, and while it didn't seem like I put much effort into fighting her, I knew I'd been applying pressure for her to open up to me. I knew she fucking wanted me, and I made it that way. Why?

Because I was a selfish ass recalcitrant, who went after everything I was told I couldn't have.

Bilan and I came from two different worlds. While hers wasn't blemish-free, her lifestyle was. Corruption was around her, not in her. And she was beautiful. Fuck, she was bad. Almond skin, pear shape with fixed wide hips, and the short throwback haircut worked well on her. She seemed...simple. Uncomplicated in the grand scheme of things. Smart, aloof of her environment, hidden yet honest, tainted and undeniably innocent at the same damn time. I'd never seen a clearer case of duplicity in a woman.

I needed to back down. Had to call off whatever fantasy I'd been wrapping myself in regarding her. It was only right. After tonight, I wouldn't fuck with Bilan anymore. It was best for her. Good for me...I'd been breaking all my rules for women and dating with her. I didn't date. I didn't second-guess. And I damn sure didn't apologize. Tonight wasn't my first time taking a woman to Dr. Clifford for testing. But she damn sure was the first to protest about it. Even Dr. Clifford quickly commented to me about her unease before we left with our HIV results.

I took her to get tested so I could fuck her. I wanted to, badly. She called me a demanding alpha, and my dick inflated at the last syllable! I held her hand with a grip of possession because she melted into my palm as though she was mine. The heat of her body, the scent of her desire for me, all felt familiar too fast. I wasn't a man of romantic gestures or candlelight measures. Yet, here I was, sitting in a symphony hall, hoping I was impressing her. And she didn't eat my food on the jet. Completely rejected all but a slice of bread when I suggested she had something on her stomach since she was drinking quality brandy. Other than that, half the DiFillippo's order I managed to have on our flight went to waste.

The musical selection transitioned into another, ripping my eyes from Bilan to the printed program rolled up in my hand. According to it, Ameerah was on her last piece, an original titled, "Lone Tabby." It was from her first album published under L.I.T. Music. An emotional ballad. One I found myself sipping brown juice to in a dark room when raindrops pelted the damn window. It had been a while, but watching Ameerah perform it reminded me how transcendent music is. No matter what format, great emotion could be felt from it.

My eyes traveled over to Bilan next to me and grew wide before catching myself. Streams of emotions trailed down her face as her eyes were fixed to the stage and mouth hung ajar. Something in my damn belly leaped, my arms strangely wanting to do the same. Why would I comfort her? Why would I care? Could it be because it was another piece of proof of her innocence? The same factor making me want to spend time with her, although I knew it was wrong?

The song ended and the lights came up, ending the show. The room stood in applause, Bilan and myself included. For the first time since the show began, she looked my way.

"Oh, my God." She dried her face and laughed at herself for crying at the same time. "Thank you for this. I can't believe I saw Ameerah live."

See…

There it was again. That innocence she had about her. It made my damn lungs burn. Out of nowhere, I was out of breath as bodies moved around us.

"So, you dig Ameerah?"

Bilan nodded, still emotional. "A friend of mine introduced me to her work three years ago. We were in a music class together. The 'smart kids' were discussing her catalogue, and I had no idea who she was. I've been hooked ever since. When she signed with L.I.T. Music, I was happy as though it was my deal. That 'Lone Tabby' piece is one of my favorites—probably the favorite. It's crazy she finished the show with it. Let's just say, I get what all the buzz was about." She rolled her eyes. "And, of course, I'm forever indebted to the friend." She couldn't hide her smile.

I knew I shouldn't ask. "Who?"

Her eyes widened. "Who what?"

"Who is the friend, who put you on to Ameerah?"

Bilan swiped the back of her neck, uncomfortably looking toward the stage. Then she faced me again, a gleam of defiance in her eyes. "Ready to talk about Ms. Lia?"

Touché…

Not having the words to respond with, I grabbed her hand, starting out of the theater.

"If it's not too much, I need the bathroom before we head back to the airport," I heard her almost squeal behind me, timidly.

Once I located Rory and Lamont, I tossed my chin down a hall opposite the entrance. Rory nodded, tapped Lamont and they began making their way. There was a line for the ladies' room when we arrived.

"I'll wait right over there for you." I pointed across the hall near tall potted plants. "I have a few calls to make."

"I'm sorry," Bilan recoiled. "I hope I'm not holding us up."

I kissed her forehead, unbothered by the inconveniences she may have conjured. "Take your time."

By the time I made it over to my security, Rory was handing me a phone.

"Pops," she murmured.

I tapped the phone, hitting him back.

"Yeah," he growled into the phone, alerting me of his mood.

My leaving the way I did earlier would not be forgotten anytime soon.

"You called?"

"Fuckin' Iban pulled out on one of Rizzo's capos."

Fuck!

My gaze swept across the hall, reigning in my temper. "Where?"

"In Scotch Plains, at one of Rizzo's houses."

"What happened?"

"Said he was there with Lia and the muthafucka started poppin' off disrespectful to Iban. You know we don't stand down for no under-bosses. More than that, you know how much of a fuckin' hothead your brother is!" he shouted. My father was angry. It was typical for him to be heated with Iban, but not likely to have a beef with the both of us at the same time. "And I ain't got a flying fuckin' clue what his ass was doing there. You know?"

Yeah. Lia...

"I'll take care of it."

153

There was an abbreviated pause before he pushed. "You better, or I will."

I dropped the phone, knowing my father hung up right away. It was his thing. Then I went into my text thread.

"Sadik!" someone in front of me called out in surprise. I glanced up to find Hyacinth, a face I hadn't seen in some time. "Shit! It's you!" She began to make her way over to me, cutting the sea of people trying to leave the restroom for the exit.

I quickly typed into my phone a text to my big brother.

Me: Pack ya fuckin bags. We leave in the morning.

I was done by the time Hyacinth made it to me. "I can't believe you're here," she sang, reaching up for a hug.

I reciprocated. "How are you, girl?"

"I'm good, love." Hyacinth's eyes perused my security next to me. "Does she know you're here?"

My forehead wrinkled. "Nah. I heard about the show last week and saw I had time to come through."

"You have to come back and say hello!" Her eyes were wild with excitement. I didn't fly down here to see Ameerah personally, only to catch her show. "The dressing room is right around the corner. Come on!"

Saying no would have been rude. Going wasn't the biggest deal. I glanced over my shoulder and, right away, Rory stepped up to go.

"Nah. I'll be right back." I tossed my chin. "Stay here for when she comes out the bathroom."

"I ain't no babysitter, bruh," Rory snarled. "He could stay for shortie. She'll be a'ight."

I took a deep breath, knowing how fucking stubborn Rory could be with women in my life—and Bilan was not in my life. It didn't matter; Rory wasn't fond of her.

I tossed my chin to Lamont. "Keep an eye out. I'll be right back."

He nodded as Hyacinth wrapped herself around my arm. "She's gonna be so psyched!"

She was accurate when she said the dressing room wasn't far. Before I knew it, Hyacinth was pushing through a door. Inside were people bustling around. Ameerah's little frame was in a director's chair, face getting wiped down. I remained outside, my phones blowing up with alerts and calls.

Iban: *Daddy called you?*

As I was typing a response, the door opened and a big blonde afro swept out. She was beautiful with just half a face of makeup.

Her eyes went wild when they landed on me. "Sadik?"

Those dimples were as stark as ever.

"What's up, young lady?" I reached down when her arms shot up in the air to embrace me.

"Holy shit!" she screeched into my chest. "How long has it been?"

I let go and smiled. "It's been a minute. I see things are going well for you, as they should."

Her smile deepened. "Thanks, man. You always believed in me." Her whisper was wistful.

"It's easy to with your talent. Now, you're selling out shows, and shit."

She took a deep breath, shoulders rising as she beamed. "It's been great times mixed in with the bullshit."

"Ahhhh." I nodded, pushing my hands into my suit pants pockets. "But what did I tell you about the ride of success?"

"Grind hard and you'll be hit with more good days than bad."

My nodding continued and as we gazed at each other, I could tell her memories of our friendship were fond. Mine were, too, but I didn't romanticize fucking. I appreciated great moments of chemistry with a woman and moved on. Ameerah came with a lot of baggage. I met her through a mutual friend, close to five years ago. She was doing orchestra gigs in New York City, a starving artist with a goddamn pedo for a manager. I never judged; she loved him. But he was too much for her, too hard on her. Dude was possessive. Unfortunately for him, he ran up on her one night while she was with me. He thought his mature looks and manager title would give him weight. I beat the shit out of his old, Spanish Santa Claus ass.

Ameerah didn't take too kindly to that. Even after all the crying she'd done about his possessiveness and controlling nature. He started fucking her the last night of her years as a minor: the night before her eighteenth birthday. He cheated on her, manipulated her mind to

155

sharpen her talent. She would cry in my arms at night after fucking and smoking a fat ass blunt—that was Ameerah's thing. But when he grabbed her up from a table at a club where she was with me, I had to show him I was an Ellis.

Ameerah called me the next day, saying our five-month affair was over. She couldn't "betray Alejandro" that way. My guilt was over how little I cared if she stayed or left my life. I only wanted her safe. Nonetheless, I never reached back. My life had been devoted to building a name for myself aside from my father's legacy. There was no time to play Captain-Save-Her to a broken girl, who sold her soul to her mentor.

So, as I peered down on her now, all those memories of years ago coming back in spades, I had to be proud of my decision to let her go. Besides, there wasn't much I could offer her back then. Shit. My life was such that I had nothing to offer a real relationship now. Being in love wasn't a state I was familiar with, though I'd cared for several women in my life. I guessed Ameerah could be considered one of them.

Her eyes strained as her dimpled cheeks twitched. "Let's go for a drink. I just need to shower." She licked her lips.

"Diner," Rory coughed into her hands, and I knew what that meant.

I turned to see Bilan's eyes wild and nervous as Ameerah's 'fro came into vision to her. Damn...her naivety was a fucking aphrodisiac. When she was at my side, Lamont a few feet behind her, I took Bilan at the small of her back.

"Bilan, this is Ameerah. Ameerah, this is a friend of mine—" I leaned down toward Bilan's ear. "Can I call you friend yet?"

Her eyes crawled up to mine. She blinked, slightly taken and somewhat annoyed. "Stop it," she mumbled, fighting a grin.

"Ameerah," I continued. "This is Bilan."

I couldn't look away from Bilan, still in flirt mode. She made teasing her fun. I caught her smile fade as she observed Ameerah. My regard swept over to the musician and found her, too...unsmiling.

"Thanks for the show," Bilan covered my hand with hers, detaching me from her body. "It was amazing. I'll wait for you outside."

156

When Bilan turned to leave, I caught her arm, pulling it through my palm until I clasped my fingers with hers to keep her from going. I looked over to Ameerah again, whose eyes were on our laced fingers.

"The show was amazing. Take care, sweetheart." My parting words to Ameerah were brief as to not leave an extra moment for Bilan to pull away, causing a scene.

As I passed Bilan up on the way to the entrance, I caught Rory's angry glare on me. I knew what she was thinking.

Since when did I give a fuck about the feelings of a woman I didn't know?

It was time to get Bilan home.

∞ 10 ∞

We made it to the limo in complete silence. Not even his security team uttered a word. For once, I wasn't the only one brewing after an obvious "incident" we both experienced. Similar to earlier when we left the doctor's office, Sadik sat back in his seat, the arch of his index and thumb pinching those sheen lips I tended to get stuck at. His kaleidoscope-hued eyes scanned out the window. He was ruminating—possibly upset. But with me? I didn't do anything wrong. The more time I spent with him today, I realized how one-sided Sadik's views were as far as I was concerned. He had brute tendencies, and if I didn't stand up for myself, I'd get run over by them. Once again, I found myself not caring if we hung out together again. I wanted to be respected.

"It would've been nice to get a heads up on going to see your ex-girlfriend. You got some kind of jealousy fetish?"

He scoffed, sexy smile in tow, but anger teeming beneath the beautiful mask. "Excuse me?"

"Ameerah. It didn't take a historian to figure out you've slept together. The poor girl looked as though her ice cream cone melted in her hands the moment you pulled me to your side."

"Sweetheart, I don't need to give you or anybody else a heads up about who I've slept with."

"Don't call me that!"

"What?"

"Sweetheart! It's what you called her. You can call her that. You've slept with her, not me."

"I'll call you anything you'd like. Didn't know you were keeping score."

"Keeping score of what?" I spat.

"Of how I reference people I've fucked."

"I don't know who you've fucked."

He dropped his arm and chin. "You're right, Bilan. You don't. Neither do I care for you to know. And just like you've made it perfectly clear, I haven't fucked you, so there's nothing left of the matter to speak about."

I tossed myself deeper into the leather bench, crossing my arms to hold myself. He'd efficaciously ended the conversation, and that revved my anger even more. He went back to cogitating and I brooded, wiggling my ankle the same way my mother used to when she got pissed with my dad or brother. After a few minutes, I couldn't take it anymore.

"You want the clothes back?"

Sadik's head shook as he blinked softly. "Nah, Bilan."

"They all still have the tags on them, including this fancy MEEHAR gown. So, why?"

"Because I can't fit them, Bilan."

"You can still get your money back. I'm sure the small fortune you spent could help pay for this private plane you rented for the night."

What was wrong with me? Why did I want to see him as angry as I'd felt?

Am I really angry?

Sadik exhaled, that stupid sexy smile mild, but present. "It's a jet and not just a plane. And I didn't rent the jet."

I rolled my eyes. "I'm just putting it out there. You can have the phone back, too."

His sharp intake of air jostled me as he shifted up in his seat, eyes slightly narrowed. "What can I do to make these next few hours as pleasant as possible?"

I'd chaffed at his nerves. His tone and posture gave it away.

"What?"

"This flight. Clearly, we've veered into a red area. I don't know how, but I'll be the mature party to try to navigate us to peaceful waters."

That stung. And look at me... I was sitting with crossed arms, pouting. I was sure I looked a childish sight. Aside from his aggressiveness with the doctor and introducing me to a person who'd had the type of relationship with him I'd recently fantasized about, Sadik had been very nice to me. Generous, too. Clearly, this was not the way to behave toward a man who'd made so many romantic gestures. Still, I didn't have an answer for why the Ameerah thing pissed me off.

"I'm sorry," I grumbled, rolling my eyes again.

He smiled with his teeth this time. Less energy, but a brighter disposition as he moved across the car to sit next to me.

"Well, it's nice to know I have company in the apology department." His hand slid over my arms, pulling them apart. He cupped my fist, bringing it over to his hard thigh. "I'll try to get you home without upsetting you again."

Okay. I feel like crap...

My eyes squeezed closed in the low lighting of the limo. "This is all new to me."

"What is?"

"This. The gown, shoes...clothes, makeup, celebrity stylist 'hair,' private jet, and even the invitation. I don't date."

"That makes two of us." I could feel his phones vibrating between us in his pocket, but Sadik didn't move to tend to them.

"You can answer," I referred to his phones.

"Nah. I'm okay." His tone was forlorn as he gazed out of the window opposite of me.

Yup. I screwed this up. And I had no clue when I did or how to fix it, so I sulked until we arrived at the airport. We pulled in front of the small building, where the limo was taken over by someone else. Sadik didn't hold my hand this time, but he was still a gentleman, allowing me to take the steps up into the "jet" ahead of him while he held the back of my gown.

160

By the time we sat in the middle section of the cargo, my stomach began to eat itself, I was so hungry. Jeremy appeared right away offering a beverage before takeoff. Sadik ordered more brandy while gazing into his phone. I wanted food, but was too embarrassed to ask. I checked my phone during liftoff, ignoring the drink before me. Tasche sent a few memes and my cousin, Joslyn, sent a text about her mom, my aunt Franzel, wanting to acknowledge my graduation this summer during their annual beach week at the shore. Wow…I got an invitation. I replied with an empty, churning belly by thanking and reminding her Abshir would be home this summer as well, in case she wanted to incorporate the two.

After completing that task and breezing through Facebook and Twitter, Jeremy appeared again. The sight of him made me salivate.

"Are you two ready for dessert—"

"Yeah!" I answered too hastily.

Sadik lifted his head from the laptop Rory had brought in just before we reached the clouds. His forehead wrinkled, but he didn't comment. Instead, he gave an affirmative nod to the flight attendant. When I was sure he'd gone back to his work, I squeezed my eyes in embarrassment. For more reasons than one, this guy was way over my head. As much of a Neanderthal as he had been today, I had to admit, Sadik was a man. One of class, worldly experience, and wealth. Even now, he showed dedication to whatever business he was taking care of on his MacBook.

"Here we go," Jeremy quietly announced, carrying a tray into the section.

I couldn't be happier to see his face. My hands scrambled to put my phone away and pull up the tray table attached to my chair. The most beautiful crème brûlée in an oval ivory porcelain bowl was laid before me. The presentation was too pretty to eat. However, my raging tummy said otherwise.

"I can get a pot of coffee going now, if you'd like," Jeremy offered.

"That would be great, J. Thanks," Sadik replied, thankfully.

With gusto, I grabbed the spoon and cracked the thin, glass-like caramelized sugar surface and scooped custard onto my spoon. The moment the sweetness hit my tongue, my lashes fluttered in pure delight. My tongue swiped through the pudding-like texture slathering the roof of my mouth. Unreal! I immediately decided this was, by far, the best crème brûlée I'd had, although I could never tell Nicky that. This dessert was his contribution to their family's events, and I'd been invited to one to experience it. That was good, but this...

One scoop led into three, and by the time I was on my sixth, there was only one more left. It wasn't fair. I could still feel my stomach rumble. My face began to burn, causing my eyes to roll up, hitting yellowish irises. Sadik's gaze was undeniably heated on me. He gaped at me and I peered at him for seconds long before he caught on. Then he lifted his own neglected bowl, offering it to me.

"Oh." My eyes dropped as I considered the last of the custard still in the bowl. "No thanks. Enjoy." When my taste buds connected with the neurotransmitters of my brain, I reconsidered.

He possibly read the change of mind from my face.

"You sure?" His tone so soft, inviting. "Your 'no-appetite bug' must have jumped from you to me."

I lifted one shoulder. "If you don't want it..."

That's all I had to say for Sadik to switch out our bowls, but not before I spooned the last scoop from mine. I took more time savoring the second serving, though my opinion hadn't changed. It was really an amazing recipe.

"Did Jeremy make this on here?"

Without looking at me, Sadik shook his head as his honeyed regard bounced from his phone to his laptop screen. "DiFillippo's."

Oh...

I recalled Pastor Carmichael mentioning the place, and was disappointed when the second bowl was cleaned, though now my palate was satisfied. Not too long after Jeremy collected our bowls and offered coffee, which we both declined, Sadik stowed his laptop and worked his way out of his suit jacket. He settled in to relax with a glass of brandy. My cell battery had died, so I began to take small sips of my Mauve, though nothing dedicated. Thoughts of the following day began to flood my head. I had an exam and an application for grad school that were due. Before I knew it, time had lapsed and I realized how quiet it had been in our section.

Sadik tended to his phone, and I got lost in inspecting his profile. Seriously, this guy had exotic features synonymous with beauty, a word not typically used to describe a man. However, beneath the translucent eyes, smooth russet skin, and well-articulated tongue was indisputable ruggedness. Proof of it was the indented scar on his left eyelid and the raised one just beneath his bottom lip. Even they added to his appeal. Did women like Ameerah feel the same? Pretty boy features had never been a draw for me as far as guys went. I couldn't tell you what was, but could never imagine being excited over an orange beard or kaleidoscope-hued eyes. What was it about this—

Those feline eyes were on me.

So lost in thought, I missed when Sadik glanced up from his phone. My head whipped to the right and I set my gaze in the dark sky. I heard him snort, but wouldn't dare acknowledge it.

"I can tell you want me, at least half as much as I want you." His tone was soft, yet so confident. My heart thudded in my chest, groin fluttered wickedly. "What I can't figure out is why you're holding back."

I sucked in a breath, suddenly embarrassed. That was when I realized the need to get honest with him about what was going on in my mind.

Shaking my head, I tried explaining. "This is happening fast. All of it. I just met you three weeks ago at work when you happened to come in to order one of my desserts for your pregnant—" Lifting my brows, I shook my head again. "Whatever the woman is to you. Then you so happened to be at the same concert my girls and I were at. And yesterday, I walked out of a high-end boutique in Manhattan with thousands of dollars' worth of clothes! This morning..." With animated eyes, I dipped my chin for emphasis. "I sat in a hair stylist's chair that was just occupied by Oprah's best friend. Then the doctor's office visit." From my peripheral, Sadik's head reared, engaged. "We had no begin point." Foolishly, I peered him directly in his eyes.

Sadik's full attention was on me, as it always seemed to be before I snapped on him tonight, after the show. His full lips with a light sheen from Chapstick, and the cupid's bow portion slightly thicker than either side, brushing together captured my attention yet once again.

My lids collapsed and face contorted. "Would you stop? I'm trying to have a moment of honesty here and explain this isn't my real life. This..." I gestured the jet. "...does not happen to me every six to eight months."

His brows met as he smirked. "What could I have done differently to ease you into...this?" His regard paid a cursory glance around the cargo.

I took a deep breath. "I don't know..." My arms flew into the air. "Maybe if we had seen each other a few times before your buying me a four-figure gown and having me cleared for HIV, there would have been a pace set and I would feel..."

"Feel what?" His expression was now stoic, though his posture was lax.

Sadik's legs were stretched in front of him as he reclined in his chair. He made this seem "everyday" for...us.

"Feel earned."

"By whom?"

"By me. You seem to be a generous guy. I can admit to enjoying the attention, but I don't want to take advantage of you." And I hate the thought of you with other women—pregnant and not!

For a while, he just gazed into my eyes. I wondered if I'd said something offensive in my honesty spiel. Perhaps I reminded him of our reality. Sadik didn't know me. And I didn't know him to be spoiled with his money. I turned for the window, once again, feeling embarrassed.

"Taste or touch?"

I turned to him, surprised by his even tone, clearly not fazed by my awkwardness. Immediately, I decided to play along.

"I bake, so definitely taste. Touch..." I shivered, simultaneously flashing my tongue and turning up my nose in disgust.

"What's up with that?"

I shook my head, grinning shyly. "Touch has never been a big deal to me."

Sadik sat back in his seat, letting out a weary breath as he swiped his nose, facing the window to the left of him. "Taste and touch can go hand in hand."

"Wha-what do you mean?"

Hiking his right brow, Sadik appeared tired. I could understand; it had been a long day and was late.

"Well, when fuckin'—good fuckin'—you can enjoy taste and touch in the same event." My whole frame went rigid, toes curled as I stared straight ahead. "Shit, Bilan!" he breathed. "You're over there blanching?"

My hands flew to my cheeks. "No!"

"You are," he droned, leaning toward me. "Coyness ain't never been my thing, but yours is adorable." His hands clutched beneath the layered fabric of the gown behind my lower legs, pulling me into him.

Then he lifted my chin and brushed his soft, warm lips against my mouth. I pushed into him, wanting the opportunity to kiss Sadik again. My suction in the peck was slow to show him I wanted it. God, I wanted it. My eyes opened in time to see his lids slowly separate.

He moved into me again. "Shit, Bilan..."

Sadik's lips caressed mine just before his tongue pierced my mouth and I opened for him. I had no idea what came over me, but I met his every lick and swipe, greedy for his taste. My hands went to the sides of his face, holding him to me as I explored his sweet mouth. His moan made my spine shiver, and his breath hitting my face had my nipples stinging in the tight corset. I couldn't breathe as I matched his thrashing with my own aggression.

Even when I felt his body shifting, though his mouth remained in a dance with mine, I didn't stop kissing him. I couldn't. I wanted to drown in the magic of his scent, heat, and oral pleasure. I didn't realize he'd knelt in front of me until his hands were pushing up my legs beneath the gown. When they reached my thighs, my legs contracted and jerked embarrassingly.

He retracted his tongue and whispered while meeting my throbbing lips. "Relax, baby," My chest heaved as I sloughed in air. I couldn't believe the weird things my body was doing at his touch. "I can't promise I'll wait until the results come in, but I'm going to try."

165

He breathed the words into my face. "Tonight, I wanna show you taste and touch can be one in the same."

Underneath the layers of the gown, my panties were given a light yank. "Lift."

On instinct, my eyes roved around the quieted plane and saw no movements on either side of the partitions now drawn by curtains. His honeyed eyes seduced me as his hands teased my jumpy skin. My panties were pulled over my sandals and tucked into the pocket of his trousers. He gathered the fabric of my gown, rolling it up toward me. Then Sadik lifted my legs in a manner more illicit than I was used to. A draft of air hit my pelvis, followed by a warm slithery muscle snaking up my slit. On their own accord, my thighs tightened to the point of closing. Sadik gently pushed against them.

He reared back, peering over the fabric. "Did I hurt you?" The croak in his gentle voice had my heart trembling. Biting my top lip with squeezed eyes, I shook my head. "Then just relax," he groaned lowly before ducking his head beneath the mountain of layers.

Oooh...

Sadik peppered kisses up my right thigh, tickling me shamefully. He repeated the same sensual torture on my left thigh. My hands curled into tight fists. When his tongue roved between my labia again, my belly leaped. Trying to relax into it to not further embarrass myself, my breaths were ragged. It was almost impossible to breathe in the tightness of my corset while having an experienced man between my legs.

I felt his hand move up and sucked in air when a finger pushed into my flesh, rounding and rounding inside, rimming me. His tongue busied on a bed of nerves, shooting zings up my groin. My mouth stretched wide, eyes squeezing from unfamiliar pleasurable torture. Then his finger was at my mouth, brushing against my lip. I opened and he pushed it inside. My lids flashed wide at the salty, astringent taste.

Sadik's shiny head lifted, eyes heavy while holding his finger in my mouth. "Suck," he whispered huskily.

He didn't wait for me to start before heading back down under. My back bowed as his tongue began to clobber that bed of nerves down

166

there. Pathetically, I was twenty-eight years old and had never felt a sensation like this in my life at the hand of a man. It was powerfully euphoric, and Sadik's efforts felt so intentional—even if I didn't know the destination. I began to suck on his finger, feeling…crazy. Nasty.

And that's when it hit me. Taste and touch worked together to bring pleasure. Only, we weren't having sex. This wasn't intercourse, and, still, I was prepared to lose my mind, sucking in more and more of his finger. Quickly, I was encroaching on an urgency my body couldn't resist. My mouth suctioned, tongue moved under his digit in an impassioned stroke. My groin lifted and lifted, constrained nipples tingled to a vibrating sensation. I sucked hard as an intense insistence took over me and a bomb of pleasure imploded without warning, leaving my entire frame vibrating in bliss. Floating. As euphoric flutters took over my body, I glided in space.

I couldn't decide how long lightning pleasures zipped through my frame before I fell into the seat boneless. When I was able to open my eyes, I was met with those that were green, yellow, brown, and black. Scowling, his half-mast lids made me wonder if he'd just experienced the pleasure I did. His mouth and dusted chin glistened more than his skinned head. And in that moment, I felt a connectedness to him I'd never felt before. It was a degree of vulnerability as I lay slouched, opened to him, allowing him to expose me to his staff as he took pleasure from me.

"You taste amazing," he barely uttered. My chest heaved and I swallowed hard, fighting to keep my eyes open. "You okay?"

Struggling to catch my breath, I managed to nod.

"You're stunning after an orgasm, too."

I felt weakened by the desire heating his gaze. The hallmark of affection I'd never felt from a man. An expression of earnest was in his eyes. Something tangible, I couldn't deny. My chest heaved, goosebumps still peppered my skin, and my heart stammered at what was being transmitted between us.

"Sa—"

Before I could finish his name, his soft lips were on me, tongue expressive inside my mouth. Yes. He was aggressive, all alpha, and while that concerned me before, it thrilled me in this manner. That salty astringent taste was now seasoned with Mauve, mint-flavored lip balm, and distinct Sadik. It emboldened me, made me needy for him. My hands pushed up to his stubbled cheeks, holding him to me.

"One more," he whispered after pulling back.

My tongue laying distended from my mouth as he did. Then I watched him lower his torso and dive beneath the rolled layers. His mouth on my labia, tongue teasing the plumped tissues. My head rolled back onto the plush leather chair, eyes too heavy to keep a watch out for his staff. Mind too lost to care. His warm hands splayed at the back of my thighs, ears caught in between. His mouth dangling me between two galaxies.

With an arching spine, I began to move against the rhythm of his tongue on my clit, pleasure so intense I wanted to scream, cry, beg. Still, I rode out the pleasure. Even against the pains from the restraints of my chest, my lower body moved, feeding myself to his busy mouth. When another wave of urgency blossomed in my groin, I panicked, feeling heavier than I did before. But I was powerless to the magnitude of the detonation, and mewled weakly. Second by second, I was lost to the current and washed away in bliss.

We pulled up on her quiet Woodland Park block. Bizarrely embattled, I pulled myself from beneath Bilan's sleeping frame to exit the limo. She stirred, slowly awakening herself. By the time I stood from the car and glanced back inside, she was gathering her things. I extended my hand, helping her out, throwing my arm over her shoulder once she was on her feet. Immediately, she melted into my side as we trekked to her house, then hiked up the stairs.

I waited for her to pull out her keys and noticed Bilan kept her head low, not looking at me one time. She looked tiny draped in my suit jacket over a poofy gown, hiding her face. When she pushed her door in, Bilan turned to me, head still low.

"Thanks," she whispered awkwardly. Then she brushed the back of her tapered head. "Sorry about the show. I..." Bilan hesitated.

No. I'm sorry...

I lifted my hand to her face, and swiped the underline of her bottom lip with my thumb.

"Thanks for tonight. I enjoyed you." I brushed my lips over her forehead. "Go get some rest." I nodded toward her open door before taking off.

My shoulders were heavy as I skipped down the stairs to the limo. I sat on the opposite bench we were in on the way from the airport. Not even two blocks from pulling off, my mind began to churn on overload and my phone rang. My brother's name lit the screen. I answered it and tapped again to put it on speaker as I rubbed my tight eyes.

"Yeah, Ib?"

"Just got a call. Marco's crib just got blown the fuck up."

Marco was Salvatore Rizzo's son, Lia's brother.

I rubbed my head from top to bottom, exhaling along the way. "How?"

"Bomb. Somebody must've planted it."

"Was he there?"

"Nah. That muthafucka lucky his lady and kid wasn't there. The house was empty, but they said it's gone."

"Hmmmm..."

"Yo, where you at?"

"On my way to my office to pick up a couple of thumb drives." My assistant packed documents on them while I was out of town today. Shit I didn't want on the system. "You packed?"

"I guess. Monica in there, throwing shit together."

"Three weeks. You'll be gone for that long. As we can see, timing couldn't be better."

"Shiiiiiit," he croaked into the phone. "I told Pops the same fuckin' thing."

"I need to stop by Julius' in Paterson to sign some paperwork before the flight out."

"What you doing with Julius Richards? Ain't he running for mayor?"

"Yeah."

"The fuck you doing with that?"

"Donations." I cupped my chin, still feeling dried traces of her around my mouth.

"Oh." Iban's tone was flat.

"I'll see you at the airport in a few hours."

"Till then."

The line closed. I sat back, exhaling again.

"Yeah," Rory groused from the front seat. The open partition just above my head. "Eating that girl's pussy'll have yo ass tired ass fuck, my nigga."

I rolled my eyes, a flurried sensation zipping through my chest.

"Fuck you, Rory."

"Nah. That's what you wanted to do to that girl. Had her ass sounding like she was fuckin' crying back there."

Of course, she'd know. Nosy ass...

Lamont snickered, smart enough not to let a full-on laugh slip. Rory got away with shit no one else on my payroll could, and it was well known.

I tapped the pocket of my pants before pulling out cotton thongs with lace trim. I hated cotton. They had no place on a woman. Too bad that wasn't a "Sadik-ism" I'd be indoctrinating her with. I crushed the panties into my fist as I gazed out of the dark windows, watching the street lights shoot past.

That was it...
It was time for this shit with Ms. Bilan to come to an end.

∞ 11 ∞

May

Sadik

THREE WEEKS LATER...

Pelicans jerking their wings over the roaring waves played the background as I scrolled down my iPad. My other hand brought a bottle of Corona to my face for a pull.

"Aye." I glanced up to see Tiffany glide over to the fridge, pulling a silk kimono over her bare shoulders. Her thick thighs shifted with each step she made. Her smile couldn't be missed even on the quickest glimpse. "Ain't y'all meeting before we leave for the airport?" She opened the door and browsed inside.

My attention went back to my screen, mind recessed again, surfing pictures.

"We ready, Deek." Iban's tanned frame filled the doorway of the cottage.

I nodded, moving for another sip of my beer before tapping my device to sleep and standing to my feet.

On my way to the door, Tiff asked, "Y'all eat all that Beluga caviar last night?"

I shrugged. "Probably Diane and Nena and them."

She sucked her teeth. "Dad need to teach them bitches community," she hissed. "They're not at the Elliswoods Palace in Hunterdon County."

Ignoring that reasonable complaint, I headed out to the small table on the porch where my father was sitting, gazing out at the turquoise sea several yards out. Iban was near, puffing on a stogie, the wind pushing his open beach shirt behind him. He approached the table, taking a seat.

"What do you think, Sadik?"

"About this island?"

He nodded.

"This shit dope as hell," Iban interjected animatedly. "I can't believe you finally ready to buy a island, Pop. You been saying this shit forever. I like the last one. Shit was big as fuck."

My father's green eyes landed on me, once again asking for my opinion. We'd seen four islands in the past two weeks. The first two were in Central America and the last two, here in the Caribbean. Grenada was our last stop. He'd planned this time to start looking at them from the top of the year, being sure to have me clear my schedule as well. Iban wasn't originally in the plan. It was supposed to be my father, his attorney, Marion, and me. I wasn't even sure if Iban knew we were making the trip. But with the issue of him pulling out a gun on one of Rizzo's men, I couldn't leave him back in the U.S. without supervision from my father or me, the only two with influence over him.

"This one is nice, but too far from a developed island. Just like Marion said, we'd have to clear the area of savages before building anything here."

"We got the manpower," Iban asserted. "Shit, me and you can come out here for like two-three weeks and clear this bitch of anybody who ain't 'posed to be here." He took a pull of his cigar.

Ignoring that statement, my father asked, "So, the cay in Belize or the double island in Honduras?"

"The cay in Belize isn't developed at all. It'll be a mean expense to get the type of plumbing and wiring for even the designated house

173

area that you'd be comfortable with. And the twin islands in Honduras may be the least expensive and have construction already, but those shits are dumb small. You won't have an ounce of privacy from fellow residents or voyagers."

He nodded in deep consideration. I had to admit, I was happy for my father, too. This move was a good look for him. He was inching toward seventy years old and needed more leisure. He deserved it. Even looking at him now with his yellow chino shorts, open silk button-up exposing his belly bump and salt and peppered chest hairs, and Ase Garb thong sandals—all of which I was sure his young diva girlfriend, Nena, picked out for him—brought the vision of him relaxing on his own private island.

"And the thing with Salvatore's boy?"

I heard from my FBI connect, Jefferson, with the news last night while on a neighboring island for dinner.

"Damien," I answered.

"What?" Iban leaped in his seat with wide eyes.

My father, too, sported an expression of shock, though not as animated as my brother.

I nodded. "Damien received a patch of skin he recognized as Tank's." My hard and knowing eyes ranged over to my brother.

Iban cowered in his seat, looking busted.

"You can't just kill a muthafucka and let them take every piece of their flesh to hell with them, can you?" my father barked at his eldest.

Iban mumbled something beneath his breath with the stogie hanging from his lips. We'd been on him for years about discretion. My brother preferred his bloodshed be public knowledge.

"The good news is, those two have each other to be busy with," I advised. "That'll give us time to do what we need to gather the info needed to take Damien down."

"Fuckin' finally," Iban grumbled, looking toward the forest of palm trees opposite the ocean.

"My concern is Lia and the baby," an unusual cry of concern spilled from my father. He'd never spoke fondly of a Rizzo. He and Salvatore went way back, and while they were cordial now, beneath

174

the peace of a treaty was a sea of shared resentment. "You see how Marco's house was hit. Who's to say Lia's won't be next?"

"Man, Damien's fruity ass know not to touch a ghost of a Ellis! He don't want no smoke with this family." Iban was too confident with that false notion.

He'd already robbed my father's warehouse of tens of thousands, which led to the death of three of his men. But I wouldn't be the one to bring us back to that fact.

"Just calm the fuck down, Iban!" My father's breathing turned uneven. "I'm trying to get out of this shit with peace of mind. I don't need the attention."

"You right, Pops." Iban nodded, still facing the opposite direction. He was upset, and of course couldn't see how he created problems for himself when he pissed Earl Ellis off. "You right. I'mma chill. Let this shit play out how it's gonna play out."

There was a moment of quiet, allowing both men to calm down.

"Antigua would be my pick," I circled back to our original topic. "Close to fifty acres that includes barren land and foliage for privacy. You can have a piece for your family and possibly build commercially for added retirement income." I shrugged, gazing out to flying terns. "But you're bringing Mommy out for her pick of your top two."

"Yeah." I heard the smile in that one syllable and glanced down to have it confirmed. My father's beam was undeniable. "My Irene's gonna love this sun and water shit. I remember her first time on a beach with clear water. Damn!" He breathed. "The feeling I got knowing I was the man to bring that to her. You know?" He gazed up at me with so much pride—and love—in his eyes, thinking about that woman.

I averted my eyes, proud he still had a level of affection for her. I wanted that one day. I wanted to bring wonder and adventure to a partner. I would have loved to be a first of ventures.

That led my thoughts to three weeks ago, when I sucked the sweetest nectar from trembling Somali legs. She felt new to having her pussy tasted, but it was hard to believe a woman with her style and self-awareness would still be a virgin. I, myself, was too old to expect

175

to run across a virgin at my age. But I could damn sure run into a woman I could show new things to.

"As corny as it sounds, it's a fantasy to spend the night at the beach."

Her.

But I let it go. I'd heard from Bilan a little over a week after the Ameerah concert. She texted me about returning my suit jacket. I was at a tiki bar in Belize, drinking with Iban when the text came through. I was both excited and annoyed. The girl was prideful. She was disappointed by my absence, I was sure. But instead of saying so, she tried playing it cool.

Bilan: *You were generous enough with the women's apparel. It's clear you don't want them back, but what am I supposed to do with a man's tuxedo jacket. I can drop it off to you. Or mail it.*

Bilan: *Let me know.*

Bilan: *I can donate it if you no longer want it.*

I'd been with enough women to know she was uncomfortably intrigued. What was crazy was, I was sure it was half of what I felt. I wanted that girl, but had to let her go before anything kicked off.

"Yeah," my father breathed. "A private island to have my grandbabies run wild on. And I want more. When I finally get my grandson, I may die after that. It's the last thing on my list of wishes for my life; a grandson to extend my legacy." He laughed. "Now, I see what your mother felt like until your sister, Taaliba, got here. I got two granddaughters I gotta have tea parties with. I need a boy I can show how to shoot a rifle, man." His grin was longing.

"When does Lia find out what the sex is?" It took a few seconds to realize the question was posed to me.

"Uh...I think she finds out soon," I answered honestly, trying not to look at my brother. The last I remembered, she'd be having a gender reveal party. No one mentioned a date to me, so I doubted it had taken place. "She wants a gender reveal party soon."

"Ahhhh..." Earl groaned. "As much as I don't want no attachments with the Rizzos, I'd be happy with a little boy from you, Sadik."

Damn…

I knew that was hard to say. My father had been having a difficult time with this pregnancy thing. Even my mother had noticed. Hearing him accept this had guilt gripping me in a vice-like chokehold. Iban and I finally met eyes. I was the first to look away.

"Aye, Pops." Iban's cheerful tone caught my attention. He faced my father, body fully turned now. "I know you been wanting a lil' boy at your kneecap. I just wanna let you know Monica's pregnant again, so hopefully you'll finally get your wish." His smile was accomplished.

It annoyed the fuck out me.

"Well, damn," my father sighed. "I gotta get my shit in order. Two on the way! My boys don't play!" He reached over and gave Iban a firm shake, nothing of what I got when I announced Lia's pregnancy. Iban wouldn't know that. He wasn't there when I broke the news. "This shit is wonderful. Next, Sadik'll be telling me he's finally settling down and getting married!"

He didn't laugh at that ridiculous prediction, because he didn't mean it as a joke. My father and mother would have loved that for me. For them. For the family.

"I see Tiff still here." My father's expression turned boys club on me. He was a man. He knew what Tiffany was after when she flew out here two days ago, saying she'd gotten into a fight with her man, Larry, and needed a break. My father was no fool, likely knowing she'd been sharing a bed with me since arriving. But he was also no baby and could understand what simple fucking was. "Maybe I'll get two grandbabies out of you and have you make my goddaughter an honest woman." He winked.

"Nah. That's a lot and ain't gonna happen," Iban replied. "Shit like that take focus. Deek too busy contributing to campaigns and shit."

My eyes slammed into him hard. Why the fuck would he bring that up in front of our father?

"Campaign?" Dad predictably asked. He turned to me, confusion etching his face. "What campaign?"

"Julius Richards," Iban answered before I could.

"Your boy from Silk City? What's he running for?"

Iban's brows lifted. "Big dog; mayor."

My father's expression matched his oldest son's. "He running for mayor in Paterson? I ain't know that."

"He announced it last week," I finally spoke.

As he peered up at me, I could see so many thoughts shooting through his mind. Yes, I could contribute to an election campaign. My legal businesses and reputation allowed me to do something my father couldn't, even if he was interested.

And there it was, another strike of disappointment for a decision I made in my life.

Dad stood from the table. "Let me make sure these girls got me packed up. We should be leaving soon." He strolled into the house.

I moved toward the waters, needing to get a distance between Iban and me.

"Yo, Deek!" Iban yelled. "Wait up, man."

I didn't hear him gain on me so quickly, so when he grabbed my left arm, yanking it hard, I swung back with my right on a hard twist, connecting to the corner of his mouth. Iban flew back, landing on his ass.

I bent over, cocking my arm with a balled fist to jab his ass again, but Iban's arms flew into the air.

"You got the power, man! You got the fuckin' power!" he shouted.

I knew I had; I was ready to put his fucking lights out.

"Fuck you!" I grated, wanting to kick him in the fucking face while on his back. "Eight fuckin' months! Eight fuckin' months and your punk ass still ain't coppin' to this shit. The baby'll be here in two. The fuck're you waiting on, Iban? You gone wait for your wife to get pregnant with her fourth child before you tell her about your third?"

A sharp whistle sounded, causing my head to whip up toward the cottage. My father's new security, Stewy, was charging toward us, but stopped at the harsh sound. He looked back, and a tiny ass Rory in little jean shorts and a bikini top rolled her index finger in a circle.

"We don't involve ourselves in those, new blood!" her coarse voice carried across the gentle tropical breeze.

Stewy looked confused, but in a few seconds was convinced and began to back away. He was new and more familiar with Iban than me, so that could have gotten ugly real quick.

"Why the fuck you trippin'?" Iban shouted, trying to keep his voice low while holding his jaw. Blood trailed his chin. "I told you, I got this!"

"When?"

"Soon! With all this shit going on, it ain't been the right time!"

"But you take advantage of the time when he's fuckin' broken hearted over shit I didn't do. That's cool, though? When he's fuckin' bleeding over his legacy being tainted by Rizzo blood, thanks to me, you hit him with the news of another baby in the family and how I'm contributing to a damn campaign. Bruh, that's some foul shit!"

Iban lifted himself from the sand. "I ain't mean it like that. But we brothers. We hold each other down! It ain't like I'm compromising ya marriage, or shit like that. I keep telling you, you don't know how complicated this shit is. It's just fuckin' inconvenient, man!"

"And what the fuck you think it is to me?" I shouted.

"Deek!" Rory barked.

My eyes rolled up to find my father on the porch of the cottage, watching us.

"Fuck this," I exhaled, taking off.

"Where you going, man?" Iban asked with outstretched arms.

I called over to Rory as I trekked toward the side of the cottage to the jeeps. "Grab all my shit. I'll meet them at the fuckin' airport!"

"C'mon, Deek!" Iban shouted from behind me, wisely staying the fuck back.

Bilan

I rolled my neck in circles, feeling each tender muscle stretch. My entire body was sore and I felt drained.

"I 'on't know how you gone get through this shift, yo," Tasche observed from across the table while on her phone.

I pinched the innermost corners of my eyes, gripping the bridge of my nose. What I really wanted to do was rub my tired eyes, but refused to disturb what was left of my eyeliner.

"I'll make it. I do it all the time."

"This time different, though," her chords gravelly. "You been on one thousand at school lately."

She was right. As we sat deep inside the diner, opposite of the entrance and away from the front counter, I tried killing time while I waited on my banana puddings and peach cobblers to finish baking so I could put the sweet potato pies in. Maria and Pedro were back there, packing the aluminum pans with pie crust now. Their help would ensure a faster assembly time, then I could hopefully leave by five...this morning. It was now just after three in the morning. Tasche opted to have her "dinner," which was breakfast for most, here at the diner instead of taking it to-go.

"Daaaamn, I could use a fat ass spliff right now!" She rolled her eyes dramatically. "I'm sleepy as fuck."

"Is he coming over?"

Tasche was plotting on the guy she'd been DM'ing for a couple of months now.

"I'm still waiting on that nigga to respond. His shift should be up by now. Damn!" she moaned, scratching her head.

I tried stretching my arms above my head, but winced when I felt the first zing of pain.

"Uhn-huhn! You all fucked up, yo. You sure the gym did all that?" Her eyes twinkled with girly mischief.

"Girl, please. I hadn't been to the gym in a couple of weeks because of finals and work at school. My body reminded me of it today in my workout."

"You sure that's the only session you got today?" she teased.

"I tell you a guy went down on me one time, and you think I get all this play now."

"Girl, he ate ya pussy on a private plane! The entire fuck you mean?"

I shook my head, lungs shuddering as I exhaled. Thinking about Sadik hurt. I still hadn't figured out why. It had been three weeks since he dropped me off on my doorstep, drugged from an emotion created through intimacy. That's the part I didn't discuss with Tasche when I was sure to tell her not to share a sentence of the story with Randi.

I messed up whatever Sadik and I were on our way to establishing because of my stubborn tendencies. Yeah, the doctor's office thing was extreme and rude. I would have gone on my own if we decided to take it there. But it didn't have to be a deal breaker. Then the Ameerah thing. Not only was I disappointed by her reaction to me, but it bothered me that he'd take me to a show of one of his former lovers.

So many things went wrong that night, and out of all the times my mind replayed those incidences trying to measure my actions, I couldn't convince myself there was no connection between Sadik and me. That was until over a week had passed and he hadn't reached out. That hit at something so vulnerable in me. So, I sent him a text—from the phone he bought me—offering to return his jacket.

Your Friend: Thanks. I'll have it picked up. Will hit you with details when I'm back in town.

That was it. I didn't even know how to extend the conversation. It was sterile and not of a man who went down on me—twice in one night. So, for close to two weeks now, I'd been privately sulking while taking exams and working both jobs. I decided to hit the gym at six in morning before heading off to school. Most of my day was spent on campus between classes and departmental work. I clocked in here at ten last night and had been busy baking since. Tasche here was a welcome distraction.

"Look at my lil' mommy, yo." Tasche held a picture of an infant to me on her phone.

"Awwwww! She's cute. Who's that?"

"My little Mia Grace!" A high-pitched girly voice wasn't a common act of Tasche.

Her preferred persona was coarse.

My face tightened. "Whose baby is that?"

"My girl, Lex-dawg. You don't remember her from that church service in March?" She went back to cooing over the picture.

"Oh! Lex and the eclectic, palm-reading husband." I balled my mouth. "She was cool, though. How is she?"

I wanted to ask how could she be married to such a strange man—no matter how good looking he was.

"Girl," she sang. "Hookin' off on bitches in the fuckin' prayer line!" Tasche dropped her face toward the table so hard and fast, I thought she'd hit it.

"What in the world is she fighting in church for, Tasche?"

"Them bitches that be wanting her man. She starting to go with him more when he preaches all over the damn world. He was at this church in Cali, and some bitch was trying to act like she had the Holy Ghost—you know, the way them church people be falling the fuck out, and shit. Well, Lex said it was mad people at the front of the church, everybody wanted Ezra to pray for them, and shit. Then ol' girl started coming at Ezra like she was ready to bumrush him, and shit. Lex saw that shit coming from a mile away and moved from behind Ezra as ol' girl was coming in front of him. Lex circled in front of him quick enough to hook that bitch by the neck and knock her over. The bitch snapped out that fakin' shit and swung on Lex." Tasche laughed. "It was over after that. Lex went Harlem Pride on that ass, and had to be pulled off ol' girl."

"Oh, my God! What did her husband do? Say?" I couldn't imagine him going for that.

Tasche shrugged, rubbing her nose as she yawned. "Lex said he was hot for a minute about it, even though the church kept apologizing to him and Lex. They said they had problems with them bitches in there doing shit like that and was embarrassed they showed out when they guests was there."

I shook my head. I thought church people were better than that, especially in church.

"There you are, Bilan." Georgie from the kitchen walked over to our booth, handing me my phone. "It was going off back there."

"Thanks," I murmured, curious as to who was reaching out to me at this hour. "Oh, my God!" I chirped.

"The fuck wrong with you?" Tasche asked.

I scrolled down my text thread.

Your Friend: *Hey. I'm finally back in town. I'm coming to pick up my jacket. I should be at your place in five minutes.*

That was more than forty-five minutes ago…

Your Friend: *I'm outside.*

"Oh, this nigga finally hit me back," Tasche graveled across from me, but I barely followed, so wrapped in these text messages.

Your Friend: *I'm gonna stop by the diner just in case you're working. I'll come out back.*

That was sent twenty minutes earlier. My eyes swung round and round in my sockets, doing the math.

I leaped on the leather bench. "I need to go check on something!" My tone was animated as I clambered out of the booth.

"A'ight," Tasche acknowledged, frantically tapping into her phone. "I may bounce myself in a minute. This nigga talking right!" She flashed her tongue.

I almost missed it, tripping over my feet to get to the counter in the front of the restaurant. When there, I paid a deep gaze out the window in the front, but saw no ruby black Mercedes-Maybach. With added speed, I pushed inside the kitchen and zipped past a couple dozen bodies for the back door. My pulse banged in my neck and limbs trembled from overwhelming excitement at the door jamb when I recognized the sleek-body sedan. Rory's short frame squatted on the hood, lighting a cigarette. Her buggy eyes low as the flame curled inches from her face.

The back door opened, and his russet frame stood from the car, holding a phone to his ear, honeyed eyes intensely on me. He moved to close the door and made a few steps in my direction. I could feel blood rush through my ears as I prodded down the stairs and headed straight for him. It was him. Finally, I was seeing him again, now realizing how much of a privilege it was. On the way, an abrupt thought hit. Just before our toes met, Sadik lowered the phone, his regard no less intense on me.

"I don't have the jacket with me," spilled from my lips pathetically.

And God, did he smell amazing. Scented, groomed, with a broadness to him I'd forgotten in three weeks. I throbbed below.

His cheeks spread and eyes narrowed. "I didn't think you'd carry it to work every day."

"I've slept in it, so bringing it in wouldn't be much of a stretch."

His forehead wrinkled while his beam remained. Sadik now looked confused.

I closed my eyes while shaking my head. "I'm kidding. But if you realized I wouldn't have it at work, why did you come?"

His hands pushed into his track suit pants as his chin dipped. "I just got back in town and wanted to see you."

"At three in the morning?"

He nodded. "A couple of hours ago, but yeah."

"Haven't seen you in weeks." I hated those words of weakness the moment they left my tongue.

"I've been out of town since the night of the Ameerah show."

My chin dropped this time. "Really?"

Rubbing the orange stubble on his jaw, he nodded. "Took a redeye out to China and spent a little over a week there in Qingdao, meeting with a client and courted a potential one. Then I flew to Central America, where I met my father and his attorney, who's looking to acquire property."

"Property in Central America?"

He shrugged, looking too tempting. "Property. We started in Central America...was there for a few days before jetting over to The Caribbean to look there, too."

"Wait." My forehead stretched, lips pouted, and eyes rolled a three hundred-sixty degree circle in their sockets. "Is this like some kind of litmus test to see if I can handle your family's wealth or something?"

He exhaled. "Kind of."

"I thought you got a few positives on your STD report and changed your mind," I quipped.

As his eyes perused my face, Sadik shook his head. "Got the email a couple of weeks ago, All negative here."

I nodded, remembering mine as well. This turned awkward fast.

"Listen, Sadik..." My eyes rolled out into the distance, brain stumped for words. "I'm sorry about—"

"We're not doing that apology shit today. We can save them for the future." He snorted. Future? He shifted his weight forward on his toes, telling of his unease. "I want to spend more time getting to know you, Bilan."

"Really?" I was ghosted.

He nodded, struggling with something. "I don't know where it'll go or how far, but let's see."

"Then why the seriousness?"

"Because I'm not an easy man to have 'relationship' expectations with. I own three damn companies—and not all in the same industry. My damn schedule is impossible. There aren't enough hours in the day to satisfy it. I have a business with international legs. My family commands so much of my attention—even when it stresses me out. But they're my identity and nonnegotiable when it comes down to dividing my time. And then there's me."

"I don't get it."

"I'm demanding, Bilan. There may be times I require you to be up and lively at four in the morning when you're not working." He lifted his hand to my face, his thumb drawing a feather caress from the outer corner of my eye to my cheek. "In eyeliner and lip gloss for me to fuck up." I swallowed hard before my jaw dropped. "Or just to rub my back until I fall asleep."

"I can be a night owl," I murmured.

"Or you'll meet me at the airport just to drive me to a meeting because I'll be there all night, then on a redeye, out of the country for a week or two."

A pang lanced my belly.

"Are you trying to tell me to run? Do you want me to be turned off?"

He shook his head, a scowl playing at his face. "I want your expectations to be reasonable. I don't want to be the bad guy on the other side of this."

"On the other side of being your friend?"

A beautiful smile spread across his face. Sadik used his thumb to scratch the patch beneath his bottom lip as he averted his dangerous gaze.

"Yeah." I nodded haughtily. "I've researched your name. Sadik means he who is a friend in Swahili. Who knew you'd use the meaning to get girls?"

"Touché." He snorted, appearing impressed by my obsessive snooping. "But I told you I don't do this. I think you should consider yourself lucky."

What?

"Lucky! Now, I know you really don't want anything real with—"

My 'oh, no you didn't' read of his arrogance was snatched from my tongue by Sadik's soft lips. It was slung around by his aggressive tongue. It was destroyed by his big hands holding my face. The memory of his taste returned. The ghost of his touch became fresh again as my body melted into him. I felt myself shifting on my feet, but was too lost in the desperation of his taste to know for sure. Sadik crushed me with his weight, pushing the swelling of his erection into my belly. My legs wobbled, but thankfully I didn't succumb to gravity. We enjoyed each other more than we thought to breathe. I got lost in space as our mouths moved in sync and we created a pact of possibility.

I couldn't open my eyes when he pulled his mouth away. His thick impression still on my belly.

"Beelon!" I could hardly make out.

186

"I think you're being called." His silk alto was clearer.

"Who?" I whispered, still lost in space.

"Yo, they calling you," a coarse, boyish voice announced. Rory...

That's when I finally opened my eyes and saw I was pushed against his car, and Sadik's attention was to the back of the restaurant. Maria waved her arm to get my attention.

"Beelon!"

"Shoot!" I leaped on my feet, causing Sadik to relieve me of his lush weight. "My stuff is ready. If I don't put my pies in right away, I won't get out of here until day break."

I pivoted just slightly when it dawned on me. "Can I call you?"

"I hope so." Sadik swiped his lips with his thumb. "I have a crazy few weeks ahead, but we'll be in touch."

I walked backward, oddly hating to be leaving him so soon. I mean... Did he really just show up at my job to say he wanted to give it another try? This was unreal. I didn't even know the man and suddenly, I felt like I was walking on clouds of joy. I only turned back when I made it to the door. Rory was inside the car, starting the engine. Sadik was still in the same place I left him, his honeyed irises on me with that intense gaze.

∞ 12 ∞

Bilan

"Hey!" I shouted. "Chill. I'm coming!"

My hands worked to open the plastic Michelle's Diner bag where grilled chicken wafted from the Styrofoam container. Dog was growing…too much. He was salivating and all. But it was his growling that scared me. It had been months and he still frightened me. He'd been growing every day, too. Before his leaps landed him on my leg. When he almost knocked me over while I pulled out the knot, my heart dropped to the floor.

I stopped and turned to him, forcing Dog back on all four. "I'm going to feed you, you know this. You need to calm your butt down, boy!"

He barked, causing the floor to vibrate beneath us.

"Stop!" I issued a leveling glare until he took a few steps back, unusually acquiescing.

It was late—close to three in the morning—and I was bone tired. Instead of life slowing now that I was a week away from graduation, it seemed as though my responsibilities on campus had doubled. Jason said it was because they were trying to squeeze all the cheap labor out of me while they could. By the time I made it to the diner tonight, I saw my trainees starting my recipes. When I asked what they were doing, Marie explained Nicky told them to do it before he left. That was strange. I made a note to ask him about it on my next shift.

I dumped wasted pieces of chicken into a bowl I had for Dog in the house. "Here." I placed it on the floor near a wall. "Wait!" He almost knocked me over trying to get to the bowl.

I backed away, seething. Why did I have a dog? My mother would freak out. And what would I do with him once Abshir came home? I shook my head, walking over to the sink to wash my hands. Before I was done rinsing, my phone vibrated loudly in my bag.

"Shoot!"

I tried rubbing them together faster to hurry the process. It was a waste of time. By the time I finished drying my hands and dug through my bag for it, it stopped.

Sadik...

My hands moved like they were on steroids to hit him back.

"Hey," his velvety alto chimed.

"Hey..." I breathed, winded by it all.

"I catch you at a bad time?"

"No!" was delivered too forcefully. "Not at all. Perfect, actually." I rolled my eyes as I pulled out a chair and lowered myself to sit.

I hadn't seen Sadik since that popup visit at the diner. We'd been in touch almost every day since, texting or calling at night, and he even sent a delivery to my campus. He'd been traveling since then, even FaceTime'ing me from San Francisco a few nights ago. So far, he didn't lie about his excessive traveling.

"Thanks for the flowers." I smiled too hard.

"Again, you're welcome." I texted it to him from class when I had to rush out of the office after signing for them. "You never said how the chocolates were."

"Are you kidding? They were Guilty Pleasure. Excellent! Unlike the bouquet, they never made it to my house. I devoured them in class and work that day."

"So, sugar."

"What about it?"

"That's all you eat."

"Not really."

"That's all I've ever seen you enjoy while with me. Interesting."

I rolled my eyes, not wanting to go there. "Where are you?" I quickly amended, "If you don't mind me asking."

"Toronto."

"Canada." I mused out loud.

"Yeah. Just leaving my sister's art exhibit."

"Oh, nice! She's an artist?"

"This month, yeah." I laughed. "Acrylic painting. My family flew up here to support her on her latest venture." His tone deflated, playfully annoyed by the short attention span of his baby sister.

"Well, you know I feel family support is everything. I think it's cool you all backed her." I scratched the back of my neck, combing down my tapered hair. "I hope I'm not keeping you from them."

Sadik made it clear how close a unit his family was. Suddenly, I felt like an interloper.

"Not at all. I...uh...I actually stepped away from them, not wanting to wait till tomorrow to reach you."

"Everything okay?"

There was a pause. "Nah," he finally spoke. "I've been horrible at this shit."

"What?"

"You?"

My pulse began to race.

"What do you mean?"

"As soon as I told you I wanted to spend more time together, I skipped town twice. I miss you." There was a slight growl in his delivery, taking my mind to that night a month ago, on the jet. This time, I was speechless. "Dinner."

"When?" I asked too quickly.

Too desperate.

"Thursday."

I blinked. "This Thursday?"

"That'll be the one. We need to talk about how we can sync our schedules. The semester is ending for you and I have no idea what your post-graduation plans are." That makes two of us. "I need inspiration to take some time off. Maybe you can help me with that."

I chuckled shyly, not knowing how to respond.

"Okay."

"I'll text you the reservation tomorrow."

"Okay," I repeated.

"My people are passing me, heading to the limo. I'll hit you later."

"Ok—" My eyes squeezed closed. *"Goodnight, Sadik."*

I took a deep breath, eyes wandering subconsciously until they landed on the beautiful bouquet of exotic flowers on my kitchen table.

Dog barked, and I rolled my eyes.

"You burp like a beast, and I lose my good sense and forget to ask him about his soon born baby."

"Damn." My brows shot into the air as I held the phone to my ear with one hand and swiped through reports on my iPad with the other. *"And how many they got off on Low?"*

"I hear only one, but Low caught it on the body somewhere."

"Damn." I breathed again, eyes scanning the restaurant, awaiting my guest. *"And Sub lost one."*

"Yeah. Just Nintendo," Iban confirmed.

Damn…

Hearing it from my brother gave it a new reality. We had to speak like this over the phone, always moving as though our lines were tapped. Names changed, but the players didn't. Iban called while I'd been waiting in DiFillippo's for Bilan to show, telling me Damien and his peoples pulled up on Rizzo's crew at a pub they were known to hang out at in Elizabeth, and rang out shots. Low was Damien,

191

because he was on the low with his sexuality, though we had proof of it being fluid. Sub was Rizzo because we referred to sandwiches as submarines, as in Italian subs. And Nintendo was Luigi, one of Salvatore Rizzo's top men, because Iban and I used to be true Super Mario Bros. fans as kids.

"That's fucked up."

"Yeah, well," Iban sucked in a loud breath before letting it out. "I'm good. Fuck both them niggas. They can swallow the drain of my fucking toilet. Off each other in the same shootout for all I give a shit."

My scalp began to prickle, ripping my attention from my report and the telephone conversation. I glimpsed up and saw her strutting my way in heels. It wasn't for a few seconds, when she was closer, that I could see Bilan rocked booties just inches above her ankles. Her damn legs were out in long, fitted denim cutoff shorts, stopping just at her kneecaps. They were high-waist, accentuating her wide hips and narrow midsection. She covered it with a green sweater duster while a yellow crossover purse lay at her hip.

I. Noticed. Everything.

Now, each detail of Bilan intrigued me, including the small silver studs in her ear. She grew closer, as I did anxious.

"The nigga upstairs think we should take advantage of this chaos and tell the commission about what Low did to us six years ago and—"

"I gotta go, Iban." I shifted to move out of the booth as she approached.

Not waiting for a response, I tapped to disconnect before dropping the phone to the table. A timid smile formed on her face when she finally saw me. I didn't give Bilan a chance when she arrived. I pulled her into my arms the moment she was within reach.

Those fucking freckles are gonna be the death of me...

She didn't cover them with makeup, and that thrilled me. Quietly, I inhaled her flowery scent. This was fucking troubling; me being this taken by a woman.

"You look angry," she murmured in my arms.

I pulled back, observing her smile. Then I brushed my lips across hers. "Quite the opposite. You look good."

192

If she could blush, it would have been in that moment as her eyes dashed down my body. "You always look good. I hope I'm not underdressed."

"Suits are synonymous with looking good?" I offered her a seat across from me, but knew it would be a challenge maintaining the distance for long. "Don't tell me you're one of them?"

Her smile broadened. "One of who?"

"The women who think a suited man is a distinguished one."

Bilan's brows met. "I think you're a distinguished man, and that has nothing to do with your suit." She winked.

"I like that." I nodded. Bilan spit out a laugh, confirming her charm. "Ego-stroking will get you everywhere with me."

She sucked her teeth. "Like women don't flirt with you on a regular basis."

I scratched my head, preparing to lie. "They don't. And not the ones I want."

"How many do you want, Sadik?" One eyebrow shot into the air.

"Just one who bakes her ass off for a popular diner. She's about to get a degree next week and do God only knows what with her, already limited, schedule. Therefore, I need to get ahead of it so I can be a part of it."

"And how do we do that?"

My agenda had been set since I decided to see her tonight.

"I'll get to that, but first, these." I pushed a double shot of tequila to her.

"What?" she sputtered a laugh.

I nodded, finding myself smiling. "Yes. Don't ask why, just trust me. And you have to drink all of it."

Bilan chewed on the corner of her lip, considering it. I was surprised—and pleased—she didn't spend much time dithering. It took her three gulps, but she got it all down.

My girl…

With the burning esophagus face, she fanned herself. "You know I have to drive back to Jersey, right?"

"You don't have to. I can have you driven. Never worry about drunk driving with me."

Bilan sat back, deeply peering at me.

"Pull out your phone." I grabbed mine, needing to get to the next task. When Bilan's was in hand, I asked, "First, when do you start work?"

Her face tightened. "What work? I'm not picking up more hours at the diner just yet."

"For your job...in your field. I'm sure you have a job lined up. When do you start?"

Her head shook softly. "I don't have one."

"Really?"

"Where have you applied?"

"To grad schools." She laughed softly, as though embarrassed. "Still undecided about which one."

"Why?"

"Because I haven't decided what I want my master's in." She bit her bottom lip.

It was clear Bilan wasn't comfortable talking about it, so I decided to move on.

"Let's start with graduation. When does that happen?"

"Next Thursday, at ten."

Shit...

My eyes shot up to her.

"What's wrong?" She looked just as concerned as I felt.

"I'm in a staff meeting that entire morning. It'll be a working office anniversary party." My staff had been planning it for months. I wasn't supposed to know that a few of my clients from all over were going to call in. "And I have a mayoral fundraising ball that night."

With a tight smile, Bilan shrugged. "It's not like you were invited no ways," she joked.

Or is she?

"Were you planning to invite me?"

Another beam glowed from her. "Yeah."

Why the hell did I feel relieved by that?

"Okay." I went back to my electronic calendar. "What plans do you have for Saturday?"

"My friends are giving me a party."

"Where?"

She shook her head and shrugged at the same time. "My house. Nothing fancy."

I went back to my calendar, rubbing my head.

"The following weekend?"

"My family is meeting at the beach. They want to acknowledge my graduation..." She shrugged, rolling her eyes.

"Is it just for the day?"

"Yeah."

I went back to my calendar, counting days of miss-able events. Perfect...

My attention went to her. Bilan's head was down, observing her phone, too.

"Please tell me your passport is in good standing."

"Why?"

"Because I'm taking you away to celebrate your achievement."

Her eyes shot wide. "My graduation?"

"Yes."

"For how long? Where?" Her eyes were wild and mouth agape.

"For a few days. I have no idea where yet." I rubbed my head, mumbling, "I'll figure something out."

I already had an idea, but wouldn't say. This could be good for the both of us. I needed leisure.

Waiters arrived at the table. Our food was finally here. Bilan reclined, making room for them.

"I came early to place the order since I have to get ahead of traffic."

"Oh," she chirped while somewhat frowning at the food being laid before us. "Your niece's recital. How cute! I wish I had a niece or a nephew. Kids are so adorable!"

"What about having your own?" I teased.

Closing her eyes dramatically, Bilan shook her head. "No time soon. I crave being an auntie, not a mother. Even though Abshir is a pain, I used to look forward to the day when he came home telling my mother he got some girl pregnant instead of the other crap he hit her with."

"Will that be all?" the waiter asked.

Bilan's eyes swept the table, looking overwhelmed.

"We're good. Thanks," I dismissed the men.

One nodded. "Enjoy, Mr. Ellis."

"What's all this?"

"Food." I swung myself to the middle of the circular booth. "Food you're going to enjoy, but let's get you one last shot."

She sputtered again. "Are you trying to get me drunk?"

"No. But it is my goal to loosen you up." I pushed another shot her way. "I'll take another with you." She went for her glass. "Ready?"

She began to giggle. "Okay." She took a deep breath. "One…two…three, and go!"

We tilted at the same time. I took mine to the neck, and Bilan needed two tries to empty the glass. That tickled her, too. Not drunk girl style, but with lowered inhibitions. And that's what I needed from her.

"Come here, Bilan." I couldn't curb the authority in my tone. With her, I had to be careful. I waved her over, next to me in the center of the circular booth. Wearing an infinite smile, she licked her lips and with little hesitation, she scooted my way. "Food is a huge segment of socializing. Your parents were restaurateurs; you should know. I want to socialize with you more; therefore, I need you to eat."

Her head swayed dramatically as she rolled her eyes, her smile never fading. I enjoyed its presence. It couldn't co-exist with her comfort companion, timidity. I wanted to rid her of that personality flaw. She had too much going on for her to exhibit uncertainty. That was akin to insecurity. I slowly pulled cloth napkins onto our laps and rearranged the plates and dishes on the table.

"Now, these are all my DiFillippo's favorites. Last month, for our flight to Miami, I ordered based on what I didn't know of you. Now that I'm convinced you don't like much without a high sugar content, I know I have my work cut out for me."

Using a fork, I cut a piece of stuffed mushroom, observing the way the cheese stringed as I pulled it apart. I ate that piece, turning toward her as I fed myself.

Delicious…

Then I forked the other half and brought it to her full brown lips. "Open," I murmured.

Bilan steeled in her seat. She didn't want to eat it. Not thinking too hard, I put the fork back in the serving dish and pulled her soft body into me, leaving my arm around her shoulder. I used my other hand to grip her chin, gently turning her face to me. She was beautifully stubborn. I leaned in and kissed her softly. When I pulled back, Bilan's eyes were still closed.

"I like your kisses. They're transporting."

Her eyes blinked open.

"What does that mean?"

"They take me to places. Happy places."

I hoped she didn't feel the unease that caused me. I liked Bilan and was intrigued by her, but was very clear on the lack of potential between us. This was supposed to be selfish fun for me. Making her happy did that for me.

I went back for the fork and brought it to her mouth. Bilan's forehead creased as her eyes were on me.

"Please, baby," I whispered. "Trust me."

"I do." Her response just as soft.

I nodded toward the fork. After a few seconds, Bilan opened her mouth. My dick twitched as I pushed the half a mushroom inside.

"Now, chew."

Bilan closed her eyes and chewed slowly. I watched her closely as she breathed out, humming.

"Good?" I held my breath until her head bounced in short movements.

"Not bad at all," she murmured.

"Another one?"

Bilan nodded. I repeated the same actions as the first time, breaking the mushroom in half and feeding myself first, then Bilan with the second.

"Let's move on to the mussels." I removed my arm to prepare. "I prefer them in red sauce, but have enjoyed them in white. Do you eat pork?"

Bilan's face wrinkled as she chewed the mussel. I ate one myself while waiting for her to speak.

"No. We're Muslims. My mom never cooked it." She shrugged with her mouth. "We never served it either."

I cut a piece of chicken and forked it with risotto.

"What do you think about the texture of that mussel?" With a screwed face, Bilan shook her head. "Okay. Let's stay away from soft meats for now. Here's baked risotto with chicken thighs. It's flavored with lemon and scallions."

I brought it to her mouth, and Bilan slowly opened for me. I went back to the dish for myself.

"I know your mom was in utero when her family came to the States. She may have only experienced American culture if they didn't return home often. Did your mother cook mainly Somali dishes?"

Bilan licked her lips in between chews, her eyes shifting. "A lot, but she dabbled with American dishes, too." She sputtered a laugh. "We used to get on her about adding her usual spices to spaghetti and macaroni and cheese. Her culture cooked with lots of turmeric, coriander, cumin, and curry. I guess it's hard breaking old habits."

"Here." I handed her a glass of water. "That should help clear your palate a little."

I cut a piece of parmesan chicken for myself, then her. It was fried, and the firm texture could work for her.

"This should be good." I fed her the chicken. Bilan chewed this faster than the previous ones. "Good?" She smiled, nodding. "You said last week how the recipes you make at the diner came from your mother. Those are southern desserts."

"Her mother. My grandmother had a good friend—Black woman who was a colleague. She shared a lot of her recipes with my grandmother, but my mother only took the desserts. Those, she stuck to the recipes with, and it got better with time. I would cook them with her and eventually, for her at their restaurant."

"I have some seafood Alfredo over here." I reached across the table, rearranging dishes to bring new ones closer. I twirled creamy pasta in a spoon with a fork when I glanced back to find her peering over my shoulder. "This is considered a commercial recipe, but it's delicious." I fed her some. "Tell me you've had fettuccini Alfredo before."

Bilan licked her lips as she chewed again. I was happy to see her smile again. "Not this good, though."

"Good, right?" That shit excited me. "DiFillippo's has a range of authenticity. They have their traditional Italian recipes, and even the American renditions of them. This is a combination here."

"Can I have more of that?"

"Baby girl, you can have more of anything you like here." I twirled more on the fork to feed her.

We talked as I fed us from one fork. Bilan didn't like every dish, but she didn't decline anything. When she began to relax into me, her palm curled over my thigh. And when she laughed, her hand would cup my chest. I couldn't decide if it was the company, good food, or the shots I had her take relaxing her. Either way, I wanted to see more. However, I knew time was of the essence. I would have to leave soon.

Bilan tapped out before I did. The waiters eventually came and cleared the table to make room for dessert.

The waiter pointed to dishes. "Tiramisu, chocolate amaretti cake, lemon ricotta granita, zeppola, sfogliatelle, and crème brûlée." He bowed. "Enjoy." Then he left us to it.

"Crème brûlée is actually French," I offered, reaching for a spoon. "I have no damn idea why they brought this when I asked specifically for only Italian desserts."

Bilan squeezed my thigh. "Stop it, Sadik!" she whined.

I knew she liked the crème brûlée from our flight back from Miami last month, and wanted to tease her. I broke off a piece of the chocolate cake and tasted it. "I'm serious. I'm in my laboratory here, trying to conduct a scientific experiment and need controlled conditions."

"What controlled conditions?" she demanded.

I waved my hand over the table. "Italian foods. I need to see if my subject: one, has aversions to specific foods. Two, has a problem just eating around me. Or three, has an eating disorder."

Bilan shook her and rolled her eyes, her smile fading. "I'm perfectly healthy."

"That's for damn sure." I playfully perused her frame. "Those hips tell me that."

She slapped my arm. "Stop it, Sadik," she cried in a baby tenor.

"I'm just fuckin' with you—while being honest. Here. Let's try this lemon ricotta ice cream stuff before it melts."

I spooned some for her. Bilan's mouth opened before I made it to her. She was ready.

"Mmm!" she chirped.

"You like?"

"It's dessert. What's there not to like?"

"Oh, so your preference is sugar? That's how you got those hips. Not those spices in your mother's recipes."

While she laughed, I used a fork to cut a zeppola in half. When I fed it to her, Bilan moaned. She fucking closed her eyes and moaned. It wasn't looking good for me. The woman preferred sweets over food. I still didn't know why, but would enjoy the knowledge.

"Tell me something. A secret you wouldn't tell the world."

"Hmmmm... A secret for Sadik." She giggled. "I'll share for some of that tiramisu." Her smile so bright, her teeth were exposed.

I really like this Bilan...

It didn't take long for me to prepare the tiramisu and feed it to her.

Her eyes closed again, and she hummed too sensually for public. And I started to grow in my damn pants.

"Go for it." I dropped a piece of tiramisu in my mouth, game for whatever.

"A couple weeks ago...while you were on a world tour, I went to your friend's club."

"What friend? I have lots of them, you know." I went for my water.

"Energy." Shit... "I think her name's Tiffany?"

"Why would you go there?" I tried playing cool as I pulled the crème brûlée closer.

"I don't know. Randi told me you two were really close and... Well, as you could tell with the Ameerah situation, it appears I have jealous tendencies when it comes to you." She shook her head against my shoulder as she mused. "I guess I wanted to see you, even if it was a different side to you. You're still such a mystery to me."

"I'm trying not to be." I fed her, her favorite.

I'd had enough, appetite dissolving after her "secret" was shared.

Her head shifted so she could peer up at me. Yup. Her slanted eyes gave her slight inebriation away.

"I hope you aren't. I don't want games, Sadik." She paused, eyes possibly trying to read mine. "I don't deserve it. And I don't want drama either. I've had enough for a lifetime, which is why I haven't had boyfriends. At least when I'm just occasionally dating a guy, I don't see him enough to set any expectations. You know?"

"Tell me another secret," I murmured while feeding her more.

I waited for her to clear her mouth, closely watching those lips I wanted wrapped around my throbbing cock.

"You feeding me is a bizarre turn on. I'm horny." She howled in laughter so hard, she rolled to the opposite side of me, curled over in the booth.

When she was able to calm herself enough, she glanced back at me, catching my smile.

"That makes two of us, and there ain't shit I can do about it."

The humor drained from her face. "What time is it?"

I scooped more of the ice cream for myself. "I have another fifteen minutes to torture you with sweets."

That made her sit up and sober her humor. "Then I should kill the silliness, huhn?"

She made a show of straightening herself in her seat. Bilan was tipsy.

"I'll have Lamont drive you home in your car. He can make sure you get in safely, and he'll get a ride home."

"Lamont will be boring. You know, I don't think your security people like me. And I swear Rory heard us in the back of them on the jet that night. She rolls her eyes at me when I see her now. Even earlier when I was outside. I smiled at her and said hello. She didn't even look my way while pointing me to the door."

"I don't need my security to like you, just to protect you."

"Oh!" Her palms lifted in the air, wiggling. "Protect me from what? What do you need protection from? You're completely legit. I'm sure of it now."

My brows lifted in shock and piqued interest. I was glad to hear that.

I pulled her closer to me. "You, my sweets who loves sweets, will never need to know." I nuzzled into her neck, kissing her. "I'll talk to Rory about laying off the mean girl act."

I fed her more, enjoying how she nestled under my arm again.

"And Bilan."

"Hmm?"

"I don't frequent clubs. Please don't go to any looking for me."

Her eyes shot open, and the typical timid and unsure Bilan returned. I didn't prefer it, but if that's what it took to get my point across, I'd have to be okay with it.

Bilan

"Fuck, Ricardo, you flexin' over that bullshit?" Randi shouted into the phone over the booming music streaming through the house. "I told you I thought it was money you left for me. You act like you ain't did that before. Why would you do that? Why wouldn't you do that?" She paused for his response. "Fuck it. I won't touch another dollar in your place no more!"

Taking a deep breath, I scanned around the dining room. My home was pretty packed with so many I didn't know, and others I couldn't care less celebrating with. Tasche and Randi made sure to fill the place with bodies.

"Can we just talk about this shit when I get in?" Randi yelled to her boyfriend, Ricky. The way her eyes grew wide and wild gave me an idea of his equally spirited response, and I turned my head. "Don't fuckin' bother coming? The fuck that mean?"

That was my cue to walk away. When I passed the living room, I saw Tasche giving a lap dance to Ruben Kline, an associate professor from my school. I was beyond surprised to see him at my home. Randi reached out to Jason from my school, and he invited a few people from campus—professors included. Kline was the only staff who showed. He was given what Tasche's coworker, who worked the bar in the kitchen, called Honesty Juice. I guessed his honesty was he enjoyed black erotic dancers because his pink face was buried in Tasche's dark chocolate bosom as he gripped her hips around his lap.

Rolling my eyes, I decided I needed fresh air. On my way to the kitchen, I ran into the "bartender" in the hall.

"Oh, shit!" he trilled. Then he recognized me. "Oh, you! You sure you ain't ready for this Honesty Juice yet? You done with school, so fuck it: let it all hang out." He laughed.

I raised my plastic cup with a tight smile. "Still working on this Moscato."

It was punch'ish. Too sweet for my taste, but I needed to look like I was attempting to loosen up.

"Okay. Well—" He raised a pitcher of purple liquid. "It's ready when you are, shawtie."

I continued on my way to the back door, where I was able to escape onto the back stairs. After closing the door behind me, I squatted on a step. My phone burned the pocket of my cropped blazer. I planted my cup on a step between my legs as I pulled out my cell. My hands tapped, now used to the new layout of the device, until I made it to his text thread. I scrolled until the image appeared. It was a picture of me on the stage at The Prudential Center, accepting my faux degree. The shot was pretty decent, capturing my smile as I shook hands with the provost.

He'd come. Sadik came to my graduation. By the time I'd made it back to my seat and checked my cell, there was a text waiting for me. It was the picture and a note.

Your Friend: *Congratulations, Ms. Asad-Yasin on your commencement ceremony! Glad I didn't miss your moment.*

Even reading it again—for the fortieth time—my belly fluttered. I closed my eyes, frustrated by my feelings. I found the man wildly attractive, could sense darkness around him, and had been downright angry with him since we met. All of this, and I wanted more of him. Sadik wanted to go away together. That scared and thrilled me at the same time.

And he fed me at DiFillippo's...

I now understood what sexual frustration felt like. I wanted him so bad and didn't know what exactly I wanted at the same time. I wanted to have sex with Sadik, but didn't understand why or what I'd gain from it. It made no sense, and yet I wanted it anyway. And now, he was away—again—and I didn't have the opportunity of his *time. Taking a deep after dark, spring breeze breath, I blackened the face of the phone.*

Then my nose spreading, I sniffled.

Is that...

I turned to my right and in the darkness of the shadow, next to the staircase, the flame of a cigarette glowed from a deep pull. Only it wasn't a cigarette.

"Who is that?" I grated.

Stepping out of the shadow was Jason from school.

My neck whipped. "You're back here?"

He blew out a string of smoke. "Yup. Me, Mary, and Honesty Juice." He lifted a blunt and a plastic cup.

My brows met. "I had no idea you blew trees, Jason."

He didn't seem like that type—or did he? Jason was tall, at least six foot. His almond skin wasn't as blemish-free as someone else I'd grown partial to, nor was Jason's glow like his. But Jason was handsome in his own right. His light skin, and coiled hair worked for him. He always sported a door-to-door salesman look: khakis and plaid button-up or polo shirts. He'd typically tote a black IT utility duffle bag around campus. Jason was articulate and engaging in the few classes we'd shared over the years. He was typically reserved, but attentive.

He snorted with tight eyes. "I've done better at not letting it be a part of my identity. Back in high school, I'd smoke a "L" before school, at lunch, and at least two more before going to bed at night."

"Just when you think you know someone." With one hand, I slipped the phone back into my blazer, and I used the other to lift my cup to my face.

"My Somali queen has her Honesty Juice!" he joked over the muzzled music pouring from the house. "This can be fun."

Swallowing, I shook my head. "No Honesty Juice for me. That stuff is probably lethal. He works at a legit bar in Paterson."

Jason heaved from his blunt and spoke without breathing. "Nah. It won't have you talking to the wall or ready to jump off the roof, but it is potent." He blew out the musky smoke. "This is your graduation party. You gotta get shit-faced, Bilan."

I shook my head, smiling. Embarrassingly, I had no idea why I was so uptight. Having people in my, otherwise, empty house didn't bother me. I was growing numb to the memory of what the place used to be since the foreclosure letters began. I was powerless to the process of losing the house. Maybe it was because I wasn't used to being here so long. Over the years, since losing my mother, I only seemed to have slept and washed here, never resting. Shoot, I was scared to sleep here. To be here. So, having the house full was okay. Still, I had no idea the cause of my unease.

"Loosen up, Bilan," Jason demanded while casually passing me the blunt. I hadn't smoked weed in some time. It was something I'd do on occasion with Tasche, and even Randi. But that wasn't something I was prepared to do with Jason.

I shook my head, declining. "I have to get up early tomorrow. Can't afford to get messed up tonight."

His arm recoiled. "Get up early? This is something I've wondered for four years. You only talk about work—either on campus, for the department, or at the diner. You don't have kids, don't belong to a sorority, don't go to campus parties." His shoulders dropped, exhausted of his points. I worked out. That was my leisure, I guessed. I was too old for all that other crap he named: a non-traditional student. Those things didn't appeal to me. "What do you do for fun, girl?"

My brows and lips drew up as I pondered how to take that on.

"Me," a thick, velvety alto proclaimed.

My head whipped up to find a suited, russet bald head with yellowish cat eyes.

Sadik...

I shot to my feet. "Hey," I could hardly produce.

Sadik dropped down a few steps, eyes behind me on Jason. His hand cupped the back of my neck and he pulled me into him, brushing those soft lips across mine. A pocket of air pushed from my nostrils when my brain registered his scent and heat.

"Hey," he murmured close to my face.

"I—" I cleared my throat and licked my tingling lips. "You were out of town."

He snorted softly in my face. "I guess I found a way to sneak off to be with the graduated...again."

"You're here for my party?" That was so dumb!

"Am I not invited to this, too?"

My forehead stretched and brows tightened. "Yeah—"

"Bilan," my neighbor, Rashida, called from the backdoor. This time, I heard the blast of music pushing from it. Oddly, I didn't when Sadik came out that same door. "Somebody spilled a bunch of shit in the dining room. Randi cleaned it up with towels, but don't wanna go put them in the washing machine because that big ass dog is down there."

I rolled my eyes, remembering Dog. He was probably down there going crazy with all the noise over his head.

"I'll take them." I nodded toward Rashida before she went back inside. Then I turned to Sadik. "I'll be right back. Okay?"

"What's this?" He grabbed the cup from my hand possessively.

"Nasty punch."

"Punch?"

I shook my head. "Moscato. I'll be right back."

Without waiting for his response, I went into the house. Cutting through bodies in the kitchen, I made it to the hall for the dining room when I saw Randi standing in suspension. She held soiled towels in her hand as she stood motionless.

I rounded her to see her face. "You okay?"

She tossed her chin behind me. "What the fuck they doing here?"

I craned my neck to look behind me first, then my body shifted. Lamont and Rory stood at the front door, heads swinging left to right, absorbing the place. They couldn't have been more polar in appearance. Rory's tiny frame stood lax in a black suit, resting on one hip with her right hand clasped onto the belt like in the movies. Was she carrying a gun? Her buggy eyes had a permanent animated look to them. Her hair pulled back into a ponytail. Lamont wore all black, too: a button-up shirt and slacks with his hands entangled at his pelvis.

Sadik's accessories...

207

They looked so out of place. So sinister and somehow, I preferred their presence over every other one in the house because theirs came with their boss'.

"You're fuckin' Sadik Ellis."

I grabbed the towels, ignoring her stuck presentation. "I'll take these. Didn't Tasche say there was a cake to be cut?"

Quickly, I hurried to the back of the house for the basement. Dog was barking non-stop from his cage. He only quieted when I came into his view near the washing machine.

"Would you simmer the heck down! I have company." He whined, sitting back on his hind. "Thank you!"

I tossed the towels in the machine and jogged back up the stairs, hearing Dog bark behind me. Sadik was in the kitchen when I made it up. His feline eyes were on me while several in the room were on him, one could argue because of the suit he wore and the formal aura he possessed in a room full of tipsy people. But I knew it was because the women appreciated the view. Their goofy smiles and excessively blinking eyes confirmed it.

Like being drawn to a magnet, I glided straight to him.

"You have a dog?" he asked when I sidled to his side.

A wry smile stretched on my lips. "More like security." My face hardened when a thought hit. "You want a drink? I doubt if we have Mauve here, but I can see about a brandy."

Sadik glanced at his wristwatch and considered the time for half a second. "I'll take a beer."

"Oh, okay." I went to the fridge where there were a few brands. "Corona good?"

Sadik's gaze on my ass was heated as he took his time to shift it to my face. He nodded.

"Thanks for stopping by." I handed him the bottle.

"You're welcome."

"And for the graduation pop up," I added.

Sadik opened the bottle like a pro. "My pleasure."

"How were you able to pull that off?"

He snorted before taking a sip of the beer. "Conducting a conference meeting on mute and hoping I wouldn't be asked a question while I was listening for your name." My hand flew to my mouth, eyes went wild. "The timing was perfect. Rory told me when they were near your name and I zoned out of the meeting so I could hear it. Thank God you're an 'A.' I thought I was good until I was walking out and was asked a question appropriate for only me to answer. I sent a text to my staff, telling her to stall a minute. I was good once outside in the parking lot."

I couldn't fight a smile. "Must be nice to be the boss," I teased. Sadik smiled as he shook his head. "I saw you checking for the time. What are you off to do next?"

"My brother invited me over."

"Yeah?" I guessed that was normal, non-illegal behavior. "Like, to just hang out?"

Sadik nodded, his eyes on the room. "I told him I'd come as soon as my flight got in."

"Well, aren't I special," I joked.

Sadik turned to me, face implacable and eyes intense. That knocked the sail out of my boat.

"So, this party tonight and next weekend, the beach with family?" It took a moment for me to catch his reference.

"Oh." I shook my head. "Got canceled—well, pushed back until next month. My aunt wants to invite her in-laws in upstate New York, who won't be available until then."

But she didn't ask when Abshir would be home. I hated that it bothered me.

I hadn't realized Sadik's body completely turned to face me. His scowl-like expression set when he murmured, "So, you don't have plans for next weekend?"

Lost in those eyes, I shook my head.

"Bilan," Tasche's raspy voice called across the kitchen. I turned to see her waving me to her. "Let's cut this cake. Everybody in the dining room."

I turned to Sadik, and his expression lightened. "Cake time!"

I chuckled before following the crowd into the hallway. It took a little time, but we were able to pack it in there, and I weaved through bodies to the head of the table, where the cake was. Randi and Tasche were there waiting on me, too.

"I guess this the part where we say how proud of you we are, shawtie," Tasche rasped. "Y'all, I only met this bitch a few years ago in the diner when I moved here from Harlem. She was cute with them freckles and bad as hell with the Halle Berry cut." I rolled my eyes. "And smart. Bilan is so smart…she different, yo. Cut from a different cloth. She innocent, but she ain't. She sweet, but ain't the one to sleep on." Tasche was getting emotional. "I remember thinking, after I told her I was a dancer, that she wouldn't be nice to me and kick it no more when I came in after my shift. She told me she was in college and all. But I swear, Bilan ain't never act funny style with me. She started inviting me to chill with her friends, and shit. Now, I still don't know 'bout them!" She rolled her eyes dramatically as people laughed. "Nah, I'm just fuckin' with you, Randi." No, she wasn't. "But here's to a real one. May God give you the bag, the bread to put in it, and the boo to fuck you right!"

My head reared as I hooted.

Sooooo Tasche!

I wrapped my arms around her for a tight hug. That was so sweet and kind of her to do. Tasche never failed to surprise me with her heart. I loved her so much and was sure to tell her so.

Someone clearing their throat caught my attention as I was pulling away from Tasche.

"Now, from her day one," Randi embellished. I'd met her right after high school. She rolled her eyes, but I accepted that, too. Tasche and Randi hung out with me very amicably, but did not claim each other as friends. Being able to chill together and plan a party for me spoke to their level of maturity. Women have been unable to accomplish less together. "Bilan, I'm happy you got this shit done. I know it wasn't easy, busting ya ass to go to class and work after your moms passed away. There was a few times I thought you was gonna burn out, but you proved me wrong. We been through a lot of shit together. A lot of shit." My brows met, and simultaneously, my eyes rolled up and landed on honeyed ones who mirrored my expression. I didn't know he'd come into the room. "And we still friends till the very day. Not many can say they go through so much together and still be friends with the same bitch. So…I 'on't know what you gonna do with this degree, but I know you gone be great, 'cause that's what we do!"

Her cup was in the air as she ended that totally embroidered speech.

"Hold the fuck up!" someone shouted. When bodies began to move, I noticed it was the bartender headed to the front of the room with his pitcher and cups. "This the graduation girl. She ain't have the house punch yet!"

As a few cheered, I rolled my eyes. Tasche and Randi encouraged me to do it as I laughed. This time, I did look at Sadik and caught the smile in his eyes. It was almost like approval. Oddly, for the first time tonight, I felt comfortable enough—secured—to let my guard down.

"Fuck that!" Tasche shouted. "Take a shot first."

The bartender pulled out a bottle of tequila from his apron pocket and poured what had to be more than a shot's worth into a plastic cup.

The room started to chant. "To the head!"

Again, I tossed my regard to Sadik. With his intense eyes on me, he switched stances, resting his head to the side. A flutter of excitement ran through my body and I tossed back the cup, unbelievably getting it down in one shot. The things peer pressure could do.

Or Sadik's approval…

As the room shouted their cheers, Randi was lighting the cake with my name and a cap and tassel. The cup was being pushed into my hand again, this time filled with purple Honesty Juice. Tasche's hoarse vocals began the ditty, "For He's a Jolly Good Fellow" but customizing it to a woman. The room followed and I raised my cup, shoulder dancing along.

"Make a wish!" Randi shouted once they were done and I needed to blow out the melting candles.

Once again, my eyes roved up to Sadik, who stood at the opposite end watching with a pleasant, but stoic expression. I closed my eyes for seconds long, then began blowing hard, relieved when Tasche assisted. As Randi began cutting the cake, I strolled over to Sadik. The room clearing out made it easier than coming in.

"Is my time up yet?" I asked when I made it to him.

He smiled with narrowed eyes. "What do you mean?"

"Your brother's. I know you have to go soon."

"Oh." He shook his head.

"Good." I hooked my arm around his. "More time for me."

His smile broadened as I took a sip of the purple potion to find it wasn't harsh at all. In fact, it had a bitter tang to it I liked.

"Mmmmm!"

"Good?"

I nodded, feeling the first woosh from the shot I took. When I was able to swallow what was in my mouth, I called for the bartender. "What's his name, Tasche?"

"Billy," she answered, plating cake.

"Billy!" I shouted, thankful the music hadn't resumed yet.

"Damn, Bilan. That shit got to you already?" Randi hissed.

I turned, shifting closer to Sadik's handsomeness. "Maybe it's not the drink."

Sadik laughed, and I gulped my drink.

"Deek, you dickin' my girl down like that?" Randi's accusatory tone had me leap around.

"What?"

"Damn, yo!" Tasche admonished her. "How you know she ain't fuckin' the shit outta him?"

Randi's mouth balled to the side. "She ain't built for that."

"The fuck is you saying?" Tasche challenged.

"Why would you say that?" I demanded.

Randi stood straight, raising her palms defensively. "We all adults in here. I'm just playing." She sucked her teeth. "He done figured it out by now anyway."

What?

I turned to Sadik and took him by the wrist to leave the room.

"Sadik, don't fuck with my girl," Randi called behind us.

I felt him stop behind me, and turned back.

"Easy, Randi," he warned. "My ignore game has been generous."

212

My eyes widened. Tasche's expression mirrored mine, and Randi stood frozen with her face screwed and mouth open. But she didn't utter a word. Not knowing what to say or do, I pulled Sadik behind me out of the room. The music had returned, drowning out the collective sounds of dissonant voices. We made our way into the living room, where the single sofa was free. I offered Sadik the seat and squatted between his legs.

"Sorry about that." As I tried addressing it, his phone rang. I turned away, facing the room.

After a short break, Sadik observed, "So, this is your childhood home?"

His eyes brushed around the room at the sparse Islamic art work on the wall. Family pictures on the wall unit and artificial flowers I never thought to change since my mother passed.

"Yup." I took a couple of sips from my cup, head beautifully whirring.

"Is that you as a baby?" He stood over my head, reaching for a framed picture over the bookstand. "Damn, you were pretty!" he breathed. Sadik placed his beer bottle down and traced the glass of the frame. "Those freckles aren't here."

My eyes popped out of their sockets. What was up with him and my freckles?

"I didn't get them until I was about six or so."

His phone rang again as those orbs met my face, clearly going over the freckles. "You think your kids will have them?"

He tapped to silence it.

"I don't know. My parents didn't. My brother's are faint."

As I took another sip, I saw Rory in the hall talking to Professor Kline. A giggle sprouted from my lips.

"What's so funny?" he asked over my head.

"Rory. Why does your security need guns?"

"Because my enemies have them?"

I turned to him, goofy expression splitting my face as I rolled over to my knees. "You have armed enemies in customs? Do they ride up on the ships wearing eye patches and scarves around their heads?"

"Yup. Pirates," he'd caught on. Sadik snorted, going back to the picture. "Dangerous pirates."

"Do you carry a gun?"

He shook his head, tapping to silence the phone now vibrating. "Don't need to. I pay those two to do it."

I shifted closer to him, voice uncontrollably husky. "You know how to shoot a gun?"

Sadik's eyes shot into me, causing the energy around us to stiffen. "I only shoot one type satisfactorily."

My mouth dropped.

"Aye! Aye! Aye!" Tasche danced into the room, pulling Kline behind her. "It's a party, y'all."

Tory Lanez's "DrIP DrIp Drip" played as she dropped down into a deep squat and came up in a rhythmic twerk. Between Sadik's promising threat, his scent, seeing my adjunct getting yet another dance by my friend, and this Honesty Juice, I was effectively tipsy. As I watched the two in the center of the room along with everyone else, so many things ran through my mind, including how fast I was growing intoxicated. Kline seemed to be having the time of his life, trying to hold on to Tasche's lithe hips.

I heard a vibrating phone from over me. "I need to take this," Sadik murmured close to my ear as he squeezed my shoulder. He swung a leg over me and ambled out of the room to the front door.

Immediately, my empty cup was being replaced by a full one. Slowly, my eyes peered down and saw the purple juice. I brought it to my mouth for a sip as I turned to see who it was. Randi plopped down on the sofa behind me. She wouldn't even look at me. I turned back toward the action, sipping more.

Lace, another dancer from Tasche's job, jumped in the dance; now, Kline had two Nubian queens grinding on him.

"He's gonna spray his pants..." I whispered into the cup while watching.

Then Tasche leaned down, extending her hand to me. "C'mon, yo. Let them see what an educated woman dance like."

"Tasche!" I cried as she pulled me up. "Most of your colleagues are degreed and make a better living than I do."

She took the cup from me when I was on my feet. "C'mon. Do what I taught you."

"What?" I observed her heel kick and hip-sway before I caught on.

Rolling my eyes, I repeated it. We swung in a circular motion with me trying to keep up with and emulate her skilled hip thrusts. When her friend jumped in line behind me and slapped my ass, I burst out laughing. It was so bad, I had to grab Tasche's shoulders in front of me to keep up. In fact, laughter rang out in the room.

Tasche turned to face me, trying to transition into another dance. It was a familiar one she'd taught me before. Once again, I mimicked her movements, thrusting my pelvis while rolling my torso back.

"Fuck it up!" somebody shouted, I couldn't tell who.

Then as I was curled over, spine arched and I could see behind me, Tasche came out of nowhere, providing support beneath me.

"That's right, B!" she yelled. "Now, flip that bitch."

Without thought, I extended my hands until my palms touched the floor, pushed off my toes, and flipped over into a split. Tasche went crazy, screaming and pumping her arms into the air. In fact, several people cheered as hard as she did.

I, on the other hand, struggled with dizziness. Slowly, I leaned forward to pull my right leg around. Before I could figure out how I'd stand to my feet, my body was lifted into the air. I smelled him immediately; feeling deliciously delirious, I fell into his hard chest, laughing.

"That's enough performing for you," Sadik advised in my ear.

"You okay, yo?" I could hear Tasche, but not see her behind my closed lids.

I couldn't help my giggle. "I can't see you, Tash!"

"Damn. You fucked up that quick?" she guessed correctly.

"She ain't eat shit all day." I recognized Randi's voice.

"Shit." Sadik's chest rumbled against my face.

My arms pushed up and circled his neck, eyes still closed. "I got something for you to eat, though."

I couldn't stop laughing.

"Alright. That's enough." Sadik grumbled. "Where's your room? You're done."

Pressing down on his shoulders, I climbed his frame, shocked by how quickly I did it.

Continuing with my incessant humor, I laughed, pressing my lips against his.

"Fuck," I heard and felt him annunciate.

"Her room's the first on the left, yo," I heard Tasche direct. "I'mma get everybody out. Come on, Randi. Let's end this bash."

I felt my body float as I clasped his hard frame.

"What're we doing, Deek?" My head popped up from his neck.

"Rory?" I asked as though I didn't know she was here. I laughed at that, too. "Why are you hounding him? He's with me. I know you don't like me. Why? Is it because you like his baby's mother better? Huhn? You think I care?" I stuck my tongue out. "He won't leave me alone. Make sure you go tell her that. He likes African juices better than European, bitch!"

Rory's eyes grew impossibly larger when Sadik grated, "Y'all just chill until I get this settled."

As we continued down the hall, I stuck my tongue out at a waiting Rory. And of course, I laughed at that, too.

"This it?" Sadik asked, I doubted looking for an answer because we walked into my bedroom. "Where's the light switch?"

My head vibrated when the room illuminated. He walked me to the bed and bent over to place me on it. There was nothing funny about being on my back with him hovering over me.

"You gonna fuck me now?" I heard the chirp in my voice.

Sadik shook his head. "Nah, Bilan."

"Why? You got me tested. Look!" I pushed past him for my dresser drawer, where I kept the printouts from my results. "Here they are. Chlamydia, herpes, syphilis, HIV, and gonorrhea—I'm clean, baby!"

Sadik took the papers from my hand and placed them back into the open drawer.

"Take off your shoes, Bilan. You need to get in the bed and sleep this off."

"Not until you fuck me and make me forget!"

"Forget what?"

"That you have a baby coming. When was the shower? Why didn't I get an invitation?"

His thick brows hiked. "Bilan..."

"Bilan," I mocked him. When he didn't laugh, I kicked off my shoes, then pulled my t-shirt over my head. I glanced down at my bra. "You like satin? You probably don't. You look like a lace man." I started toward him, trying for a sexy strut. "Or do you like nothing at all?" My brain didn't have the chance to communicate anything to my arms. My hands were already behind my back, unfastening my bra. When I pulled it off, Sadik's eyes closed to a squeeze. "You like this melanin, Deek?"

I pushed my lips into his, feeling him exhale from helplessness. I was drunk, I knew it. I'd be ashamed in the morning, I was sure. But when would I get to explore this thing I knew nothing about?

When my hands pushed down to his waist, I worked fast to unfasten his belt.

"What the hell are you doing?" His tone was pleading.

My head flipped up to face him. "I need to know something."

I went back to his belt.

"What?" he demanded, tone low but affected.

I let out a dramatic breath, closing my eyes momentarily. "I need to know if your pubes are orange, too!" I matched his low, yet dramatic tenor.

"No."

"No?"

He gently pried my fingers from his fancy belt buckle. His neck stretched forward for emphasis.

"No, Bilan. You're going to put on your pajamas and go to—"

My heaving and slapping my palm to my mouth had his face hardening.

"You're sick," he stated, not asking.

I nodded.

"Shit!" He moved quickly to remove his jacket. "Where's the bathroom?"

I felt the heated material cover my skin as I was being pushed toward the door.

Her soft body beneath me twisting had my eyes opening. The sun was barely up, but the glow of a new day pushed through the shade of the lone window in her room.

Bilan whimpered as she shifted under my suit jacket, her hair spiked in every direction. Her smeared eyes tight, and one crusted in the outer corner. She was fucking beautiful in the morning, giving me visuals of intimacy my body was responding to. She opened her eyes when her hand hit my dick.

"Dog!" she slurred.

My face balled and head shot back against the pillow. Bilan's eyes closed and she shifted from me, leaving the bed.

"Oh, my God. Dog!"

She made a quick work of going to her closet door for a flannel robe and tossing it on. She tied it on her way to the door. I heard her footsteps jog away from the room. Needing to go, I shifted, sitting with my feet on the floor. Smelling her did me no good. My dick ached. I tried rearranging it in my pants when a knock sounded.

Rory was in the doorway, shaking her head as she rubbed her one eye. "You wildin' the fuck out."

"Yeah." I shook my head, not in the mood for it. "Yeah."

"Double E Bags fucked up, you missed that meeting last night." It wasn't an important one. I'd decided around one in the morning it was a good look for me not to go if I wanted to show them I was done with that shit. "Got the call last night her brother got rocked in his cell."

That had my head shooting up. "Ab?" She nodded. "By us?" She nodded again. I took a deep breath, having to accept it. I arranged for someone we had at the same prison as Bilan's brother to put pressure on him to finger Damien in the warehouse robbery. I knew if it went bad, violence could occur. "Ab up or down?"

"Down."

"Bad?"

She shook her head. "Just a few bruises. But the nigga ain't talk." I nodded, eyes averting, thinking about my next move.

"Yo, Deek, what the fuck is you doing?" she whispered hard. "She dope. I get it, but you know she ain't possible, big homie. You know this shit fucked up!" Rory rubbed her neck. "Got me sleeping in the fuckin' car. I ain't do that shit since ya Blakewood days."

"So, you more upset about me going after her or getting paid to sleep in the car?" Rory gave me the finger. "You weren't supposed to be sleeping."

"Fuck you. I ain't get notice I'd be on some stakeout type shit either." As she spit her shit, Rory gazed to her left and right in the hall.

"I need you to reach out to Vincent Ricci."

"The brothers running Michelle's Diner?"

I nodded. "Vincent, in particular. Remind him of the deal he made with Double E Bags." I was sure to lower my voice. "I need Bilan's schedule more flexible moving forward. When she asks for time off, I don't want them giving her pushback."

Rory rolled those big ass eyes, now swollen from fatigue. Then she backed out farther into the hallway. "You got it, sire." I soon learned it was to give Bilan room to enter the room. "Yo," she called to Bilan. "The bathroom down here. Right?"

Bilan nodded, not even looking her way.

"I'll be ready to go in five minutes," I called behind Rory's disgruntled ass.

Bilan reached down to pick up the bra she shed last night.

"Close the door." My delivery intentionally hard. She gave me a long look, then wisely obeyed. "You do that shit often?"

"What?" Her face still tight from sleep.

"Invite strangers over to your house party and get drunk, wanting to fuck."

Bilan's mouth dropped. "I don't have parties here! This was my first like this, but that's none of your business."

"It's not? Would it have been if I fucked you last night like you begged?"

Bilan rolled her eyes, nostrils swelling. "I'm sorry. I was drunk!"

"I know!" I watched her hard eyes falter. "What I want to know is what if it was your college boyfriend here when you stripped last night instead of me?"

Bilan raised her arm. Her index finger pointing to the door. "If you're going to belittle me while I physically feel like shit, you can go now."

I stood from the bed. "Clear your schedule for Thursday."

"Why?"

I didn't look back when I answered. "Because we're taking a trip, and won't be back until Monday." When I made it to the door, I turned to her. "And Bilan, you will eat when you're with me. You won't get drunk from two sips of a cocktail because you had nothing on your stomach. And then, when I do finally fuck you, you'll beg me to, but it won't be because you're pathetically drunk."

I left her room, closing the door behind me.

∞ 14 ∞

The jet steadied and I took a deep breath, looking for paper or a napkin to spit my gum into. Taking off on a plane was no less an event, no matter how many flights I'd taken. I rubbed my tired eyes, releasing another long breath. Pensive. Fucking tight all over with big ass question marks in every area of my brain.

I'd been in search of black therapists with a specialty in post-traumatic stress disorder in the North Jersey region. My customs business was just hit with a lawsuit I'd been struggling not to take personal. However, all of the strain I was feeling wasn't from work either. That part of my stress was what had me fucked up. My mother received a call from Catena Rizzo, Salvatore's wife and Lia's mother. She wanted to know why she had missed Lia's baby shower. My mother had to honestly answer she wasn't aware of the event, that I hadn't told her. The problem with that was I didn't know of the shower. Lia hadn't told me; neither had Iban.

Catena told my mother Lia was upset the entire day about her lack of support from the Ellis family, despite the packages my mother had delivered to her months ago. That part fired me up because fucking Lia understood exactly why she didn't have the support of my family: she was the other woman. A part of me wondered if she believed the lie of which brother's baby she'd been carrying. Had it been mine, there would have been more involvement from my family. But it's rather complicated to share in the joy of a new baby when his father's identity has yet to be revealed.

Needless to say, my father called me, bitching in my ear about how thick the tension had been at the last commission meeting, where he

221

sat across from a seething Rizzo. Double E Bags wanted to come out of his suit and reach across the table for Rizzo's neck. But that would have been unacceptable in the setting, and prohibited, even, outside of their meetings, according to their rules. Shit turned personal as soon as Lia got pregnant by an Ellis.

And of course, Iban stirred the pot at the end of the meeting, in the parking lot, by asking Rizzo if his capo was paid enough to approach an Ellis. He was referring to the capo he pulled out on in Scotch Plains when he was creeping off to see Lia. And of course, that set off a scene of threatening posturing and warning gapes between my father's crew and Rizzo's.

It vexed my father, which meant he leaned on me. As a result, I began planning a small baby shower between the two families next week. Lia was due in July, and I still had no idea when Iban was going to clear the air.

If that wasn't enough, that particular meeting was about the Rizzo and Damien beef, where the men were able to establish Rizzo had nothing to do with Tank's death. Damien apologized for the blood and, as a means of amends, pledged to have a luxury car delivered to each man in Rizzo's crew who was hit in the shootout in Elizabeth. And for Luigi's death, Damien would pay a premium in cash to Rizzo and Luigi's family. That may have been an ego-stroke to Rizzo, but a ticking time bomb for me. Damien would learn it was my father and brother who killed his lover soon enough. There were few in the state with the balls to do so. And before that happened, I needed to be prepared.

Or else more will die…

"Mr. Ellis," the flight attendant's soft voice interrupted my thoughts. Lynn, a thin woman of Asian descent, leaned over with a professional smile. She'd worked my flights before. "We've cleared ten-thousand feet. Can I get dinner started for you and Ms. Asad-Yasin?"

My eyes rolled across from me as Bilan's regard left the dark window and peered over to the two of us. She was so goddamn gorgeous, even when foolishly stubborn. The position she sat in accentuated her narrow waist. Her legs were crossed, exposing the

222

plumpness in her left thigh as she leaned toward the window, cupping her hands. Her fingernails were a hot pink, and I bet her toes matched. I couldn't be so sure because they were concealed in her pointy-heeled pumps. But those full lips were a brownish maroon, highlighted by matching speckles across her face.

Damn...

Bilan's regard hit me before shifting over to Lynn.

"You can call me Bilan," she softly corrected.

"Okay." Lynn straightened, broadening her smile. "Can I get you dinner, Ms. Bilan? Or should I start you off with a drink?"

She hesitated. "A drink would be fine. Thanks."

"A cocktail?" Lynn clarified.

Bilan glanced over to me again. "Mauve is fine."

"Okay!"

"We'll be ready for dinner in about thirty minutes, Lynn," I asserted, eyes locked onto the stubborn woman just a few feet away, springing her ankle in the air and causing her foot to bounce and body to vibrate.

It was close to eight o'clock at night, and I was sure she hadn't had a decent meal recently, if at all today.

"Okay. I'll get those drinks started now." Lynn turned toward the front of the jet.

I located a napkin on the table across the aisle and spit my gum into it.

As I balled the napkin, my gaze shifted over to Bilan. "We have five hours on this flight. The time is now to jump on it to make it pleasant."

She turned from the window, brows perfectly arched over her eyes. "Is that your way of initiating it?"

"I did when I picked you up."

"'Hi, Bilan' is a pleasantry?"

My forehead wrinkled and lips pushed out. "Is it a diss?"

"No." She shook her head. "But judging me for having a drink is, Sadik."

Oh...

223

My head swung back. That's what had her so distant all week. This was the first one Bilan didn't call or text. Typically, we'd both reach out to each other daily, whether to say hello or have a full blown conversation. I realized in the bustle of my week, how she hadn't initiated communication. I'd been too busy to fully examine it, but her actions tonight on our flight confirmed it.

"You had more than one drink. When I walked up on you and your one of three, you were working on one."

Her face folded. "One of three what?"

"The guys you're seeing."

Bilan snorted, eyes rolling. "We are not going there," she mumbled. "Unless you're ready to talk about your baby. By the way, when is he or she due?"

Anger shot up my belly. I unbuckled my seatbelt and sat up in my chair. "Sweetheart, I'm a man of little leisure, but lots of labor. At some point, the strongest of my kind needs a break, and as impossible as it is, it's a matter of health for us to find time to retreat for a reprieve, even if it means creating it. This weekend, I cleared at least nine engagements to take some time for me." Bilan's head dipped, eyeing me keenly. "I'm in need of a major escape: mentally and physically. A selfish one where it's more about me than it is you. Not of a sparring partner on my dime. I'm not short of women who could fill the role of companion for a getaway."

She leaned over her crossed knees. "Yet, for some random reason, I'm the chosen woman for your retreat. I've even passed the tests by way of your proficient doctor." She scoffed. "I mean... You stalk me at my job, trying to get my attention using a Christina C. Jones book. Then you so happen to be at a concert my friends and I were at." She began counting off on her fingers. "You wined and chatted me at a romantic jazz concert in the park. Then you treat me to a shopping spree when you send me to pick up a two-thousand-dollar MEEHAR gown. And, to be honest, I don't want to revisit that night of the Ameerah concert, but let's move on to how you show up to my graduation unexpectedly. Then finally, you pop up at a graduation party my friends are giving me, where I accidentally get drunk to vomiting proportions and try to fuck you, then fall into a crying fit

224

about missing my parents and knowing I'm about to lose their house in foreclosure. Did I mention the crying fit lasted for two hours and I was topless and clawing at your neck, begging you to not leave me or let me go?"

My eyes rolled away as I took a deep breath.

They told her...

"Yes. Tasche told me about what happened. She mentioned the bath I would only allow you to give me after throwing up on the way to the bathroom, and how I tried to fight you for using my dead mother's washcloth instead of my own. Yes!" Tears welled in her eyes. "She told me every embarrassing detail. And, for some insane reason, you still want me with you on this—" She used air quotations. "—selfish vacation that is about you rather than the initially labeled graduation gift you posed last week."

Bilan did all of that, and more than she mentioned. Possibly, it was because it sounded less tragic than it played out. As I washed her face, she pointed out several towels and washcloths on racks in the shower and over the toilet, and explained who they belonged to. Toothbrushes were another object still in place. By my estimation, they hadn't been used or cleaned in years. I offered to buy the house for her, feeling physically struck by her outpour of emotion. Oddly, while blubbering the pain she'd been carrying from feeling alone in the house, Bilan shared she didn't want to save the house. According to her, her mother told her not to spend her money saving the house because it was cursed and filled with so many bad memories.

There were so many questions I had. Quite a few things her girl, Tasche, didn't address when I questioned her after finally getting Bilan to sleep. That Tasche understood the art of protective silence. She seemed to be loyal to Bilan, and that strangely comforted me. But whatever she told her friend had this woman in a panic, and so unnecessarily.

"Yes. I did choose you to take this trip. And I did say it was your graduation gift, because it is. But there was nothing insane about my selection of you or this trip. There's a bigger picture. Doing this as a way to celebrate your accomplishment satisfies me—"

"Why?" she demanded, chords flaring in her neck.

225

"Because I can afford it. That's why. Making a woman I find incredibly appealing is fuckin' stimulating for me—"

"Well, I'm not just any—"

"AND DON'T YOU EVER FUCKIN' CUT ME OFF WHEN I'M SPEAKING!" I barked.

Bilan's scowl deepened, and Rory was at the door of our area of the cabin.

"Did I fuckin' call you?" I asked, not needing her shit when I already had enough on my hands with Bilan's.

Rory backed away, mumbling something she knew damn well to keep to herself.

I turned back to this frustrating woman I still couldn't understand my draw to, past her fat ass and fascinating freckles. She shot me a glower, chest heaving and breathing almost audible.

"Now, I'm not the type to dance around shit," I explained to Bilan, deliberately lowering my tone. "Yes, I saw some concerning shit that night, and maybe it is embarrassing to your sober mind right now. But clearly, it couldn't have been that bad to me if I'm still wanting to spend my fuckin' personal time with you. I told you, I don't do relationships. Compromising with someone other than my damn parents isn't a luxury I bestow generously, but I'm trying here, damn it!"

A single tear fell from her eye, and Bilan quickly swiped it away. Shit...

I didn't mean to make her cry or upset her. I was just wound tight from all the shit I'd been juggling. There was no room for this back and forth shit. Frustrated, I decided to let it breathe. And maybe that was why Lynn decided to finally come with those drinks. I took a huge gulp, taking back almost half the glass right away. Bilan didn't touch hers. She leaned toward the window again, sulking. After a few minutes, I powered up my laptop and began drafting a letter to my staff about our current legal posturing. It was something my attorney advised I do right away, and of course, that didn't mean when I returned from my miniature vacation.

"I want to escape this weekend, too," she murmured.

226

I glanced up from my screen where I was prepared to click Send on the email for the draft to my attorney. Bilan's lips were twisted, her sad eyes faltering when trying to focus on me. It dawned on me the time lapse I'd just experienced while working. Maybe she'd had enough time to think about what I'd said while I worked. Either way, seeing her dejected pulled at me. I clicked the tab and closed the laptop, placing it into the pocket on the side of my chair.

"Come here, Bilan." I flapped my fingers, motioning her.

My dick jolted when she jumped into action right away. I received her in my arms and allowed her to bury her face into my neck. As I rubbed her back, her soft hand pushed up to my face and grazed my jaw. I felt her breathing against my skin and her heartbeat against my arm. We stayed that way for a while, and I experienced an odd peace in holding her. When I realized her strokes became soft scrapes against the stubble on my face, I peered down at her. Immediately, the muscles around Bilan's eyes relaxed to a close and her lips parted. Then on instinct, I kissed her.

Right away, she clawed at my jaw and her body went rigid in my hold. But her tongue fluttered, swiping my lips. My hand pushed to the back of her head, fingering through her short hair. I got lost in the sorrow of her kiss, the temptation to consume her. Bilan was fragile in a way she didn't know. This thing between us was more dangerous than ever.

She pulled away first, her soft eyes beseeching. "I'm not seeing three guys—" Her eyes flashed wide. "Is that why Jason left early? I told him when he called me the other day I don't remember seeing him since I left you two on my back steps!"

I dipped my chin and stared at her for that stupid ass question. It was a fact.

"You told me in the park you were dating two guys."

"What did you say to him?"

Fuck him...

Bilan completely ignored my inconvenient recollection.

"What did he say to you?"

Her eyes bounced around. "He asked if you were my boyfriend."

"And what did you say?"

227

She shrugged. "I told him we'd been getting to know each other."

That thwarted my ego. "Not that we're friends—I am your friend. Right?"

"Why is it so important for you to be my friend, Sadik?"

"Because friendships between a man and woman are underrated and underutilized nowadays. Friendships can be beautiful, uncomplicated...meaningful."

"As opposed to what?"

"Meaningless fuckin'."

Her face fell, not expecting that. Her reaction reminded me of how little I knew Bilan. She was a walking conundrum. One I wanted inside of so damn bad: literally and figuratively.

"Here you are, Mr. Ellis and Ms. Bilan." Lynn returned with a rolling tray of food.

"Mexican!" I announced as though surprised.

I could hear Bilan groan as she tried leaving my lap.

"No." I tightened my arm around her waist and pulled her back into me. "We'll eat."

Bilan's timid regard shot to Lynn first before she murmured. "But I'm not hungry. You eat while I do something else."

"Something else like what?"

She shrugged. "Maybe explore your 'jet' now that I see you have one of your own." I guessed she was able to figure that out when we were boarding.

I shook my head. "Enough of that shit, Bilan. While you're with me, you'll eat."

Her mouth dropped. "How much?"

"That's up to you, but even if I have to feed it to you, it's going down." She needed to understand this.

"Fine, Sadik," she acquiesced.

"Good." I rearranged her on my lap to free my arms for the task. "Now, tell me about your issue with your aunt canceling the beach gathering."

I didn't look at her for a reaction as I began to squirt hand sanitizer in my hand before preparing tacos I hoped she'd finish.

Costa Rica...

I couldn't get over being in Central America. The flight hadn't been long enough for me to feel I'd left the country. That could be because it was spent in Sadik's mouth, whether we kissed or he spoke while I curled in his lap. It was a patterned dance we did, Sadik and I. We fought for short stints before he found a way to navigate us to safe waters.

As I followed behind him while we were being led to our bungalow, it felt beyond midnight, but wasn't quite that considering the time zone change. I was restless, excited beyond measure about it all. Sadik, and alone, on a Central American coast for four days? What would we do?

And the property was gorgeous. The glow of bright lights over winding hunter green palm trees complimented by red foliage. A marriage of cherry wood planks and stones was the thematic presentation of the property. To top it off were the sounds of the ocean, exciting my senses. I was overdressed, clacking in four-inch Valentino Rockstud Noir slingbacks I'd gotten from JAGMisha Boutique. Lucky for me, I decided on a simple Ase Garb t-shirt and cropped jeans. Sadik was no more prepared in a track suit, minus the jacket he'd left on the *jet, though he knew the destination. His bald head shun against the outdoor lamps leading to the back of the place.*

A pamphlet-worthy image of a lit pool came into view. It was lined by tall plants and concrete structures, giving a grandiose ambiance. We stepped onto the first of a three-level deck. The staff of the property led us into sliding doors, where we landed in a lounge area. Contemporary furniture sat along the walls, and candles burned in every corner. Immediately to the left was a small bar stocked with glasses of colorful liquids. Straight ahead was a wide staircase, leading to the second level.

"Mr. and Mrs. Ellis, this is your lounge area," one of the men informed. "We'll take you upstairs to the living room and kitchen."

"Mr. Ellis and Ms. Bilan," I corrected.

Sadik's eyes slowly glided over to me as his body turned to face me.

Sheepishly, I added, "Asad-Yasin is harder to remember for most."

His expression remained placid.

"Very well," the nice man agreed and turned for the stairs. "This two-thousand square foot unit built with intimacy with nature in mind should be most pleasing to you..."

As he went on, Sadik reached for my hand before taking the stairs, too. We were shown a cozy, yet lavish living room with plush furniture and floor-to-ceiling windows overlooking the pool. Down the hall was a full kitchen, though the man ensured all of our meals would be prepared for us, occasionally made in the unit. There was a short set of steps for the final level that opened to a humongous, four-poster wooden bed with thick, twisted manila ropes stretching across the canopy. A long sofa sat against the wall adjacent to an open bathroom.

Sadik led me, hand-in-hand, to an open, double-sliding door with a majestic view of a mountain. On the deck, you could see the pool beneath. Sadik didn't speak as my eyes ate up the surreal vista of paradise where a group of birds could be seen flying against the moonlight. He walked back into the bedroom to the opposing deck. It was out here where the moving ocean could be seen directly ahead. A large, netted catamaran bed stretched out over the shallow ocean.

Shapeless clouds glided over the mirrored water. Patterns of small ripples moved peacefully underneath me. The experience of it all seized my lungs. The view was surreal.

"You okay?" I could smell his proximity, feel his heated frame.

I nodded. "What is this?"

"The beach," he murmured uncharacteristically low.

My eyes flew open and lungs filled. "Sad—"

"Your luggage has arrived, Mr. Ellis." The man swung his arm to the center of the room, where more uniformed staff were placing suitcases against the wall near a fireplace.

Sadik approached the one narrating the tour, speaking at a volume too faint to hear. I turned back to the view. Excitement shot through my belly. I couldn't believe how beautiful it was.

"Let's unpack." Sadik reached for my hand. "Luis, this is great. Thanks for seeing us in. We'll take it from here."

As we ambled into the cosmic room, a tray topped with champagne flutes was placed on the cocktail table near the sofa. Candles were being lit near the bed, similar to the lower level.

The man whose name I now knew was Luis commented, "Your staff's unit is not too far from here. Just take the walkway on the east end of the bungalow to find their villa."

Sadik nodded, and Luis instructed his crew to leave. As they did, Sadik sauntered over to the cocktail table and grabbed a flute. As I examined the décor of the place, he handed me the champagne.

"Let's see what Bilan packed for her graduation celebration," he playfully voiced as he strolled over to the luggage and grabbed my lone suitcase. "Drink," he ordered, lifting it onto the bed.

My brows narrowed as I pulled the glass up for a sip. I considered the light and crisp flavor as I watched him unzip the suitcase, swinging the flap open.

"Well, I can tell you now, you overpacked." He pulled out a turquoise robe and tossed it onto the bed. Next were my jean shorts and a cardigan for at night if we were to be out. I always got cold in the evening. "These will never do, baby." he conveyed as though speaking sweetly to a child lifting bras and panties. Sadik made a point of turning toward me. "As you can see, we're in a tropical climate where you'll wear mostly swim gear."

My face tightened as I tried swallowing what was in my mouth. "At night. I could use them when I sleep at night." Sadik shook his head, disapproving. "Underneath my pajamas," I tried further explaining.

He took a deep breath and his chin lifted. "When you share a bed with me, Bilan, you wear nothing."

My neck gave loose and face dropped to the floor. "Not even underwear?"

"They're useless." Casually, he turned back toward the bed. "This is cute." He lifted a tube sundress. "I'd love to see you in a maxi." Then his head fell to the side as he further examined the dress and mumbled to himself, it seemed, "I'd love to see your thighs in short dresses, too."

"You're pretty much done rambling through my things." I rolled my eyes, gulping more champagne.

I quickly decided I liked bubbly. A lot.

"I had to, to see what needed to be replaced." He was back over by the luggage, where he lifted one of his, and traveled it over to the bed to open it. I turned back for the ocean, hoping it didn't disappear. Ah... "This is cute. Right?"

I twisted my neck to find a beautiful black and white-striped maxi dress. Sadik laid it on the bed, then pulled out a hot pink, silk spaghetti-strapped mini. My mouth dropped when he unfolded several more dresses and wide leg pants with a matching midriff top.

"Why didn't you tell me to just pack toiletries?"

A wry smile formed on his face. "There was no way I'd risk your company out here."

"Sadik..."

"Bear with me. I can be a bit..."

"Of an ultra-demanding alpha?"

The most adorable diffident smile broke on his face as Sadik snorted, eyes falling. Then he went back to the clothes on the bed.

"To show you I do have tact, I'll fold your clothes back up and bury this suitcase in the back of a closet downstairs." I chuckled, lifting the glass to my mouth. "Let me just make sure you don't have anything in here you may need." I returned to the vista out back, the imposing mountain looming with breathtaking beauty.

"Wonder what's the name of that thing," I mused out loud.

When I didn't hear a response, I glanced back at Sadik. My eyes ballooned at the sight of him holding two boxes of condoms. I tried breathing and swallowing at the same time. That resulted in a light choke.

His bemused gaze met me. Sadik's thick brows narrowed and he pouted. "Quite presumptuous, aren't you?"

I tried clearing my throat before I explained, "I didn't know which brand you preferred. Figured going with two would cover it."

He lifted the one box. "Snugger Fit?"

Crap...

"I didn't know your size and didn't want to..." I couldn't find the words. Embarrassed couldn't begin to describe my sudden discomfort. I did an extensive Google search on penis sizes and popular condom brands. "The average size is six inches—"

My ranting ended when Sadik tossed both boxes into the suitcase with the discarded clothing and zipped it up.

"You tired?" He kicked off a sneaker, then the other. "I'm wired, but I'll be crashing soon." His shirt came off over his head.

I stood straight, unreasonably flustered at the sight of his ripped chest. His skin was...golden, a small patch of light brown hair dusted his chest. My eyes brushed over an inked shield covering his right pectoral. They fell away as I transferred the weight of my hips.

"No." I cleared my throat, glancing down at my shoes. "Not at all."

My regard roved back up to Sadik as he pushed down his track pants. "Good. I'm going for a swim." Next, his thumbs hooked the waistband of his boxers and he peeled them off, too. The grooves in his inked back flexed as he bent over, pulling them under his feet. His socks were removed next. I clutched the flute to the point of pain. He stood straight, baring his full naked frame. I couldn't look away. Clothed, Sadik was of a modest build, and while he was the same bare, he was deliciously cut all over. His thighs were columnar, as were his arms. His abs were swollen, and belly button oddly beautiful.

I wanted to avoid it, but couldn't. It was right there resting with confidence. His dick was... I didn't have the words. It was mean. Intimidating and buoyant. And his pubic bed was just as tangerine as the hair on his face.

My eyes shot up to his face. Sadik's expression as blank as if the weather forecast called for rain. I closed my mouth.

"You coming?"

He didn't wait for an answer when he began walking toward the front of the bedroom, where the ocean lay before us.

His ass!

Two muscles moving rhythmically in his casual stroll.

"Bilan?"

My head shook, and I took a deep breath. "Yeah."

"No clothes in the ocean, either."

Sadik ambled out to the deck, where I could see him, in perfect form, dive from the third level into the water. I dashed out there and peered over the ledge. It was clear where he landed, but it took a full patient minute to wait for him to reappear, flailing his arms to float.

"You can't come with a glass of champagne!" he called up to me.

I backed away, feeling an uncanny sense of excitement growing as I set the glass on the table. I pulled out of my shirt, unhooked the slings of my shoes from my ankles, then kicked them off. Ignoring that small voice of fear about what he thought of my body, I shredded all of my clothes and jewelry and toed out to the deck.

"Can you swim?" he asked, floating in the water.

"A little."

"Shit..." I could hear him cry out when I reared back, then ran toward the ledge and jumped in.

Yup. I'd officially lost my mind, eradicated all good senses and precautions, just to be in the moment with Sadik. Never had I felt so safe around a man pursuing me. It had been years since I felt protected from my father. But as I held my breath and flogged my arms to come up from the water, I didn't feel an ounce of fear. Not even when arms circled my frame, propelling gravity.

"You're about to give me a damn heart attack out here, girl!"

I cleared my eyes and let a giggle rip from my lungs. That turned into full blown laughter. Soon, I was delirious with them. Even in my elation, I could appreciate the warmth and silkiness of the water. It glided over my skin like fabric.

"Hold on to me, silly!" he commanded.

In my laughing fit, I was able to obey, tasting the salt water trailing into my mouth. Sadik backstroked somehow, moving us.

"I didn't think you'd come."

"Me either," I admitted.

"Glad you did, though. Can you really swim?"

"I used to at the Boys & Girls Club."

"How long ago was that?"

I shrugged, unable to stop smiling. "When I was thirteen…fourteen maybe."

"Shit!" he grounded out. "Don't get out here and drown on my ass, Bilan."

"So, I can do it when I get back to Jersey?"

"Don't be a smart ass either."

Sadik's temperament was lighthearted. I decided I liked that facet of his personality, too, perhaps more than the demanding, bossy one.

"I see you can swim."

"Of course. My mother made sure I learned a little bit of everything. Swimming was one I couldn't avoid. There were pools everywhere we vacationed, even in cold climates."

"Indoor pools?"

"Yup. Can you stand now?"

I looked around the moonlit water and saw we were closer to the house. Letting go, I swung my arms and stretched my legs until I felt the sanded floor beneath.

"You don't believe me? That I can swim?"

Instead of walking into an intended fight, Sadik neared me. His attention was on my head with his hand reaching for my hair.

"It's curly," he murmured, fingering through it investigating.

"It's wet." Duh…

"It's beautiful." His words were but a whisper.

Still kicking my legs and arms to float, I laughed. "It's a black girl thing."

Was he so used to Lia that he didn't know coarse hair drew up in water?

"Are you being a smart ass again?" he growled, grabbing me in his arms. "You don't want to be that way with me." I sputtered a laugh when he spun me around like a ragdoll beneath his arm. "Apologize!"

"No!" I felt intoxicated with mirth, unable to stop laughing.

Even when Sadik lifted me in the air and dunked me into the water, I came up howling. That inspired him to do it again and again. Horse playing in the water with Sadik. That's what we did for a countless spell, engaging in unmitigated fun.

At some point, my lungs slowed, as did Sadik's swimming. It was gradual, organically timed.

"Hang here. I'll go get a towel," he ordered, moving past me to leave the water. "Time to turn in."

I followed him fixedly, shamefully ogling his glutes that were amazing in the nude. He sauntered over to a trunk, where towels I was sure weren't there some time ago appeared. They must have been delivered while we were at play. With casual speed, Sadik wrapped a towel around his waist before waving me over. Like an obedient child, I began to wade toward the shore. He met me in the water, the line at his ankles as he held the towel open. His eyes were unapologetically all over my frame. I tried not to falter in step.

Sadik wrapped the towel around my body, then pulled me into his hard frame for a kiss.

"Let's get showered." He took me at the hand. "You hungry?"

"No," I murmured behind him, taking off.

When we made it to the bedroom, I saw the mess he made of the clothes he'd purchased for me.

"You want to go first?" Sadik referred to the shower as he pored over his phones on the nightstand.

"No. You can go. I'm going to fold these clothes you threw all over the bed."

Sadik nodded, attention to his one phone before sauntering off to the bathroom. The shower had glass walls and was only separated from the bedroom by a partition and not a door. So badly, I wanted to look, but forced myself to get busy with hanging up the pretty dresses and unpacking my toiletries. By the time Sadik was ambling back into the bedroom area, I was done.

"You sure you're not hungry?" His eyes were tight; Sadik was tired.

"It's late. I just need a shower and a bed." I took off to start just that.

In the shower, I washed and conditioned my hair before tending to my body. The water pressure was amazing, but I forced myself out when I was fully rinsed. After drying off, I awkwardly stood in the mirror. He said no pajamas or underwear. What was I supposed to change into? Romance could be weird, I quickly decided.

"Sadik?" I called for him.

"Out here."

I turned and noticed the main room was dark. With the towel around me, I toed to where a trail of rose petals and tealights led. It was the deck with the netted tarp extended over the water. Sadik was there, laying on what now looked like a bed topped with white, oversized fluffy pillows, sheets, and a comforter. The sounds of the wavy ocean played the backdrop.

"'Bout damn time," he complained throatily. Sadik rubbed his eyes as he flipped over the comforter, inviting me in.

The new view revealed his sinewy upper torso and his black fitted briefs. My jaw dropped. Sadik flicked his chin as if to ask me what was the hold up.

"I have to sleep naked next to all of that and you get to wear underwear?"

Sadik yawned, looking sexily youthful doing it. "My rules. Blame it on the ultra-alpha thing, I guess."

He wasn't relenting on this. It was clear by his impatient disposition. I rolled my eyes and tossed the towel to the side before toeing out onto the deck. The moment I laid down on the firm, yet yielding foundation, Sadik lifted me over his body so I was closest to

237

the water. Within seconds, I was swathed in soft and freshly scented linens with a man snuggled at my back.

"You see that?" he mumbled, pointing directly ahead over the water.

"The mountain?"

"It's a volcano. The Arenal volcano. It's seven thousand years old. The last eruption was in two thousand eight."

I gulped hard.

"Sheesh." I croaked.

"Goodnight, Bilan," he droned so sweetly behind me.

My eyes fluttered closed, and I hummed contently. "Sadik..."

"Yeah..."

"Thanks for this."

His response was a spine-chilling kiss at the nape of my neck.

∞ 15 ∞

My eyes opened to sounds beneath us, unrelated to the waters we slept over. I pushed myself up to peer over the ledge of the catamaran net. The chef and her crew were letting themselves into the bungalow. I had to get used to their silent provisions. This resort was beyond luxurious. It was noted to be stellar with its services and amenities. While I made it clear I didn't want people on the premises without my knowledge—because I planned to have Bilan naked around here every day—I had to allow for their presence to serve us.

I rubbed my eyes, feeling my dick throb from the smell of her. Shit… This would have to be the last morning of waking up to her naked body and not emptying inside while fucking her senseless. But the wiser of me chose patience. I had no idea how much, but it was clear to me Bilan was grossly inexperienced. I could tell each time I touched her. She'd now grown comfortable with my kiss and even reciprocated greedily. She wanted me, badly. But there was still something innocent about her that could backfire on me if I wasn't careful.

With the least amount of movements I could make, I crept off the tarp and headed to the bathroom. It took a minute over the toilet, holding my erection but after a while, I was able to calm and relieve my bladder. I washed my hands and dried them before slipping back beneath the covers. To my right, Bilan lay on her side facing the water. She looked so peaceful against nature. Sexy with her short cut that was now a dry nest of messy waves. Vulnerable because she was hiked in the air naked. And innocent because I made her sleep that way. She looked like a woman who should fall asleep on the water any time she felt the need. She should be kept that way. Bilan would be surprised to know she held that type of aura. I wondered if my father was able to see that in my mother. Some women were built to be spoiled by men of wealth.

I turned toward the deck for a phone, any phone. The sudden need to capture this beautifully erotic seascape in a picture felt imminent. I snapped several, ignoring the alerts popping up on the screen.

"Sir." I turned and found one of the cooks. She smiled. "We're here and will have your brunch ready in about ten minutes," she whispered.

I nodded, swiping my palm over my face. Then I turned on my side to face Bilan's back. My hand hooking over her waist, I caressed the tiny pouch at the small of her belly. It made me wonder how it got there. The woman never ate—at least, not around me. Caressing her soft skin wasn't a good move, considering my heightened state of arousal. I couldn't remember the last woman who created such a strong need in me.

Bilan stirred, her arm swung over her head before she turned onto her back. Those freckles were plentiful on a makeup-free face. Damn, I could wake up like this more often. She was beauty personified.

When her eyes opened and settled on me, Bilan quickly began to shift back toward the water.

"No!" I caught her at the waist, hooked her, and pulled her back to me.

She squirmed against me, not helping my condition at all. "Aw, come on! I haven't washed my face or brushed my teeth yet!" she squealed.

"Neither have I." And that damn sure wasn't going to stop me. I grabbed her at the chin, forcing her to my mouth and kissing her. She punched my shoulder with the side of her fist. And I pried her mouth open with my tongue. I wouldn't fuck her, but would damn sure take all the comforts only a woman could provide in the morning. I could taste the initial morning staleness in her mouth, but it all faded away with her participation. Within seconds, Bilan softened beneath me, her palm now clutching me as she let go of a hum. "See. That wasn't too bad."

She squeezed her eyes closed and shook her head. "That was so not right." I smiled at her stubbornness. "I need to pee."

"Go. Food will be up soon."

Torturously, Bilan crawled over me to leave the tarp. I watched her ass jiggle all the way to the toilet room that was enclosed by a door. I used the time to text Rory to check in. I asked her to make arrangements for my day with Bilan. Then I called my queen.

"Well, hello." She picked up almost right away.

"You miss me?" I smiled.

"Always. Are you just waking up?"

I rubbed my eye, feeling my body relax. "Yup."

"Long night, I see," she teased.

"Not answering that."

"And you'll be back on Monday?"

"Something like that. Yeah." Moving along, I asked her about work. "How's that replacement coming?"

"The director's role?"

"That's the only one you're concerned with at your level."

Being the owner of fifteen charter schools in the state, my mother had a solid staff to manage them all. She recently lost her Director of Operations to the public school system. We'd suspected an admin on the board of education had been trying to sabotage her charter program for years now.

"Nothing. I've interviewed six people in the past week—one from Oregon—and no one fits the role. Of course, the generous pay and benefits are attracting the masses, but this is a key role and should be filled by someone with the right educational background, as well as a, lack of burnout from the system. I almost prefer someone without public school experience, hoping they'll bring in fresh ideas and fervor."

I nodded, understanding. "I feel you. I'll keep my eyes open."

She giggled into the phone.

"What?" I asked.

"Like you know people in education."

"I make it my business to know people in every industry, lady."

She snickered at that, too. "Your father was upset about you missing a meeting with him again."

He could get used to it. I wouldn't even give that topic of his disappointment in me a moment of thought today.

"Was Dad the first guy with money to seduce you?"

"Honey, your Dad was the one and only dude with money seducing me." She laughed.

"Was he aggressive with it?"

She hummed. "I suppose. He had a little something back then, nothing like now, of course. But Earl Ellis only knows one way, honey. I don't think he's capable of going slow or pacing himself."

I took a deep breath, agreeing. From the corner of my eye, I saw the food arriving. I motioned them to bring the trays out on the tarp.

"Let me guess, you can't shake your natural inclination to be yourself out there."

"I'm damn sure trying."

"Why?" Her tone was curt.

I scratched the back of my head. "Because I like her."

"Then don't be Earl. Extinguish that part of your DNA so that the other dominant facet of Sadik can lead the way, and go at her pace." My brows shot up as I considered that. The last of the food was laid out on the comforter, and the staff quietly and swiftly left for downstairs. "This heffa better be something," my mother warned.

That's when Bilan walked out of the bathroom to the vanity to wash her hands and face.

"Oh, she's something," I assured watching her. "The question is, is she mine?"

"Wow," she breathed. "Are we going there?"

I took a deep, cleansing breath. "I gotta go. Just wanted to check in with you."

"Okay. Be safe and have fun."

"Love you, baby."

"Love you more, honey bunch."

After hanging up, I slid the phone onto the wooden ledge and glanced around at all the spread. I took another deep breath, looking

242

out into the ocean. This was just what I needed. A break from the bullshit. An escape with her.

"And who's going to eat all this food?" Bilan was standing next to me, one hand covering her pubic hairs and the other arm holding her tits.

I reached for her to help her back into bed. She quickly covered her breasts with a sheet when seated next to me.

"Feeling better now?"

"After not sharing my morning funk with a man and risking turning him off? Yeah."

I shook my head. "It's kind of hard turning off a man with something he's requesting."

"I'm not too sure about that. Guys ask for things they turn out not liking after all."

"Not men," I made clear. "You eat eggs?"

She gave me her typical faint shrug. I started with the plate of scrambled eggs. It was an American spread today. With Bilan, I kept food simple, trying to appeal to her.

"Just a little," she noted, watching me.

I forked a small chunk and fed it to her. Then I had some myself. As she chewed, her regard was across the water.

"This is paradise," she mused out loud. "I can't believe I swam in an ocean not crowded with seaweed and cracked shells. Even with mostly the moonlight last night, I could see clear to my feet." She shook her head and turned to me, where I had a piece of French Toast waiting for her to eat.

Bilan pulled it off the fork, then I cut a piece for myself. It was okay; I'd had better.

"So a customs firm," she commented, referring to my profession.

My brows lifted as I considered she was accounting for the expense of the trip.

"I said 'for starters', I have a customs firm—or third-party logistics is the appropriate term." I bit off a piece of turkey bacon, then brought the remainder of the stick to her mouth. "You got hung up on that topic, and I didn't get the opportunity to continue."

"What do you mean?" she asked before taking a bite herself.

"I have several businesses."

"Well, what else do you do?" One of her brows was higher than the other.

Bilan didn't trust me, which was another reason I resolved to go slow with her.

"I own a dispensary—two, actually. Open." I fed her home fries.

"As in marijuana?" she asked around her food.

Of course, that would be the first thing to come to mind for her.

"That would be the product."

"Is that a part of your father's business?"

I swallowed the eggs in my mouth before answering, "The marijuana dispensary industry is heavily regulated by the government. My father is a felon and wouldn't qualify for the license to grow it."

"How long have you been in the business?"

"About ten years." I raised a piece of crepe to her mouth. "These are delicious."

After seconds of her chewing, she asked, "That long?"

"It was a promising trade. I saw that coming. Got started with the one in Colorado—"

"You have a dispensary in Colorado?"

I nodded, going for a glass of orange juice. "Then bought the second in California a few years ago. That one just started earning consistently."

"Wow," she breathed as I handed her the glass.

I cut into the pancakes, hoping they'd be better than the French Toast. "Yup. That is what I do, too," my tone wry.

"And, what else?"

"Investments."

"In what?"

"Several things; primarily technology, though. I have a company that invests at the seed stage for things like app developers and receives a portion of the profits when it's sold."

"You're a venture capitalist," she trilled, understanding.

I nodded. "Mmmm…" I plucked a piece of pancake and offered it to her. "These are incredible."

I watched for her reaction while she chewed. Bilan gave nothing away as she held the sheet to her chest, the curve of her left breast unknowingly exposed. I needed to get out of these beddings with her or I'd lose my damn mind.

"I like the French Toast better. Better than everything. Can I have more of that?"

"You can have whatever you want." I cut into that plate, then poured more syrup. "Let's finish this so we can get out and explore the area. That okay with you?"

Bilan nodded, attention fully on the egg-battered bread. That obvious slight thrilled me.

Sexual frustration had hit an all new plateau for me, one I had never experienced before. We went skinny dipping, slept naked over the ocean, showered in view of each other, and he'd hand-fed me breakfast and hadn't tried having sex with me. For all things holy, I'd seen the birthmark on his upper thigh, though I pretended not to when he stalked out of the shower before we left the bungalow earlier. All of that, and he hadn't attempted sex. It didn't make sense for the guy who took me for drive-thru STD testing on our first official date.

"Ready?" His silky alto rang next to me.

I'd been staring blindly out the window as we rode in a jeep to a pier. Sadik mentioned wanting to boat today.

"Yeah." I cleared my throat and followed him out of the truck.

Rory was with us, looking all of a male pre-teen in her short-sleeved Hawaiian button-up and distressed jean shorts, cut at the knees. She didn't greet me when we left the resort, and for the first time, it wasn't a big deal. That was likely because of my preoccupation with her boss—even now as we trekked out of the pebbled parking lot.

We stopped at a walkway leading to docked motor boats. Sadik turned to Rory.

As she lit a cigarette, she mumbled, "I prolly won't be here when y'all done. I'mma go look for something to get into around here."

"Alright. Take these." Sadik handed her his phones. "Drop them off at the bungalow if you get back before I do."

Pulling in a draw so deep, it narrowed her fishbowl eyes as she held it in, Rory nodded as she took off. Sadik took me at the hand and continued the path onto the dock.

"This is us, I think." He slowed at a boat.

Seconds later, a tall, caramel man with curly salt and pepper hair and a checkered smile waved from the side of the boat. Sadik led the way until we met the man, who jumped onto the dock.

"Mr. Ellis?" His accent faint.

"Yes." Sadik gestured to me. "And this is my Bilan."

My Bilan?

"I'm Sammie." The man gave a neck bow. "Welcome aboard the Outter." He swung his arm and Sadik climbed onto the boat, then assisted me. "For what you have in mind, she'll be perfect. Get comfortable and we'll get you out to the peninsula for some adventure, huhn?"

The boat wasn't too big, but it was nice and clean. Sadik and I sat on one of the white leather benches. Before we took off, a woman was carrying a tray of drinks to a nearby table. Sadik had a beer, and I opted for a white wine. My eyes barely left the trail of disrupted water from our powerful speed. This was heaven.

"You good?" he asked into my neck.

My eyes automatically hit the woman now laying out towels across from us. Heat creeping up my toes, I nodded while clenching the stem of the wine glass.

"I never asked how you slept last night."

A smile crested upon my face. "Like a baby. And you?"

"The worst part was waking up to a warm, naked body and a painful erection."

I shuddered, eyes closing and all. Sadik felt it and snickered.

"You're weird," I hissed.

"Nah. Just crazy about Bilan."

I rolled my eyes, unable to fight the grin inching on my face. The mild shouting from Sammie on the upper level of the boat caught our attention, causing Sadik to let up off my shoulder. The woman pointed out to the water.

"Dolphin!" she relayed.

Sadik pointed for me, and I followed his line of vision to several dolphins leaping into the air, performing impressive somersaults.

"Wow…" I breathed.

This was amazing, nothing I'd ever seen. I was awestruck. Sadik's pulling me into him by gripping my thigh told me of the bubble I'd found myself in. I turned to him and found those honeyed eyes of understanding and…peace on me. I couldn't resist caressing the side of his face with my hand. He leaned into my touch.

"Thank you," I breathed.

For the next few minutes, while we jetted off to our destination, I was able to admire the picturesque sights of the Pacific Coast. Then the boat came to a stop. Sadik stood and accepted gear from the woman assisting Sammie.

"What's that for?" I asked.

"Do you want to scuba dive?" Sadik's eyes gleamed with an energy I couldn't name.

The idea made me nervous. "Can I watch?"

"Sure." He began to put on a mask and was assisted with a backpack with a tank attached. So much equipment for leisure? I didn't like the way he stepped to the lip of the boat before jumping off. That was when I jumped to my feet and went to the ledge myself to see where he'd gone. The water was a lucent greenish blue, but eventually I saw no sign of him.

"Would you like to go with him?" Sammie was at my side.

With a tight smile and animated eyes, I chirped. "No. I'll just watch."

I turned back to the water to wait. Nothing. I turned back to the bench, where my bag sat with things Sadik packed while I was changing into the bikini he laid out for me to wear out here. I thought to pull out my phone and take pictures. After several of them, I began to grow uneasy.

"How long can he stay down there?" I asked Sammie, who was peeling off the skin of some fruit with a pocket knife and chomping away.

"Hours if the fish don't get him." His accent was a little thicker that time, and I accounted for that being the reason I didn't get the joke.

I went back to the ledge and waited for signs of him. A sign. Any sign.

Nothing.

"Your husband?" Sammie asked.

I shook my head.

"Boyfriend?" the woman asked, tongue thicker than Sammie's.

I shook my head again as I checked the time on my phone. It had been close to thirty minutes since I'd taken the pictures.

"He called you his." Huhn? I turned to Sammie. "Mr. Ellis called you his when he introduced you." He pointed to the woman, who smiled affectionately. "She no like the water when my girlfriend. She need the water...now my wife." He laughed.

I turned to the woman squirming against the wall of the stairs. She loved him; it was palpable.

"You two married?" I asked, pointing at them both.

"Twenty-two years. Even lived in America for three. She needed the bus then." He laughed.

I got the joke. It was really funny. But... Sadik was down there too long, and he didn't have security.

I tossed my finger over my shoulder. "Do you mind?"

The woman ducked her chin and hopped to a chest, where there was gear. Less than five minutes, with a quick 101 of scuba diving in hand and at least fifteen pounds later, I was wobbling toward the ledge, then leaping into salt water.

The sound was different down here, and so was my agility. All I could hear was my breathing and racing heartbeat. The lower I dropped, the darker it became. That reminded me to turn on the flashlight Sammie's wife had given me.

"Ah!"

I swung my body aimlessly when a school of tiny rainbow fish swished around my head. I kept twisting around for more before seeing they were all gone. That was it: I was over this already. Where was Sadik? I glanced up and could still see the bottom of the boat. Sinking deeper, I saw colorful corals and groups of the tiniest fish. I had no idea they existed in these miniature sizes.

The one thing I didn't like was feeling so weighted. In water, you can't move quickly and for self-defense reasons, that concerned me. I tried channeling my mental and physical energy toward finding a russet-skinned, bald head, kaleidoscope-eyed man. Certainly, I'd be able to find him amongst sea creatures.

I glanced up again to be sure I hadn't floated away from the boat above. Then I swam toward a shaded object. It turned out to be old wreckage: a piece of a car it seemed.

That's it. I'm going back...

This was beyond my world experience. I know I said I wanted to explore the ocean, but this was outside of my dreams. I had no business being down here. Maybe Sadik had returned to the boat since I'd left. The moment I turned to find the boat, I felt a gentle swipe of my ass. I tried jerking around and collided with a body. A human body. My flashlight revealed the top of Sadik's head and my heart dropped.

I was relieved and startled at the same time. I wanted to scream at him, but remembered I couldn't speak. He extended his hand to me and I took it, believing he would help me up to the boat and we'd be done with this excursion. But as I glided behind him, I saw new sea figures. There were fish of larger sizes and varying colors. More *exotically hued coral reefs. I was legit spooked when I saw a humongous stingray. It was monstrous, even at a distance!*

I learned Sadik had a camera when he motioned for me to stay and the camera aimed at me flashed. We did that a few times, swimming to different places close to the floor of the sea. We came upon a wrecked bus. I couldn't tell the model of it, but we were able to swim inside, where there were fixtures resembling seats. The steering wheel was even still intact. Sadik had me sit on top of it or pretend to by clamping my hands into the frame of a couple of windows as he snapped away.

We were off again and, after a while, I realized our time down under had come to an end. Just before our final ascension, Sadik held me with an arm wrapped around my lower back, underneath the tank. He pointed ahead and after I swiped away a tiny worm-like creature, I saw it growing in size.

A shark!

My body tensed and Sadik's grip on me tightened. I was ready to lose it, but was concerned about drowning. If I breathed wrong in the tube, I'd be in a world of trouble. I was able to exhale when the big fish didn't come our way. It made a beeline in the opposite direction. Sadik tapped my hip to get my attention. With his hands, he motioned for me to watch him. I nodded, telling him I understood, then watched him flap his arms and legs in two rhythmic motions. He began to move further away from me, toward the boat, leaving behind bubbles. Thankfully, I was able to get a good look at his technique to mimic him. It wasn't as easy as he made it seem, but I developed the coordination and push upward. At some point, I passed Sadik, or at least I thought until he was next to me, working to the surface.

The point became clearer, and the lighting increased the closer we drew to the surface. The moment I reached for the boat, my legs were seized and pushed up. Seconds later, my arms were pulled up and my body propelled too quickly out of the water. I landed inside on my stomach. By the time I was able to right myself, Sadik was on the boat and standing to assist me. The transition from water gravity to that of air was immense. It took me a while to balance myself.

"Up you go," I heard, likely from Sammie.

His wife was busy releasing me from the book bag-like apparatus on my back. I pulled the mask off, and she helped with the fins from my feet.

"What did you see down there, Mr. Ellis?" Sammie asked, helping Sadik remove his gear.

"Lots of shit," Sadik grumbled. I eyed him closely, feeling a yearning strange for our dynamic. "Barracuda, whitetip reef sharks, cuttlefish and whale sharks…manta rays."

"Wow!" Sammie whistled. His wife sighed in amazement. Sadik worked to remove all of his gear, looking so bad ass to me. I ached all over, just to touch him. "They were out today, huhn?"

"Yup." Sadik was less animated with his responses. His attention was locked on me. "Great day," he murmured on his way to me, his brows furrowed, golden face beautifully scowling. "You okay?" he asked, hands at my waist.

I nodded, breathing hard. My hands acted on their own accord and pulled him in by the head. The moment my fingers touched him, I knew. I wanted him, my body humming with need. I heard nothing, saw not a thing. I only tasted the salt of the earth and flavor of a worldly man with experience I could only read in a textbook. Sadik revealed another side of his sophistication to me today. His knowledge down there, his braveness. It all made me feverish all over. My mouth worked to communicate that. I urged my hands to remain on his head and face only. My pulse banged in my ears as I sucked his tongue, and my pelvis pressed into him unabashedly. Once again, I lost myself to Sadik.

A purr of contentment managed from my lungs as our tongues twirled around each other. It was the magic of the moment: his heat, his touch, the winds brushing across my back covered by just a string, the sun glowing around us, and the powerful transmission of promise pinging in our enfold as he held me.

When Sadik pulled back, he smiled softly. "I think our boat ride is over."

I glanced around and saw we were, indeed, docking.

Then I faced him again, joining him in humor. "I see it is. This was fun, Sadik."

My soul was light on the water. My spirit calmed. Sadik's hand grasped my hip possessively as he gazed into my eyes. I was convinced it was his way of communicating reciprocity. And that didn't need verbal affirmation to be felt.

"Maybe tomorrow, you have time to fly over Whale Bay. It's shaped like a whale's tail." Sammie laughed as he nodded. "Lots of whales there, too."

Sadik's gaze met mine. "Is that something you'd like to do?"

Overwhelmed with excursion options while on "vacation," I shrugged with a sheepish smile. I didn't care what I did, as long as I did it with him.

"Go," Sammie's croaky chords advised. "Make love. It's always a good time to here." When we chuckled at the awkward command, he noted, "Why do you think we're a top Blue Zone in the world?" His brows hiked suggestively.

"Blue Zone?" I was thrown by that one.

Sadik snorted, grinning. The corner of his eyes crinkled against the rays of the sun. "The natives tend to live past one hundred years old."

Oh.

My face exploded. "Ohhh!"

Sadik was at my side, rubbing my back with long, comforting strokes, expressing it was time to leave the boat.

"Let's grab a snack on our way back to the bungalow," he advised, kissing my neck chastely before we hopped onto the pier.

Hand-in-hand, we strolled down the sanded shore to the jeep.

"Thanks." I smiled at the woman arranging a tray of pastries and beverages on the table out on the deck.

She offered a bow before heading toward her cart near the side of the bungalow. Now showered, I felt calmer than I did on the boat, but still unsettled. Sadik was busy getting cleaned from our excursion while I retreated out here to the pool area. The view of the Arenal volcano from a distance was breathtaking. I struggled to not get lost in its vastness. Its dangerousness. As an active volcano, it could erupt, spilling over danger and destruction to anything and anyone around. Like Sadik. He'd been different out here. His attentiveness was affectionate. There was no barrier to his fixation on me. Deep down inside, I wondered and worried if it had to do with my drunken meltdown last weekend. From what Tasche mentioned, I shared so much.

Taking a deep breath, I admonished myself to leave that mess I made in last week where I made it. Sadik was right: if it was that bad, I wouldn't be here with him enjoying this gorgeous view of ultra-hazardous nature.

The sudden presence of a fruit pastry in front of my mouth had me leaping over the barstool I sat on.

"Bite," his deepened alto demanded.

Slowly, I opened my mouth, obeying. The bread was flaky, the jellied fruit too sweet. But the tip of his nose skimming the back of my neck had my eyes fluttering closed and my spine arching.

"You like?"

I shook my head as I swallowed the small piece I bit off.

"Try this one," he whispered in my ear.

My eyes fluttered open to find a cheese Danish topped with fresh fruit baked on. I took a bite and was rewarded with a delicious balance of breading, cream cheese, and natural sugar from the fruit. At the same time, a sensation rocketed up my inner thigh when Sadik's fingers feathered my skin. I pulled in a heap of air from my nostrils.

"Eat, Bilan," he ordered directly in my ear.

I took another bite, barely tasting, distracted by my racing pulse. His hand stroked my thigh, and soft lips brushed against my neck. When his tongue swiped into my skin, a moan pushed from my chest.

"Another," he referred to the pastry, and I chomped off a smaller piece, appetite effectively killed.

There was no way I'd give him an inkling, afraid he'd stop. God, I wanted this. Needed this next level of whatever we'd been building sexually. My head rolled back helplessly when the knot at the neck of my bikini was released. The small breeze caressed my compressed nipples, and I could feel them sprout like buds. That's when my breathing turned erratic.

"More," he whispered.

I opened and took a bigger bite. The quicker I ate, the faster I could get the feeding session, that had been turning me on, over with. His snaked arm pulled back, and his busy fingers were on the knotted string at the left side of my hip. As should have been predicted, it unraveled. As I worked the food in my mouth, Sadik's hand pushed down my crotch. Two fingers navigated between my labia.

"Open."

Right away, my thighs parted.

"No," he corrected throatily. "Your mouth."

My shoulders collapsed with disappointment, but I obeyed and was happy when those two fingers furthered down, grazing my nub I could feel growing. My belly leaped and spine jolted. When they made it to the opening of my sex, I could feel how wet I was. And when those fingers dipped in what felt like a puddle down there and brought the wetness up to my clit, my jaw fell.

"Swallow, Bilan."

Gradually, I was able to command my brain to continue processing the food in my mouth. His fingers moved in a circular motion, immediately heating the pads of my feet. I grabbed the edge of the stool, bracing myself. His mouth was on my beating neck, and I forgot to breathe. A tsunami began to stir in my groin, causing my hips to move against his efforts.

I felt him against my lips.

"Suck," he ordered.

Without opening my eyes, my lips parted and his two fingers pushed inside. The cool taste of Jell-O slipped onto my tongue and I began to explore it, breaking it between his fingers and the roof of my mouth. Once each piece dissolved and was swallowed, I focused on his fingers. It wasn't long before I realized my sucking instinctively mimicked his motions on my tight nub. My head rolled against his shoulder, chest heaved to growing proportions.

His fingers slipped from my mouth and brushed over my pebbled nipple. My body isolated, all but my pelvis tense and frozen.

"Oh!" ripped from my lungs.

I was on the precipice of a deep fall, I knew this from him. But this time, there were so many moving parts attacking my sanity. Foreign sounds shot from my mouth as I pumped sensually—and desperately—into his hand. The pressure deepened on his fingers between my legs, the two on my nipple worked like scissors. Then his tongue swirled on my neck again.

"Sadik," I coughed out.

"Mmmhmm," he assured with that simple hum. "Let it rip, baby."

Rip?

What did he mean by ri—

"Uh!"

My body vibrated in every corner. Pleasure danced on each cell. Ripples of splendor sprang out in my groin, rendering my body possessed. By him. As my frame quaked over the barstool and against his chest helplessly, my lids parted just enough for me to see the Arenal. It was then that I felt a connection to the vast mountain. I was spilling over violently, possibly in the most danger of my life. Exposing it all to Sadik.

Movement returned to my pelvis first as I rocked slowly against his fingers, belly still spasming. I was able to pry my palms from the sides of the stool and grip the arm controlling the stroke against my sensitive clit. My body had, had enough. I couldn't endure another moment of sensation. Thankfully, he took the hint and moved to hold me at the waist with both hands. My arm snaked behind him to bring his face down with my hands. Sadik came willfully, feeding into my sudden need for his mouth on mine, his tongue on mine.

He worked his way around, until his hips were between my thighs.

"How do you feel?"

With my eyes closed, trying to regain myself, I bit my lip and nodded.

"Look at me, Bilan." The authority in his chords had returned, even while sounding seductive. My heavy eyes sprouted open. "How do you feel?"

I swallowed. "Good?"

His brows met, and a smirk curled on his lips. "Is that an answer or question?"

I didn't know. I had no clue how to articulate what I was feeling. In the moment, I felt needy, vulnerable.

"I want you close," fell meekly from my lips.

"I'm not going anywhere." Good. I wrapped my arms around his neck and pushed my sex into his waist. "I've got a question for you, though." That had me peering up into his eyes. "I want you to be honest with me and not feel embarrassed. Okay?"

I nodded. Fear struck my chest, but I wanted whatever was coming. That powerful orgasm sedated my defenses. I was open...ready.

"Are you a virgin?"

My eyes blossomed, and an unexpected giggle pushed from my lungs.

"As in intercourse? No!" I continued to laugh.

Sadik didn't, but nodded. "C'mon, baby."

In two gentle tugs, I was off the stool, and straddling his hard frame. My soaking sex slapped against his abdomen. It was unrelenting torture rocking against him while he walked us into the bungalow, taking the stairs. I could only lay against his sculpted shoulder, mouth agape as I endured the spikes of pleasure from my clitoris.

My arms and legs tightened around him when I began to recline. I flashed my eyes open to find we were in the bedroom, crawling up the bed. He lay me gently on the mattress and I unhooked from around him. Sadik backed away on his knees, until he left the bed. I felt bereft instantly. But he didn't go far, just to the foot, where he pulled off his trunks. That ripped chest and those hilly abs intimidated and aroused me at the same time. My legs closed on their own, rubbing together.

With a blank expression, Sadik reached over and parted my thighs, his feline eyes beaming directly on me. He climbed the bed again as I watched him over a heaving chest. My eyes struggled to remain open, groin roiling deliciously again. His aplomb face dropped between my legs, and his tongue landed directly on my throbbing clitoris. My back arched over the mattress and face stretched wide as my eyes squeezed. How could it feel so sensitive two minutes ago and be so needy now?

He thrashed with a demanding speed and pressure. His palms pushed the back of my thighs up until my kneecaps were toward my ears. He sucked and beat with hurried speed.

"Oh, god..."

Without notice, I felt it in my shoulders first when one whipped hard and fast into the mattress, then bombs imploded in my groin. As prickles of pleasure detonated all over, I began to cry out in volumes of insanity. And it wouldn't stop. My thighs shook uncontrollably around his head. Shoulders flapped with fury, and my teeth chattered.

Still enduring small trembles, I was able to crack open my lids. Sadik was standing on his knees—oh, my god—erect cock in his hand, stroking. It was a monster and alive: swollen bulbous head, mean veins running indiscriminately around it. And his sac... Dear god, it was huge, loaded, and hanging from the silky bush of tangerine wiry hairs. And there was hair around his curvy, muscular thighs spread wide between mine.

My eyes roved back up to his face, passing his fondling hand and monster penis. His full lips were glossed with...me, and his eyes seared my skin feverishly.

"I got another question," he croaked, the muscles around his eyes straining, pecs flexing. "It's kind of non-negotiable."

I swallowed, not believing the levels of arousal I'd experienced with a man. Still heaving, I nodded, telling him to go.

"Bareback."

There were a few seconds of processing that phrase for me to catch its meaning. That was a challenge as I watched the tip of his raging dick glisten at the eye.

Bareback...

I nodded, granting him permission. To be evident, I widened my legs. We were both recently tested for this reason. Right? Then he leaned over me, eyes closing as his lips met mine. The taste of them was lewd, musky, erotic, and downright intimate. I licked his tongue, pulled on his lips, and did it all over again. My heart galloped in my chest as it became clearer this was the moment. I'd finally have this private side of Sadik. I was finally giving him a piece of me that could never be undone. I didn't care. I wanted it. Needed it.

My hands were at the sides of his face when I felt the first intrusive thrust. His hips made wide an usually uninhabited area. My eyes opened, and he continued to kiss me.

"Breathe, Bilan," he whispered against my lips. "It's how you're going to relax."

I was heaving again, hips locked. "Okay."

Slow rocks into me didn't get him very far.

"Bilan?"

"Hmm?" I felt so tight, I couldn't breathe.

"The first night I met you..."

"Mmmhmm..."

I guessed the small smile he offered, peering directly into me, was to disarm me. His gaze went over my head before I lost his eyes.

"I saw those freckles, big brown eyes...round mouth, and I knew I'd have you," he husked in my ear, then kissed my temple. "That didn't sound all that romantic, did it?"

"Uhn-uhn," I answered, feeling infinitesimal drives into my core.

This was harder than I fantasized. Sadik was a real, for real man in my arms, pushing into my womb.

"When I left the diner that first night, I couldn't get you out of my head. It took a few days, but I swallowed my pride and went back. I had to get your attention."

"Via Christina C. Jones?" I grunted my sarcasm.

Sadik chuckled lowly, kissing my chin. "That didn't work out well for me, did it?"

"No." My lungs held.

"Call it psychic powers, but I knew you'd be a tough push—no pun intended."

"Stop it. This pressure is no—" My lungs hiccupped. "—joke."

His hips circled. "If you would let me finish, I'll tell you I cheated."

"On Lia?"

"No..." he croaked playfully. "On my unfailing skills at getting the attention of a woman."

My eyes bounced around, over his head and shoulders. "I don't get it."

Sadik didn't speak for a beat. "I didn't run into you at the Pixie concert. I knew you'd be there."

"How?" I felt myself contract around him.

He kissed my neck, rocking into me. "The night I saw you reading the book, I'd been there for over an hour waiting on you. I was in the booth behind you and your girls when you were discussing your tickets."

What?

If this were true, it meant Sadik had stalked me before I had him, after the Ameerah concert when Randi and I went to his friend's club. My mind began to reel back to that night, looking for any sign of his presence. I recalled Tasche being upset about the quality of the seats, remembered Randi's cold comments when I asked to borrow a few of her things.

"Damn, bitch, you need panties and a bra, too?" Randi was being shady, as she could do at times.

While I gave Randi a hard gaze, Tasche mumbled, "Who the fuck is that sitting over there?"

"Oh, my... Fine ass fuckin' Sadik."

Sadik...

A gush of holding air pushed from my lungs. Randi said his name! That fact thrilled me. It was vague in my memory chamber, but there. He was there. Sadik was at the din—

"Uh..." I whimpered when hit with a tingle of sensation in a place never felt before.

"Goddamn, Bi—lan," he chopped up my name, thrusting into me. "Yes..."

He moved over me like a single muscle, plunging into my core with riveting hip drives, reaching deep. My hands clasped onto his sculpted back, trying to anchor the sensation I couldn't name against the enduring pressure.

"Don't do that," he droned, lunges increasing. Pressure easing. Pleasure isolating. But I didn't know what to stop doing. "Shit, baby..."

Sadik thrust into me hard twice more, filling me to the hilt before holding suspended while cupping me in his arms. A mewling cry emitted from his nose as he shuddered over me, the muscles in his back flexing considerably. My eyes flew open and body tensed at the feel of him coming apart over me...inside of me.

I waited for him to still before breathing again. Slowly, Sadik began peppering kisses down my chin and throat.

"I'm sorry about that." His pitch was desolate.

I licked my lips. "About what?" The fullness?

"My bareback'ing backfired on me." His eyes roved up to me and I swear, my heart skipped a beat at the glow he exuded. If it were possible, Sadik was even sexier after sex. His russet skin beautifully luminous. "I wasn't expecting you."

"What does that mean?"

Sadik's brows furrowed. "When was the last time you've had sex?"

My head reared back into the mattress. "When is your baby due?"

His eyes narrowed. "Don't do that now, Bilan," he growled, expression crestfallen.

"Then why would you ask me that question?"

He lay plank over me, out of breath, and gaping for a while. I had no idea how this beautiful moment took a bizarre turn. I could still feel him pulsating inside of me.

Then his face descended and Sadik kissed me softly on my lips. "This isn't what we do after magic like that, baby. I don't want to fight with you."

"And I don't want to either." I exhaled. "Look... Clearly, there are some things you're not ready to open up to me about. I don't like it, but I've accepted it. Give me the same boundaries. I'm so out of my element here, Sadik. And no matter how far out I go with you, I can't seem to stop myself."

His chest was still heaving when he asked, "What does that mean?"

"It means I'm out 'there.' Okay? It means I'm more vulnerable in this thing with you than I was out there in the lows of the Pacific without any experience. Can you believe I jumped in there just to find you? How insane is that, Sadik? I don't even know you!"

"Yet." He reared, pulling out of me.

That single move caused my sex to pulse around him; I was so sensitive down there. Sadik left from between my legs.

"Where are you going?"

"To get ready to take you out to dinner and a show. Suddenly, I'm inspired to get out 'there' with you and let you get to know me."

My eyes bulged and jaw collapsed as he climbed off the bed.

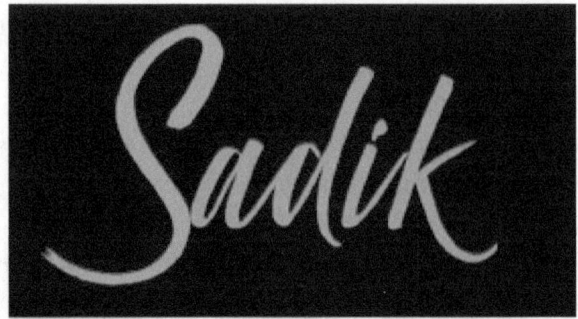

The entire audience was up on their feet, applauding. A few whistled and some shouted. Bilan clapped with inspired enthusiasm as the curtain closed on the final act of the musical presentation. When I had enough, I motioned for her to take her seat. Not too long after, those around us did the same. I went for my drink at the table in front of us as jazz music began to pour into the air.

"You liked that?"

Bilan smiled, stretching her eyelids while adjusting her dress in the sofa chair. "More than I ever thought I could." I pulled the tumbler to my mouth. "So, you like classical music?"

"I enjoy music. Period. Always have." I took another sip, then placed the glass on the table in front of us.

"Is one of your parents a musician?"

"Nah." I stretched back in my seat, enjoying the breeze coming into the makeshift night club on the beach in the style of old world cabaret. Dozens of tables formed rows of a U-shape in front of the stage. The lights were low and red, and the ambiance sensual. It was dope. The tables were small enough to create a room of intimacy, but large enough to serve dinner before the show got started. The music was decent, too. "But they made sure all were exposed to music."

"Nice." She shook her head slowly. "Do you prefer classical?"

I took a moment to consider that. "My ear is moody. I appreciate instrumentation without the layer of vocals. They can sometimes be distracting. But I like hip-hop. R&B's my first love. I dig gospel, too."

Her eyes balloon. "Gospel?"

I chuckled. "Of course! It surprises you that I believe in God?" Averting her eyes, Bilan shook her head. "Are you a Believer?"

"Muslim." She reached for her glass distractingly.

I was quickly reminded of her dominant culture. Bilan was Somali. The official belief in Somalia was Islam.

"But your parents spent their childhood here in the States. They were primarily raised here."

She took a sip of her drink, nodding before she swallowed. "But they held to their roots." She shrugged, eyes on a nearby waitress dressed in heels, fishnet stockings, and sleeveless and legless bodysuit. "My father's practices faded a few years before we lost the restaurants. My mother tried to keep going, taking us to the mosque for Juma'a, and things like that. But then..." Her voice faded. She cleared her throat. "Then she had to take care of my father when he got sick. Eventually, she got sick, too. We didn't practice much, even though I know better."

"Don't beat yourself up. You're technically second generation American since your mother was born here. I'm sure you and your brother were more influenced by American culture than you were Somali."

She scoffed. "That's for darn sure with Abshir. That dude had not an ounce of cultural pride in him." Her brown eyes rolled.

I nodded, taking a sip of my drink. "What took you so long to go to school?"

"Her."

"How so?"

"My father got sick when I was in high school. Trying to keep up with him... Caring for him was a full time job for her. She did it alone, being a private woman when it came to her marriage. I applied for schools and got accepted to a few. But he was really bad at my graduation. So bad, my mother looked...old. I think I knew then I couldn't leave her." She shrugged with her head and a pouted bottom lip. "I pushed it back. He died about a year later. Not too long after that, she got sick. It all happened back to back. Abshir got arrested, then sentenced. She passed while he was in custody. I think she gave up." Her head shook faintly. Then Bilan took a deep breath. "Right after her funeral, I applied to schools again and got in."

The topic saddened her. It was counterintuitive for her to be upset. I needed to navigate the conversation.

"Elementary education. What made you pursue that degree?"

"I always wanted to teach. My mother wanted to teach. It was all I ever said I wanted to be. So, I went for it."

"And now?"

"What do you mean?"

"What do you want to do?" I recalled her struggling with this on the jet, but I wanted to know.

Bilan took her typical deep breath when wrestling with a thought, her eyes to her lap. "I don't know. I do know I'm not ready to be in a classroom. It's too routine for my life right now. I like the irregularity of my schedule. But I want to get my master's. Believe it or not, in my family, my parents were underperformers. Their mediocrity in education made them black sheep—well, some of the reason. My mother wanted me to get both, and back to back since I'd been letting the time slip past."

"I think you should get an MBA."

"Really?" She twisted her mouth.

"You have something else in mind?"

"No. I've applied to a few programs. I hate that I honestly don't know what lies ahead for me." She laughed. "I'll be homeless with a degree and no real job."

No, you won't...

"I'm serious. You should go for the golden master's."

"Why?"

I took another sip of my drink. "Because it's so versatile and gives you the basics of business. It can open up your understanding of entrepreneurship."

Bilan's eyes on me narrowed, but a smirk played on those lips. "Who said I want to have my own business?"

I lifted my palm in the air. "I'm just recommending options here. It, apparently, is in your blood. Your parents had a thriving business for a number of years. Right?"

She didn't answer, but her gaze remained on me. She lifted her glass to her lips for a drink. "What industries were your exes in?"

I wanted to laugh, but managed placidity.

"Several."

Her face fell and neck rolled in a "duh" manner.

It was my turn to shrug. "The most recent was law."

"Oh, yeah? Practicing what?"

"Real estate."

She nodded, poker face shitty as hell.

"And the one before her?"

I scratched my nose, slightly uneasy. "A veterinarian with a specialty in internal medicine."

Her lips pushed out ruminatively. "The one before that?"

I took my time with the last of my brandy, then glanced around for a waiter. "A tenured real estate agent."

"You mean the lawyer?" She damn near croaked.

"Nah." I shook my head. "She's how I met the lawyer."

Bilan's eyes flashed wide. "So, you like boss women." Her whole aura deflated.

"I like smart, ambitious women." I abhorred "boss women" in the way the kids used the phrase today. "I adore supportive women."

"Supportive as in what?"

"The women drawn to me tend to aspire to the life of a kingpin's wife—a former kingpin's daughter-in-law." This was true. It was the biggest stigma in my personal world. "I adore women who prefer to build with their man instead of taking titles from him." Even though Bilan stared at me, perplexed, that was some real shit. "My mother built alongside my father. He plucked her young, when she couldn't give a shit about what he had. My brother chose his wife, who owns and operates liquor stores throughout the state. These women were selected and bore crosses, they don't just flaunt crowns."

Although I'd come across women established in their careers, all they ever vocalized to me was early retirement and raising my children. That hadn't been enough for me. I needed more in a woman's ambition as far as I was concerned.

"Women tend to use you," she murmured, turning her head. "I never considered that." Then she turned back to me. "That's awful."

I waved it off. "No pity parties here. I'm sure it's a tear in the bucket for women every day, who constantly have niggas approach them for ass."

Bilan shrugged with her lips, and I laughed. That propelled her giggles.

"Am I right? Is that what your plight is like?"

Grinning hard, she peered over to me. "What? Like guys trying to sleep with me?"

"Yeah." I pouted before smiling.

"Stop it." She shook her head, hand on her forehead.

"What?"

"You're trying to pry again." She couldn't hide her smile. "You want me to talk about my sexual history!"

I damn sure was, and couldn't give a single fuck about my curiosity.

"You have the prettiest pussy I've seen, and I can't help but be obsessed about knowing who's seen it before me."

Bilan turned away again, self-conscious. She shrugged—again. I watched, tortured as she played with her lips contemplatively. That foot and leg crossed over the other, bouncing in the air.

She hummed I don't know before turning to me. "I think you should be more concerned about having it in your possession now than who had it before."

My head pushed back on my neck, brows rose. "Did you enjoy the best thirty seconds of my life, Ms. Asad-Yasin?"

She winked, fucking blowing my mind with unusual sensual aggression. "It was more like fifty-eight seconds, but I'm into second chances." How could I not find that funny? "How about we order flan to take back to the villa, you feed me, then we'll give you a second run?"

When I could do nothing but gaze at her, Bilan broke character and chuckled.

"Mmmmmm…" I moaned, head falling back over my shoulders between my elevated arms.

The bristle ends on the manila rope scraped my areola again. My groin stirred, open thighs squeezed and pelvis went rigid at the sensation.

Amazing…

"Look at me, Bilan," he commanded.

My eyes bolted open, and I was able to roll my head upright to face those darkened honeyed irises. They gleamed with sexual wickedness. Intense. His gaze on me was blazing, weakening me.

"Your nipples are beautiful, too." The tip of his tongue circled my left nipple before he kissed it. With the right, he continued slapping the stubbles of the rope against my sensitive breast. I still couldn't believe he'd snatched down four of the ropes stretched over the canopy. One, he used to tie my wrists together. Two, he tied together to create a rope to raise my wrists over my head. The last was used to sensually torture my skin. "Your breasts are fuckin' perfect, baby. The perfect shape of rain drops." His tongue stroked my nipple again.

I was teeming, body vibrating. Desire firing on all cylinders. Perspiration sprouted all over, and my core throbbed with incredible need. I was tied up. I let a man tie me up as I straddled the bed, my sex exposed.

Sadik's wicked mouth trailed down my belly, and my spine couldn't keep still. His teeth clamped onto the bed of my hair and yanked. The pain was unexpected, then my brain was jostled when his lips caressed the crease between my thigh and pelvis.

"Uhhhhh..." My body quaked, pelvis pain fizzled now.

"You don't like to express your pleasure, Bilan." Sadik's wrinkled forehead hinted his mood. "I like to hear how you feel, baby. Okay?"

He was sexy. Golden skin glistening against the candles that were magically lit when we arrived back at the bungalow. The glow revealed each stroke of ink on his casing. His orange stubble on its way to a full beard any day now, and I loved it. Sadik presented as a sophisticated, articulate corporate man. But underneath the scholar was a slick and cunning goon. The correlation became clearer the more time I spent with him. Sadik had layers to his soul.

He dipped his head and yanked my bottom lip with his mouth. "Bilan, answer me."

My eyes squeezed as I nodded, though it was false assurance. I didn't know how to express pleasure.

Then I felt strands slapping against my sensitive nub. A sleek grin grew on his face, and I knew he was teasing me down there.

"Whew..." I grunted, head collapsing backward again.

"Look at me, Bilan."

I struggled to force my head up again, and when I did, I caught Sadik's cut frame, bearing only black Calvin Klein boxers, rounding my body. I could hear him behind me, but didn't see him again until his head appeared between my flexing thighs. I sighed, tortured by the sight.

"Your pussy really is pretty, baby," he groaned before his palms gripped my hips, pulling me to his face.

"Ah!" My pelvis lifted when his tongue swiped over my cleft.

He pulled them back down and rolled his tongue between my labia. His smooth head twisted, licking all around, reaching nerve-endings I tried not to react to. Sadik's hand caressed my butt as his mouth busied on my sex. My body flapped and tightened against the pleasure,

268

brain delirious from the sensations. When I could feel him draw in my clit, suckling with sensual effort, I began to roll over his face, riding the waves to my orgasm. I knew it would be the next destination. My fists tightened, shoulders flexed as my groin stirred, building for my climax.

"Sadik..." I cried, ready to release in the crudest way to date: on his face.

Then he pushed my hips up, causing me to widen them in panic. I was completely disturbed by the abrupt ending of my ascent, my body vibrating with the need to release. Sadik snaked his body down the mattress, until we were pelvis to pelvis. I felt the hot flesh of his dick at first against my cheeks, springing like a rod. The sight of him reaching between us for his erection made me lightheaded. Those biceps curling, chest bubbled and strained, and abs flexing as though he was in pain.

He rubbed the bulbous head against my slickened lips back and forth, coating himself with me. His navigation slipped, bumping it against my clit and my spine arched.

"Ahhhh!" I cried, pebbled nipples rising toward the canopy.

"Shit..." he swore, movements beneath me sped until I could feel him breach me below. Initially, I wanted to panic, remembering the fullness earlier. "Ride me, Bilan," he whispered, chords hoarse.

"I don't know—" My eyes rolled closed at the first spike of pleasure from him drilling into me.

My hips began to move, exploring. Chasing traces of pleasure. They were down there. He was so thick, rubbing against sensitive spots I couldn't quite locate, but certainly felt.

"Yes," he susurrated. "Use me for your pleasure. Every inch of me. Any part of me. I'm here to satisfy you."

I was full. Oh, so full, gyrating in awkward increments onto him. But, already, echoes of pleasure rang out on my groin. Promising prickles of sensation shooting up my groin.

"Help me," I demanded with squeezed eyes.

"Come here, baby," he groaned, lifting midway in the air.

His hands clasped onto my hips, lifting them and driving me into him. Biting my bottom lip feverishly, I went into my head to adapt to

269

the rhythm—the pleasure. It was there. The more I grinded, the more my walls relaxed for him. The more he sucked on my nipples, the creamier my walls grew. The more he coached, the more fluid my independent strokes became.

"You feel me deep, baby?" His helpless groans melted me each time.

Sadik's eyes were closed, his face completely relaxed.

I did feel him deep, deeper than I knew this thing could go. Pleasure sparked and expounded in my groin. I rocked against it, feeling it grow. Even the motion of my hips intensified it. I couldn't believe emotions could be mixed with physical gratification like this. Had no idea pleasure could be mutual during intercourse. I let the fire inside me ignite and rocked, and rocked, and rocked, and roc—

"Oh, God!" slough deeply from my lungs, and my hips began to buck on their own accord.

"Yes," he breathed directly in my ear. "Get it, Bilan."

My entire frame shuttered as I imploded, energy on hyper-drive. I could feel my walls contract around his fullness as I drove up and down…up and down. It was a resounding reverberation all over my body. Sadik plummeted into me from beneath. He banged into my core, reviving the echoes of pleasure. My mind went numb with unadulterated bliss. I was so gone.

Completely.

Utterly.

Lost.

"Goddamn…" Sadik swore as he continued to buck into me.

His arms rounded my back and squeezed me into his bedewed chest. The powerful beat of his heart banged against my abdomen. He thrust into me slowly, several times more before freezing, holding me in his embrace. I couldn't stop shivering, my chest heaving against his head.

"You okay?" he murmured.

"No," I croaked honestly.

I felt off, couldn't control my shakes or breathing.

Sadik's torso reared. "Fuck!" His arms lifted to my wrists and worked to unknot the rope. "My bad, Bilan."

270

My chest continued to heave, face folded and I knew. The knot was untangled, my wrists dropping mechanically too fast. Pain thwarted in my shoulders, and a sharp howl pushed from my belly. Crashing against his chest, I began to cry.

"Hey..." He gathered me to him, lifting us into the air to rearrange me without my help. It took a few tugs but eventually, I was nestled into him with closed thighs. "Tell me what I did wrong."

"Nothing," I whispered, tears in my voice, too. My body shivered. "I just feel..."

"Feel like what, Bilan?" There was urgency in his tone. "You have to tell me."

"Just...raw." It was true. This was new to me, too. Everything concerning Sadik had been a new experience. I hated it. Instantly, I wished I didn't reserve myself so much, just so I could be prepared for this moment. With him. "It's stupid."

"It's not!" he bit back, rubbing my back. "What can I do better?"

"Nothing. You were fine." Perfect. "Just give me a minute."

He steeled. "To yourself?"

"No!" I barked. "Here. Right here." I broke down again.

What the hell is wrong with me?

His snug grip resumed. I felt sick with neediness, and from him. Only from Sadik. I hated it. It had to stop.

I began to peel from his hold and climbed from the bed.

"Where are you going?" His face twisted with frustration. Confusion...

I managed a smile, a cheery one. "Let's go take a dip."

"What?"

I waved him on. "Come on. Let's take the plunge!" Sadik's brow line lifted and chin dipped. "Aw, come on! I bet you've never jumped into the Pacific after sex." My forehead rose to challenge him.

Sadik considered it, or pretended to. My nervous giggle had his eyes shooting to me again.

"You sure you're good?"

I waved off the notion. "Just a little emo-phobic."

"Bilan," he tried.

"Come on!"

271

After taking a deep breath, Sadik slid down and stood from the bed. I took him by the hand and ambled to the deck off the front of the house, facing the ocean.

"One…" I began to countdown, hand in his. "Two. Three!"

Together, we jumped off the ledge in the darkness of the night, leaping into water. The doosh didn't alarm me as much this time as I sunk down toes first. The silky warmth of the water wasn't a new discovery either. Not even the stillness of sound bothered me. It was when I surfaced with closed eyes, I swiped them of the running water, and the first thing in sight was a glowering Sadik. I must have taken too long to spring up. He'd been waiting. He was concerned.

Before he could utter a word of complaint, I blubbered, "You gave me my first orgasm. Okay?" I managed to shout with limited lungs.

Sadik rolled his eyes, a dramatic reaction, making me feel even worse.

"Bilan," he droned before taking me at the arm and swimming closer to the shore.

When we were able to stand, he towered me, scowling. "You couldn't have said that upstairs in our bed?"

I rotated a shoulder, still feeling the ache from them being suspended over my head. Confusion was etched over my face. "The water seemed like a safer place."

It was sarcasm. Really!

"Look, it's clear to me you don't want to talk about your sexual history. I get it, but you're making it damn hard to avoid doing shit like this!"

"Why?"

"Why— Because as a man who wants to please you by way of orgasms, it would have been encouraging to know after it happened up there. You don't think I need that feedback?"

"For what? To add to your already pompous state?"

"What the hell are you talking about?"

"This trip—escape—is for you and not about me. Remember on your 'jet', when you told me to get in line?"

Sadik's globular shoulders dropped as he exhaled, and his eyes rolled. He swiped his nose, glancing away.

272

"I'm sorry about that. I lost my temper…had a lot on my mind this week, leading up to this trip."

"Like what?"

"Business…work."

"That's it." I stated rather than asked.

"It's nothing that concerns you."

That stung. Bad. I took a deep breath, slightly turning in the water, too.

"And I'm supposed to believe those things still aren't on your mind?"

Out of nowhere, I heard, "An employee—the same one that was the cause of me having to cut our picnic short at the park. I fired her, and now she's suing me. I had to type up a letter to my staff about our position regarding it."

"I'm sorry," I grumbled, brushing my hands over my face.

"It's not your fault."

"Yeah, but like you said earlier, we're not supposed to fight after doing what we did up there."

He scoffed. "Can you even name it?"

I shot back, "Can you?"

His head nodded softly. "Mental therapy. A connection, I hoped."

Like a child, I was speechless, without a clue on how to proceed.

"Did I do anything wrong?" His tone was softer. Blow my mind, yeah. I shook my head. "Is there anything I could do different?" I shook my head again. "Anything I can do better?" Again, I shook my head. "Were the ropes too—"

"Again, Sadik," I blurted again. "I wouldn't mind doing it again." And again.

Why was I reduced to a child around him?

Probably warranted…

Only when it came to sex.

He pulled me into him, making a splash when our flesh met in the water. It was instinctive for my hands to round his tapered waist and lay into his neck.

"I can't guarantee what's to come," he murmured over my head. "but I can promise to be completely honest with my feelings for you moving forward."

"Even if it means breaking my heart?" I joked dejectedly.

He shifted and took me at the shoulders. "Even if it means you breaking mine."

My mind attempted to tackle the meaning of that as we strode up the beach and back into the villa.

"Oh!" I cried out, enduring delicious thrusts from behind.

Our skin slapping, the fat of my hips—and everywhere else—flapped to and fro. I felt more helpless in this position than any other one. I couldn't see his face, measure the "connection" we were supposed to have when engaging in copulation. But I felt him. As he pounded into my core, gripped my hips with desperation, and splattered sweat onto my back, I felt every inch of Sadik. He was thick and long with ridges to tease delicate nerves of the walls of my sex. Deep inside, his impression resounded all the way into my womb.

And when my groin began to stir that familiar motion, I knew no matter the early hour of the morning when I rolled over to him, meeting his erection, I had to have him. When I tried to leave the bed to brush my teeth and wash my face, Sadik flipped me on all fours and buried his face in my butt, licking me senseless. Then he entered me from behind, and I didn't know how to receive him.

He was right; sex with Sadik was some form of therapy. This was our last morning in Costa Rica, the place where, oddly, my sexuality had been awakened and deeply disturbed. I knew I'd never be the same after this getaway. Sadik had given more than a graduation gift. We'd been at it all weekend, spending Saturday in the bed, cancelling the scheduled excursions. Then yesterday, after a late morning *rendezvous in the shower where Sadik used the faucet as an implement of pleasure, we were able to make it to a cooking class—yes, a cooking class. It was intimate, just the two of us with a world class chef. It was a fun and romantic way for Sadik to increase my desire for food. He hand-fed me along the entire experience, and by the time we were done, I was so revved up for him I couldn't keep my hands off his body. I had no idea where that facet of my personality came from, but I felt free to express sexual needs. To remedy that, Sadik pulled me into a pantry for my first session of clandestine sex where I had to choose between breathing and screaming during an orgasm.*

But now, minutes into his deep thrusting, I had no choice but to receive him. I was coming apart, thrust by thrust. My core jolted, spine dipped more, inviting him in. The soft fabric of the bedding teased my erect nipples, intensifying my senses. His helpless grunts over me propelled my launch as I pushed back into his drives.

"Goddamn, Bilan," he cried. "you're swallowing me..."

Before he was done, I was lost to an earth-shaking orgasm ripping me at the core. My pelvis rocked back into him, fingers clawed the sheets, and teeth clenched as I endured the indelible explosion. Sadik rocketed into me, pumping hot semen I'd wanted to taste, mumbling a string of expletives.

I groaned against his slow strokes, knowing he was momentarily depleted. Hearing his wheezing confirmed that.

"You can go get washed up now," he joked, slapping my hip.

I squirmed, giggling. "We're leaving," I croaked.

"Wanna stay a few more days?"

"We can't." I slammed my face into the pillows.

"I can. You just say the word." He used his palm to wiggle my butt. "Your ass is so sweet, Nalib."

That sent a cackle from my belly into the air. "Lin-what?"

"Nalib. You're not the only one researching names," he panted. "Yours is unique, too. Bilan means 'first born' and is given to the first born baby girl in a Somali family."

"Right. So where does that other name come into play?"

"Nalib is my nickname for you. It's your name spelled backwards. It means my last."

Humor drained from my face.

"You're stiffening." He palmed my cheek again. "Don't—"

"Your last what?" My wide eyes rolled all around the crisp white sheets beneath me.

Perhaps this position did have its benefits.

"My last everything," he groaned with charm as he circled a stroke, still mildly erect inside of me. "Don't close up on me, Bilan. I can't take that shit right after sex. You know this now."

"I—" I closed my eyes, squeezing them. "I just don't know what you mean by your last."

"My last girlfriend, Nalib. My last lover...hopefully."

I swallowed hard, growing lightheaded. "You want me to be your girlfriend?"

"You are my girlfriend, just a stubborn one I have to give time to get adjusted to it." No way I could gather the words to reply to that edict. Things went quiet for a spell, my mind whirring with questions—logic. "Bilan..."

"Hmm?" My eyes went wild again.

"I have a connect for an MBA program in Jersey. A friend of mine sent me a link yesterday. They have online and in-class courses, making it a flexible program for someone like you, who likes irregularity in your weekly schedule."

And when he said things like that, providing a balm after dropping a bomb, I was able to breathe again. I leaned forward, ejecting him from my body and turning to face him.

"You know the chairperson?"

He shook his head, wiping sweat from his brow, swollen chest still heaving, but mildly. "I have a connection to him. I can send an email this morning with the request. And before you ask, the request is just a meeting for you to get an introduction to their program, and for them to see if you're a good fit, too. It would be on your own merit: I don't know the people at the school. I doubt my friend has any control over their enrollment or practices at all. I just know he has the ear of the chair."

His tone was soft, eyes direct and sincere. An MBA program? I never considered it, but his adamancy influenced the possibility.

276

I nodded. "Okay," the word but a whisper. "I'd like that."

Sadik reached over and brushed his lips against my forehead. "Okay, Nalib. I'll do that while you shower, but first, I need to take a leak."

He hopped off the bed, managing a last smack to my rear. Just as he took off, one of his phones vibrated near me on the nightstand. Sadik turned back toward the bed.

"Damn." His brows met. "I thought I powered them both off."

I settled onto my side, peering over the nightstand. "Not this one. It's Lia."

"Shit." He grabbed his hanging penis. "Answer and tell her I'll be with her in a minute." He continued to the bathroom.

My face folded. Answer it? Your unborn child's mother? I bit my lip, challenging myself to be an adult about this. It was clear Sadik and Lia had, at most, just a sexual affair and created a baby from it. They were in agreement about it being over. If he asked me to answer it, it was because he wanted transparency. As the phone continued to ring, I gathered a sheet around my body, leaving the bed for the deck. At least when she saw my bare shoulders against the ocean, she'd think I was dressed for the beach rather than just finishing sex with the person she was calling.

I slid the virtual bar to answer. It took a couple of seconds to connect, which allowed me to prepare my greeting.

Lia's face appeared. It wasn't enhanced by makeup the way it had been the night we met. She looked even paler than the night Sadik FaceTime'd her at The Garden. Lia looked ghosted, shocked by me answering. That was understandable.

"Hey, Lia!" I tried for cheery; she seemed so down to earth the night of the Pixie concert. "Sadik's in the bathroom. He didn't want to miss your call and asked me to ans—"

Someone in the background spoke, causing Lia's regard to peer over the phone. That's when I noticed her eyes were pink at the rim, lips swollen, and cheeks puffy to Botox proportions, something I knew was out of the ordinary based on just the two times I'd seen her.

"I asked who the fuck is that?" a man shouted, and I believed at Lia.

She didn't speak.

"Honey, answer your father," a woman urged.

But Lia didn't speak. It was as if she couldn't from fear.

"Give me that goddamn—" I couldn't hear the rest from the whishing and crackling from the phone being snatched from Lia.

"No, Daddy!" she cried, but I could no longer see her.

Coming into view was a robust White man, thick dark brows, dark circles under his eyes, mostly salted hair, and a flaming red neck.

"Who are you?" He squinted with palpable energy into the screen.

My heart began to gallop and suddenly, I felt indecent, tightening the sheet at my chest. His unwavering scowl was bone-chilling. It was scarier than Sadik's undercurrent dark energy because with him, I felt an odd and uncanny sense of safety. This man's vibes told me he could harm me and sleep exceptionally well at night.

"Answer me! Who the fuck are you!" he barked into the phone. I couldn't speak to answer, my throat closed tight with fear. Tongue with a bitter coat of silence. He snarled, "Do you know who the fuck I am, bitch?"

"Daddy!" Lia cried behind him. "No!"

He continued, "I will find where you live, where you work, where your mother lays her head at night and make you regret dropping your panties for those exotic eyes, bald head, style, and that smooth talk." I blinked, utterly shocked and shaken. Lia tried calming him in the background, as did another mature female voice. This man didn't seem like the type to yield to compromise. "You hear me, you dumb cunt—"

The phone was snatched from my hand, making me recoil, and I dropped onto the wooden planks of the deck. My heart fell from my chest, and my entire frame vibrated with fear as I found Sadik standing over me as naked as the day he was born. His scowl more baleful than it had been in our worst fight, his eyes darker than they'd ever been when aroused.

"I don't give a shit about why your fuckin' face is on my screen," he growled, tone too calm, too deceiving. "That fuckin' point is moot at this time. What I will give you is the opportunity to apologize to my lady for your irrevocable disrespect."

The man scoffed. "Are you fucking kidding me? I will not apologize to no bitch you're romancing on a fucking beach. I see the background, you asshole. My daughter is here pregnant! All fucking alone while you're gallivanting God knows where with random whores—"

"Salvatore." Sadik was just a pitch over the man, but dominant in his tone. Commanding. "You don't know me."

"I don't know you?" The man seemed flabbergasted. "I knew your father before your dumb ass was ever born! Don't you ever tell me—"

"I'm not that Ellis." His tone still calm, threatening.

"What Ellis?"

"The Ellis you want to ruffle."

"The fuck do you mean! You bring disrespect to my daughter all these months since you knocked her up. Didn't even have the decency to tell me, like a man you were seeing her, and you want to talk ruffled feathers? Fuck you, you asshole!" His Italian accent was sharper the louder he shouted.

"When you're ready to apologize to my lady, you have my number. Get it from Lia. And speaking of Lia..." He bent over, resting his elbows on the railing. "I know you can hear me, Lia. You know this was unfair and inappropriate. You're not holding up your end of the bargain. But it's okay, sweetheart." His tone menacing. "We'll both get what we want real soon. This shit ends here."

Sadik tapped to end the call. After seconds of gazing out to the angry waters, his honeyed eyes fell upon me slumped against the rails, wrapped in a sheet stained with our weekend therapy.

"Let's shower so we can get out of here."

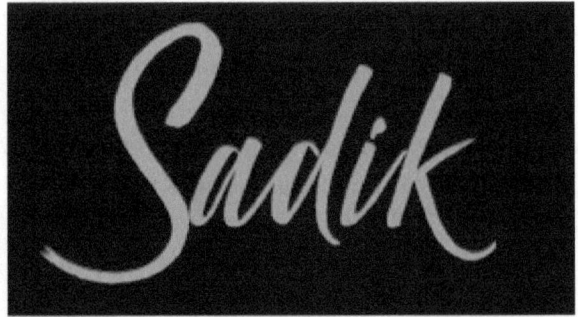

∞ 17 ∞

The captains greeted me and bowed their necks as we took for the stairs to board the jet. With my hand on the curve of her hip, I skipped up the steps behind Bilan. She went straight to the set of chairs we flew in on and plopped down. Without even looking at me, she went to the cloth bag she carried as a purse and dug out earplugs. I lay my Louis Vuitton Astralis on the sofa across from us, watching her plug her phone, then her ears, then select music.

It was clear: Bilan was upset. Although she willingly followed me to the shower, received an orgasm I pulled with my mouth from her sweet pussy. Even though she let me choose her clothes to fly home in, feed her breakfast before getting dressed. And despite the way she giggled at my joke when I wiggled the unopened box of condoms while packing our things, Bilan didn't give much outside of moans, obedience, and mirth. She was upset.

"We're not going to do this." I peered down at her, chin low and voice clear.

Bilan snatched a bud from her ear to ask me to repeat myself.

"We will not do this."

"Do what?"

"Go home angry. Not after the weekend we've had. We won't go home the same way we came out here."

Her head shook softly. "I'm just looking for music to get me comfortable. I want to sleep."

"Okay." I could understand her needing rest. We'd kept odd hours all weekend. "I have a bedroom in the back. We can nap after takeoff." The jet had begun to move on the runway, so I began to buckle up.

"It's okay to zone out after the weekend we've had, Sadik. It was pretty intense."

"And it will stay intense! Because that's how my feelings run for you!" I barked, causing Bilan to push back in her seat. She stared at me, eyes wide with fear, and I wanted to kick myself for losing it.

The shit with Rizzo had me buzzing with volcanic energy. I wanted to kill him. Put a fucking bullet in his head myself in front of Lia and Iban. That would teach them both to not involve me in their bullshit. And ol' Salvatore had just signed his death certificate. He'd soon know.

I rubbed my eyes, suddenly feeling drained my damn self. "I'm sorry."

"You don't have to apologize, but please say something about what happened."

I dropped my arm and looked her directly in the eyes. "What do you want me to say?"

Her hands shot into the air. "Something of assurance. Make me feel as secure as I did before they called. Manipulate me again so I can resume thinking it's okay to spend time with you, knowing you have a baby on the way."

I forged a smile. "I'm your boyfriend, remember? You have to spend time with me."

Bilan took a breath, ready to respond, but was interrupted by the captain announcing takeoff. I pulled out gum from a side pouch on my chair to help with the air pressure. When I glanced up to offer Bilan a piece, her eyes were still on me and mouth balled.

"What?" I asked.

"My assurance. I may have accepted your baggage, but I won't set the precedent for you treating me just any way. Give me the respect of transparency if you want my acceptance, Sadik."

Shit...

I dropped my face into my hands.

"Wasn't it you who made us girlfriend and boyfriend?" The jet began its course down the runway, speeding before we launched. "You're not making this an attractive deal."

My chest and mind roared with the same force as the jet. I felt pressure like never before. The desperate need to make shit right. For the first time, I actually gave a fuck. Without reservation, I wanted Bilan. More than I wanted the big account I'd be acquiring in a couple of days, more than I cared how my family would feel about it, even more than I wanted the shit with Iban and Lia cleared up.

Then we were off, in the air and I couldn't take the pressure anymore.

As the sound from the jet lessened, as did the pressure, I reached over and grabbed her by the hands. "Salvatore and my father are old associates. They've known each other longer than you've been alive. Underworld bullshit. He considers it a slap in the face, having his daughter pregnant the way she is."

"Because you're black?"

"Much of it, yes. The other part of it being our families just don't cross socially. So, as you can imagine, there has been tension over the past few months. Lia knows how delicate the details behind her pregnancy are. She also knows her father's anger has blinded him from thinking logically." I took a deep breath. "I'm leaving out a lot of significant details because it involves family, but I swear to you, the moment all is revealed, you're the first person I'm running to with each of them."

Bilan snatched her eyes from me, looking out the window.

She let out a breath. "Thanks, Sadik." Her eyes finally met mine again.

"So, you can understand?" Why the fuck was I so desperate?

She nodded. "I respect your privacy. I just need to know I'm respected, too."

"You are." I swear it.

We remained in that position, holding hands until the captain announced we were free to move about the cabin. I pulled Bilan up and walked her to the back, where my bedroom was. We stretched out on the bed and talked about her love of reading until she passed out first. She'd been reading books since eight, and her taste had evolved over the years. As I considered the types of books she liked and obsessed *over how I could use that to my advantage, I slipped into slumber myself.*

"Now—what, now?" My father leaned his ear in my direction as I sat in a chair in front of his desk.

Iban, in the chair next to me while facing him, grunted, "I knew you had some bullshit with you! When do you ever just bounce the fuck outta town with some bitch?"

I was two seconds off his ass and had to remind myself I'd deal with him later.

My attention went back to my father on his throne. "I said I'm dating the kid, Abshir's, sister."

"The one that works at the diner?" he asked, visibly surprised.

"That would be the one, sir." I cleared my throat, adjusting the collar of my shirt.

"How the hell did this happen?"

I took a deep breath, knowing what I had to do. "A few months ago at the diner."

"The night of the Energy anniversary party," he recalled.

"Yes." I nodded.

"But you were with Lia. I don't understand this shit, Deek." He sat up behind his big wooden desk.

I braced myself, scratching my brow. "Yeah. That night, I took Lia to the diner to pick up some desserts. Bilan was there working. That was the night I met her."

"Then you start fuckin' her, flyin' her out to Costa Rica and shit?" Iban griped. "You know how dangerous that is? She know her brother a dead man as soon as they fuckin' release his ass, and it'll be by a Ellis gun?"

"No." I couldn't even look at him first. "She doesn't know any of that, at least, not from me. She doesn't even speak of her brother much. I doubt they're close at all. She's practically been on her own since the warehouse was robbed."

"What does she do?" my father asked.

"Other than the diner? She had a part-time student role on her campus. But she just graduated, and is looking to start graduate scho—"

"Oh! That's the bullshit!" Iban laughed while pointing my way. "That's the hook to your ass. You like them educated bitches. It don't matter her brother a robber. Shit! How the fuck we know she ain't one herself, just not in the drug game."

"What other game could she be in, Iban?" I had to know.

"The getting niggas—setting up goofy niggas game." He waved me off dismissively, tossing his head back. "Man, cut that shit off, Deek."

"He's right, Sadik," my father agreed. "That pussy, Ab, will pay right along with Damien, who hired him, for robbing me and killing my men. It's not my style for them to even be breathing six years later. You want a grieving girlfriend, crying over her dead brother, too. Have you thought about how that'll affect you?"

I had. A lot, too. So many scenarios shot through my head about how this could all play out. My father's revenge would be carried out with or without my input. Ab was on borrowed time. But even that wasn't enough to deter my interest in this girl. I'd claimed her this weekend, with open eyes. Announcing it to my family was the final act of ceremony for Bilan being my lady.

I stood, buttoning my jacket. "I thought it was necessary for me to tell you as soon as I realized it turned into something."

Iban pushed air from his mouth. "As soon as it turned meaningful," he mocked. "How nice of you, Sadik."

"It's what I do," I snapped. Iban's wild eyes hit me. "I'm frank, honest, forthcoming with my shit. I don't hide. As a man, I don't have to. And I don't make messes."

"This sure seems like a fuckin' mess to me," Iban shot back. "You fuckin' falling for a chick whose brother we finna kill. If that ain't mess, I 'on't know what the fuck is."

"It's an inconvenient truth, Iban. But I deal with them head on—"

"Enough!" my father barked, standing from his desk. He walked around it toward us. I was his stop. "I know you. Know when you get your mind fixed on shit, ain't no turning back. But you know me, too. Know that same stubborn shit comes from your daddy." His chin dipped. "So you know, you'll be going to a goddamn funeral to hold this girl's hand."

Our eyes bounced against each other's, back and forth. I didn't like that prophecy, and he knew it. But I understood it was inevitable and there wasn't shit I could do about it. He turned for the door. "Your mother's waiting for us to eat." He closed it behind himself, leaving us alone.

"Maaaaaan," Iban started until I leaped in the air, doing a one hundred-eighty degree turn with my finger to his face.

"The end of the fuckin' week!" I growled. "You have until then to come clean about this baby or I'm doing it myself." I turned for the door.

"Deek, man,"

"Fuck you, Iban!" I faced him. "There's nothing I wouldn't do for you, man. Nothing! And you know that, and use me like this."

"I'm not using you!"

"You don't hold me down in front of the old man. You turn the fuckin' knife in my back every time you create strife or disagree with a move I make."

"We never agree on shit!"

"But our brotherhood! We always protect each other, Iban. And for months, I haven't felt that shit reciprocated."

I didn't give him an opportunity at a rebuttal when I opened the door, leaving him to himself.

"Well, Ms. Asad-Yasin, this was...astounding!" the Dean of Business stood and offered his hand.

His assistants followed suit, leaving me as the last to take to my feet.

I met his palm in a firm handshake, then theirs.

"I appreciate your time, Dr. Chung. This was enlightening." My smile was measured, unequivocal, yet soft.

"Most enlightening." His unbridled smile widened, and his grip was strong and spirited.

With a neck bow, I offered, "I appreciate that."

The small group consisted of five attendees, most of whom were staff of the School of Business, and two were students. The interview went far better than I thought; my nerves cleared after the first fifteen minutes. Although they were impressed with my GMAT score, if I was honest, I thought I'd flunk this "meeting" completely because I didn't have a business plan or general aspirations for business. Thankfully, Sadik emailed me talking points about management and entrepreneurship to prepare me.

"I'll walk you out," Dr. Chung offered when the round of goodbyes was over. "Do you know your way out of here?" he asked as I collected my things to go.

"I do," I breathed, standing with my briefcase. "Thanks."

As we took to the door, Dr. Chung commented, "We look forward to hearing back from you. I think our program would benefit from a bright and innovative mind such as yours."

We stopped at the conference room doors, where I gave him a final handshake. "Again, I appreciate your time and reception, Dr. Chung."

His final smile made my lungs hike with excitement. My stride out of there was on clouds, that's how light my bounce was on the way to the elevator. I couldn't contain my smile. Three days ago, I stepped off a private jet, back from an exclusive tropical vacation with a man I found to be absolutely intriguing and unbearably attractive. It was becoming sickening, even to me. I couldn't scrub his facial expressions, grunts, or scent from the back of my eyes or my nostrils. See! Even now, after a seemingly successful interview, I was thinking of him.

As I boarded the elevator, I realized it was unsettling, but I couldn't ignore it anymore. Sadik had gotten beneath my skin. Was this normal? Did this make me weak? Could I now count down the days until disappointment came with him?

I sure didn't want to. The man was kind…smart, worldly, and resourceful. Not to mention he was rich and awfully sexy. Those last two shouldn't have mattered, but I couldn't deny them. It was easy to become intrigued by a "rich" man. It told of his drive and focus. And attraction didn't come easy for me. Most guys were full of so much game, it covered their physical features.

My eyes swept down to my feet. They were comfortable and cute in Yves Saint Laurent. The olive skirt and ivory blouse he picked out somehow empowered me, propelled my confidence all the way into this meeting. My appearance annihilated my fears and doubts as I presented myself up there.

Did he know it would? How?

Once I arrived in the lobby, my mind ran in a different direction. I wanted to see him. I threw myself into work hours after landing in Jersey. The demand on the job has shifted. Nicky had his new hires, Maria and Pedro, making more of my desserts. When I asked him *about it, he gave some excuse of needing them in case I decided to quit now that I was done with school. It was so unfair, seeing I told him I had no plans to. This meeting boosted my confidence after being in that tense environment at work these past few days. And I owed it all to a dear friend—boyfriend. I'd suddenly had an increased craving for Sadik.*

How does this happen?

My heart began to bang against my chest, my mouth salivated, eyes went wild swinging from left to right as my brain conjured erotic scenes of days ago. I could hear my pulse in my ears, my breathing turned choppy.

I rubbed my lips together while blindly watching people enter and exit through the revolving doors. Before I knew it, I pulled out my phone.

"Bilan?"

"Hi, Rory." My eyes bounced left and right as my pulse pounded. "Are you busy?"

"You need something?"

"Yeah." I bit my lip. "Where's Sadik?"

"At the office. Want me to call him for you?" I couldn't decide if her tone was laced with suspicion or concern.

Several things had happened since our return. Sadik sent boxes of designer clothes, shoes, and bags from JAGMisha Boutique to my house. They arrived the following morning before my shift. Apparently, my new "boyfriend" had a fetish for dressing me, and his style was impeccable. No more borrowing clothes from Randi for a while. The other thing was he gave me access to his assistant, Rory. He was sure to emphasize that I was to contact her during any emergencies if he was unavailable. Apparently, Rory was with Sadik the most. Now, on my first attempt of her services, I wasn't so confident this was a good idea.

"No!" rushed from my lungs. I tried rebounding quickly from that curtness. "Do you know how long he'll be there?"

Rory didn't answer for a while. That's when I realized she'd been suspicious. And how could I blame her?

"He here all day. You sure you 'on't want me to call him? If something wrong, Bila—"

"No! I... Uhhhh..." I grabbed my forehead, eyes squeezing close. My pelvis throbbed with unrecognizable need. What was going on with me?

"Be careful, girl. Niggas like that will wine, dine, and fuck the sanity out your ass. Then you're left behind, looking for your wig when he move on. And I don't mean your hair. It's your mind that go when he do."

Randi's words of advice still rang in the back of mind as my eyes bounced as fast as my mind moved. But I couldn't yield to that heeding. Something more—bigger—was compelling me into an unusual daring place. And that's where I wanted to be. I wanted to risk my pride to feel the exhilaration I did each moment I spent in Sadik's presence. Once that truth was out in the universe, I was free to make my choice.

"You think it's possible for me to sneak up on him?" My eyes had narrowed, mouth dried.

"Like..."

"Like pay him a surprise visit. I've got great news to share with him, and I want Mr. Cool's surprised smile today."

It felt like hours of silence on the line. I couldn't hear what was going on around me, only the sudden ringing in my ears.

"I'll come scoop you. Where you at?"

My eyes blossomed with fresh hope. I glanced all around, searching for an answer in the figurative sense.

"He's in a meeting happening in there." Rory pointed straight ahead to the closed doors of a room labeled Conference on the plate posted on the wall.

A whole hour later, I was standing in the hall of Ellis International, the office of Sadik's primary business. It was a modest unit inside a business park, modern in design. Most doors were frosted glass, the walls contemporary gray hues, and carpet a strong blue. The scent stirred my belly. The place smelled…professional, intimidating, and possibly because I was uninvited in a facet of his world new to me. But everything about Sadik was new to me. Even craving him in the middle of the day.

This is insane…

I approached the doors, then turned to find Rory still looking my way. With dramatic effect, she turned and walked off with both hands tucked inside the pants pocket of her big boys' suit. I rolled my eyes back toward the doors. Through the opaque glass, I could see bodies moving and hear voices. I pushed in one and glanced around the room. A man standing at the head of the conference table continued speaking to the room, yet most others turned their attention to me. It didn't take long to find Sadik. He sat at the other end of the table, a laptop open and a mountain of paperwork in front of him while he tended to one of his phones.

"Our 3PL wing has expanded over thirty percent this last fiscal year, and we've been able to identify and adjust on all customs laws and regulations. Acquiring this next account would put us beyond our goal for this quarter." He finally stopped and glanced over at me, too.

Eventually, a woman of Hispanic descent asked, "Can I help you?"

That's when Sadik's golden head pulled up from his device. He didn't speak right away as I hoped. But the muscles around his feline eyes relaxed. His suit jacket clad elbows came up to rest on the table, his chin planted on one of his palms as he waited.

My nostrils expanded from nervousness and annoyance. He was going to make this hard for me. I managed a smile as I lifted my chin.

"Hi, I'm Bilan. I apologize for interrupting what looks to be an important meeting. I'm looking for the owner."

"May I ask for what?" Sadik turned the heat up.

"I brought her lunch."

The whole room reacted, most of which by laughing. Some of those laughs included confusion. My face broke into an unbidden smile. Sadik finally stood and rounded the table, making his way toward me.

"Continue, Rashad. I have that Kolwaski next." His gait was confident, aura powerfully uncompromised.

I backed out as he neared me, and Sadik closed the door before taking me at the small of my back.

"Everything okay?"

I nodded, unable to hide my girlish grin. "Yup."

"Just stopped by to meet the owner?" His grin was adorable, my walls constricted.

He took me at the hand and led me down the hall.

"And tell her how today was crazy successful. Dr. Chung is the sweetest man. He was so nice and smart. Oh, my God, I was so nervous, but by the end of the meeting, I was so happy to see it through. He told me to submit my application and he's sure I won't have any problems." As I gushed, ambling next to him, Sadik didn't speak.

He was stopped by a young guy, Black and professionally dressed. Sadik answered questions about their warehouse. When that was done, we rounded a corner leading into an office. When Sadik closed the door right behind me and I gazed around the large room, I knew it was his office. The artwork was sophisticated Black. Sadik crossed the room for his desk while I got lost in the décor. Sepia images of Black figures on all walls. In the corner, on a waist-level and all-glass pedestal, was a gold sculpture of Jesus Christ on the cross. Its fine details astounding.

I walked across the office to view the contents on his desk. Every item was spaced from each other. No clutter, all organization. But there, at the right edge was a digital picture frame. I watched patiently as pictures appeared of people I didn't know, most of which bore similar features to Sadik. Some had sandy blond hair, a few had his nose and cheek structure, a couple even had the feline eyes trait. They were beautiful people flashing across the screen. My heart skipped a beat when I saw pictures of me on a beach, swimming in the water, fast asleep on a netted tarp over the water, diving into the water, and in scuba gear on top of a wrecked bus.

At the edge of his desk, he wordlessly gazed my way. His inspection began at my head and roved down to my "Amber" Yves Saint Laurent sandals.

A faint smile lightened his face. "You came all the way out here to tell me about the meeting?"

I nodded…a little too eagerly. Sadik's eyes narrowed into slits, and his grin broadened cheaply.

"Is that the only reason you pulled up on me in the middle of my day?" His full lips twitched.

An involuntary deep pull of air vacuumed into my lungs, and I pushed it right out. My face tightened with contemplation and eyes fell, but I couldn't find the words. I tried to ignore it, but couldn't. The pictures…they sent me over the top in emotions. I was included in the slideshow with his family. It was the sweetest gesture ever.

Then I was yanked forward. My body smacked against the hardness of his suited frame. His warm hands were at my hips, then moved forward. One shifted up, pulling my head toward his. The scent of his cologne at this proximity fluttered my eyes closed.

His lips were against my ear when he whispered, "I've been thinking about you non-stop, too."

The pictures were proof.

I sucked in a breath. My eyes rolled behind closed lids when I grated louder, "Not the way I've been thinking about you."

That emotional admittance made me want to cry.

"You wanna bet?" His lips were on my ear again.

I swallowed deeply, felt a sudden need come over me and rushed him, meeting his lips with stark impatience. I felt his deep groan push from his lungs and hit my face. My tongue pushed through his soft lips. His mouth tasted of jelly beans and Bvlgari. Quickly responding, his tongue swept mine. I refused to be afraid as I had been the first two days in Costa Rica, my lips and tongue moved aggressively…faster, wanting to taste his soul.

His groan echoed around the room, then he pulled back. His eyes were half-masted, lips full and glistening. "Don't do that, Bilan," he begged, vocals gravelly.

Sadik was out of breath and…disheveled. He stood to his feet and sauntered with grace to the door and twisted the lock on the knob as he peered over to me. Then he slowly took to his desk, sitting behind it and picking up the phone.

"Hold my calls. I'll be ready for the meeting with Kolwaski in a minute," he murmured, then listened in. Sadik nodded. "Alright. Thanks."

Before he could hang up, I reached for him, not having a clue what I was doing or where the boldness was coming from. I only focused on the need. I needed this man unlike anything else in life. As I went for him, he pivoted in his chair and reached for me. My lips were on his, his hands were at my legs, roving. The hem of my skirt raised to my hips as I moaned into his mouth. Cool air hit my backside and his fingers were on the string of my panties, roughly pulling them down. I opened my thighs to him with ease. Our tongues swiped and teased one another's. My hands went to his neck, feeling more confident than ever to roam his person.

I lifted each foot to be relieved of my panties. A clanking sound caught my attention and before I could withdraw to see what it was, Sadik was pulling me onto his lap. I swung my right leg over his and straddled him, my arms circled his shoulders as I sucked on his tongue. I could feel his hot hands rounding my back before pushing down to my bare cheeks and squeezing. I tried stifling another moan.

"Bilan…" he called against my busy lips. "I'm gonna fuck you right here."

I couldn't decide if it was a warning or a tester. My head reared from his face and our eyes met. Sadik's expression was deadpan. I didn't think for a second, didn't want to hesitate. My shaky hands went to his waist in search of a buckle or latch. A guttural growl pushed from his throat as his hands went to the sides of my face, pulling me to him. His mouth was more aggressive this time and I tried to keep up. I didn't know what had come over me. Where did this bold Bilan come from?

My hips moved over him, needing him. One hand left my face, and I could feel him between us. His mouth went to my neck and my head rolled back, giving into the tickling pleasure. Taking me at the waist, he lifted me as I held onto his desk for security. When he lowered me again, I felt him. My eyes flew open and between it was the bullet head of him. My chest thundered, and the pits of my arms misted in a flash.

His lips moved against my neck. "I'm waiting on you."

My hands clutched his shoulders, squeezing as my body tensed all over. "I wan—" I swallowed the sudden excess liquid in my mouth. "I want...you." With closed eyes, I lifted from my feet planted on the floor. "I want you, Sadik," my voice a trace of a plea as my eyes were squeezed closed. "I don't know what to do."

I felt his hand beneath me this time, the mushroom head of him brushing against my aching clit. I sucked in air, then again when I felt him at my opening. Without invitation, I pushed down gently, but greedily.

"Easy, baby," he warned in my ear.

Fullness. Already, I felt full from his girth. He took me at the sides of my face again, gracing me with a tender kiss. His tongue worked at a more patient pace, his lips followed suit. I felt tender and center stage on his lap, in his arms. I felt versed with his body this time. My friend was becoming my lover, and my body loosened to him. Yielded to him. He was filling me by the second as my straining walls settled onto him. My neck gave out, eyes fluttered closed. I could feel my excitement for him as I glided down. My need.

My hips began to move of their own accord. It was as though my body had its own destination with him. I could feel his erection throb inside me, his clammy hands now at the curving of my hips.

"Are you okay?" I asked, somewhat panicked.

He let out a heavy breath against my neck. "I don't remember you being this wet without me eating you first," he heaved.

I rocked, feeling tiny sparks of confusing pleasure against the pressure of his fullness.

"Help me," I panted.

I was still a novice at this. His palms clawed my hips, lifting me to stroke him. With curled toes, I rolled my pelvis over him, changing his pace to meet my need. The pleasure expanded in my groin, and so did the ache. It increased, just like my thrusts. Sadik's spiked face scraped down my chest to my cleavage. One arm wrapped around my backside, and his other hand palming my breasts. He kneaded through my blouse to the lace of my bra. His hand rounded until his fingers found my pebbled nipple and squeezed, enhancing the ache and propelling my hips faster. I could feel his protective arm behind me, encouraging my thrusts.

Then pleasure bloomed in my belly at cyclonic speed.

"Oh!" I squeaked, pushing my sex into him.

The cheeks of my butt squeezed, pushing into the pleasure. My entire frame seemed to gravitate to the point of ecstasy: Sadik. His arm, fingers, mouth on my neck. And his cock... It was the base of bliss.

"Sadik—" I couldn't breathe to speak, emotions flared.

"I know, baby," he panted, mouth moving to my ear. "You're coming for me. Just ride it out." I moaned into his shoulder. "You're doing so good, Nalib," he whimpered, moving his pelvis against mine.

I flopped on his lap, inspired anew, face tense, and tears slipping from the corners of my eyes. This was too much. I was too open, too raw. No man should be able to strip me like this.

Oh, God...

"I'm gonna come with you," he groaned as though in pain.

Sadik crushed me deliciously in his arms as he thrust into me from below, grunting as he did. Even against the slight pain of his grip, I felt protected and empowered. I felt purposed in his arms. Needed and belonged.

"Shit, girl," he swore, crushing me into his chest.

I felt complete exhilaration there, boneless. The moment he began to come down, his arms loosened from around me. A heap of holding air I was unaware of flew from my lungs. That caused me to choke on a cry.

"I came in you again..." he grumbled, not panicking and not proud.

I sniffled, wiping my tears as I backed away, needing to see his eyes. My brows met as anxiety poured over me, as did the tears. "I've only been with one guy...before you." I lifted my gaze to measure his. Other than the relaxed muscles around his eyes given what had just happened, Sadik showed nothing. His expression was aplomb, eyes darkened. "I was seventeen and it was with my brother's friend, Derrick." I could feel his thighs stiffen beneath me. I'd been sensing Sadik's jealous streak lately. "He was cute, and I thought...different. I don't want to get into it, but it was horrible—all three times. And it wasn't just the...sex. It was the experience." I took a quiet, yet hefty breath, feeling him still throbbing inside of me. "Honestly, I was in no rush to do it again..." A shaky breath left my mouth. "Until you."

He lifted his hand to my face and thumbed my wet cheeks. His soft lips brushed against my mouth sweetly.

I rolled my eyes at what I was about to share. "Randi told me not to trust you. She said you'd get bored with me as soon as I got comfortable with all the spending, attention, and sex." I took a deep breath. "But I want to let go. I want to trust you." My forehead wrinkled. "I want to be your girlfriend. Your real friend." As my bottom lip quivered, the pad of his thumb grazed it. "I want to trust you about the baby, the illegal stuff about your family. I wanna let everything go and let you be a friend."

Sadik didn't speak right away, all tension seemed to have left his body. His soft lips brushed mine again.

"Let me cook you dinner tonight."

"You cook?"

He chuckled softly. "Nah. But let me have a moment to lie." My head tossed back as I laughed. "I'm trying to impress you here."

After a final howl, I admitted, "You are—you did." I wiggled on his lap.

"Shit!" he mumbled, lifting me. "Easy," he warned as I balanced myself in my heels, my legs slapping together from something leaking from my inner thighs.

Sadik shot to his feet, holding the crotch of his dress pants with one hand and cupping the tip of his cock with the other, then tottered to a small room in the corner with his pants and boxers collected at his ankles.

A bathroom?

I heard water run for a while before he returned with a wet cloth. Sadik dropped on his haunches and ran the warm fabric up the center of my legs.

"You can go wash up. There's a small closet with washcloths in there."

I grabbed the cloth from him and wobbled into the bathroom. He under-spoke of how well the bathroom was stocked. It was small, but contemporary in design. There was a small shower, marble vanity, and a linen closet filled with bar and liquid soap, washcloths, and towels. Physically and emotionally spent, I washed up with a gazillion things running through my mind.

When I stepped out of the bathroom, Sadik was hanging up the phone. His honeyed eyes met me in inspection.

"You good?"

I nodded. "I have to work tonight. Dinner'll have to be postponed."

"Bullshit," he declared. "What're you about to do now?"

"Bum a ride home and take a nap. I'm tired." That subconsciously prompted a yawn.

"I'll get you a bucket of coffee and a ride home. You forget I know you make your own hours at the diner?"

I snorted as he made his way to me. "It doesn't exactly work that way, but there's a bit of flexibility involved."

His lips were on my neck again, warming me. "Work now." His voice was breathy against my skin. "Play and rest with me later. I still want to taste your pussy."

My groin roiled deliciously.

"Sadik..." I whimpered when the tips of his fingers gripped my scalp.

"Agree to it," he grated playfully with tight lips. "And pack a bag. You're gonna stay with me for a few days."

I sighed, licking my lips. "I get to see your place?"

My lips were just inches away from his. "You're my girlfriend. It's about time you do."

∞ 18 ∞

"Before we close, I'd like to make a deal with you, Ellis."

Extending my arms the full length of the armrests, I nodded, encouraging his proposal.

"I have a brother-in-law. He lives in Paterson. My only sister's husband. Half Polish like us, and half Irish; second generation. He's a supervisor of the dock workers there at the port. Abram Murphy. He hasn't had a raise in over seven years, and I've been told he was looked over for a position rightfully his by some Italians who have more connections in this area."

Salvatore Rizzo.

"I'd like for him to have his hard work reflected in his home as far as what he can provide for his family of six." He shrugged. "And he likes the seaport. That's where he feels he belongs. I know you have some influence with the board controlling them."

I tapped my fingers on the leather armrests. Silence rested over the room for a stretch of time as I considered all the moving parts.

"Then it sounds like a deal."

Kolwaski nodded, taking a deep breath while scowling pensively, it seemed. His men around him stood guard with fixed blank expressions, staring at the walls with their hands linked behind their backs. It wasn't customary for me to have clients or guests needing armed security on my premises, but this one was necessary because of my need of his alliance.

Kolwaski was a powerful businessman in Poland. He had several industries catering to the American market. His reputation was solid, but his ruthlessness largely unknown to most. When he approached

298

me a month ago, I saw, in more than one way, how this relationship could be beneficial.

He lifted his head, and his index finger waggled my way. "Although you're a multi-million-dollar company in your own right, I need you more than you need me." He sat up on the sofa. "See, Ellis, I've done my homework on you. Yeah. We've heard about your father's alleged underworld, but if you've not been investigated or sought after for involvement, I don't give a damn." He tossed his hand in the air dismissively.

He was saying I was the type of man who didn't run at the sight of an illegal matter. Kolwaski would likely smuggle small amounts of prohibited goods in his orders I'd be responsible for clearing in customs, receiving, and storing in my warehouse before delivering it according to his companies' preference. I've never allowed smuggling in my customs business. Ever. This opportunity was one I'd be remiss to turn away.

"You getting me as an account will take your company into the billionaire status in a matter of three to four years," he continued. "For me, it'll give me the boutique type of customer service I feel my companies deserve."

I stood first. "As do I." I offered my hand. "I can assure you the A1 customer service you're due."

He stood, broad smile in tow. Kolwaski met my palm in a firm shake. Midway, a gut-pushed laugh belted from him and was followed by his assistant. I didn't kiss in business. I didn't laugh, either.

Bilan

I toed barefoot down the cool marble white and gray veiny floor. It was the same flooring throughout the entire apartment. The hem of his black tank I tossed on gathered into my palms as I voyaged his home. Who knew this luxury apartment building existed over here? The high rise was nestled behind trees, but just a few blocks away from Route 22 highway. It was a hidden gem.

The walls had to be, at least, fifteen feet tall all around the place. There were just three bedrooms, but the apartment could swallow my parent's single family home and be hungry for more. The unit was just one level, but generous with room sizes. And just like his office, Sadik's home was meticulously decorated. The in-ceiling light fixtures made the place look sexy last night, and the sunlight pushing through the floor-to-ceiling windows in some rooms made it intimidating. Even the bathroom in the master suite had glass walls overlooking a small forest.

I strode into the kitchen, passing the entrance of the spacious dining room, where a vast, intricate crystal chandelier hung over a ten-seater table. Just amazing. Again, his home was intimidating. I knew for me to feel at home here, I had to take initiative and be domesticated, so I opted to cook breakfast—for Sadik. I'd make coffee for myself. But first, I had to find the coffee maker. Of course, a state of the art kitchen would have one.

"Magnifica. Hmmmmm…" I whispered to myself as I physically examined it to figure out how to use it. "Okay…"

Hard arms circled my waist, and soft flesh pressed into my neck. A familiar and alluring scent filled my nostrils.

"You left my bed," he murmured into my skin. "What are you doing?"

My lashes fluttered. "Trying to make a cup of coffee."

"That's an espresso machine. The coffee's down there."

I glanced down the long countertop. "All these toys," I whispered, enduring his tongue against my pulse. "Almost as nice as your home."

"Come back to bed and feed me." He bit the bottom of my earlobe.

"I came to make you breakfast."

"I have a cook to make me breakfast." He rubbed his erection against the small of my back. "I need you to feed me."

"Sadik..." I tried.

I didn't need the feel of his arousal against me any more than I needed the reminder my "boyfriend" had a cook. Last night, I arrived later than I thought, thanks to so many callouts at the diner. Not only did I complete my usual tasks, but I had to assist Nicky and the floor staff. It was a grueling shift because the family of Lenny, who had gone missing over a month ago, held a vigil for him a block away, driving traffic to the diner. And of course, when there were young black men at the diner, I had to serve as a shield. By the time Rory picked me up and brought me here, Sadik's cook was putting the final touches on our dinner for two in the dining room. She was younger than I would have imagined a cook to be, but very professional. Sadik asked her to keep dinner warmed while he "washed his girlfriend." I nearly died on the spot. And without an awkward reaction, Kimmy, a medium-build mocha skinned, Black woman agreed to it.

"Bilan," his tone was clearer, less affectionate. "just as there's a 'no clothes in my bed' rule, there's a 'no leaving my bed until I've had you' regulation."

I turned in his arms to face him. "Regulation?"

"Yes. Unless I dismiss you, I may need your body to help regulate my mind for the day." And there was the deathly serious scowl he'd wage effectively.

"You're serious."

"About this? Hell yeah."

I crossed my arms. "So, what do we do now?"

He unraveled my arms and grabbed my hand, leading me across the massive apartment for his bedroom. Sadik pulled the black tank over my body and head then tossed it onto the floor. His t-shirt and boxers followed before he took to the high mattress set on a platform fit for a king. His mouth landed on me first, and his heavy cock plopped next on my belly. A hungry need stirred immediately. My hands roved all over him, starting at his smooth crown. They moved down his neck and shoulders as my thighs opened to him.

"I want to taste you," I panted.

Sadik froze over me. My racing heart and the pulse of his erection were the only two things to be heard and felt.

"Have you ever done that before?"

I squirmed, immediately embarrassed. "No," I grated.

I told him how little experience I'd had. After a few seconds of self-doubt, I felt his body lift. He laid out next to me, then patted his stomach.

"Come here, Nalib." His tone so soft, I hardly heard him clearly.

However, I acted right away, lifting to my knees and facing him.

"Turn to face my feet," he murmured.

Awkwardly, I obeyed.

He grabbed my right thigh. "Bring this over my right leg."

I had no idea the destination of these orders, but I was too excited to even question it. I brought my right knee to the other side of his right leg. The minute it was planted, he took me at the hips and pulled me backward to his face, his hardness dragging beneath me until it was under my chin. My eyes were wild with wonderment at being this close to his dick. It was even more intimidating than when I'd first seen it.

Abruptly, my spine dropped and shoulders caved when I felt his mouth between my cheeks. His tongue lapped down my slit, the sensation had me leaning into him. Air pushed from my closed lips and my head collapsed, falling on steel covered in a smooth velvet casing. His musk aroused me, nipples tickled by his skin beneath the pebbles. My hips rolled over his face as I felt his tongue dip inside what I knew wasn't my sex.

"Mmm…" My moan stifled by slight shame.

Pleasure shouldn't be felt in that zone. Yet Sadik proved it to be erogenous. My eyes rolled closed and I lay a kiss against the ridge of *his hardness. As he licked and lashed behind me, I kissed, grabbed, and stroked the length of him. In no time, he was in my palms and mouth as I fondled him. Feeling his abs constrict beneath me made the thought of his cock friendly. I controlled his pleasure with my technique, and he guided the technique with the way his body responded.*

It took time, but I had a rhythm I knew he enjoyed by the growls elicited and the wild thrashes of his tongue reaching my clit. Sadik sucked on it, sending me on a gyrating bliss. I struggled with the task in my hands and mouth, when the zings of pleasure grew to proportions I couldn't control. Then his body went rigid, mouth withdrew from the creases of me. His hand pushed down beneath mine, assisting my strokes. His thighs widened around me, pelvis pushing into my face. With little ability for full breaths, I maintained the rhythm. Sadik made it hard when his thrusts into my mouth grew erratic. Then came an explosive slap on my ass followed by a guttural cry of ecstasy, and hot creamy liquid squirting into my mouth. My hands slipped around him, but remained in motion.

That was until my torso was shifted back, disrupting my balance. But his mouth returned, licking wildly until I was squirming in his tight hold. Sadik gripped me so hard, locking me in place. I was forced to endure the pleasure. I moaned hard, riding his face. My head fell against his abs, toes curled, and back trembled until a rope popped and I exploded in his face. My screams of mercy were less crazed than the body tremors. And I still couldn't move far, his grip strong, mouth busy delivering bliss. I rocked against the waves of ecstasy until my body collapsed against him in utter depletion.

Sadik

"Did you hear me?" the softness in her voice curled around my dick, tickling it.

The hot water beating on my head, neck, and back felt amazing as I leaned into the wall with one arm. An endless number of details, fine and broad, running through my head. It was something I was accustomed to happening when alone at my place. What I wasn't used to was sharing headspace with someone. The benefit she had over my preferred headspace was her influence of my body and chest space.

After an unusual morning nap once done with our six-nine session, I woke up before Bilan and ran a few miles on the treadmill up in the gym. When I returned, I warmed up quiche my cook whipped up last night for breakfast. I woke her up, hand-feeding her a late breakfast. I showered, then got a few things done in my office before Bilan strolled in there distracting me in my robe, asking about marketing strategies pertaining to her graduate program application. That conversation ended with me carrying her back to my bed and driving into her plush ass until I was drained of vitality.

Now, here in the shower, I turned to her. Bilan sat on the bench across from me with crossed legs, an elbow resting on the high knee as she pushed back her cuticles.

"What did you say?"

"Your STD drive-thru clinic." Her smile lightened my chest. "I went a couple of days ago."

"For what?"

"Birth control, dude." Shit... "We've been reckless."

No, baby. I've been reckless. You've been lost in lust with me...

"I took the full GYN exam and got a prescription. Didn't even have to wait long as a walk-in. When I gave my name and they ran it through their system, they remembered me. Wonder if they're going to bill you. When I asked about how to pay, the girl said I'll be billed. But she never asked for my insurance information."

Dr. Clifford wouldn't charge her. His staff would likely bill me.

"Do you have insurance?"

Bilan shook her head. "Not anymore, but I was prepared to pay."

"Can I ask you something?" I'd been wondering since I met her in the diner.

"Sure." She lifted only one shoulder, uncomfortable.

"How much do you earn annually?"

Bilan's eyes averted right away. She pinched her fingers while licking her lips. But she rebounded quickly, facing me again.

"Last year, I cleared just over forty."

My brows shot in the air. "From the bakery?"

She nodded. "They pay me fairly." Then her face wrinkled. "Even though I don't know what my future there looks like."

"Why?"

"Nicky—my boss—is letting my trainees run my recipes when I'm not there." She shrugged. "I'm sure my recent requests for time off justifies it. He'd been asking me how long would I be there after graduation. It's like he doesn't trust me to give him fair notice if I'm going to quit."

"I have an opening at Ellis International, I'm sure you're going to say—"

"Nope!" She stood from the bench, nearing me. Of course... "I know nothing about customs, and I'm already too preoccupied with you to have to see you at work, too." Her arms pushed around my waist. "Did I do that right earlier?" Her voice but a whisper.

My forehead wrinkled. "What?"

"You know. With my mouth..." Her hand brushed over my dick. "...here."

I snorted. "Why would you ask that?"

"Because you aided."

"I got lost in your hand and mouth work." I kissed her lips.

"You sure that's the only reason? I'm feeling a little... You know. Insecure about it. It's new to me."

And I'm so fucking happy, baby...

"And that made you perfect. I almost lost my damn mind." I peppered her face with kisses, trying to land on each freckle.

"Nalib," I whispered.

Her eyes were closed when she answered, "Huhn?"

"We're going to my parents' for a couple of nights."

Her eyes appeared. "A couple of nights?" I nodded. "Why?"

"It's time you met them. You're my girlfriend, and they haven't been happy with me leaving town with someone they haven't met yet. I got chewed the hell out by my mother for even having a girlfriend she hasn't met."

"Oh." Her eyes fell blindly to my mouth. "I didn't think about that. You kind of sprung that title on me, too."

I laughed at her honesty.

"I did. So, it's time for me to merge my worlds. There's no need to delay the inevitable. You have to meet and blend in my family. They mean everything to me."

"When?"

"Tonight."

"Oh."

"Oh," I mocked her, unable to help my laughter.

"For a few days?"

"Yes." I kissed her chin. "You'll be fine. You're gonna see the girls, too. My nieces are going to love you." I swiped my tongue into her mouth. "But not half as much as I do." My hands reached up and pulled her body into me as I took her mouth with full force.

Her little hand gripped my bicep as I ravished her.

Bilan

He cut the engine and turned to me.

"You ready?"

My eyes bounced all around at the regal entryway of what looked like a historic library, but with a fancy driveway.

I turned to peer over my shoulder to where we'd just drove at least a half a mile from. "That was the security station for your family's home?"

Sadik shrugged, his yellowish eyes regarding me heavily.

"Sadik, where are we?" We'd driven for what felt like two hours.

His head bounced back in a muted chuckle. "In the middle of nowhere."

"I see!" My eyes ballooned. "Are we still in New Jersey?"

"Yes." He gave a gentle yank to my earlobe.

"Where, exactly?"

"Elliswoods."

"Where in the world is Elliswoods? I've never heard of that."

"I know." There was a long pause before he shared, "Because it was just incorporated as a township twenty years ago, here in Huntington County. Before then it was a rare and small stretch of the state the neighboring towns didn't claim."

"I don't understand."

"Twenty years ago, my father bought twenty acres of nothing here. The owner was some German guy that's long been deceased. My father purchased the land from his estate. It took years of bringing the state along because of its bastard status—"

"And I'm sure your father's reputation," I urged.

Sadik nodded, one free hand in the air defenselessly. "And his former lifestyle. Yes. But when all was approved, he cleared out about sixteen miles of forest, then hired builders to begin this estate. He said it's his last home and he'd have enough space to accommodate his family."

My eyes were on what I could see of the expansive property. My god, it looked like a cathedral! The entire structure was lit beautifully from beaming spotlights. The cemented steps leading up to the front entrance guarded by two brass lions had my pulse racing.

He got out and rounded the car for my door. I stepped out, peering between the man in all black, similar to Sadik's security, and the entrance with double doors. Sadik greeted him by name. I could hear him tell Sadik our things would be brought inside shortly.

"You grew up here?" I asked as we took to the stairs.

"Not really. I was going into college when he bought the land. I was well on my own by the time the house was built. It doesn't feel like it, though, because I'm here, sometimes, several times a week."

For dinner. I remembered him telling me during one of our first conversations. Being here made me nervous. What if I wasn't fancy enough for them? Sadik's hand intertwined with mine could be so much of a point of comfort.

The doors were opened for us when we were three steps from the landing. We were greeted by another person in all black. Sadik seemed familiar with her, too—

Holy crap!

The place was beyond a mansion, it didn't even feel like a home. We were hit by a glow of lighting in the broad foyer. Cathedral ceiling, shiny marble floors, enormous chandelier intricate in design sparkling over a round dining room sized table topped with fresh flowers... I mean... I didn't have the words or knowledge to describe the décor. I could only think of one: grandeur. The opulence couldn't be captured in a picture.

"Welcome to Elliswoods Palace, Nalib," Sadik whispered softly in my ear.

He was so close, so sensitive to my shocked state. I was grateful for his understanding. If it wasn't obvious when we pulled up to an armed guard's booth I was out of my element, it was deafeningly clear now.

"Stacy, where's my father?"

"In his study, Deek."

Sadik wrapped his arm around me, prompting me ahead. "Let me introduce you to my father first."

We walked down two hallways that were more like galleries. Colossal artwork framed in gold cases were displayed on the walls.

"You got your love for art from your parents, I see," I murmured, striding at his side.

"My mother. She's a big fan of the Harlem Renaissance—the original and the children of the original Renaissance—and Abstract Expressionism. She has an extraordinary collection in her library. I'd like to show it to you while we're here."

We stopped at a set of doors and Sadik opened one, inviting me to go in ahead of him. The room was large, brown leather furniture set in the entrance. Old school music streamed into the air. A man crooned, "Do they turn you on all night till dawn..." There was a mood in the atmosphere, giving the place personality immediately.

Farther into the room was another lounge set of sofas and coffee tables, only larger. To the right of that was an enclave with a pool table sandwiched by two mounted flat screen televisions. Beyond that was a large office setting. But it was in the billiard area that I found what looked to be a private dynamic that had me turning and bumping right into the muscled flesh of Sadik.

"Right over there, baby," his voice was soft, masking strain as he pointed.

With him now in front, leading me by the hand, we ambled deeper into the enclave where a slender, dark-skinned woman, with a short cut similar to mine, lay stretched out on the side of the pool table, taking selfies. A man stood at the front of the table, leaning over another slim woman with a skintight mini-dress on as she attempted to hit the billiard ball with the stick. His chin was planted in her neck, his right fingers trickling up her thigh.

The woman giggled. "Earl, stop it. You're gonna make me mess up, Daddy."

The man's attention was on us first. His eyes—familiar feline eyes—roved up my frame with palpable indifference that chilled my bones. *Slowly, his spine erected, and my breath hiked at the DNA revelation. It was him. Earl Ellis. His son's resemblance to him was uncanny in person. His eyes, they were greener than his son's but just as mesmerizing, and far more daunting. He rounded the table in his approach while his gaze was glued to us, the tips of his long fingers grazing the leg and thigh of the first woman splayed on the frame of the pool table. It reached high near her pelvis, clad in silk shorts.*

"Sadik." He reached for his son's hand.

"Mr. Ellis." They shook hands with an air of formality that made their chemistry pretty cool.

"Glad you're home again," Earl greeted.

"I am," Sadik grinned, then air stroked his arm from me to his father. "With Ms. Bilan Asad-Yasin." He regarded me from behind, his head over my shoulder as he grounded me with a firm palm at my hip. "Honey, meet my overseer, Earl Ellis."

My shaky arm pushed out for a shake. "Nice to meet you, Mr. Ellis." My voice just as unstable. "Your home is beautiful."

"As is my son, Ms. Asad-Yasin. We can't deny that." He pulled my hand to his face for a kiss. "Welcome," he delivered in a softer tone before releasing me. His regard went back to his son. "I think we still have some time before dinner. You want to embarrass your old man on the fake green?" He gestured the pool table. "Nena just whooped my ass, and my lil' Diane over there's right on her way."

"Nah," Sadik answered. "I want to take Bilan around to meet everyone before dinner. You guys have fun." He acknowledged the girls, who were observing intently and eagerly waved at us.

"I think your mother made seafood salad for the kid." Earl waggled thick, shaggy brows he gave his son as he chuckled. "Be careful; that's how she's able to work her magic on your old man." He winked, and I gulped down air.

"We'll see you in a few, man," Sadik offered before prompting me to go.

I was muted, sauntering out of Earl's "lair." Stunned into utter silence. With my hand nestled in Sadik's, I simply followed his lead as we traveled the opulent palatial halls, our footsteps rhythmically synced until we turned into an open room with carpet and soft toned furniture and décor.

"Uncle Deek!"

"Uncle Deek!" two petite voices cried successively.

Little bodies dashed toward us. It was them. His nieces, and boy were they gorgeous in living color. One was taller than the other, both dressed in pretty A-line dresses. The oldest wore yellow Converses with white, ribboned ankle socks. The smaller one with the same socks, but with Mary Jane style shoes.

Sadik dropped to his haunches. "Hey, Ivy! Whaddup, Eshy!"

I watched him greet them, their evidentiary love for this man on display. Quickly, I felt like an interloper and averted my attention to the two adults in the room. A stately chocolate woman sat curtsy on the sofa with one heeled foot ahead of the other. Her spine was upright and her smile dazzling. I could tell, even from her sitting posture that she, too, wore an A-line dress. Black with white polka dots and a yellow belt at her tiny waist. Her dark, crinkled hair shiny and pushed back into a tight ponytail.

On the other side of the room, dressed in a suit as he always was in the Googled pictures of him, Sadik's brother held a tumbler of clear liquid as his elbow rested on a hanging ledge. His chin was low, eyes narrowed. He watched silently, seemingly unaffected.

"Iesha, Ivana, you remember Bilan?" Sadik asked the girls.

"It's Ms. Bilan," the woman, who I believed to be their mother, lightly scolded Sadik.

He took it well, smiling at her playful scowl.

"Ms. Bilan," he corrected. "You remember her?"

The little one nodded. The oldest one played with the lapel of Sadik's suit jacket as she answered, "Yes."

I remembered her being a little less welcoming than her younger sister. I guessed I would, too, if I had an uncle dote on me the way Sadik did them. And I now understood his doting: he took them to Disney to celebrate progress reports from school, and took me to Central America to celebrate my graduation with passionate sex and mind-blowing orgasms. I now, too, felt a bit territorial myself. I quickly decided to build an alliance with both girls and not allow the awkward wedge between the oldest and me to fester.

I dropped to a knee alongside my boyfriend. "It's nice to finally meet you face to face." I asked the smaller beauty, "Are you Ivana?" She shook her head. "Then you must be Iesha. My best friend back in grammar school's name was Iesha. She was the first friend I made. I was sad when her family moved out of state and we lost touch. It's nice meeting a new and prettier one."

Iesha's shoulders went up as she unleashed the biggest smile.

"And you, Ms. Ivana," I turned to the oldest. "You have style. I love how you paired those 'Verses with this gorgeous dress." I smiled at her.

Ivana shrugged, eyes still on her uncle's person. "My mommy picked it out."

Her father snorted across the room.

Ignoring that dig, I explained, "But it takes someone with the right amount of grace and finesse to pull it off. Mommy's always know best. And we can see yours is no different. You look very pretty, Ivana."

Finally, her pretty, jet black button eyes were on me, and I could sigh out loud if I wasn't so nervous already. Sadik, beside me, stood and placed a supportive hand on my shoulder.

"Monica, Iban, please welcome my Bilan."

Iesha came to my side and took my hand as I stood nervously for what I believed would be an awkward introduction. Iban pushed against the ledge with a lazy neck, his head dipping as he made his way to his wife, then they approached us in a joint manner.

"Bilan, honey, this is my big brother, Iban," he informed.

I forged a smile and offered my hand. Iban, like Earl, was taller than Sadik. Iban's eyes were a light brown, at best. Like their father, he had all his hair. Only Iban's was honey blond mixed with brown like his younger brother's, creating an orange hue; a low cut with a precise shape-up. He was inarguably handsome and did resemble his brother.

Iban met my palm with a nod. "Bilan."

"And this is, Monica, the best sister-in-law I could ask for, for my big brother and nieces," Sadik charmed Monica, but spoke directly to me. "We're expecting another."

"Oh," I breathed.

Two new babies for the Ellis clan...

"Do we know what it is yet?"

Monica shook her head. "Not yet. But I'm so happy to finally have a fellow sister brought home by an Ellis son." She actually ignored my proffered hand and took me at the shoulders, pulling me into a hug. "It gets better day by day. They're not as tough as they appear, outside of the streets. You'll be fine," her words so faint, I almost missed them.

I returned her enfold, confused yet undeniably comforted by her forged sisterhood. We released one another and immediately resumed the tension in the room.

"Your shoes are pretty," Iesha complimented next to me.

I glanced down to my shoes, forgetting I had any on for a moment.

"Oh." I stretched my ankles, observing the nude "Choca" Christian Louboutin sandals Sadik had waiting for me after our long shower, a few hours ago. When I toed back into his bedroom, they were propped on the bed next to the cropped black suit and ivory blouse I was wearing. In fact, Sadik had several ensembles and shoes for me in his two-level walk-in closet. He wasn't around when I discovered it, I guessed to avoid my questions of his generosity—or fetish—of women's fashion. "Thanks. They're pretty comfy, too, thankfully." I smiled down at her.

"Oh, look at this bullshit the wind blew in," Iban teased, and a friendlier tone sounded behind me. His smile wide. "Lil' ass troublemaker thinking she moving out. I got something else for that ass, though."

"Auntie!" Ivana shouted before taking off.

"That's our Auntie Taaliba," Iesha explained, hand still inside of mine.

"Oh, nice!" I turned, as everyone else had for the incoming attraction.

Like me, Taaliba had a pixie cut. Hers longer at the top, thick spikes curling up and toward her forehead. It was wild and incredibly cool. As she swung Ivana in a circle by the entrance of the room, I observed her mocha skin so unlike her father and brothers. She was slender, too, even more than Monica. Taaliba covered her frame in an oversized, feminine cut t-shirt hanging from one shoulder, blue boyfriend jeans, and cherry red Ase Garb loafers. On her wrists were layers of bones and skulls, beaded bracelets of varying materials and colors. Her ears were bare, neck decorated in a red choker.

When her eyes finally came up from her elated niece, I was able to see she, too, had yellowish eyes. I couldn't tell if they were comprised of the green, yellow, hazel, and a cloud of orange like her brother's, but knew it was a strong possibility. All three Ellis siblings were identifiably related and shared a DNA pool, they all just didn't present with the same features.

Taaliba received Iban first as he was now closer to her. Monica advanced to the duo and was greeted next. Iesha was off to her auntie for love when her mother was finished. Taaliba stopped en route to Sadik. Her stance was like a dude's, though her essence was of a young woman. She was almost like Rory, but diluted in boyish mannerisms.

"Whitcho cool ass," she hissed with a blank face.

"Get yo' pretty ass over here," he returned harshly and affectionately as she continued his way with extended arms.

Taaliba dove into his chest like a child. He received her, embracing her little frame with closed eyes as he kissed her forehead.

"Costa Rica, huhn?" Taaliba asked. "Did you know out of— maybe—one hundred thirty volcanoes, they have about ten still active? You couldn't invite a bitch. Coulda blown some proper leaves with you."

"I was blowing alright. Just not leaves. And we had a clear view of one. Meet my Bilan," he murmured over her head.

Taaliba's grip still appeared tight as she returned, "She's dope, Deek—not that I expected anything less. Still can't believe you brought someone home."

He scoffed. "Then tell her that shit. Greet my lady, knucklehead."

"Sorry," Taaliba finally acknowledged me. "I haven't seen my big brother in a while."

Monica interjected. "It's been less than two weeks."

"Feels like an eternity. I'm sure you know," she addressed me. "Taaliba, this guy's favorite sister."

I chuckled at that as I met her splayed palm and returned, "He's right; you're gorgeous, Taaliba. I'm Bilan."

"Thanks, B. Nice to meet you. You're gonna have to give me lessons on how to arrest the attention of a dude like this one." She used her thumb to gesture to her brother.

My eyes grew wide. I was effectively embarrassed. That was hard to do when I didn't know how I'd gained Sadik's attention in the first place.

"What the hell ever," Sadik graveled, taking my side, his palm protectively at my hip again. "We have a few minutes. Let me go find the queen and let her bless my lady before we break bread."

We left out of the grand room as the siblings exchanged familial jokes on the way.

"Monica is sweet, and Taaliba's cool," I noted out loud to him as we trekked the halls I could easily get lost in. "Iesha likes me, but I still have Ivana and her dad to win over."

He pulled me into his hard frame by my shoulder. "You were perfect, baby. Give them time. They'll be fine."

His confidence warmed me. As we traveled, it dawned on me how varied the Ellis children's personalities were. Iban's was, undoubtedly, the coarsest. Taaliba's delivery, like her middle brother's, vacillated between lax and articulate. Many would say the same about Abshir and me. My father said it was because I stayed in books, broadening my vocabulary versus my brother, who cured his boredom with video games. It was as though the Ellises had different educational backgrounds.

Just as I was about to ask Sadik about that, we turned a corner just a few yards away from a couple in front of a mirror on the wall. The woman held her hair in the air while the guy, intimately close to her, latched a necklace onto her neck. He ended the task with a kiss of adoration just above where he settled the fine jewelry.

As we traveled closer, I could hear them.

"Okay," she breathed, gazing into the mirror. "Sadik should be here. I wonder if they're unpacking upstairs."

His hands were at her shoulders, fingering through her blonde tresses. "You're nervous. You serve your family dinner three times a week, and tonight you're nervous." He kissed the side of her face. "You're perfect. Dinner'll be perfect, too. Just relax."

The closer we drew, two things happened: Sadik's clench around my shoulder deepened, and the man began to resemble someone I knew.

"You always say that," she snorted.

The man reached down and whispered something into her ear, his pelvis now embedded in her ass and hands on her shoulders. The woman giggled, no doubt at salacious words of promise to her.

"You say that just before I serve my family," she shrieked girlishly, though her vocals were as deep as a seasoned woman.

We were on them when it was all made clear.

"Queen," Sadik greeted after clearing his throat.

She turned our way, and so did her obvious lover.

"Tom Banks?" I trilled lowly.

"Oh. Hey, Bilan!" His animated eyes bounced from Sadik to me. "What are you doing here?"

"I could ask you—" My eyes went to a woman who was, without a doubt, the mother of my lover. She didn't give him her dark brown eye color, but she had naturally blonde hair; it sprouted from her thin sideburns and tinted brows. But her skin was a rich, radiant brown. Just odd genetic traits.

"You know him?" Sadik asked rather low. Too low to say there were two other people just feet away.

I couldn't speak at first. Tom Banks was the boyfriend to the old friend, Iesha, I just told his niece about. I went to school with this guy. This night couldn't get any more bizarre for me.

"And so, this is Bilan?" the woman mused out loud. Her laced fingers were at her pelvis line as she flashed the smile that made my heart do somersaults each time her son unleashed it on me. "Welcome to my home. I'm so glad to finally meet you, dear."

Behind her, Tom looked uneasy each time he regarded Sadik. The way Sadik's body was angled disregarded him.

Okay, so we're in agreement this is grossly inappropriate?

∞ 19 ∞

The Ellis family was certainly a beautiful group. I tried to recall a family with so many exotic features without the evidence of European mixing in their bloodline. The undertones of both Earl and Irene were of Black people. Even Sadik, with both striking eye and hair color, didn't resemble anything but a Black man.

That was the one thing I tried to focus on while at the immaculately decorated table topped with candles, gold rocks, crystal goblets, fine china, and fresh flowers. The table sat fifteen people and required five staff members to serve. Along the table were bowls of all types of dishes that, apparently, Irene prepared with her kitchen crew. On my plate was seafood salad, roasted asparagus, and grilled swordfish. The aged Malbec Irene had flown in from some winery I wasn't familiar with was far more appetizing than anything on my plate.

Over and around me, conversations flowed fluidly. No one affected by the obvious breach of marriage the parental Ellises had been committing. Earl was at the head of the table and Irene at the foot. To the left of him were his young girlfriends, Diane and Nena, who lightly participated in conversations with people other than themselves and Earl. To the right of Earl was Sadik, then me. It was very clear to me already that Earl was fond of Sadik. The way he looked his son in the eyes when speaking to him about casual topics was with fondness and admiration. Next to me was Iesha, chowing down. Her sister sat next to Nena, across from us. To the left of her were her parents. On the right side of my Iesha was her aunt, Taaliba, then Tom. Of course, Tom sat next to Irene.

317

The most uncomfortable time was during seating. Both parents wanted Sadik. Palpably hesitant, he chose his father, citing business talk being the reason. Ironically, not a word of business was discussed. I knew because I ear-hustled, wanting to see if Sadik lied to me about being in business with his father. What had I gotten myself into? Why was I here? Another night at his lush pad would have been perfect for me. Just the two of us. No...mess.

"Baby, try the fish with mango sauce," Sadik requested softly with loads of endearment.

I glanced up from my plate and collided with yellowish eyes shooting uncompromised energy. He held a fork of fish to me. Sadik noticed I hadn't eaten. I didn't like the idea of being fed here. The last thing I needed from his father, who hadn't spoken a word to me since we made it into the dining room, and his brother, who shot me the nastiest glances at times, was them knowing about the handicap I had with eating.

"Please, Nalib," he begged beneath his breath.

I opened, and he pushed the tasteless food into my mouth with rapid service, but with care as well before continuing a conversation with his father. I kept at pushing food around on my plate with the occasional scan of the table. This time, I found Iban smiling sinisterly.

Awwwww... Great!

I put my fork down and sat back. As if on cue, Sadik was handing me a couple of pieces of forked pasta.

"Try this seafood salad. My mother makes her own mayonnaise. It's the kicker."

If I wanted the seafood salad, I'd eat the bit on my plate!

I wanted to shout at him, feeling irritable. His family seeing him feed me couldn't go over well.

"That wasn't a request." His tone was with full authority.

The kind I responded to, always. It wasn't out of fear, rather respect. I hadn't been able to put my finger on it just yet, but there was a foreboding component to Sadik's makeup. Experiencing the aura of his father and brother encouraged the inkling.

I ate the pasta and tasted no more than I did with the fish.

"Thank you, sweetheart," his delivery endearing again.

A clinking of glass caught the attention of the room. Irene, down at the other end, leaned into the table.

"I know it's early yet, but we need to discuss the holidays. I've found an accommodating property in Aspen, but Earl wants us to break in the new island property he closed on last week."

An island?

I grabbed my wine glass for a big gulp.

"Everybody ain't here for us to handle that, Ma," Iban asserted.

Taaliba made a dramatic show of gazing up and down the table. "All Ellises aren't present? Who are you missing, Ib?" She sent him a saucy expression.

"Nah," Iban disagreed. "Tiff ain't here." With a sinister grin, he plucked fish into his mouth. "You know she'll have Deek's ass if family plans are made without her. Real talk."

Taaliba sucked her teeth. And Sadik sent a long gaze his way.

"That isn't necessary," Monica interjected as the plates were being collected.

Thank God this was the end.

Earl cleared his throat, reclining in his high wingback chair. "Nah, he's right. Baby girl's input still matters in this family." Then his golden irises brush against me briefly.

Who is Tiff?

I couldn't see how the name "Tiff" could be pulled from Lia.

"Well, those here can begin to decide on their choice," Irene made clear.

"Not everybody here," Iban countered. "Y'all forget how many chicks I brought home before I got my hands on Monica?"

"Oh, stop it!" his wife demanded. "We all know you're not Sadik. Let's not make Bilan feel ostracized by reckless comments like that."

Sadik's hand was on my thigh, weightily stroking it up and down for consolation.

"I agree," Irene shared with feminine authority. "Why don't we have drinks in the garden and welcome our guest with more intimacy? Let's retreat out there with just the core."

People began leaving their seats, beginning with the girls.

"I have a call with a gallery in ten minutes," Taaliba announced as she left the table. "I may have to miss this." I watched as she made her way to her mother for a hug similar to the way she did Sadik.

"I'll be out there right behind you. Girls, let's go." Monica ordered. "Just give me a few minutes, Irene."

We all began to file out of the room as I wondered what Irene meant by just the "core." I followed the group down the hall with my brain speeding.

Sadik's mouth was at my ear. "I have to take this call I've been avoiding all day. I'll meet you out there."

The soft kiss on my neck sealed the deal.

As I followed the small group outside, I glanced behind me to find Sadik ambling in the opposite direction, fixedly on his call. That's when it dawned on me. The core meant minus the lovers. Tom, Nena, and Diane were no longer with us. There was a strange set of dynamics in this family.

"Come on, Bilan." I turned to find Irene with her arm stretched and a warm beam. "The garden is gorgeous. One of my favorite features of the property for the family."

I smiled and continued ahead. Earl led the way, and I was low key surprised to see Irene catching up to him. I stumbled when his hand stretched as he reached back for her, anticipating her presence. Iban strolled with one hand holding a drink and the other in his pocket, his posture almost as intimidating as his younger brother's. He was definitely brooding. I wondered what was his deal.

We journeyed quite a way under the glow of tall lamp posts along a cement walkway. To the left of us was an open, deep green, manicured lawn. Its details were hard to make out at this hour with the sun being down. To our right were high artificial boxwood hedges.

I was tempted to reach over to pull a clover, but decided on good judgment. The Ellises were legit in every facet of their lifestyle, other than their reputation.

The group eventually made it to the lounge, centered by a fire pit bowl. The flames were blazing against the mild wind. This cozy area was illuminated by the fire and light posts around miniature stadium-style seating.

"Have a seat," Earl offered as he took to a curved bench himself.

Irene followed him, planting herself to his right. Iban took the area to the left of his parents. As he sipped his drink, his glower on me couldn't be missed. My eyes averted from unease and I tried to smile.

Irene's regard swept our small group. "I'm going to call for a cocktail. Earl, I can request Mauve for you and Sadik. Bilan, can I order something for you?"

Why did my eyes balloon? I didn't know what to say at first. Order?

"Ummm..."

"She'll take more Malbec," Sadik's smooth alto boomed with authority out of nowhere, golden head glistening against the flames of the pit.

His expression was blank as he strode in with a cell phone in each hand. Irene nodded warmly, taking to her phone. Instead of taking a seat next to me, Sadik walked up to the bench above mine and sat behind. His muscular legs surrounded me, knees on either side. Immediately, I felt a sense of comfort. And when he pulled me back and into his crotch, my contented hum was almost audible. This visit was harder than I imagined. The family intimidated me just as much as the compound.

"So, you're from West Paterson?" Earl asked as Irene spoke quietly into her phone.

I gazed up to find his regard on me. "No." I cleared my throat. "I guess you can say I'm from Newark."

"Oh, yeah?" His eyebrows hiked.

"Yes." Placing one palm over the other, I weaved my fingers together. "My parents had a restaurant there by the time I was born.

When I was about six, they opened a second location in Paterson and settled there."

Iban scoffed. "I thought you were gonna say Woodland Park."

"Oh, noooo," I breathed. "That was a big issue with my neighbors, but for me, the name switch didn't change the neighborhood. I still say West Paterson in conversation. And up until a few years ago, I had to remember Woodland Park when filling out my address."

"How did your father feel about the change? I know those folks had been trying for that for years. It was that big of a damn deal for them to separate themselves from the hood. Did Sadik tell you I'm from Paterson?"

My head shifted up to Sadik. "No. He didn't." His response was a tender kiss on my forehead. I turned back to face Earl. "The change was officially made in maybe...2009." After my father's passing. "I don't think he was into the politics of the town."

"Too much into running those restaurants, I bet." Irene smiled.

"No." I let out a breath. "We'd lost them by then."

It was a dreadful period. We struggled so hard around that time, living off my mother's wise savings from when years were plentiful.

"Running a business is hard," Irene attempted to save me.

"If being a businessman is a part of your attraction to Sadik, you on point, shawtie." Iban took a sip of his drink.

"This is true," Earl chimed in. "My son's a Blakewood man." Iban's head whipped over to his father. "His mind is one of the brightest." He nodded decidedly. "My son."

Sadik went to THE Blakewood University?

I had no idea. I'd never asked him which schools he went to, only about some of his experiences. This deepened the gap between us. BU? Was he being modest about his pedigree or simply withholding pertinent information?

Like the fact that his parents' house is as big as my whole block?

My head shot up and found Sadik's blank expression, though I was confident he knew I was surprised.

"That's enough of embarrassing him. Let's talk about something else," Irene tried with a warm expression.

Sadik began to rub the tension, he likely sensed, from my neck. I loved the intimacy of his touch, didn't even mind it in front of his family.

"The only other pressing topic I can think of is our family vacation this winter. And seeing how Sadik brought someone home, I think it's appropriate to get to know Bilan, Irene," Earl noted. He opened his palms. "This is us: our unit, our family."

"Or maybe we reading too much into this," Iban voiced.

"What do you mean?" his mother asked.

Iban shrugged. "Maybe my brother is finally acting his age and just...dating." His brows lifted as he peered over to his brother above me. "Things're about to change in his world. Like it or not, this may be how he's dealing with it." Sadik's legs tightened around my arms, and his hands froze on my shoulders. The baby. He was referring to Sadik's baby. "Let him be a young man." Iban shrugged again.

We were now both sitting in front of a crackling fire, tensed from agitation. It was pathetic how easily I could forget Sadik was an expectant father. How could I agree to being a man's girlfriend when he'd be having a baby soon? A man who clearly doesn't like using condoms—because he doesn't with me—and didn't just a few months ago with Lia.

His magical hands began again, and as good as they felt, I didn't lean into him this time.

"What did I miss?" I heard sang from my right. Monica swept into the pit area wearing the biggest, most distracting smile. She carried a tray of the drinks Irene ordered. "The girls are tucked away in their room and should be dozing off any minute now." She lay the tray down on the table portion of the pit.

"Oh!" I perked up. "The girls have a room here?" I guessed so, seeing the place was large enough for a small army.

"They share one now, but in a couple of years when they're funky teens, they'll separate and have their own room," Sadik explained, unusually tender. "Everyone has a room here."

"Easy," Iban warned, nose in the air and eyes narrowed our way. "Only family."

I spit, "Of course. For family." I laughed nervously, trying to rebound from his hidden message.

"Yup," Sadik added coolly. "My room was just remodeled last year. It's enough space and grandioseness for you, I'm sure." Humor sprinkled between his words. "One day, our babies'll have their own room, too."

Monica's torso swung up and her head whipped back to face us. She wasn't alone in her shock. Earl's arm held, extended in the air from when Monica handed him a tumbler of brown liquid. Irene's mouth hung agape, and Iban's chin was to his chest. We were all agog with Sadik's forecast.

"Babies? Are you two planning a future together?" Earl trilled.

Sadik kissed my forehead again. "Of course, it means we'll be married first, but yeah."

Monica handed me a glass of red wine.

"The hell! Is this the way you tell us?" His father pushed. "Randomly, after a family meal?"

My breathing became shallow, and my pulse pounded my neck.

Sadik's hand moved affectionately over my head, neck, and shoulders. "Me bringing a woman to my family home and to our dinner isn't random, and I believe you know that." His voice was eerily calm, just a hint of agitation in it. "Bilan is my future. It was time for me to bring her here. Hopefully, in the morning, Monica can show her around the estate."

My eyes flew to Monica, whose expression hadn't changed.

"So, this is you proposing?" Iban bit out, clearly angry.

"Nah, but I'm taking her away in a couple of days, and we'll have a timeline soon after," Sadik responded to his brother, but the tenderness in his tone was obviously for me.

My head whipped around to see his eyes gleam with a fire I'd never seen of him.

"We just got back. I have to work, Sadik."

He lifted my chin with his index finger and kissed me, pulling my lip when he withdrew. "I know, baby. You'll have to quit."

"Quit?" I echoed.

"You're done with school anyway. How long did you think you'd keep that gig? Nicky was right. You're about to be a graduate school student." His eyes were soft, completely loving as he admonished me in front of his well-heeled family.

"Holy shit," Monica cried, still in shock as she plopped down next to her husband. "This is serious."

Iban's irises shot bullets; this time, I saw they were landing on his brother. I'm not sure I'd ever been as uncomfortable as I was in that moment—and I'd been uneasy a lot recently. I couldn't help but wonder if this all was some sick joke. And by the way Sadik's father and brother were gaping at me, I could assume they wondered the same thing.

"I'm happy for you, Sadik," Irene proclaimed proudly.

"Are you?" Earl barked. "While he has a child on the way with a fuckin' Rizzo? You think it's okay for him to be littering the state with my goddamn legacy?"

That was it. I stood to my feet and slammed the untouched wine glass down on the tray it came from.

"Excuse me." I turned to Monica. "Could you show me to the room I'm staying in tonight?"

The exit was so corny, but the only one I could think of to get me out of the twilight family.

Shooting to her feet, Monica scurried to place her bottled water down and began out of the lounge area. "Sure. This way."

I sat there in the wake of her scent with my head hung, pinching the bridge of my nose. I did the countdown thing, trying not to lose my shit on these two.

"We should have kicked it about this first, Sadik," Iban grounded out.

My head swung up in rapid speed. "Muthafucka, I've kicked it with you enough about my future! Don't fuckin' go there."

"Sadik, your mother!" my father shouted.

I shook my head. He was right. I couldn't give a damn about him, but my mother didn't deserve me spazzing the hell out.

Squeezing my eyes closed, I begged my temper to slow. "You better hope I can rebound from this." My eyes shot to both Iban, then my father.

I paused, holding the knob, fortifying myself for what awaited me on the other side of the door. After a deep breath, I pulled the lever and stepped inside, closing the door behind me. My eyes swept the room until I found her at the other end, pacing with crossed arms. Bilan noticed me almost immediately and began her trek toward me.

"What the hell was that?"

"What?" My aplomb game was strong, she would soon learn that, even for matters concerning things closest to my heart.

"Let's start with you bringing me up here to this..." She swung her arm around toward the open balcony. "This fortress, and basically telling your family we're engaged!"

I dipped my chin, eyes beseeching for her logical thinking. "We both know I didn't tell my family we're engaged. I said we're going to get married, sweetheart."

"That's the same thing!" Both her arms shot into the air. "How could you get me in front of a whole bunch of strangers...on a freaking arm-guarded compound and decree my future like that?"

I inhaled deeply, my eyes closing momentarily. "Bilan, I only gave you what you asked for, but presented it in front of the most cherished people in my life. I don't see what the big deal is."

"What did I ask for?"

"A family. Remember that?" My eyes narrowed and head tilted. "Is that not what you said you wanted more than anything in this world. A family, similar to what you used to have as a small child? I can give you that. My family is that and more. We're a stringently woven unit. Loyalty is a part of our teaching. Nothing comes before my family." I took a deep breath, standing straight, and stretching my neck. "Until you."

A wave of tears fell down her freckled cheeks. "Don't manipulate me, Sadik. Don't do it!" That knocked the fucking wind from my chest. "You took my words of vulnerability...admitting to wanting to risk my feelings for you, to trust you an—"

"I'M FUCKIN' IN LOVE WITH YOU!" My whole body quaked with volcanic rage.

The tumbler I held vibrated, spilling brandy all over my hand. Sweat sprouted from the pores of my head and my chest heaved, lungs working vigorously. I needed space from her. If I didn't leave, I was afraid I'd be stripped of the last of my dignity. She was fucking clueless! How could she not know?

With a quivering frame and hands covering her mouth, Bilan sauntered backward. "You never said."

"I did! Down there in front of the people I love the most. And now I'm here, like a fuckin' clown, telling you. I'm fuckin' in love with you, Bilan. I want to spend the rest of my life being your friend, lover, leader, and protector. I want all of you. I want your damn hips to birth my babies. I want to fight with you and for you for the rest of my days, but not just as we are now. I need more of you. All of you." I began to back away my damn self. "But I guess I'll just have to wait for you catch the fuck up."

I marched the rest of the way out and slammed the door behind me.

My heart thundered when he opened the bedroom door, casting a stream of light from the hallway. Closing it behind him, he trekked until finding his way into the bathroom. I lay there listening to the shower go, counting down the minutes until I had to confront him again. My heart ached and mind somersaulted with questions and probabilities and scenarios and doubts. The one thing I didn't have was assurances.

I sucked in a breath when I heard his padded steps nearing the bed. That's when I realized I'd taken a mental trip—again—tonight. Sadik was lifting the covers with one hand and reaching for me with the other. Once he was satisfied with my location, he slipped beneath the linens and spooned me, chastely kissing my shoulder. I twisted around to face him, effectively guiding him to lie on his back, then straddled him. Leaning over to meet his face, I kissed him sweetly, shuttering when I felt his cool palm on my hinds.

"Look, Bilan—" he tried when I withdrew, my fingernails scraping down his five o'clock shadow.

Then I crawled backward down his hard frame until my face met his crotch. Swiftly, I flipped around, bringing my knees over his chest so my head was toward his legs and my feet near his shoulders. Sadik growled with animalistic fervor as he leapt in the air, burying his face in the seam of my butt.

I scooted up and hissed over my shoulder, "No! Lay back."

Slowly, he obeyed, laying back. I knew what I was doing, understood the torture of it on his part. Sadik loved nothing more than me spread for him, but tonight, I had my own agenda. I began with soft kisses on his member swelling in my palms. I reverenced everything about the man, from his brain that stimulated me to his appendage that pleasured me, and his feet that wanted to lead me. My tongue ran greedily across its bulbous head, then pulsing veins zagging all the way to the root.

That quickly, I decided I enjoyed this; it was my pleasure. Sadik's body beneath me was tense and vibrating. He didn't enjoy being in timeout during intimacy. And I added to his torture by wiggling my ass, making my cheeks clap so he could smell me.

"Yo, Bilan," he groaned, warning in a way that would threaten an unknowing party.

But not me.

I took him deeper into my mouth, tightening my grip on his thick root. Then I jerked him, slapping his head around my tongue. The sound was libidinous and I felt emboldened. His rigid legs kicked out, then pushed back together. I cupped his sacs, feeling how loaded they were. My fists moved faster, jaw suctioned harder, tongue moved with more aggression. Doing this not only pleased Sadik, it brought me immeasurable pleasure, too. My sex danced in the air, lubricating with need. The thicker he grew in my hand, the more drenched I became, and the harder I worked.

My commitment was to the whole night if that's how long it took him to find a release in my mouth. I moaned over him, loving his warmth around me, relishing in his natural scent, aroused by his heat. The apex of my areola rubbed against his bubbling abs like they did this morning, driving me insane.

"Shit!" he swore. "Bilan, please..." he cried. "Just let me touch you, baby. Let me make you cum."

Stubbornly, I stroked faster, harder, and rocked my hips over him more, releasing more of my aroused scent into his face. Seconds later, his body began to quiver violently beneath me.

"Bilan..." he groaned. "I'm sorry, baby." His cry grew imminent. "Hold up!" he choked out, his legs lifting, pelvis pumping to my face. He moaned deliciously as I worked with vehemence. Then his palm was on my neck, pushing the head of him farther down my throat. "Fuck!" he croaked.

Seconds later, I felt warm cream squirt into my mouth, down my tongue. It was easier to process it this time. Sadik's heavy arm didn't let up so easily. I had to manage the water hose of his hot release and breathe, but his cries of helpless pleasure made it all worth it. He let up when he couldn't take my onslaught any longer.

I crawled down his legs to sit next to him on my knees. Sadik sat slumped over as though inebriated on a street corner. His heavy breathing was violent, chest heaving visibly. Swallowing the last of him, I wiped my mouth as I waited.

An index finger raised in the air. "Don't. Ever. Do. That. Shit. To. Me," he growled between breaths.

My face opened alarmed. "What?"

"Manipulate me with sex. Don't make me powerless!"

"I didn't—"

"You did!" he shouted. "You took advantage of my..." He couldn't catch his breath. "...vulnerability because...you know you fuckin'...can."

Is that what I did?

I shuffled closer to him, my hand going to his clammy, taut back.

"That's what I thought you did to me earlier. I thought you took a piece of my inexperience and vulnerability and manipulated it for your selfish agenda. I was deliberate, yes. But was I selfish and manipulative? No."

"Then what the fuck was that, Bilan?"

"Miscommunication, I now see."

"What?"

I rolled my eyes in the darkness of the room. "While you were gone, I had time to think about your announcement of being in love. I don't know when it happened, but you never shared it with me when it did. And when you thought it had happened to me, you took the next logical step—in your mind—and brought me home to meet your family. They were left in the dark, too. Those people had no idea what I was doing here."

"What's the fuckin' point?"

"My point is: we need to communicate more. Better. You began developing deep feelings for me at some point. You should have told me, just like I told you when I realized it yesterday."

"Bilan, I told you, I'm not a man of a lot of words. I say what I mean and that's it for me."

"But what you're proposing of me doesn't work with that attitude or state of mind. Marriage, Sadik? Kids?"

"And? What's wrong with that?"

"The fact that marriage is a partnership. I don't know what type of union your parents have, but mine was crappy. My father dictated. My mother knew he wasn't that strong of a leader, yet followed anyway."

"What the fuck are you saying?"

"I'm saying I need time. I'm saying even though I've been laying here in bed for over an hour, mulling over scenario after scenario about where your mind was when you made that announcement, I finally came to the conclusion there was no malice on your part. You saw me crack and took your shot. The thought of you having deep feelings for me warmed me. It made me feel..."

"Loved?" he hissed.

"Pursued in earnest." I held my breath.

Sadik croaked a laugh, grumbling, "Fuckin' asshole."

He grabbed me, lifting me onto his lap in two rapid movements. A guffaw ripped from my lungs as I was being manhandled. He kissed my exposed throat.

"What's it going to take for some reciprocity here?" He bit my ear.

"Time." Another thought flashed. "And assurance."

"Assurance of what?"

"Assurance that you don't want an arrangement: you want me exclusively."

He snorted. "What else would I want?"

I paused, choosing my words wisely. "Sadik, why does your father have not one, but two girlfriends? Why was Tom Banks fondling your mother in the hall of the home she shares with your father? And at dinner, he sat right next to her. And your father... He kissed both those girls, dismissing them after dinner. You can't tell me that was appropriate."

After a long breath, Sadik used his remarkable strength to pull us up to the head of the bed, where he leaned back on the mountain of pillows. Then he arranged me comfortably in his lap.

"My parents are...unique in their union, but they're very much committed to their marriage."

I scoffed. "That's clear."

He nodded, pacing the topic. "For years, my father struggled with infidelity. Some months, he was totally faithful to my mother. When I became an adult, he once confided in me, after Taaliba was born, the longest he'd abstained from other women was a year. His needs changed, his appetite broadened. She knew it and fought with him in the earlier years, according to her, until she got tired. She packed up her things and moved to the other side of the house—had a second master bed added on. My father allowed it to happen. What he didn't realize was while he was out fulfilling his physical needs with women, he neglected my mother's emotional ones. For years, she said she didn't even desire sex, just companionship."

"Whoa..." I breathed, lost in the story.

"My father saw she'd taken on telephone and texting conversations with other men and okayed it, believing them to be harmless. The trick with that was, when she began to have her emotional needs satisfied, her physical ones returned. My father approved of platonic relationships and even would allow Jake, my mother's first friend, to come by. That was until he caught them on camera in the pool."

He shook his head, blinking hard. "I don't know the details of what he saw, but it was clear my mother and Jake's rules of engagement had changed. That's when all hell broke loose. For three years straight, they fought, and hard. The weekly dinners were tense and sometimes canceled. They wouldn't look at each other and only used vile words to communicate. My father cleared out all of my mother's closets and drawers one Valentine's Day and burned them a mile away from the house. My mother had his Trinidadian girlfriend, at the time, deported from an expired visa."

"How did she know?"

Sadik chuckled dryly. "Money gives you resources. She hired a private investigator. But yeah." He took a deep breath. "It got ugly. So bad, Taaliba started acting out. If you ask me, she still hasn't recovered and this was years ago. They made it perfectly clear divorce was off the table. My father threatened her life if she left. My mother threatened his freedom if he walked. So..." He dipped his chin. "I hired a therapist. An intense one, who moved in for half a year. It took that long for her to quit and tell me the best way for them to live amicably would be for either my father to stop his cheating or allow my mother to have male friends."

My eyes ballooned. "She proposed that?"

"In jest—well, frustrating jest. She had no idea they'd make that agreement a month after she left, and all alone. They sat down and laid out rules."

"What are the rules?"

Guilt pricked my chest the moment those words left my mouth.

Sadik shook his head softly, eyes out into the distance. "I really don't know. I never asked. To me, inviting a third lover into your bedroom if you have an exclusive love with a woman or man will invariably begin the timer on the bomb."

"So, you don't approve?"

"Hell no!" he grated bitterly. "Never. But we were taught to always view our parents as leaders and ourselves as lower-ranking members of our village. We had no choice in the matter. I saw that even though my father's girlfriends—that will rotate—mostly lived here, he would still take my mother on vacations with just the two of them. He still buys her gifts and surprises her with them. They'll return to the original master suite on occasion. And when it comes to decisions and events about the family, their lovers are left out."

"But they weren't tonight. It was made clear to me, my being here was an occasion. But their lovers were included in the family dinner. That's insane, Sadik."

"That was my call."

My head jerked hard to shift my body to face him. "What?"

"Their...lovers are not at most dinners. Even if they're on the premises, it's understood they sit out dinners. I requested they be here tonight because I needed you to see us at our dysfunction. I didn't want to surprise you with our dynamic later and make it more awkward."

"Is that why you were so cold with Tom?"

"Tom isn't accustomed to breathing the same air as me. He's wisely stayed away since my mother shared with him how Jake got his jaw wired after strolling around the compound leisurely one day I pulled up. My father may allow the queen her spoils, but for me, she'll always be untouchable. I don't need to see her imperfections, and that's precisely what happens when I see her...lovers." He cringed again at that word.

This had to be hard for him to share. And I couldn't bear many more details about his confounding family.

"Where are you going?" he asked when I shifted to leave the bed.

"To brush my teeth."

"Nah." He reached over and pulled me to him. "You're going to get on all fours so I can fulfill my needs, too. Then you're gonna come in my mouth while crying your devotion." He tossed me until I was straddling his waist.

I turned back to him with a racing pulse and throbbing clit. "Crying what, exactly?" I murmured over my shoulder.

Sadik kissed my left cheek. "That you'll stick this out until you fall in love with me."

If I had a reply, it was effectively vanished from my brain at the first long stroke of his tongue in my slit.

20

I'd been up for over an hour before I decided to shower. Sadik was still lost in slumber as I slid out of the massive bed. Once I was cleaned, I decided to curl my hair and get dressed. When I came up to the room last night, our suitcases were here inside the walk-in closet; not as big as the one in Sadik's apartment, however, just as lavish. Without his assistance, I decided on blue distressed jean shorts, a black spaghetti-strapped tank, and a yellow cropped blazer. The blazer was for in case these people dressed formally in the morning, too. I pushed my feet into Ase Garb heeled mules, and slipped out of the room quietly.

When I thought I may find the girls and hang out with them, I was faced with their father instead. Almost right outside the door, Iban stood in slacks and a button-up, holding a mug of coffee.

I pointed behind me. "Sadik's still asleep. I can wake him if—"

Iban shook his head. "I thought I'd see him coming out first. The nigga never sleep late." His eyes roved indecently up my body. "But after he made it clear how good the pussy is, I can see how he breakin' all the damn rules." He did a reverse nod with his head. "C'mon. Let me walk you out to the veranda to get some coffee. You drink coffee?" I nodded. "Good." He began his stroll.

After I made the quick decision to obey, I realized I'd never been this close to a known murderer before. My armpits prickled with perspiration.

"Yo, I 'on't know how much you know about my family, but I bet you know I was locked down and why." I didn't answer as he sipped from a fancy porcelain mug. "I 'on't wanna get into what sent me there, but I can say this: it was behind family. I 'on't give a shit who,

where, what, or why; when it comes down to the Ellis name, I'm murkin' niggas to keep the legacy. Don't nobody come before my pops, mom dukes, brother, baby sis, and kids. Errbody know that shit—my fuckin' wife included. And for this family, I guard over the emperor— my pops—and the regulator, my brother."

He patted his chest as we turned a corner. "I'm the fuckin' enforcer. Bitches always think money and power when they see the Ellis sons. They think we their come up. Nah. That shit 'on't go down. It took me years to choose my wife. I watched her, learned about all her friends. Shit." He blew out a breath. "They had to go. Her shady family members. Them niggas see her maybe once a year. Being the wife of a Ellis man means you live, breathe, and die for us."

I was relieved when we turned another corner and the bright blue sky appeared in the opening to a balcony.

"See, a small-town girl like you don't belong here. You ain't built for this life. We move different, sweetheart. The shit we be on'll have you fucked up. Even being in this house a goddamn privilege. And it better not be no shit on social media about the place either."

My forehead stretched. I raised my hands in the air as we crossed onto the veranda. "I don't even have my phone on me."

"Good." He nodded toward the left at someone. I looked and saw Earl sitting with his legs crossed, facing the beautiful vista of a garden while smoking a cigar. "Coffee's served," Iban mumbled before walking off.

My chest heaved, lungs worked so hard, my head spun.

"You okay, dear?" I could hear Earl, but couldn't answer just yet. "Sweetheart," he called again.

"Good morning, Mr. Ellis," I chirped, managing to open my eyes.

"You can call me Earl. Come have a seat. You look a lil' pale." My feet began to move, and I found my way to the empty seat next to him. He pointed over the balcony. "You see that Violet Love tree down there? The little one with the purple and white blooms?" I nodded. "It's new. My wife wanted it. Been begging for it for years. It didn't fit in with the rest of the garden, I knew it." He shrugged, taking a puff from his cigar, those honeyed irises narrowed to endure the smoke. "Me being a reasonable man, I gave in last fall. We had it

planted, and just like I knew it would, it bloomed out of order." That's when his regard landed on me.

"I don't understand." I had to say something.

"The moody lump of wood don't bloom with the spring blooms, don't exactly bloom with the summer ones either. It blooms randomly and don't keep with the family of trees I personally chose for my property. It doesn't fit in."

Oh, no...

My hand rose to my nose.

"I taught my boys a long time ago, honey, just because something's beautiful and attractive, doesn't make it perfect or complete. It has to align with their goals and ultimate visions set for their lives. But as a parent, I had to learn correction lasts well into adulthood—even with my wife." He pointed again. "Look at that damn tree," he urged with charisma. "And you know what she's going to say? Just plant a few more so it won't be the only one blooming when it does. And that, honey, is why I shouldn't have allowed the first one to be planted. More would be expected to follow and before I know it, I've lost the vision of my garden."

Earl turned to me, pulled strongly from his stogie and blew it out. Clouds of smoke covered his face, keeping him veiled...from me. It was his barrier. His mysticism. I bit the inside of my lip to distract from the impending tears. It was clear. Sadik's family didn't like me. I wasn't wanted here.

I thought this stuff only happened in movies...

"Why is coffee on the east veranda this morning instead of the usual north?" a woman asked. I turned to find Monica dressed in a fitted sweat suit with her voluminous dark hair now down and blown out. Her eyes met mine, then swung over to Earl's. "Dad, you can't do this."

"Do what, baby?"

Monica came my way almost in a rush. "You cannot intimidate her like this. Does Sadik even know you're here with her?"

Earl blew air from his mouth, hand stretching into the air toward the garden. "I came out here for the magnificent view. I don't know where my son is now," his voice with child-like innocence.

338

"Come on, Bilan." Monica brushed my shoulder affectionately. "I'll walk you down to breakfast. Irene should be done soon."

I stood to my feet, nearly stumbling over them, and followed her back into the house.

"I'm so sorry about that!" she cried.

My breathing was erratic as I paced the marble floors with her. "I thought men were supposed to get threatened and bullied when meeting the family." The joke felt right at the moment.

"You'll soon learn two-thirds of the Ellis men in this family believe control is the only way to get along with people. I was relieved to see the youngest of them had some reasoning to him." She sucked her teeth. "Irene would have his head if she knew this."

"Did Earl do this to you?" I asked, my body still pumping adrenaline.

She didn't answer right away as we stopped at an elevator. An elevator! Monica pressed the button for a call.

"My introduction to this family was way different from yours. I'm from Newark. My father and Earl knew each other before I was born. He worked for my father-in-law for years. I didn't meet Iban until I was nineteen. I didn't even make the connection, but he knew me." She shook her head as the elevator door opened. "We were just one of those things that got ahead of me and twelve years and three kids—" She rubbed her almost not there bump. "—and a string of liquor stores later, we're here."

We stepped onto the elevator that had the nerve to be playing Muzak.

"Look, Bilan, you seem to be a sweet girl. I'm sure to you, these people are either scary or crazy."

"Try both," I mumbled, pulse still racing.

"If Sudik brought you home, you're likely the real deal to him. Lucky for you, he may be the younger male Ellis, but he's the most influential to senior." Her wry smile expressed a million things. We stepped off the elevator and began down familiar hallways I'd seen last night. This place definitely felt cathedral-like in prestige and size. "You're the first woman Sadik has brought home. He's almost forty, and hadn't mentioned being interested in anyone." She tried to

339

chuckle and brought her arm around my shoulder. "You must have his damn nose wide open, girl!"

"Then who is Tiff?"

Monica stumbled. "Girl, another heap of bullshit."

We turned a corner, sauntering into a commercial-sized kitchen with quaint home personality. It was beautiful with an open floorplan and half a dozen people working and scurrying about.

"Bilan, Monica," Irene sang from over a huge ceramic pot as she stirred. She banged the spoon on the edge before placing it on a utensil trivet. "Good morning!" She headed our way, arms outstretched for Monica.

"Morning, Irene," Monica greeted in her arms.

I noticed she called Earl Dad, but Irene by her first name. That was strange.

"Is it okay that I hug you?" a cheery Irene asked when she approached me. "You don't look well. Everything okay, miss?"

I forged a smile and nodded softly. "I hug," I lied, not really knowing what I "did."

She wrapped her arms around me. "Oh, you feel so tense. I know everything isn't okay, but I'm not the type of mother-in-law to pry. Isn't that right, Monica?"

"At all, although I am married to your oldest child," she joked.

Irene rolled her eyes and sighed, "This is true. I was so ready for that guy to get a partner. You have no idea!" They laughed. "Bilan, do you know how to make grits? It's a must for my Deeki." She waved me over to the stove she once manned. "My advice is to use Country Crock instead of any other butter, and definitely not margarine. I tried that when they were small and the little guy barely ate half his bowl. Oh! And he likes his in a bowl when it's good. When he's cutting back, he'll have it on the plate with the rest of his breakfast, just not as much as he does in the bowl."

"And not 'quick' either," Monica amended.

"Oh, no! My king doesn't eat quick style grits or packaged ones either." She turned her nose up, stirring the pot of white grains. I believed I'd tasted grits before at a friend's, but had not actually eaten them. "He'll do quick steel cut oatmeal, though."

They spoke at the same time, "But only from the round box." Both women giggled.

God, I was expected to keep him sexed and fed on food I didn't eat? It was overwhelming.

"Yeah," Irene shared. "He won't eat packaged oatmeal either, only the dry ones from the cylinder box. The one you have to add sugar to. I got up early to make cheesecake for him." She shook her head. "The things you do for your loves." She sighed.

Monica smiled, nodding in agreement. "That man loves to eat."

I took a deep breath, rocking on the balls of my feet. "Yeah," I murmured. "That he does."

More than you two possibly know...

Their narrowed eyes landed on me at the same time.

At the breakfast table, there were no lovers. Only the Ellis family proper were seated or taking to a seat, including me. The seat to the right of me was empty, but little Iesha was sure to take the one to my left.

"Nana and the cooks made me confetti pancakes with strawberries," she whispered to me. "They're delicious!"

If I wasn't so preoccupied, I would've hooted at the table. She was so adorable, sitting with her little hands crossed on her lap. But no. My mind was on her father, sitting across from us and her grandfather, finally taking his rightful place at the head of the breakfast table. He walked in with Taaliba in his arms before she went to sit close to her mother at the other end. This room wasn't the one we had dinner in last night. Monica said this was Irene's breakfast room. It was smaller and had a skylight ceiling.

"Where's Sadik?" Irene asked.

All eyes flew to me. It felt like hours since I'd last been in his protective company. I shrugged, going for the glass of water belonging to my place setting.

"Here he is!" Ivana shrieked. "Sit next to me, Uncle Deek!"

Sadik came trudging through the archway in a heather gray t-shirt with the royal blue Blakewood University logo, white and black sweats, black socks, and Gucci slide slippers. His stride made me squirm in my seat, my body excited, my mind overwhelmed. Gorgeous brows a bushy mess, his kaleidoscope-hued eyes dark and searing on my face, and full lips pursed. My heart galloped as he neared, mouth went dry.

"Can I speak with you alone, Bilan," his tone soft and frightening.

My eyes inadvertently swept the table. Most regards were on us.

"Can it wait?" I wheezed, hardly squeezing out the words.

"Abso-fuckin'-lutely not," he grated almost as low.

Stiffly, I stood from my chair. Sadik began the way out of the shushed room, and I followed. We walked a short ways into the kitchen before his body swung to face me, arm pushed above my head, palm planted into the wall as he bent to get eye level with me. I shrunk immediately.

"I gave you two rules of intimacy with me. The first is no clothes in my bed. The second is to never leave my bed without relieving me or being dismissed. Why the fuck did I wake up and you weren't there?"

I recoiled beneath his seething gaze.

Piping fucking hot.

When I got out of bed this morning to search all of the eight hundred-plus square feet of my bedroom and in-suite bathroom with heavy sacs and a throbbing cock, and had not found her, it fucked up my disposition. For a minute, I thought finally revealing my feelings and plans for her hadn't happened last night, and I had to continue to live in the torture of wait again. Bilan may have lived inside her head, but she was undoubtedly an independent thinker and a strong woman. I hated the idea of her disobeying two simple rules.

Now, peering down on her caramel, peppered face and full satin balm lips, I saw something other than the reaction to being accosted by me. I saw palpable fear. And not the type I'm capable of ensuing on her. There was something scaring her. My eyes closed, and I sucked in a deep breath through my nostrils. My next set of words and actions had to be measured. Beneath her pliant presentation was a reactionary woman. I hadn't forgotten that.

My forehead dropped to hers and I breathed. "I'm sorry."

Almost immediately, her little hands gathered my shirt at the hem. "I forgot. I'm still learning."

My heart warmed at her realization. Acceptance.

"You still have time," I assured her.

"I hope so," she croaked so low my eyes shot open.

There were no tears, but by the way her lips trembled as her eyes were downcast, I knew for sure my Nalib was shaken. I pulled her chin up by my index finger and placed a light kiss on her cool lips.

"Come on. I'm hungry." I let up off her and grabbed her hand to go.

She sucked in a quick breath. "Sadik..." I glanced over my shoulder at her. "Don't feed me. Okay?" I didn't respond at first, growing angry at the scent of her fear. "I'll have some toast or a few pieces of fruit, but please don't bring attention to me not eating."

I didn't want to lie to her any more than I'd been withholding from her. It's not what I wanted for us. I tugged her hand gently.

"My family's waiting on us to eat, baby."

When I turned to head back to the room, she didn't hesitate. The room was quiet when we made it back. I pulled out Bilan's seat and kissed her forehead when she sat in it. Then I took to my own seat.

"Grace," I announced with my palms out.

Seconds later, the room quieted and my father proceeded with prayer. The table echoed 'Amen', and the food was served. The cooks brought out serving bowls and special orders. As usual, the family dug in. My first grab was a bowl. My mother's creamy grits were placed directly in front of me. On a plate, I loaded eggs, sausage, and French Toast I planned to feed my girlfriend.

Iesha danced in her chair as she forked a piece of her favorite pancake with fresh strawberries. My father cut into his sirloin, and Monica asked me to pass her the serving bowl of grits.

"The hell took you so long to get out of bed?" Iban asked, biting into fried catfish. "You care to share with the table?"

"Don't start, Ib!" Taaliba groaned, recognizing his childish antagonism.

My eyes were on my plate as I cut the slices of French Toast.

"Nah." I grabbed the syrup. "But I do think it's necessary to check whomever addressed Bilan without my permission." My eyes rolled up to my brother, then my father. Iban's 'deer caught in headlights' stare gave him away. My father's strong ignore game was his confession. I dropped the glass syrup dispenser onto the table. "Let's make one thing goddamn clear: she may be new to you, but she's it for me. As long as she breathes, she'll never have a reason to fear if I'm walking the earth. And in my family home, she will be safer than a fairy tale princess in a goddamn fortress." My fist banged the table, temper getting ahead of me, no matter how much I tried to reign it in, in the presence of my nieces.

344

"Uncle Deek!" Ivy shot from her seat and ran to me.

On her way, her mother grabbed her, whispering something in her ear.

"All this necessary?" Iban asked.

"I could ask you the same thing about speaking to my girl!" I was two seconds off his ass. "What the fu—what made you think it was okay to say anything other than 'good morning' to her?" Iban's face was tight as he stabbed his fork into the plate. "Do I ever address your wife in an abrasive manner? Or you." I shot my heated regard down to my father as Monica ushered the girls out of the room. "Have I said anything other than 'hello' or 'goodbye' to your bedroom evangelists?"

My father cleared his throat, sitting back in his chair, bringing his hand to his chin. Iban pouted like a big ass fucking kid, a palm cupping his fist over his breakfast.

"Then fuckin' respect my space! This will be the last time I'll have to address this shit or, so fuckin' help me, the usual interfacing in this family is about to fuckin' change!"

I eyed the two intently, waiting for a rebuttal. Iban would have been dealt with one way and my father another less aggressive manner, but effective nonetheless.

"I hear you, Sadik," my father mumbled, going back to his plate.

"A'ight, man," Iban acknowledged, regard to the corner of the room.

After another deep breath, I forked a piece of French Toast, dipped it into the syrup, and turned to my equally culpable party, for not being forthcoming with this when we spoke privately, and implored, "Now, please try my mother's French Toast. She bakes the bread herself and the syrup is purchased directly from a company in Vermont."

My tongue pushed into her lax mouth. I moved with patience, swiping, teasing, and ultimately prompting. I kept my hands on either side of her thick thighs, clasping the cement ledge of the pool. I needed her to choose. I didn't want my greedy need of her to force her hands in this instance. I needed her willingness. Soft strokes, tasting inside of her warm mouth, savoring remnants of the candy the girls shared with her when I found them after breakfast to apologize with Bilan in hand. Gentle sucking of her supple bottom lip as I kept a distance from her body, though I was between her open thighs as she sat on the ledge and I stood inside the pool, was strategic. I wanted her to feel safe and that she had a choice.

Bilan chose me when her breathing hiked, and she grabbed my shoulder with one palm and squeezed. She joined my echoes of tongue strokes when she began to chase mine with something resembling desperation. My heartrate sped and dick twitched in my trunks. It was mid-afternoon, and after what felt like a long breakfast to get food in to her after my explosion—that wasn't a real explosion because of the girls being there when I got started—I was able to get her to eat the equivalent of a whole French Toast slice.

My mother stayed behind with us as the staff cleared the table. She, too, was livid by what they did to Bilan. She offered my girlfriend an apology, which Bilan swore wasn't necessary. My girl was playing tough, but I knew deep down inside, she was frightened by it all. The one thing I had on my side was she really wanted me. Whether it was just my body to further explore her sexuality or more than that, I knew she tried sticking in there because she didn't want this to end. After I apologized to my mother, we all left the kitchen area and Bilan and I went to search for Ivy and Iesha. They were on the balcony off their parents' room having a tea party with Monica, where I apologized to them over tea and candy. My mother bought them real china recently, and they hadn't tired of the set yet.

After that, Bilan still seemed in her head, not saying much to me. So, I took her back up to my room and told her to change into one of several bikinis I packed for our impending trip. Lucky for me, she didn't give much resistance. No slick ass "fetish" comments—something I observed her hurling a lot—and no questions. She stepped into the bathroom while I changed in the closet, then made a furtive call for a few arrangements. Then we came down to one of two indoor pools on the main level of the house. I chose this one because no one would be using it at this hour. My nieces never hung out in here, opting for the other indoor pool with child-friendly slides and such. This one was designed with romance in mind. Gold brass fixtures and blue tiling all around. Candles stretched the length of twenty-four by eighty foot, L-shaped lap pool, though none were lit now.

We took a few laps around the pool before she began to initiate touch by sliding onto my back as I floated in the water, or smiled as I yanked at the knot of her bikini top. Then I asked her to sit on the ledge so we could talk. Talking led to me kissing her, needing a physical connection to calm the insecurity from the detachment.

So lost in her reception, I didn't catch Stacy plant the boxes until she was tiptoeing away from us. I pulled back from her busy mouth that went lax as I did. Her eyes opened with disappointment. Bilan was enrapt in passion, too.

"I'm sorry, Nalib," I whispered, creating a staccato reverberation around the area.

She took a deep breath. "Being with you is a lot, Sadik," she murmured.

A smile spread across my face. "I can only imagine what being my girlfriend is like."

I enjoyed teasing her with the girlfriend bullshit. At my age, I was too old for a girlfriend. Truthfully, I didn't know what else to call Bilan but mine. In some ways, she didn't have a choice. If she didn't run, I'd take that to mean she'd be what I wanted her to be. One thing was for sure, I had to call her something to make sure she knew this thing was exclusive. No more Jason.

No more Damien…

"I have something for you." My smirk was still at play. Those dotted freckles did shit to me.

She rolled her eyes. "Forcing me to call out for more days isn't enough? Do you have any idea how impossible it is for a baker to call out of a twenty-three hour diner for one shift, let alone days at a time?"

She was fussy. I didn't want her there. So, I gestured to the right of her, where the red boxes were. She followed my line of sight and reached for one.

"Cartier, Sadik?" she squawked. "I call you out of the blue, I get a MEEHAR gown. I go pick up the gown for our date and get a shopping spree at JAGMisha Boutique. I go away with you as a gift for my graduation and get more designer clothes. I come back from said vacation to get more clothes. I spend the night at your place for the first time and get even more designer goodies. And now, I get the cold shoulder from your father and brother and I get Cartier." She smiled ruefully. "You gotta stay consistent, bud."

That caused me to laugh as she opened the box.

"Whoa!" she breathed, head going back. "Are you serious?"

I kissed the side of her neck, ignoring the question. "Open the other," I whispered in her ear.

Bilan reached back for the second and opened it. "LOVE bracelets?"

"For you," I whispered again in her other ear.

"Sadik, I can't reciprocate. What can I do to return the gesture?"

"Give me the one piece of reciprocity I've been fighting for."

"What's that?"

"Your heart," I whispered into her lips.

When I pulled back, observing the unsmiling expression on her face, Monica came into view."

"Sorry to interrupt, love birds—Oooh! Cartier!" she tweeted. "What is it?" Monica bent to look between us. "LOVE bracelets! Awwwww! I want one!" she pouted playfully. Bilan cracked a smile. "Stacy told me you two were in here. The girls are down, and I'm now free to show you around the compound."

Bilan turned to me with apologetic eyes. I slapped her thighs. "Go. I've got shit to do I've been avoiding all day."

"You sure?" she asked, hesitating.

"Positive. She's saving me a bunch of descriptions and other tourist babble needed for that task." After kissing her lips, I began swimming backwards to the ringing in-house phone on the interior of the pool.

On the way there, I heard Monica giggle, "We can grab you a glass of wine before we start."

My eyes were on Bilan's dimpled ass as I picked up the phone. "Yeah."

"Oh, you are in the pool?" my father questioned with sarcasm.

"Yup. I'm down here," I returned with the same naiveté.

"I know you plan on leaving tomorrow. I need to talk to you. Meet me in the gun range."

"About?" I swiped my nose.

"I hear Rizzo's spazzin' the fuck out over the Lia bullshit. He's threatening war."

"Fuck him," I groaned. Her, too... Lia was wrong for calling me for him. The shit was out of line, and I planned on addressing it before Bilan and I left town. "I'll deal with Lia on my own terms. Iban has been wanting to unleash on his crew for a minute now. If he wants smoke, sic your son on him. Anything else you need from me?" I was unapologetically curt.

Earl knew we spoke the same language. When it came to temperament, I was most like him. When you crossed the line of my grace, god help us all.

"Yeah." His throat seemed strained. He sighed with humility. "With grown ass sons, it's like beefin' with your best friend. You gotta dead that shit before it festers."

"Word?" My forehead lifted. "How many times you have to apologize to your bestie, Iban?"

"Less than I have to kiss your ass," he grumbled.

"Actually, I have a conference call I've put off all morning to try to undo the damage you and your eldest ensued on my lady. Right now, I need to pay the bills."

I needed to shower, then dress for the call soon.

"Alright. Hit me when it's over. I'll be in my study after I'm done in here."

"You got it."

As I took to the third and final landing of the elaborate Elliswoods Palace staircase hand-in-hand with Sadik, I felt much more relaxed. Much of my confidence had returned since breakfast. Monica was fun. She was sweet and funny as she showed me around the property. She had stories—good and bad—about the different amenities of the place. And boy, were there plenty of them with over thirty-thousand square feet of the house and detached structures like a gun range, small farm, state of the art gym, a coffee shop for just the family, laundry building, bowling alley, skating rink, basketball court, a movie theater not to be confused with the theater room inside the house, and a landing strip for aircraft. And there was more to come. Earl had several projects he'd been working on this year alone.

After our tour, she walked me back to Sadik's room when I realized how much of a set-up this morning was. Because of the size of the house, I learned each Ellis practically had their own wing between three floors. Not much was on Sadik's side in terms of community, outside of his mother's art room she hardly used. The veranda the family used for morning coffee was closer to the center of the house. It was useless to get upset all over again, though. While out, touring the property, we ran into Earl as he was leaving the gun range. Without his eyes and while he cleared his throat, he apologized "if" he said anything to make me feel less than welcomed. He couldn't take back the fear I felt, but I appreciated the attempt. His son, according to his wife, Monica, had been off the property all day. So thankfully, I didn't have to run into him.

Now showered for the third time today, I was dressed in floral, silk cropped pants, an off-white blouse, and strappy sandals. Sadik was in a two-piece suit again with an open-collar white dress shirt. At the landing, there was a small gathering. Taaliba was there with Monica.

"We meeting in the foyer for drinks?" Sadik joked.

The ladies chuckled as Earl neared the circular area with his granddaughters.

"No. The doorbell rang as we came down here," Taaliba answered.

"Yeah," Monica added. "Iban went to answer the door."

"Who's here?" Earl asked, finally amongst us.

Iesha took my hand immediately. "You look pretty!"

I kneeled to her. "And, so do you. I wish I could fit that skirt!"

She smiled infectiously.

"And what about me?" Ivana stepped almost between us, showing off her black capri pants and adorable shirt.

"You're equally as stunning, as your Uncle Deek would say."

I glanced up and caught his grin as he gripped my shoulder. When I turned back to the girls, thrilled at finally having the ice broken between Ivana and me, my little Iesha broke from my hand and ran off.

"Auntie Tiff!" Iesha shouted as she lunged into the diva's arms.

She was thick. A brick house...and very stylish! Her makeup smoothed her brown sugar complexion, and the red lipstick made her teeth appear stark white. She had a line of diamond studs increasing in size from the top of her earlobe to the bottom. Her hips were round and seductively wide in black fitted, cropped joggers with the Fendi logo stripe running down the outer leg. She wore a matching short-sleeved Fendi logo shirt hugging her ample breast line and small waist. I wondered if it was possible for a woman who had to be a size sixteen, at least, to have such a small waistline. It honestly didn't matter. This woman was gorgeous, fashionable from head to toe with yellow, gold, and black strappy sandals I was willing to bet were Fendi, too.

It was the club owner. So far, Randi knew what she was talking about regarding the Ellis clan. I watched as she was greeted by the small group now congregated in the opulent foyer. That played with my head, subconsciously reminding me I didn't belong here. She seemed very familiar with everyone.

"Hi, baby," Earl cooed as he kissed her cheek and hugged her tightly. "What're you doing here?"

She moved on to hug Taaliba. "I got a invitation from your oldest. He asked me to come last night, but I had some bullshit going down at Energy I couldn't leave to those crazy asses. Heeeeey, Monica!" She reached out to hug her.

Monica appeared visibly uncomfortable reciprocating. That's when it hit me. This was the "Tiff" Iban mentioned last night at dinner. When she moved on to approach Sadik, his darkened eyes were on his brother, shooting flames. But it wasn't until her eyes met me, then brushed over to the tense arm Sadik had roped around my hip, then to his face that I knew.

"Hey, Tiff." He leaned in for a quick greeting, barely touching her. She tried smiling as she backed away, but struggled to rebound.

They were lovers. It was either past or very recently, but she'd known my "friend" intimately.

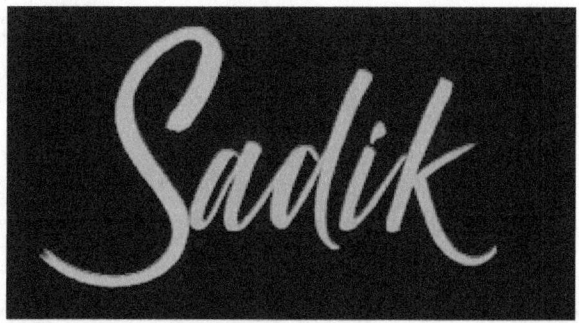

21

Bilan requested softly with a hand planted on my thigh. "More, please." I glanced down at her, practically tucked beneath me, though in her own chair. "More food," she blinked up at me this time.

Fuck!

She knew. Bilan knew I'd fucked Tiffany. It was no different than Miami, at the Ameerah concert. One look at a woman, and my Nalib knew if I'd spoiled myself in her. That was dangerous for me. It was risky. I didn't trust Bilan could accept I had a life before she sent my world topsy-turvy the night I tried to appeal to her using a fucking romance novelist as a tool.

As my regard went between her sipping on a glass of Malbec that hardly left her hand all meal as she peered across the table at Tiffany, and the chicken parmesan I cut on my plate that I used to feed the both of us, I realized we'd come a long way since that night at Michelle's. But I wasn't at ease. Bilan was still out of my grasp. I still had work to do to secure her.

I reached down to feed her the chicken, and all she gave me was the arterial view of those freckles. Her eyes were on Tiffany. Tiffany struggled, but did a good job avoiding looking at Bilan and me. I was sure she was grateful Iesha sat next to her, providing a distraction with her constant talk. She, too, was uncomfortable and caught completely off guard by Bilan's presence. My eyes roved over to Iban, who appeared completely oblivious to the tension he'd caused, leaning into his wife's ear, whispering something to make her grin.

As the staff began to collect plates, my father sat reclined in his usual seat. His discerning eyes went all around, but I was sure he was concerned about Bilan and Tiffany mixing. Tiffany was his goddaughter, and lately, his choice for a second daughter-in-law. I was sure he was in favor of that union purely to put to bed any possibility of me having more than just a child with Lia. My mother, at the opposite end, threw him glances throughout the meal I could only guess were of concern, too.

"You girls are out of school already?" Tiffany asked as though she was shocked. "You're making me wish my Ellis Academy days weren't over." She tickled Iesha.

"You didn't go to my school, Auntie Tiff!" Iesha giggled.

"I sure did!"

"She sure did!" Tiffany and Iban spoke, practically, at the same time. "You didn't know your Auntie Tiff went to all schools with Uncle Deek, even college," he had to add.

Iesha sucked on a breath, ironically, at the same time as Bilan next to me—beneath me.

Shit...

"Why don't we have drinks and dessert in the family room?" my mother suggested. "Girls," she referred to my nieces. "Nana has some tunes you can get down to!" She snapped her fingers above her head and twitched her shoulders.

The girls shouted their excitement in unison right away. The plate was collected from Bilan and me. She'd eaten more than I was used to, and I knew why. Bilan wanted Tiffany to see her being fed by me. Being a secure thirty-eight year old man, I had no problem going lengths to care for the woman I cared for. Yet I also wasn't the type of man who did shit for show.

As the table began to clear, Bilan turned to me and whispered, "How recent?"

My face tightened in confusion. "I'm sorry. I don't understand."

"How recently have you two been together?"

That was a rabbit hole my ass was going nowhere near.

I reached down and planted my lips on hers. "You're my recent, my now, and if I can catch a break, you will be my forever. Let's go."

I stood and grabbed her by the hand. Bilan stood, but did not lean into my guiding touch as I was used to. I turned to her.

"At least answer one question." I could see tears pool in her eyes. "Were you in love with her? She's beautiful...very stylish—" Her regard brushed down her frame in the clothes I purchased. "—and she seems sweet and family oriented."

I turned to her, chest to chest, beckoning her soul through her eyes. "She's never been my friend, Bilan." I gave her a minute, hoping she could process my need of friendship in a partner. It was non-negotiable for me. "My parents are the ideal partners. They've raised children and built wealth and legitimacy beside one another. But they aren't regular companions. They aren't on the same page. They aren't sick and obsessed with wanting to see the other at their optimum being. I believe, with the air I breathe, you being your best Bilan can help me be my best Sadik. And if you're your best Bilan and I'm my best Sadik, we can take over the fuckin' world. Friends. Companions. That's what I need. Trust me?"

Before she could say no, I brushed my lips against hers, then spoke into them. "Trust me, Nalib. Please," I whispered.

"C'mon, you lovebirds!" I turned to find Taaliba in the entryway of the dining room.

My little sister may have been a pain in my ass, but she'd always been able to sense my duress. She stood with a wry smile and waited with her hand out. I grabbed Bilan's hand and made it over to my Taaliba, taking her around the shoulder, under my left wing. With both their arms around my back, Bilan's lower, we strolled down the hallways to the family room.

It wasn't until we were feet away that we noticed commotion in the foyer.

"Well, what is he doing here?" my mother demanded. "What the hell does he want?"

"I don't know, Irene. Just calm down, sweetie." My father's attempt at a calm voice inherently alarmed me.

I was his preserver. No harm would come to Earl Ellis without prevention or a reaction from me.

Full. Fucking. Stop.

When the foyer came into view, the first thing I saw was Iban pacing back and forth, his hand on the burner at his waist.

"What's going on?" I asked.

"The guard's gate just called. Rizzo's on his way up."

"How many with him?"

"Just one car," my father answered. "His family."

"And I want to know why?" my mother asserted, crossing her arms.

"There are rules in place for this." Monica appeared from the family room. "Aren't I right?"

"What's going on?" Tiffany was next to appear.

"Let's just all calm down." My father's palms pumped the air. "You all can join the girls in the family room. Let us men—"

The doorbell rang in impatient successions. My father hopped to it, trekking a few yards down the vestibule to the door. He opened it with high and broad shoulders, as he'd taught us. Expectantly, Rizzo was escorted by an armed Ellis guard. While it was against protocol to bring war to any of the five alliances' homes, we still couldn't be too lax on security. Rizzo had been making threats. I saw the moment my father recognized the sprouting belly of Lia Rizzo. His hand fell from the door handle and body shifted, allowing them room inside.

Mello and Leo, our security, shadowed them inside, palms to waist.

"The fuck is going on, Ellis?" Rizzo began with arms in the air, charging inside. "I've tried staying the fuck out of this shit with these kids, but he's gone too fuckin' far!"

"Who the hell are you talking about?" my father's voice controlled.

"Who the fuck else?" Rizzo's arm swung to his pregnant daughter, cowering behind her mother like a scared mouse. "Lia and your smart ass, educated kid!"

Earl's hand pumped the air again, without animation. "Let's start with I don't have any kids. I have grown ass children. And if you're going to address my son, you will refer to him by his name." My father pointed to me, bringing my person to Rizzo's awareness.

In all the shouting he'd done within the span of seconds since he'd been inside, he hadn't realized the small crowd. When his eye landed on me, he noticed my juxtaposition to Bilan. She was still buried under my arm, chilled from the chaos.

He turned to my father. "You know, Ellis, I always respected you. Out of all the Black men I know, you've been the most disciplined, the most prideful, and calculated. I thought when your oldest got sent up…" He shrugged, lips pouted dramatically as though he was considering the right words. "…maybe it was just a fuck up that couldn't be controlled in our line of work. But then, when the youngest came and knocked up my sweet fucking Lia and did not have the gall to address me like a fucking man… The goddamn cazzo didn't have the cajones to face me like a fucking man!"

Cazzo? Wow…

Rizzo advanced my way, and I could feel Bilan's body shift, moving in front of me.

"Is this her?" he trilled, aghast. "Holy fuck! This is her!" He turned over his shoulder. "Lia, come over here and let these two address you like adults. Let him tell you why he knocked you up and dropped you like you're some trash on the fucking street and not a goddamn Rizzo!" he shouted so loud, Bilan in front of me leaped. "Get over here!"

My eyes traveled over to Iban, who watched Lia obey her father. As though he could feel my icy gaze, his regard flipped to me. If Iban wouldn't man up in this instance, it would alter the weaving of our brotherhood. This was it. This was where I would draw the line.

"Daddy," Lia choked on her tears, then slammed her face into her open palms.

She had the sense to not carry on with the lie.

This was it for me.

When the round man, Rizzo, I recognized from the FaceTime call, barked so loud, threateningly approaching Sadik, I felt protective. Violent even, if he dared lay a hand on him. But seeing this poor woman, pregnant—clearly abandoned—and in distress from the denial of her child, I couldn't do it. I couldn't forget I, too, was a woman and vulnerable to hurt, disappointment, heartache, and…being alone.

My body vibrated with an unnamed emotion as I reached for her arm.

"Lia, what's wrong?" I asked, my chin dipping to find her eyes. "I don't know what your history is, but Sadik isn't a monster. Say what you need to say. No one will hurt you." I hoped.

Her father was a fire-spitting maniac, two shouts away from cardiac arrest. But not Sadik. I'd only known him a couple of months, but I trusted him with my life. I wanted her to have that safety, too.

Lia didn't respond, and I didn't rush. There was now a timer on the bliss of my recent life with Sadik. I was sure of it. This was it for me. The time I'd have to say goodbye to it all. After a spell, she lifted her head, face red and lips trembling.

"I'm sorry, Sadik." My heart plunged from my chest at the pain in her wet eyes. "You shouldn't have been involved in this…" She could hardly finish. "I swear to god, I'm sor…"

"What the hell is she saying?" her father roared, panicked.

Lia turned to her father and shook her head, unable to stop the tears. "Daddy, I've been lying all this time. I've never had so much as Sadik's number until about a month after I got pregnant."

"What the hell?" Earl shifted in stance.

Irene held a palm to his chest to restrain him.

"Lia, baby." Rizzo took a step closer to her. To us. "You don't have to be afraid. They owe me an explanation."

"Not Sadik," she countered.

"What the fuck is she saying?" he shouted to the woman with them, I could only assume was Lia's mother.

"She's saying Sadik isn't the father of her baby," Tiffany announced.

"Then who the fuck is?" Rizzo's head rolled against every syllable.

I turned to Sadik, whose eyes were narrowed on his brother. Iban's expression resembled anger, too.

Oh my god...

His just wasn't the type that would pop out and strangle someone to death like his younger brother's.

"What the fuck is this, man?" Earl demanded. "Somebody better explain this shit to my muthafuckin' wife! Now!" His shout was more threatening than the Rizzo guy's.

Earl's command made the floor shake.

"No!" Monica yelped from behind me. I turned to see her hands shakily reach her face as her eyes widened with perceptible astonishment. "Noooo!" Irene clutched her collar in similar shock. "You heartless motherfucker!" Her scream was of agonizing betrayal, tears falling like a faucet. "You haven't changed a bit!"

Oh, no! Monica...

The moment she jogged off, I went after her. My heart bled for her trouble.

"No, Bilan!" Sadik reached for my arm, grabbing me so firmly, I stumbled backward.

I couldn't stop my anger when I hauled off and slapped the bitter shit out of him. Sadik's head rocked as his family gasped all around us.

"Don't you ever lie to me again, or I swear to Allah, I'm done!" I screamed, tears escaping.

Sadik took a deep breath. I could see the muscles in his jaw flex beneath his five o'clock shadow as he tried managing his anger.

"It's time to go, honey." His voice controlled, affectionate.

"But, Sadik—"

"I said!" He caught his threatening tone, but didn't change the menacing energy in his eyes. "—it's time we go." I dropped my arm in acquiesce, my mind racing to process this night. Sadik stepped toward Iban, index finger in his face. "This will never be forgotten." After studying his brother for a spell, he made a beeline for the staircase with me clacking behind, double his pace to keep up.

The ding sounded from the public address system.

Lynn announced, "The captain has turned off the fasten your seatbelt sign and you can now move around the cab—"

Before she finished, Bilan, across from me, scrambled to unclick her seatbelt and jumped to her feet. As she stormed off, I was two steps behind her, thrilled by how comfortable she'd grown on my jet. Nothing could kill my joy right now. A weight had been lifted from my shoulders, and there were now no boundaries between my Somali princess and me.

Even if she's an ice princess at the moment...

She slipped into the bedroom, and when she went to slam the door, I caught it with my foot and then chest.

"What the hell is your problem?" I shouted, closing the door behind me.

When she turned to find me, her eyes went wild. "No!"

"Yes."

"No!"

"You think I'm going to give you a moment alone after that shit? At least when you're next to me, my scent will challenge your instinct to run. But when you're away from me, anything can happen in that pretty pixie cut head of yours."

"I can't believe she knew! You told her and not me, all these weeks I've been struggling with this!"

Technically, I never told Tiffany. She overheard me outside of her bedroom griping to Rory about it, which was how she'd known. But sharing that with Bilan would have been pointless.

"Baby, I was going to tell you. I told Iban he had until the end of the week to tell our parents, and to make this right. You were the primary reason for that! Before, I just accepted covering for my brother. I told you I'd tell you the moment I could."

"And what if I weren't there when your parents and hers found out? Your ex-lover, Ms. Diva Tiffany, would've learned that first, too!"

Jealous...

My Nalib was jealous...for me?

I moved into her, arms pushed around her waist, down her plump ass.

"Are we gonna do this?" I pushed my groin into her, kissed her neck. "Are we really going to do this?"

"I think I am." Her voice was dry, devoid of the emotional being I'd been coming to know.

But not even that could deter me.

I whispered into her neck, "Well, you can't." I rubbed my inflating dick against her again. "This is a new beginning for us. I'm so inspired now. I can breathe...finally have that weight off." My tone turned dreamy, unrecognizable to even me. "We can proceed with nothing between us. The one thing I hated about it was lying to you, seeing your sacrifice of dignity day after day as I pursued you. The way I gave you no choice but to give me a chance."

Predictably, Bilan pushed against my shoulders, an act of futility. "Oh, I had choices! You're not irresistible, Mr. Ellis!"

I let out a hard ass laugh, clutching her to me. Bilan squirmed against my firm hold. Then I reached for her mouth. She fought my kiss, and I cupped her face with my hands, and ravished her mouth with the dire aggressive need I had for her since our first conversation. As my tongue moved in her mouth, Bilan had no choice unlike she did at the pool earlier. I made it for her.

And I would continue to until she decided on me.

"Your mom is fuckin' pissed, man! Pissed!" my father trilled into the phone, reminding me how young he sounded when affected by his wife.

"I understand," I replied, clutching Bilan's hand in mine as we rode the dark streets to our destination.

"And you and Iban need to talk this shit out," he continued. "It's one thing Rizzo declared war on us, but some other shit when you two at odds. Fuck that! Nothing comes between us."

"So, I thought."

"You better fuckin' know, man. Y'all gone get this right, and right a-fuckin'-way, too. You wasn't 'posed to leave till tomorrow. Where you at?"

My eyes breezed past trees blowing, having just passed a quaint row of shops and boutiques. Then the view turned green again. The way I liked it. Seclusion.

"In these streets, tryna clear this shit up on my end." I turned to the other side of the car.

Bilan was quiet, closely watching the scenery, too, only she didn't have a clue where we were going.

"Could you at least tell me when you'll be back, bruh?"

"A few days." And I meant just a few. I wished I had at least a week down here to crawl inside and consume myself with all things Bilan Asad-Yasin. "Then I'll be headed out of the country for a few days." That's when Bilan's eyes were on me.

"Look! Call me when you touch down in Jersey. We will meet— all three of us!

"Aye-aye, captain."

I disconnected the call as soon as we turned into the driveway. Fatigue began to set in, but my excitement would give me the verve I needed for this. The car stopped in front of a two-story home with stone-exterior and yellow panels. It was lit beautifully on the inside and out, as though fully occupied. It looked better than the pictures. By the time I made it to her side, Bilan was already out of the car, expression stoic, mind preoccupied. As we traveled up the steps to the porch, the half glass and wood-panel door opened.

A smiling face appeared. "Mr. Ellis, nice to finally have you guys here."

"Paul." I extended my hand for a shake as Bilan observed the vestibule.

He reciprocated, then handed me the keys. "If you have any questions, I'll hang around here for a few. I can see myself out."

I thanked him, then took to Bilan's side. "Welcome to Macen Beach, South Carolina, Nalib," I murmured to her as she gazed into the empty living room with dark wood floors and a fireplace.

One wall was the same stony paneling as the exterior of the home, the others a light gray. The windows were portioned with the high ceilings and framed walls. Then I followed her into the dining room that was empty as well, the same flooring and large bow windows. The whitewash wall panels lining the hall gave the home personality. She stopped and peeked inside a powder room before proceeding. The kitchen lights were on.

Bright colors hit us first. Stark white cabinetry, glass doors. A cool gray on the walls and stainless steel appliances. A huge island in the center of the room with a chunky gray and white marble countertop with a splash of a coordinating gray. It was an open floorplan design, causing Bilan to turn to the right, to an empty family room. The windowing was generous and open.

Bilan recognized the coveted sounds. She turned to me with her mouth ajar. I encouraged her with a nod toward the open sliding door. I followed as she stepped out onto the large wooden deck. Other than a porch swing, the ample space was empty. I watched as her attention moved ahead to the rippling Atlantic, stealing my thunder.

She shook off her heels with impatience and skipped down the stairs for the sanded beach, stopping at the shoreline. Pushing my hands into the pockets of my pants, I watched enrapt, feeling my head fall to the side. Bilan's neck shifted left and right, apparently trying to capture it all as she hugged herself. I don't know how long we stood out there. With so many pending matters of grave significance floating through my mind—my brother's fuck up, Rizzo's declaration of war, the lawsuit on Ellis International, my upcoming meeting in Sicily with Marcu Amato, finding Derrick Little, Ab's boy, who'd recently disappeared—I could use the gentle breeze, the calming sounds of the restless sea, and the gorgeous view of her.

When she turned to head back for the house, I took a deep breath. "You good?"

She nodded, closed lids stretching. "Beyond good."

"Cool. Let's see upstairs." I took her by the hand and found our way to the staircase.

On the second floor, I followed her as we viewed bedrooms ascending in sizes. The first was empty, and had a view of the front of the house. The second was empty, too, and larger with a partial and full ocean view. The last bedroom of the three hadn't been unaccounted for at this point, but inside the second one was an extra door not belonging to the closet.

"What do you think this is?" she asked curiously.

I forged a tight smile she likely perceived as a shrug. I wanted her to discover it for herself. Bilan opened the door and hit a light switch.

"A closet," she sang. "A long one."

We sauntered inside, observing the empty shelves and racks to the right. An ocean view bay window to the left.

"Another door!" Bilan shared in her Scooby Doo voice, facial expression to match.

I chuckled at the sight of her silliness. I wanted to see more. I wanted to see more facets of her personality. I followed her into what led into the largest bedroom; the master suite.

"Oh, my goodness…" She breathed, sucking in a deep breath.

I pulled my arms behind my back, clasping my fingers.

"Sadik!" She turned to me with wide eyes? "How did you— Is that the—"

She couldn't finish her questions. I nodded, pleased by her reaction to the bed. I had my assistant rigorously hound the resort in Costa Rica for the manufacturer of the bed in our villa. It held sentimental value for me, and I wanted to hold onto the memory in some way.

Having this all arranged took an act of God to have sped up nearly twenty-four hours. The bed arrived here this afternoon. We weren't supposed to touch down in Macen Beach until tomorrow. Rory had to be located and called in right after the Rizzo explosion a few hours ago. That meant the errands I had for her had to be expedited, too, for her to meet us at the airport this evening.

Then the jet...

My flight crew wasn't supposed to be on tonight. Thankfully, the jet had been fueled, and all three crew members were available and able to clear our flight out. Her reaction to a piece of shared sentimental value was worth all the calls and furtive texts done between the time we packed our things at Elliswoods Palace and now.

Soft tickles, a gentle salted breeze, and the sounds of seagulls and crashing waves didn't mix with the stirring sensation of my groin. Or did they? It was a blissful concoction. A sudden heavy sigh pushing from my lungs had my lids flickering open. The picturesque sunlight piercing through the open veranda doors of the master suite had my eyes straining. My thighs in the air, spread eagle with a head in between had my spine arching. Heat ripped up my core, my toes curled, and jaw went lax at the pleasure.

At another attempt to peer down, I caught honeyed irises blazing into me. My hips were cupped in his palms, the sunlight reflecting off the skin of his golden head, and a full bladder intensifying the pleasure. It was all a mood.

And it happened so fast. My body warmed all over at each stroke of his tongue. Then he began to suck on my clit. My nipples tight like bullets and stinging. My hands, clawing the sheets. I lifted my head, wanting to see.

"Oh, God!" I cried huskily at the sight of his oral work.

He sucked on my clit, pulling it to a length I didn't think possible, shooting shards of pleasure to every corner of my body. The sensation grew and grew, bliss abounding. I rocked my sex into his face, unabashed. I'd come to expect this type of indulgence from him. Possibly needing it more than I needed most essentials.

"Baby..." I sobbed, rocking and rocking.

His hands on my butt stroked, my sensitive breasts providing a scenery of erotica as they moved according to my pelvic thrusts. Then it popped. Bliss shot from my core, sprouting outward. Lungs worked to sustain me as my body was wracked with a fierce orgasm. Groin rolling and rolling, pelvis lifting and dropping until my hips collapsed in satiation.

Sadik shot to his knees, grabbing himself in a stroke. His face tense, eyes dark, and jaw flexing as his other hand pulled me to the edge of the mattress. His dick grisly: swollen, bulbous head, pulsing veins running to his orange bushy root. Watching Sadik stroke himself was an intimidating turn on. But feeling him feed himself to my achy sex was a wonder to itself altogether. I sucked in air as he plunged into me. One leg astride his curving hip, the other extended straight against his tatted chest. His first thrusts were small, hips circling to drive deeper. I relaxed myself around him and opened to his pulsing erection.

The sight of the strains around his tight eyes, head tossing back, mouth agape, and pecs flexing as he drove into me made me crazy. It empowered me, made me feel supreme and needed by him. In the moment, I believed I wielded a power, which was confusing because each stroke against my quivering walls made me feel helpless to the pleasure he ensued upon me. He filled me, stretching me, dragging against the most amazing nerve endings.

This. The feel of him plunging into me against the morning sun, the sounds of the ocean, and the singing of beach creatures had my sex quaking. My core roiled, breasts flapping in the air.

"I'm gonna come again," I warned, unable to believe my boldness.

But I wanted to share it. When we touched like this, I felt the promise of friendship Sadik pledged. When he invaded my body, ravishing it for his pleasure, I felt intimacy I never wanted to be without again.

My sex lifted and body shuttered, a second orgasm rolling in.

"Fuck, Bilan!" he groaned as though in pain, teeth gritted, biceps flexing.

The roar of his cry reverberated in my core as he plummeted into me with blunt force, extending my orgasm.

This. Is. Bliss...

When he slowed, the pads of my fingers grazed the goosebumps on his lower arm.

"God, I needed that," he breathed. "Felt like an eternity since the last time I've had you."

As my body tingled, I thought how all of the drama ensued at his parents' could be a killjoy. But looking at the dew on his golden skin after a release reminded me of all sex involved with Sadik. He was a beautiful sight undone.

"Don't bite your lip like that," he grated, eyes half-mast.

I didn't realize I was until then.

"Why?" I asked, out of breath myself.

"Because I'm still hard and want to fuck again, but physiologically, I can't."

Eyes tight, I smiled. "Why?"

Sadik came down, planted a heavy kiss on my lips. "Because we have furniture shopping to do."

"For what?"

He lifted from me, dragging his heavy appendage against the sensitive walls of my sex. I whimpered.

"For this place."

"Why would a rental come without furniture?" Then I thought. "Why would you buy furniture for a rental?"

Sadik smiled too broadly. "Because I can, Nalib."

I rolled my eyes. "Yeah. I see people with lots of cents don't have lots of sense."

"You don't like the place?" he eyed me especially, sitting next to my splayed body near the edge of the bed.

My eyes ballooned. "Are you kidding me? Furniture or not, I love this place."

"Why?" His chin pushed into his chest as a posture of patience.

Sadik wanted me to explain.

"For one, because it's a beach house. Second, it's a beautiful home and very intimate...but that could be because I'm coming from the monstrous Elliswoods Palace. That place is colossal!" I giggled helplessly.

"What's so funny?"

"Monstrous. That's how I describe your...dick." I lost my lungs, laughing so hard.

Sadik glanced down at himself. "Monstrous." His forehead was stretched and lips lifted as he nodded. "New one, but I'll take it." He stood from the bed and strolled over to the open door of the patio. Sadik stretched his arms over his head, gripping the frame. I sat up on my elbows, peering at the artwork ahead. The sight of his muscular glutes and cut back made my heart skip a beat. After meeting his family and experiencing their shared traits, there was no way I believed any Ellis was as perfect as Sadik. "Bilan," he called, gaze still ahead.

My body tensed. "Yeah?"

"Get dressed. We have shopping to do."

22

I gazed out the window at the locals strolling down the street outside of the restaurant we found in town. The place was nice, low key, and slow-paced. So unlike Paterson or Woodland Park, for that matter. The people seemed nice here, everyone greeting with a smile and nod. Many of the shops catered to beach and water activities. And that was another discovery this morning: on the side of the house was an in-ground pool. It wasn't half as large or as lavish as the one I'd swam in at Elliswoods, but perfect, in my opinion. Elliswoods Palace was large and opulent, but overwhelming to an outsider.

A chirp from a device had me facing ahead. On the other side of the oversized plate of a demolished cobb salad with turkey bacon was a preoccupied Sadik, engaged in one of his phones and an iPad, typing away. He was adorable in a fitted Connecticut Kings baseball cap, plain white tee, army fatigue cargo shorts, ankle socks, and sneakers. Unaccustomed to seeing him so casual, he looked delectable. He'd been between work and selection since we left the house this morning. We drove a couple of towns over for furniture stores and, between two, were able to pick out pieces to match the bed he'd wildly purchased, and a kitchen set. We purchased pots and pans, toiletries, and linens, too.

Today had been an entirely different experience from just twenty-four hours ago. I still couldn't believe the devastation experienced between two families. And Sadik... I understood my brother and I had a tumultuous relationship unshared by most siblings, but the lengths he went through to keep Iban's secret safe betrayed a lot of people. The look on Earl and Irene's faces as they tried to figure out what was going on was striking. The tearful expressions by Lia and Monica would haunt me for some time.

"I want to call Monica. We exchanged numbers when she gave me a tour around the compound."

He glanced up, brows bunched from his task as he considered it for a second. "I think you should. Monica's a gem. I hate she's going through this."

I agreed, eyes popping out of my head. "And she's pregnant. They both are! It's disgusting, Sadik." I smacked my tongue of the bitterness of it all. "Is infidelity a morally accepted flaw in your family?"

It was a rude question, but an unavoidable one. Cheating started at the apex of their family tree, it seemed.

Sadik finally laid down his devices. His feline eyes on me. "Loyalty is taught in my family. Unity and the importance of, not just being family, but communing. You see how we're together several times a week. Iban and I don't usually stay over like that, but we make sure not much time passes in between. Taaliba's been traveling, but with a little push from me, she comes home regularly, too. My father was sure to build a complex large enough for his family to reside in, and not get restless. He just bought property in Antigua. An island for his family to have land and pride.

"We may not be perfect, but we're accountable to each other. We move with a purpose, and we love the hell out of each other."

I scoffed. "You sure do to keep that secret," my tone bitter. I'd grown comfortable around Sadik, I could tell in that moment. Speaking against his family was clearly rude. But so was the way they treated me... "You going to forgive Iban? It didn't sound like it last night."

"Of course, I am." His mouth tight, jaw flexing as he peered outside. "He's my brother. His fuck ups are mine. I just need to manage him. Give him some space for a bit."

"How long?"

Sadik shrugged. "But guess who don't get space when I'm upset?" Those felines darkened upon me, eliciting a shiver down my spine.

"Good," I tried, playing unaffected. "Good, because you sure didn't give me the space I requested last night."

"No more alone space for you, Nalib," his tone and expression deathly serious as he planted his elbows on the table. "From now on, your space is my space, and mine is yours."

I shook my head. "It doesn't work that way, Sadik. I need to be sure you're faithful to me."

"Why wouldn't I be?" He sounded offended.

"Because you have no reason to be."

"Try, because I have no needs beyond you, and I expect you to be the same in return."

Again, I shook my head. "It's not that simple," I murmured, shifting my gaze out the window. "Look at you. You're a good looking man with exotic features and amount of money. How am I supposed to maintain that if you've not been groomed for fidelity?"

And that Tiffany woman! Ugh!

He leaned into the small table, engaging me. "Look at me. I want one thick—but ironically, underfed—freckled Somali. I want to give her the world, spoil her, impregnate her—"

I swung my body from under the table to stand. "Come on. Let's go."

No way was I going to talk about children. I had way too much growing up to do. These past two months with Sadik magnified that.

In my wake, I could hear Sadik chuckling.

Sadik

"It's unearthly gorgeous out here," she whispered with conviction, eyes low from glasses of wine as her attention was on the ocean under the dark sky. "How did you find this place?"

We were back at the house after a long day of shopping, sightseeing, and arranging the few things we'd bought for the house. Rory dropped us off and went about her way to claim the small beach town. We ordered in from a seafood restaurant that made a baked salmon Bilan didn't need my assistance eating.

I replaced the two inside piles of cards as we played "Speed."

"Yeah. It's beautiful." I gazed out to the water, too, as we sat on the back deck of the house with Vesta Williams' "Sweet, Sweet Love" playing from inside. "What do you think about when you're staring out there?"

"Peace. Mental quieting. Safety." She turned to me, a wry smirk pulling at the side of her mouth. We continued to play. "I appreciate you with the beach theme."

"You're very welcome. I see it makes you happy. That makes me happy."

Her head shot up, lips poked. "You say that, but..."

"But what?"

Bilan sat up in her chair, almost like fortifying herself. I reached for my beer.

"What are your dreams?"

My eyes shot open while my mouth was full with brew. I swallowed too hard and fast. "Dreams?"

"Yeah. Like when you were younger, what did you want to do with your life by now?"

I struggled with a cheap grin on my face as I considered telling her. "A politician."

This time, her eyes blossomed. "Really? What do you know about policy?"

"Public policy?" I chuckled. "My crazy ass began studying it my first year at Blakewood."

"Really? What happened?"

"Earl Ellis wasn't having that shit."

"Why?"

I shot her the side eye. "With my father's history in crime, there was no way he could sponsor an education that I would struggle with making good on. No one would take me seriously."

"How do you know?"

"I have businesses in three different industries. All of my twenties was spent discovering the government secretly monitoring all branches of my enterprises. I had nothing to hide, but had to protect my integrity, too." Those years were miserable between discovering what was behind the excessive audits and undercover employees and applicants, and having to endure my father's 'told you so's'. "But I was determined, and it taught me how to move differently. Made me smarter, and ultimately..." I shrugged. "Had me earn my father's respect."

"That's amazing. Sounds stressful, though."

"It was—on both ends, but I quickly realized if I was going to be my own man, I had to give up on the fruitless dream and began hustling in the opposite direction: business in the private sector."

"Mmmmmm..." she hummed mellifluently—or maybe because in my eyes, Bilan was a perfect princess ready to be crowned, stained, and spoiled as my queen. "Do you know any politicians? I'm finding it hard seeing that as a goal for you."

"A good friend of mine—fellow BU alum, in fact—is running for mayor of Paterson. It's been such a dirtied, scandal-ridden seat historically. But I know he can do it. He's young, has a reserved reputation, is married with a young baby, is community-committed because he still lives and owns in Paterson, has fresh ideas, is an eternal optimist, and is a humanity enthusiast. He's the guy, and I've

pledged my support." I nodded with poked lips, convinced. "He's holding a phenomenal hand in life."

"You admire him. How dope!" She clinked her glass with my beer bottle. "Nothing wrong with that."

"Yeah. Can you believe he envied my life back in school? He would say he'd never visit home in those four years if my father didn't own a jet." I snickered, recalling those wild days with strippers awaiting us on the plane to party, courtesy of Double E. "I had to threaten my father to ignore his begging for a job as a shortcut to earning good money before he graduated. My father obeyed, and Julius Richards finished. Not sure he's making as much as he'd like as the head of Office of Emergency Management for the city, but I'm sure he's fulfilled."

"And you're not?" she asked, aghast. "Look at you!" She scoffed. "You're beyond good-looking, independently successful, and wealthy. I mean..." Her hands went into the air to gesture the property. I was stuck on her mention of my looks again, as though it held any significance. "You rent a beach house just to impress a no-named girl from Woodland Park." I laughed at that. "To be honest, I think being a mogul is a good look for you. Do you honestly believe you could be a starving politician?"

"I wanted to live the life of a public servant. I didn't need the money. My father has been rich since before I was born. By the way, men and women seated in offices like that aren't all poor." I shrugged. "I just wanted to assist...advocate, make a difference by touching the lives of the underserved." She dropped the cards in her hands, signifying her main interest had shifted to me. "That's why finding a woman to inspire me beyond sex, and maybe surface conversation over dinner has always been a challenge."

"Why?"

"Because I'm an honest man—another interpreted meaning of my name—just like I did with you, I don't hide my father's reputation. Most times, women knew before meeting me, and it was the lifestyle they subscribed to."

"But you're not your father."

"Huhn?" I turned to her. That's when it hit me, I'd been gazing out to the water...for a while. "What did you say?"

"You're not your father. I get it. You're your own man."

"Damn right." I rubbed my head. "And being my own man, and honoring and respecting him aren't mutually exclusive items. I'm damn proud of my father. He supports me and has facilitated the building of Sadik. It's just that we'll have two different legacies."

Our conversation quieted for a bit. I used the time to consider how having Bilan now changed so much for me. How having to convince my father and brother of that would be a worthwhile challenge.

A deep sigh from across the table had my regard shifting up her. A lock of her short hair at the top danced against the light, end of May breeze. Her chocolate eyes glittered beneath long lashes as she took a sip of her wine while shooting me a contemplative gaze.

"So, now I need to figure out how to support your reality...possibly work on your dreams."

My forehead wrinkled. "My dreams?" I snorted. "Baby girl, I'm too old to dream. I've accepted my fate and am working it."

"But, are you happy? Remember I asked you that?"

"I do." I nodded.

"Happiness is a misunderstood, over-exaggerated state for most. But to me, there should be a bit of it between a man and woman when they work together toward a common goal."

"What would ours be?"

She shrugged, glancing out to the water again. "Changing your outlook on happiness. Making you feel complete and accomplished as a man." Her voice was low.

"What do you know about that type of partnership?"

I was curious. Those were things only found in a strong partnership like my parents'.

"My mother. She may not have had a happily ever after, but she swore to me there was one. She told me to hold out for a man who'd love me more than I loved him, and to support him with my last strength. The key would be in getting a man who could lead." Her eyes fell from mine before ascending again. "You're a leader, Sadik.

Now, I have to figure out how to aid a man like you—if you really want me to be your girlfriend."

"My wife," I made clear. "You'll be my wife." Chuckling, I reached into the paper shopping bag from the grocery store we hit up last before coming back to the house. "Funny that you mentioned that. This is another thing I came across that I felt would be useful to my avid reader."

She breathed while picking up her wine glass. "I haven't read regularly for fun in ages, it seems."

I pulled out the book, holding the cover over the table for her to see.

"Tending to the Man Who Governs the Masses: How to Protect What He Values Most by Twanece Edmondson. Hmmmmm..." Her eyes bounced around the hardcopy. "Never heard of her. Sounds like a mouthful." She took it from my hands and thumbed through the pages.

I began grabbing all the cards on the table, realizing I'd lost track of whose go it was. It was all good, though. I enjoyed the switch in our attention.

"You know what else is a mouthful?" When I peered up, Bilan placed the book on the table, her eyes molten chocolate now.

"What's that?" I fanned the deck of cards, watching her leave her seat.

My face tightened with curiosity when she slipped to her knees and crawled over to me. I slid my chair from the table enough to give her space.

"You," she whispered. I pulled my hands back as she went for the waist of my cargo shorts. Her heated gaze on me while unraveling them. She pulled the tabs apart, allowing the ocean breeze to cool my pubes. She buried her face in the hairs and sniffled. "Hmmmmm..." She pulled back. "You know how much I love the smell of you?"

I adjusted in the chair as her soft hands pulled my swelling dick from my boxers.

"Think I have an idea." I sucked in a breath when her tongue met the head of my cock.

"Oh, god!" I screamed.

Hands roped behind my back, thanks to the canopy implement of the bed. The side of my face pressed into the mattress, and my legs curled back, heels pushed into the fat of my butt. Cheeks spread wide with his face buried deep, vicious tongue reaching my achy clit had my eyes rolling back.

I was coming again!

"Deeeeeeek!" I yelped powerfully with chattered teeth.

My body yanked fitfully with little range of motion as I bounced back onto his face. Sadik was nasty, and I'd grown addicted to it. Never in my life would I have thought I'd enjoyed being bound, let alone getting aroused as a man tied me up.

And here was my favorite part: when his face withdrew, Sadik's knees gathered behind me, his palms with a mean grip on my hips as he breached me hard from behind. No warning, no patience. Just an abrupt thrust that had my lungs vibrating and my sex quivering from the pain and pleasure combination, thanks to my fading orgasm. He pounded and plummeted, thrust and bounced on my hiked ass, grunting every blow. His strokes were vicious and possessive, just like the man himself. And here he was, introducing a new facet to my lover: the brutal one.

With one rough thrust after another, I found my groin churning again. My pussy soaked him in helplessly, greedily, and without choice in the matter.

"Come again, Bilan!" He growled. "Come for me again, now!"

I arched my back in a way I didn't know possible to give in to the promise of the rub he ensued deep inside. Within seconds, a third orgasm rolled over me. I couldn't scream through this one. No, it was so commanding, tears pricked my eyes as I held on against the tsunami of ecstasy tumbling over me.

Sadik produced a wail making my heart swell and mind blow from its vulnerability. He pounded until the waves slowed, then circled and drilled until his hips suspended and pelvis pushed into me.

When I was able to open my eyes, the bright sun was an irritant before it became a friend. Beach mornings were perfect, and especially with Sadik. I wanted to say so, but something felt awkward. He pulled out of me gently, but too fast for my recent preference. He made quick work of untying my arms and wrists, and even rubbed the circulation back into my shoulders before leaving the bed for the bathroom.

The sound of the shower told me he'd be in there for a while, so I rolled over and stretched my arms and legs. It made me try to recall the last time I'd been to the gym. Since being consumed by the phenomenon that was Sadik, I hadn't had time for much, including work. My life had become unrecognizable. No school, little work, and no gym. I'd hardly been home. Made me wonder if having a dog was worth the trouble. I'd been paying a neighbor, who so happened to be a dog sitter for a website placing them when owners needed a temporary guardian. I couldn't afford to keep paying for a service if I wasn't working.

I groaned as I sat up and pushed off the high bed. Sadik promised we'd visit the boardwalk today. The house wasn't far from it at all. As I peered out of the balcony window, I felt comfortable being in it nude, like Sadik. The next house over was to the left and more than a quarter of a mile away, giving this place complete seclusion.

The feeling of his wasted seeds dripping down my thigh had me leaping to grab a tee of his he'd tossed on the floor last night. With a rolled t-shirt bunched in the apex of my legs, I found myself wandering to the closet. The space was now littered with our luggage and clothes sprawled about. I continued my stroll to the door at the opposite end. The adjoining room was almost as bright as the master suite. There was no balcony off of this room and, unlike the bigger room, the floor was carpeted, a soft hue of blue. And it smelled freshly painted—in fact, the whole house did—

Heat at my back had me check behind me. Sadik stood in the doorjamb looking like a GQ model, naked down to his waist where a towel hung from his muscular hips. His brows deliciously messy and face scowled as I'd become accustomed to. Something was off.

Smiling, I turned to face him, uncaring about my own nakedness. "Everything okay?" I fought to maintain a bright expression. "I didn't leave your bed before you."

Sadik's scoff was without humor. He rubbed his golden head, exhaling hard.

"Bilan," My heart began to race at the softness of his delivery. Sadik was hardly listening to me. "We leave tomorrow."

"I know," I whispered, wanting him to get on with it. The longer he waited, the more exposed I felt standing before him unclothed.

"And I haven't had the balls to tell you."

My mouth went dry. "Tell me what?"

Another deep breath. "It's ours."

"What?"

Sadik stared at me, chewing on the inside of his lip. "It's—this house—is ours. I bought it last week."

"How?" I shook my head. "Why?"

"Because of your fascination with the beach."

Bombarded with emotions, a tear slipped from my eye. "Are you serious?"

He backed into the closet and seconds later, he was sauntering toward me with folded documents. With a shaky hand, I accepted them and read right away, flipping from form to form with information regarding a four-thousand square feet Cape Cod, legal jargon that included ownership listed to Bilan Asad-Yasin and Sadik Q. Ellis. The dates aligned with his story, too. My arm dropped to my thigh.

He wasn't lying.

Breathing erratic to dizzying degrees, my pulse could be heard in my ears. Lightheadedness had me dropping to my knees.

"Sadik..." I breathed.

He was on me in less than two seconds.

"Ultra-demanding alpha, I know," he murmured. "I don't know any other way."

I shook my head in my hands. "Do I need to get a lawyer?"

"For what?"

"My name is on a legal document. It looks kind of official."

"Because it is. I can help you out with one, if you need me to."

My head rolled up to those kaleidoscope eyes, urging sincerity. "What am I going to do with a man like you?" my throat croaked out.

"Be my friend."

I pushed up, knocking him over as I kissed the insanely demanding alpha deliriously. My lips and tongue moved aggressively against his, his hungry hands gliding up and down my hips. My frame bristled with excitement and I reached between us, shifting the towel.

When I stroked his dick awake, he husked, "We have a long day ahead, Nalib." Sadik licked his lips, eyes narrowing as he grew inside my hand. "Boardwalk and a show tonight. We should eat and get out of here."

When I felt he was hard enough, I pushed back and arranged his head at my opening. Still soaked of his pleasure earlier, I was able to sink down on him slowly.

"Okay," I moaned, rolling my hips to fit him all in. "But first, we christen the place."

Planted inside a small field of sea oats, I sat on my haunches, listening. I listened for cues of his movements, his proximity. I held one of the Super Soakers we'd bought on the boardwalk earlier against

my shoulder as my chest pounded with excitement. It was dark out, but for the beam of our beach home casting a sparse glow near the shore. The placement of a small lot of beach grass came in handy for play.

A sprout of water trickling over my head onto the new MEEHAR gown Sadik had covertly placed in the closet while we were out today. I shot to my bare feet.

"Oh, no you didn't!"

I only caught the quick flash of his glistening head before he ducked into the tall beach grass. I lowered myself and tried quietly stalking through the sand after him. My heart raced so fast, I thought the sound of it would give me away. From a distance, I could hear the sounding of a cruise ship horn. But I couldn't let that distract me from my target. Sadik was going to get it. I tiptoed, hating the sound of the hem of my gown against the beach floor. It could give me away. I turned a one hundred-eighty degree angle with my gun pointed when I thought I heard movement from there. No luck.

That was until a phone chirped. I jumped to an upright position, peering over the curled sea oats.

"Shit!" I heard him swear.

That gave me an idea of his whereabouts. When I turned a corner, Sadik made himself an easier find. He was closer than I thought in black suit pants, stark white shirt and black dress socks, hunched over, trying to silence his phone.

"Busted!" I sang as a warning shot just before unloading quarts of water onto him.

He turned, startled at first, not realizing the sprinkle. His hands flew in the air as I aimed for his face.

"Okay! Okay!" He fell backward onto the sand and I moved toward him, still spraying off. "You got the power! Goddamn, Bilan." He tried laughing. "You got the power!"

That's when I stopped. Turning the gun upside down and against my shoulder, I gazed down on him curiously.

"What did you just say?"

Wiping the water from his face, he chuckled. "What?"

"The thing about the power. What did you mean?"

Talk like that after all Sadik had done for me in the past two-plus months could be heady for a girl like me.

He sat up on one arm, breathing erratic, but spirit light as a feather. "When we were kids... Iban and I would fight for control. Over the remote, PlayStation, wrestling, or bets...anything kids can fight over." He tried catching his breath. "Well, when the losing or weaker party had to concede, he'd say that."

"You've got the power?"

Sadik shrugged. He then scratched his head as a goofy grin spread across his lips. "Guess I got caught up for real, huhn?"

My heart swelled.

"I guess I have the ability to bring back the days of Ellis' when, huhn?" My face folded. "What's that?" My gaze was over his left shoulder, my right.

Sadik turned to follow my line of sight. He lifted a red box dusted in sand.

"Must've slipped out," he mumbled. "It's for you anyway." He handed it to me.

Without thinking, I received the box with one hand, laying the Super Soaker against my leg with the other. The spring on the box was strong as I pried it open. The radiant ring on the inside wasn't expected at all. I was confused, shifting my hands to the right to find Sadik. I found him alright. He was on one bended knee.

"Marry me."

My knees went weak, legs wobbled.

"Sadik," I breathed, barely a whisper. "You've got to stop doing this!" I still hadn't processed owning a home. "I've only known you for a couple of months."

Without missing a beat, he proposed, "How about we make it a couple of a quarter centuries next?"

My chest expanded. "Sadik..."

"I won't take no for an answer." His countenance determined. He took the box from my trembling hands. "You don't have a father or uncle for me to have asked in advance. But I did pray last week, when I finally chose the ring, that your father and mother would approve my love for you."

"Only a couple of months," I repeated.

His golden shiny head swung left to right faintly. "Bilan, I'm almost forty; a man of my breadth and tenure doesn't need years to feel what I do for you. He doesn't need time as a factor for a proposal for a lifetime." He slipped the ring on my finger. Its radiance blinding, the fit scarily perfect. "All I need is for you to agree to give me the chance to make you the happiest woman and to help you live out the best of your days for the rest of your days." His golden gaze was tortured, the green on the outer realm pleading. "Please say yes."

Swallowing hard, I bit my lip. Then I nodded. Tears escaped and I nodded harder. My lungs worked manically, a cry left my belly, and I bobbed even harder. Sadik was on his feet, capturing me protectively in his arms. He kissed me with desperation. His forehead met mine as he released a powerful breath into my face. Smelling him, seeing him, and feeling him so vulnerable had me wrapping my arms around his tailored waist and holding him so tightly as I sobbed.

I'd gone from three successive orgasms this morning; to learning I was a first-time home owner; to fun, junk food, and games on a boardwalk; then a black tie classical music performance; and now to this.

I'm now an engaged woman?

"This is crazy!" I trilled, face soaked with evidence of fear and joy.

"This is the Ellis way, baby," he murmured in my ear.

The wind picked up around us, causing the sea oats to cheer in our new engagement. As I peered left over his shoulder to a dream home and to the right to the force of peace, I believed I had the best seat in the world—forget the proverbial house.

Sadik

I lifted my torso and kissed the dark budded nipple peeking between the layered ropes of the lariat necklace. The apex of her areolae just as decorative as all the metal chains with glass pearls, silver pendants, and strass. But the jewelry didn't bounce like the fatty tissues of her breasts. They didn't drive me toward the impending orgasm holding in my sacs. They, in fact, distracted me from it all.

This morning, Bilan woke up to me arranging a heavy ass Chanel necklace around her neck. Leave it to my neurotic ass to have to live out each fantasy I had of her. But it was worth it. She was more confident riding me now. At times, I could see she was in her head, wondering if I was pleased, but her physical gratification provided the motivation she needed to just keep at it.

And she damn sure is…

I'd been in a dream, some sort of fucking fantasy where I actually felt shit. I didn't move with caution when it concerned her happiness. I simply soared in this space of compulsion and need. Damn it, I was a selfish motherfucker. I didn't mean for us to find ourselves here. I didn't mean to become so enthralled with a basic chick from a Paterson diner. I had no idea my attraction would grow into more that night I dropped Lia off and called Mike Jefferson for intel on a local baker.

"Oh…" she moaned, head swinging over her neck.

I had no plans to be so wildly attracted to her broad vocabulary, her resistance to a force she had no idea she was up against, the speckled melanin in her face, her naiveté, her independence, and survival skills. I guessed my brother was right about a man of my sheltered childhood not being able to resist the thrill of the girl from the other side of the tracks. As my dick grew wider inside her spongy walls, I realized the definition of our tracks didn't mirror the traditional storybook love stories.

On my side of the tracks, wealth derived from the gore of the streets: drugs, murder, deceit, power, and control. From her side, those attributes were due to the absence of wealth. Bilan had no idea my struggles from keeping her brother alive all these years since he robbed my father's warehouse. She had no clue how, unless I could come up with something solid to convince my father and now estranged brother to let him live, she'd be the only surviving member of their nuclear family.

She'd been protected against the truth of Damien being the target of my family's fury as he ordered the robbery. My fiancée was clueless about how he would likely try to harm her if he knew what the ring on her left hand signified. Just like she'd have no idea of the furtive security I'd have to pay for to guard over each atom of her body until I could convince her to move in with me and ultimately quit her dead-end job.

As I enjoyed the view of sweat sprouting at her temples and the swelling of her pouty morning lips, I could feel her love coming down while she rocked my stick like it belonged to her. I wondered if she could feel that her life was about to change. Everything she'd known it to be would wither away, only to be replaced by my needs and those of my complicated world. Nevertheless, as I observed the squeeze of her eyes as she was feeling the same euphoria from the magic being made between her legs from what was between mine, I knew.

I would forever be an apologist for not being her ideal love, but being too damn selfish to let mine go.

My balls warmed, belly jolted. Her mouth swung open, eyes blinking successively.

"I'm gonna come," she chirped. "Sadik...I'm about to—"

I leaped up to capture her mouth, tasting the bitterness from yesterday, chasing it away with a sweep of promises by my tongue. Bilan bounced on me fast, and I helped drive her springs with my hands on her hips. I drove us both into oblivion, thrusting upward and pulling her into me where there was little room in between for doubt or fear.

"Fuck!" my lungs drudged, my mouth capturing her bare shoulder, biting down as I held her wide hips in place to shoot fiercely into her. "Goddamn, Bilan!" I shouted, unable to stop coming.

Her tits bounced in my face, the jewelry of the lariat creating a rhythmic jingle to my ears. Together, our bodies slowed, hopefully recovering from another powerful ascension.

"I can stay this way forever," she breathed unevenly over my head. "Just don't bite so hard, Deek."

23

I tramped down the stairs with my duffle bag in tow, the last of my luggage seeing that Sadik took everything else while I dressed. As I made it to the landing, I could see Rory's tiny frame pass a sealed gray plastic bag to Sadik.

She paused on her way back out the front door of the house, glancing at me. "Want me to take that?"

I blinked, not used to much communication from her—at least nothing polite. Although it wasn't necessary, I pulled the strap from my shoulder and handed it to her.

"Thanks."

In return, Rory mumbled something incoherent before taking off.

I shook my head, partially smiling at her peculiar ways. "Did you tell her you proposed? Is that the problem?"

Sadik chuckled, reaching for my hand. "Rory's had this ring since the jeweler was done with it. Nothing's kept from her."

I didn't ask the specifics on that comment. "What's that?" I referred to the bag in his hand resembling a package.

"Cash."

"For what?"

"It's an Ellis tradition that when we purchase a new home, we leave money inside before we settle in. It's good faith in our absence."

"I don't get it." I frowned.

"I don't know when we'll be back here. You're always complaining about time off, I have a lot of shit coming in the next few months. And because we don't know when we'll return to, at least, finish furnishing the place, we leave something of value behind in our absence. The

payoff will be that the home will always remain a safe, protective place for us until we decide to sell it."

Strange...

"Do you want to move in?"

Sadik shook his head, then glanced around the bright bare walls. "Nah. I can't leave New Jersey at this point in my career, but it feels so special here. I'd like to keep it as a second home. Maybe we'll come back in the spring to finish decorating it."

"So, what do we do with the cash? And how much is it?"

Sadik's gaze dropped to the package. "We decide right now where to hide it."

"Would it be safe here?"

"A security system will be installed in a couple of days. It'll be a four digit code. You can choose it. Text it to me. But yes. I'm confident it'll be safe here."

"And if it isn't?"

"We won't go hungry, Bilan." He wrapped his arm around my shoulder. "I can assure you of that."

"No, Mom," I droned into the phone, eyes below on her outstretched left hand on my thigh.

My index finger pushed the five-carat, cushion-cut diamond on her finger back and forth, determining if it was large enough. Prestige enough to carry the presence and sentiments of me in my absence. With her right hand, Bilan typed into her phone as we rode from the airport.

"So, when will I be able to congratulate her?" my mother demanded pleadingly. "Talk to her about what she wants for her big day?"

My eyes rolled over to Bilan again. Her short hair frizzy at the ends from showering on the plane after rolling around in my bed, mile high club style.

"Soon."

"Will she be over for dinner this week?"

"I'll check her schedule."

"For what?"

My brows furrowed as I smiled. "Work. She works, Ma." As much as I hated what she did, it was a topic I needed to address right away. "But I'll let you know. If not this week, then next."

Bilan's regard met mine. She held it for a few seconds before going back to her phone.

"Okay. Well, let me know." My mother sighed. "I'll tell Monica we'll just have to wait to have her in our fold again. But I'll see you soon. Correct?" She resumed the tone of a lioness.

"I wouldn't have it any other way. Love you, baby." I moved to end the call.

"Love you more, honey bunch."

After deading the call, I glanced over to Bilan. My palm stroking the back of her hand.

"You know what this means? Right?"

"What?" She gave me her eyes for a few seconds before going back to her phone.

Damn, that thumb moves fast...

"It means I can't go back to waking up in the morning without you being there."

"I don't get it."

"Because you're not paying attention," I scolded.

Bilan glanced up to me, finally placing her phone on her lap.

"Thank you," my sarcasm delivered smoothly. "You have to move in with me, Nalib." That was almost purred, and strategically.

Her eyes went to the back of Lamont's head in the driver's seat before swinging back to me.

"I'm not ready to do that."

"And why not?"

"Because, I don't see the need."

"For one, your safety. I know you're not aware, but my family is known by many, and infamous to even more across the New York Tristate and the Delaware Valley, at least. The word of our engagement will spread like wildfire. I can't have my fiancée at the most popular diner in the area accessible to enemies of my family."

"So, this is when your low key promise of me getting used to having armed security around me like you and your family do comes into play? Because I won't. I'm not an Ellis."

"Yet," I corrected. "You're not an Ellis yet. But I can assure you, your safety is no less important as my fiancée than it will be as my wife. Now, I believe in tradition, and wouldn't mind allowing you to wait until we're married to live together, but leaving you in Woodland Park and Paterson doesn't sit well with me."

Her face tightened and eyes widened in a flash. "So next, you're going to tell me to quit my job?" Please believe, sweetie... "No."

"Why, Bilan? Can you give me one reason why you cannot move into my apartment?"

"I have a dog, is one, Sadik. Did you think about that?"

I didn't. Honestly, I didn't know she had a dog until the party at her house. But that wouldn't deter me.

"Bilan—"

"No! I can't just pack up and leave. Remember, that's my family home, Sadik. It holds lots of family memories for me. My brother will be released soon. I need to tell him I'm engaged—face the reality myself that I'll be moving out eventually. I still have the bank to sort things out with. How long will it take to pack up the place? What to throw out? What will Ab want to keep for himself? Where will I store what I take?" She barely breathed, volume elevated too fast. Rory glanced back at us. "Do you see why I can't get off a fancy private jet with you from a quaint beach house you bought with the snap of your fingers, and decide to quit on my former life?" Her former struggle. I understood.

She sat back into the bench, crossing her arms and gazing angrily out of the window.

"No, Sadik. You may have had your way being the ultra-demanding alpha, but here's where you pump the brakes and wait for me to catch up. Now, if you don't mind, please drop me off at Tasche's instead of my place."

"Tasche's?" My temper flared. "For what?"

Her head whipped to face me. "Because, she needs her hair braided and I need to spend time with other people who care about me. And we won't start the expectation of me having to clear my whereabouts with you!"

Twisting my mouth to bite my tongue, I sat back myself. My eyes caught Lamont in the rearview mirror ahead. He tried to hide his snicker.

Not from me. From Bilan.

Turning down the dark alley on the side of my house, the hairs on the back of my neck stood straight. It felt like ages since I'd left work and came home at close to four in the morning, creeping in the backyard to feed Dog before turning in. Illumination from the street lights didn't reach back here, and the cool June air was bleaker than the coldest in the dead of winter for some reason. I whistled, approaching the opening of the gate leading into my backyard.

"Dog."

After unhinging the metal latch, I took cautious steps into the yard. I'd picked him up from the neighbor yesterday when I got back into town and had to adjust to his aggression all over again. Being away not only suspended my normal schedule; it interrupted his norm, too. It took hours to get him to stop barking last night so I could get decent sleep.

I didn't hear him.

"Aye!" I called louder, then whistled.

The sensor light should have clicked on by now. I pulled my cell from my bag with the free hand, and tapped to turn on the flashlight.

No dog. Strange. Ignoring the stench in the air, I toed over to the kennel he mostly stayed in.

Please don't step in his poop... I cringed as I tiptoed.

My feet stopped. There was a deep red liquid and a gang of flies. A high pitch scream strained my chords and I leaped backward, dropping the container of scraps. With a shaky arm, I lifted my phone to see it again.

Dog's eyes were open as splats of blood covered his coat. His throat was slit, and there was a gaping hole was in his torso.

"Shi—" I shuffled backward before turning and taking off for the house.

On the way, I managed to pull out my keys, dropping them on the step before making it to the door. Once inside, I was sure to lock the door behind me before sprinting to my room, switching on lights the way there. I skirted into my door and ran to the closet. Dropping to my knees, I crawled to the back of the small space. I pulled back the carpet covering the hole in the floor where I kept a small, metal sewing box I got from my mother as a kid. It always resembled an army box to me, so I kept things I wanted to hide in there, which was stupid because anyone could get inside of it. I opened the box and pulled out a small gun I'd purchased some time ago out of fear. As I took to my feet, I checked for bullets, then headed back out.

With my pulse ringing in my ears, I checked my parents' bedroom, Ab's old room, and the bathroom before treading toward the front of the house. I opened the linen, pantry, and other closet doors before finally turning on the lights in the dining room. The basement. Could someone be in the basement? I had no other choice. I had to check or not sleep a wink tonight. I switched on the light and made sure the flashlight function was still on, on my phone.

The sounds of the boiler unit echoed even from the top of the steps. Slowly, I took off down the stairs. Palms misting, mouth dry, joints wobbling, and heart racing. At the bottom, I clicked on another light. Moving from wall to narrow wall, I saw nothing. The laundry area and storage items seemed to still be in place. Then I traveled over to Abshir's old space. He'd made the place his bedroom when he and my father would fight all the time about his growing heroin addiction. I used the flashlight on my phone for the dark area.

I screeched again, hitting my back against the wall.

A flat, thin bloodied tongue I knew belonged to the canine outside was on the cement floor. Bile shot from the back of my throat as I paced back to the stairs, not knowing to point the gun ahead or behind me. Back in the kitchen, I slammed and locked the door.

Hefty air shot from my mouth as I glanced around, the gun down at my side. I couldn't believe this was happening again. The fear and threat of living alone was coming back in spades. I'd been the only one living in the house all these years, but had the eerie feeling I wasn't alone. Someone killed Dog. Slaughtered him in my yard.

I whispered to myself, "And how were they able to get in the hou—?"

My head whipped back. Something was off. I walked back toward the back door, and in plain sight. The security panel was ripped from the wall. Wires cut and sprouting out. I couldn't gain my lungs. My trembling hands shot to my phone as I sprinted back to my room, locked the door, and crawled into my closet.

I dialed one number that went straight to voicemail. Then I dialed the other number.

"Hello?" her male pubescent voice croaked.

"Oh, my God!" I sobbed, relieved to hear her. "Rory!"

"Aye! Wait. Wait! What's wrong?"

"Dog!" I tried to breathe. "My dog! Someone killed my dog. They broke into my house!" I sobbed at the reality of the words leaving my mouth.

"Hold on! Just calm down, shawtie. I hear you," she tried speaking over me. "Stay right there. Okay? Don't call the police. I'm calling my guy now to head over there. He gonna search the premises. He gonna shout 'black ops, black ops' to let you know he wit' us. It's gonna take us too long to get there before him because of where we at, but we on our way. A'ight?"

"Rory!"

Far away?

"Hang tight, B. I swear, you ain't gone be by yourself for long."

394

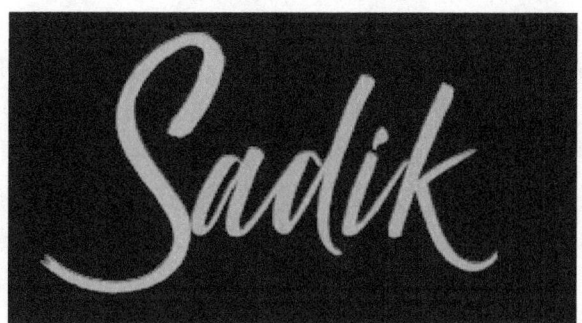

"That fat gnocchi-eating muthafucka called DEA! They shut down my fuckin' laundromats, Sadik!" My father slapped the top of the table as we stood in his warehouse. "Every last one of them shits being searched!"

And Ellis Soaps would be audited again by the IRS once the DEA completed the sweeps for drugs and paraphernalia. I knew this already, had gotten the call before my father's. I sat on the edge of the table, rubbing my face, frustrated by it all. This was Rizzo's doing. He and his crew ran the docks we all used—legally and illegally. My business was in imports and exports, but all of the top five miscreants of the state of New Jersey had some ties to those ports. They were owned by government, but run by a former mob associate. Salvatore Rizzo. He called in a favor in his legal world. He made this clear to my father in a call as I walked in here.

My father took a deep breath, planting his chin inside the apex of his thumb and index finger. His brows lifted. "We ain't got no way to rinse money now."

"I understand."

"We can call Tiff up." Iban's smirk matched his stupid ass sentiment. "You know she always down to ride for the family."

I threw him hard eyes.

"We ain't gonna involve baby girl's clubs in this," my father hissed.

"Besides," I added. "She only has two clubs. Successful or not, it's not enough to clean a day's worth of money brought in."

"We do have the three grocery stores, but..." my father noted.

"I know. They're not enough to wash all of it, either." After a beat, I offered, "It may be time we clean it through the LQs."

Iban's head shot up. Years ago, before his arrest and incarceration, I urged him to open a predominately cash operated business as a backup for their laundering. A true businessman knew you needed more than one stream of income. A true kingpin didn't always get, in this day and age of digital money, that you needed more than one system for cleaning your money. My father owned twelve laundromats in the state. My brother and sister-in-law owned eight liquor stores. When they began with the business under my advisement, I warned to keep it clean. Never to run a dirty dollar through them. That was for rainy days like this. It was my father's backup.

Iban stood straight and stretched his long arms in the air. "You already know. Just say the word and I'll have Monica—"

Rory swung the door open. Her big eyes animated with worry. "Yo, Deek." I acknowledged her. "Bilan."

Shit...

In an oversized robe, freshly showered and hair damped, I sat curled up on his couch. My puffy eyes seesawed between a pacing suited, russet baldy and the skyline vista from the floor-to-ceiling windows.

"Two days. Two fuckin' days!" he groused, rubbing his shiny head. "And this shit!"

I couldn't help my sniffles or lung hiccups. Thank God the tears stopped in the shower. I was utterly exhausted.

"You have to quit. You have to move in here." He finally turned to me, palms on his narrowed waist, suit jacket winged open.

"I can't, Sadik. My mother's things are there. Everything's there at the house."

"We'll hire a crew. You can be there as the house is being packed up. I'll pay for storage anywhere you want it. Or we can take it to Elliswoods Palace—shit, we can ship it down to Macen Beach—the choice is yours, but you're coming out of there."

"Sadik—"

His hand pushed into the air. "That's enough." That air of dark authority couldn't be missed, no matter how soft his voice was. "You told me no the first time under the guise of the dog, and I acquiesced. You no longer have a dog."

"But what about my brother? He's coming home soon."

Sadik's head was shaking before I could finish my words. "Your brother's a grown man. The house is about to be lost in foreclosure any moment now. I offered to help and you said no, which is fine because I want you here!" His finger pointed toward the marble floor. "I don't need you having any attachments to anything other than me.

You keeping that place will be a distraction from where I need you to be and that's safe, here with me."

I could feel my heart rupturing into two at that statement. It hurt so much. How could he want my childhood home gone? I understood the complication, but not at the risk of the absence. The last of my family's memory being lost...snatched away. Something so precious to me was an irritant for him.

Sadik turned and noticed me crying. He strolled over and sat next to me. As much as I wanted to be alone, his arms around my shaking frame were soothing.

"I'm sorry," he whispered. "You have no fuckin' idea how scared I was when Rory busted into my meeting and just mentioned your name." His head leaned into mine, and Sadik sighed. "I'm sorry. I know it's going to be a rough adjustment for you, but I promise, I'll work my ass off to make you comfortable and keep you safe twenty-four hours a day."

"How are you going to do that?"

"It's time for you to be assigned security around the clock."

I shifted my head. "Like, at work?"

Sadik took another fortifying breath. "I'll give you a couple of days to a week to do it, but Bilan, you're going to have to quit. It's too much of a risk leaving you at that diner. It's a high traffic area...too many people in and out of there. And while I do have the money, it's a huge liability to have armed security at that diner while you're working. You're going to have to do it. You're going to have to quit for me, honey."

And such was my life…

It had change drastically in the past six weeks. I resigned as assistant baker from Michelle's Diner. It was ceremonial; the party, cards, and tears. I, myself, cried in the backseat of Sadik's Range Rover that technically was mine as I was driven from the diner, back to my new home. Life was…different. It was enough I'd had a change since the absence of school and the addition of Sadik, but this was completely unrecognizable now that I didn't go into the diner daily.

Sadik lost an armed guard to me. Lamont was now my assigned security. Anywhere I went, so did he. Because I needed a guard, my fiancé insisted I had a comfortable vehicle for us, hence the brand spanking new Range Rover. Each day, I woke up to robust attention from a man's hands and hungry mouth. After we'd finally make it out of bed, I'd shower with him or meet him in the kitchen, where he'd feed us both breakfast. Kissing the man off to work had become a practiced science for me. I'd find something to fill the hours with while Sadik worked, and greeted him when he made it home at night.

We talked—God, we talked a lot—about his family, my future, and his business. Bonding over conversations was my absolute favorite feature of our relationship. I learned you don't know a man until you've lived with them. The man was the biggest Type A personality if I'd ever seen one. He was ridiculously predictable around the apartment, wanting his personal toiletries and clothing organized in a specific manner. All of Sadik's domestic habits, good and bad, were interesting, but nothing topped his superb sex. He'd use ropes in and out of the bedroom.

Mind-blowing...

Not having a job or school put more time on the clock I needed to kill, so I spent time with my friends. Once, I went out to a club with them. That didn't go over so well, with Lamont being so big and conspicuous in the crowd. So, I ended up leaving early. But I'd had Tasche and Randi over to the apartment, especially when Sadik traveled. I spent time getting to know Monica and the girls—on and off the Elliswoods compound. Lia delivered a healthy baby girl. I didn't hear many details beyond that by neither Sadik or Monica. Monica stayed with Iban, but hadn't forgiven him. Earl and Iban hadn't warmed to me, but they also seemed preoccupied during dinners when we'd eat with the family sometimes twice a week.

No matter how much I tried to fill in the time, I was still bored. I told Sadik I needed a job. Of course, he offered me a role at Ellis International again, to which I declined. Customs was not a field I cared to get into. He mentioned applying for a position at Ellis Academy, Irene's charter school system. While that was more of my speed because of my field, it gave me pause because that would be the finality of my independent identity. I wasn't even married into the family yet, and could easily assume their world.

And Abshir was released from prison in early July. It was a mess, but the norm for my brother and me. In the middle of a Tuesday, I got a call from the company Sadik paid to have the house secured with an alarm system. They said a Black male, brown skinned, and over six feet tall had let himself into the house with a key.

I flew over to Woodland Park, forgetting about notifying Lamont. Under the weather, I had no plans of leaving out this particular day.

When I pulled up to the house, two police cars were in front, along with a gang of familiar faces who were not all neighbors. I parked and walked inside, moving in between hoodlums, leaning on the railing and sitting on the porch.

"Daaaaaaamn," one sang, I was sure about me.

Another whistled and a few more snickered. I was annoyed right away. When I walked inside, I saw bodies in the living room.

"Oh, here the fuck Ms. America is," I heard hissed.

My face stretched as I took him in. Abshir had put on a good twenty pounds or more. He was bigger and had grown out a full beard.

"Hey," I breathed, taken by how much he'd resembled our father now more than ever.

Same warm brown skin, button nose, and even dark eyes my father earned in his last years from hard living.

"Tell these muthafuckas I live here so they can get the fuck on." He mean mugged them. "I just got the fuck out and you switching up shit, making it hard for a nigga to keep his head." Abshir rolled his eyes, sauntering into the empty living room.

"Sorry about that." I regarded the one officer of the three.

Two had followed my brother out of the room. It took close to five minutes to verify my identity, and that Abshir did indeed live there officially. The whole process felt like an hour with the way Abshir shot daggers my way and was snappy to the officers. When it was over, I saw them out. Before I could close the door, he started up.

"The fuck you think you is?" He came barreling toward me. "How the fuck you gone move and not tell me? Where the fuck my shit at? Where Mommy and Daddy shit?"

I lifted my palm, feeling weak and not up for a fight.

"First of all, it's good to see you're home, Abshir." He sucked his teeth, mumbling something beneath his breath. "Next, you didn't tell me when you'd be coming home. I specifically asked, and you told me not to worry about it. How was I supposed to know? I haven't heard from you in months. Had I known, I would have told you what caused me to pack up and move."

"The house ain't sold, so miss me with the bullshit!" He was ready for a verbal war.

I didn't miss this aggression and constant warring between my brother and me. When I was younger, I had more stamina. At this age, I couldn't do it. Abshir was angry, always combative.

"No. I got another letter stating the same status of foreclosure. I don't know when they'll ask us to leave."

"Then why the fuck you move out? Trickin' more fun when you a live-in?" The sinister grin on his face made him ugly.

"What are you talking about?"

"I heard you fuckin' one of the Ellis brothers—or he fuckin' witchu. Got you living in his crib, and shit." Abshir laughed bitterly. "You's a dumb broad if you think you his type of pedigree. I told you back in the day not to tire ya pussy out on niggas you ain't built for."

My head swung back; I grabbed my forehead as I swallowed hard. "Abshir, I moved out because someone killed a dog I bought for protection before or after they broke in here."

"Broke in here?" He scoffed.

"Yes. The security system we had all those years…the keypad was ripped from the wall. It confirmed my suspicion all this time that someone had been lurking around here for a while now."

"Yeah, probably somebody you ain't want no work with 'cause they ain't fuckin' heavy duty like that nigga you fuckin'."

My eyes closed as I tried to calm myself. "You have no idea what I am or am not doing. You know nothing about me."

"Bitch, you damn right. I don't need to know more than you out here fuckin' big wigs in these streets, and you won't be here in the house no more. Glad you moved the fuck out. You can take that new security system, too. Won't be needing that bullshit either." The disgust I saw in his eyes as he leered my way sent goosebumps shooting down my arms.

It cut me deep. Deep. But I refused to cry. He didn't deserve my tears.

"Your things are still downstairs. The washing machine and dryer are, too. Mommy and Daddy's things are in a storage facility. I have an extra set of keys for it if you want—"

"And where the fuckin' car?" He looked me up and down. "By the looks of ya Balenciaga track suit and matching sneaks, I see you getting around good."

I didn't want to part with my father's car. I made that clear to Sadik when he offered to have his people dump it. Instead, it was parked in the garage of his apartment building. Sadik also owned an apartment building in South Paterson. He offered a unit in there for Abshir should he have a housing issue once the foreclosure was completed. But there was no way I'd make that offer to him right now.

So I decided to lie. "I'll have it dropped off to you."

"Yeah." He turned his head away from me, scratching his crotch with indifference to my presence. "Do that."

"You know they'd be disappointed. Right?"

"Who?"

"Mom," I answered the obvious. "Dad, too!"

His face tightened angrily. "Fuck him," he sang. "Prolly in that box in the ground with a pipe, powder, and a lighter."

My stomach toiled at the visual.

"You're horrible. He was sick, Abshir," I choked out, refusing to let a single tear drop.

He leaped in the air, landing at the toes of my sneakers. "HE WAS FUCKIN WEAK!" he shouted at the top of his lungs, face stretched wide like an animal. "Like you, you fuckin' corny ass book worm, dummy. You fuckin' weak!"

Snickering from the other side had me looking toward the door. One of the guys sitting on the porch was there, laughing, clearly having heard what Abshir said. I turned back to see a smile spread on my brother's face in return.

"Man, get the fuck outta here, Bilan, before I end up chokin' the shit outta you." He scratched his crotch again, eliciting another guffaw from his friend.

I turned to leave, the guy standing in the doorway not moving to let me through.

"Could you tell your friend to move?" I shouted.

"Man." He pulled at the hairs of his beard, his chin angled in the air. "Let that bitch go. Should make her suck ya dick for a pass."

When the guy fell over laughing, I took my opportunity to leave. I moved swiftly down the stairs and to the truck. It wasn't until I got inside that the first tear slipped. I cried the entire way back to Sadik's and was so distraught, I forgot to grab the special box from my bedroom I'd forgotten when I packed the house up.

That was two weeks ago, and I hadn't breathed an embarrassing word of it to Sadik. Neither had I returned my father's car.

24

Aug

Sadik

"A'ight. That's it!" Iban hopped from the chair. "We doin' it. We know where Damien at. So he's gone today. I'll call in my crew now."

My father's regard bounced from Iban to me. He didn't speak, likely sensing my unease. This was it. It was the end of the period I'd been working on for over six years. It had been a long era where I'd tried keeping everyone alive despite their offenses. Damien, Abshir and, eventually, the Derrick kid had to go. Regardless of my peaceful attempts at following the NJ Commission's rules of killing a member, my father had a reputation to protect. One he believed was being tested by Rizzo, who'd still been working hard at making it difficult for my father to make money.

I was uneasy, but wouldn't say exactly why. I'd gotten a call from my guys about Damien being back in town. He'd been spending copious amounts of time in Hopewell Township, a town in Cumberland County. When in Paterson, Damien usually stayed at the barbershop he bought for his brother years ago. He'd sleep in the basement of the building he purchased in his brother's name.

But my intel on him also mentioned following Damien and his crew to an old, abandoned B-Way Burger building in Paterson. It was the second location the owners bought when they began expanding many years ago. The problem was the wiring was shot in the whole building, putting it at risk for fire. The restaurant owners didn't own the building and refused to put money into the repairs. It was too expensive, and a job they believed should have fallen on the property owner. There was a big legal battle in the papers over it. B-Way Burger decided to move. Ironically, learning from that incident, they began purchasing the buildings their restaurants functioned out of. The place had been abandoned since then.

Apparently, Damien and his crew carried large garbage bags in there last night. For what? That was bugging me. And I wouldn't reveal what I didn't understand.

"Be careful. Damien is a weird muthafucka," I warned.

"Too bad for his queer ass, I was born with a few pieces missing." Iban pointed to his head and heart.

"And the kid, Ab," my father noted.

I asked, "What about him?"

"The nigga gotta go," Iban declared. "Fuck you mean, what about him?"

My eyes drew to my father. He held them, communicating his adamancy. He wanted Abshir dead.

"Man," Iban began. "It's been six fuckin' years! Six fuckin' years and that nigga been living on borrowed time. His breathing been a stain on the Ellis brand. That nigga shoulda been shanked in Trenton State, but you kept saying we had to wait."

My brother couldn't keep still, bristling with convergent murderous energy. It was because of that a decision had to be made. Now.

It was the first week of August and Bilan's brother, Abshir, had been home for a month now. She hadn't mentioned him much, but I found it hard to believe she hadn't been in touch with him. He'd been staying at their family home and had been in touch with Damien, too, recently.

"I'll take care of him," I told my father.

My attention went to the phone vibrating in my hand. It was a text from Lamont, telling me he was taking Bilan to the diner for a party.

"Who?" Iban scoffed, causing my head to swing up. "You? Mr. Keep His Hands Clean?" He laughed. "Fuck outta here. I got both them niggas."

I glanced at my father again. "It's too much for one night. Too big of a risk to have your guys bounty hunting for two. I can put mine on it."

"Who?" my father asked, knowing I didn't reveal my sources.

But I knew he'd be satisfied with one name. "Rory."

"Deek, man!" Iban sang, spirited. "You ain't in this shit. Remember? You been making it crystal clear to Pops and me you hate even coming to our place of business." He referred to the warehouse as their office all the time. He pounded his chest. "I got this. I'm that son now. Move the fuck aside."

Again, I tried pleading to my father. "You know I can handle this."

"Okay," my father sighed, swinging behind his desk, in his chair. "Let's see if you still 'bout that work, Sadik."

I took a deep breath, grateful for a level head in him.

"Tonight!" he made clear.

I turned to leave. "Right now," I countered, lifting my phone to my ear.

When the truck pulled up to the corner, I pushed the door open. "I'll text you when I'm ready."

"A'ight, B," Lamont replied, eyes gazing around the block. "I'm outchea."

I hopped down, closing the door behind me and walking down to the diner. The place was busier than a typical weekday, and I imagined it was because of the occasion. Today was Nicky's birthday. His and his brother and co-owner, Vinny's, life revolved around the diner. This meant everything was celebrated here. Parties happened during business hours. Most gathered around for the cake, but other than that, well-wishes from friends and family happened around the clock. Because he turned sixty, the cake cutting time was scheduled.

Carina was sure to extend the invitation a week before. Completely exhausted, I almost didn't make it this evening. I canceled twice in my head, preferring to wait until Sadik got in from work tonight to finally talk to him. But Abshir sent a text asking to meet me so he could apologize for his nastiness a month ago. The diner always felt safe to me, so I thought telling him to meet me here was a one stone, two birds type of deal.

"Hey! Look who's here!" Gino, the bosses' nephew, shouted from behind the counter.

An excited smile curled my lips.

"Bilan!" Carina yelped from the register over the small line of customers waiting their turn to pay. "I should make your ass grab an apron."

I waved, shyer than usually, overwhelmed by the attention. It was clear I was missed. Saying goodbye in June was difficult for all. And the reason was so stupid, hence Lamont not coming in with me. Having security was ridiculous.

"Go around back," Carina granted. "He's going to love this."

I threaded through a few bodies to get behind the counter. A few of the waitresses spoke on the way, some while carrying heavy trays of food and drinks. When I made it to the back, Nicky was rolling dough, wearing a cone birthday hat. It read "Nicky" in gold frosting.

"Who made that for you and lived to take pictures?" I teased.

Nicky dropped his rolling pin and grabbed his heart, unveiling a rare beam. With my arms crossed, I sauntered toward him, pretending to have my nose in the air.

"I'd like a slice of sweet potato pie."

Nicky grunted. "Don't mention those damn pies." He went back to work.

"Hey, Bilana!" Vincent greeted me with a hug, coming out of nowhere.

I returned it. "You're not over a piping hot stove over there?"

"Taking a break to get some cake," he expressed in his thick accent. "Come on." He pointed toward the back of the kitchen.

People were gathering there already. A sheet cake laid out on the table was covered in an edible photo of an, even then, chunky Nicolas Ricci. It was adorable.

"I guess we're giving Super-Super business nowadays, huhn?" I jeered out loud about the Hispanic grocery stores now all over Paterson.

Vincent's face burned pink. "I'd cut my right nut off before giving them a dime of my fucking money!"

Half the crowd turned up with laughter, the other half with their own racist threats. We sang happy birthday to the big guy and performed some celebratory song from the Ricci's childhood taught to each employee at these types of parties. It was ridiculously annoying and fun at the same time. The cake was cut, employees returned to their posts, and I was pulled by one or another for small chat.

Before I knew it, forty-five minutes had passed and I felt marginally better. Having a sliver of Nicky's lemon tart helped, too.

"So, that Damien guy," Carina murmured, coming my way with a tray stacked with clean cups to store.

"What about him?"

"He comes in here a couple of weeks after your last day, rude to Stephanie when she said you quit."

"Oh, wow," was my only response. I hadn't thought of Damien in ages; my life had changed so much, including the people in it. "Wonder what that was about."

"I told her she talks too fucking much, that one." She huffed. "Just like when you were away that last time for a few days. He came in here asking about you, and the big mouth tells him you were on vacation— again. Vincent made her bawl her eyes out for running that mouth, you know?"

"Yeah. Why would she say so much to someone she doesn't know? I really don't know him."

Carina began stacking the cups in the dispensers. "She said she felt we owed him something with the way he looks out for us." She sucked her teeth. "Her ass almost got fired," she hissed. "What's going on between you two anyway? You sure you didn't fuck a time or two?" she asked on the sly.

My eyes shot wide. "I told you I don't really know him."

"Honey," she sighed, chomping hard on gum. "You don't have to know a man to have an agreement, if you know what I mean."

I shook my head while pinching the bridge between my eyes.

God, Carina! Don't let a certain Ellis man hear that...

410

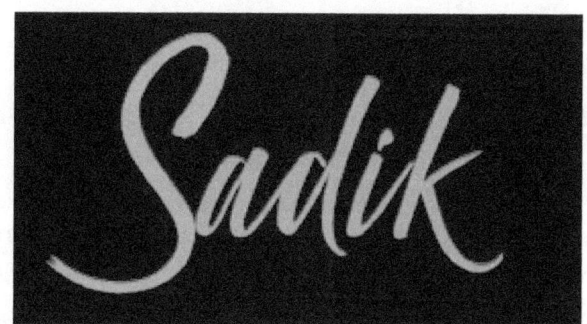

Sadik

At the back door with guns drawn, Rory, J-Dot, and Jamil glanced my way for the green light. With a nod, Jamil used the key I slipped from Bilan's ring a few days ago to unlock the door. Quietly, he turned the handle. Rory kicked in the door and moved in first. Covertly, we all toed inside looking for bodies—Ab's or anyone else's.

J-Dot signaled us. They were in the living room, but the basement door was cracked and the light was on. I pointed to J-Dot and Jamil. They moved right away. Soundlessly as possible, they took off down the stairs. We stood guard at the basement door, and at the other side of the kitchen. Within forty-five seconds, three bodies were coming back up. One wasn't as quiet as the other two and could call for attention, so I motioned for Rory to move into the hall. I covered her.

When she landed in the doorway of the living room with her pistol pointed, I heard the announcement of her presence.

"Fuck! It's Rory!"

Hearing that shouted from a grown ass man delighted me. When Rory didn't express weapons, I glided around her into the empty room. Two men were inside. Liquor and beer bottles about, tossed tobacco and bags of trees, too. Not only did the place look starkly different from the last time I was here, it smelled different too.

I distinguished Ab right away. Behind the big frame and bearded face, I saw features I'd come to obsess over in recent months. He returned the same dedicated gaze I'd given him, only I could see the rapid pulse beat in his neck.

"Wait, man, Rory!" the guy next to him begged with wide eyes and hands in the air. "Yo, I know what time it is when I see you, but I ain't do shit, man. Help me out. The fuck this about?"

"Shut the fuck up," Rory growled.

"I know what this about," Ab spoke up.

"Do you?" I grabbed an empty seat. "Pray tell."

"About that robbery we did on ya pops' warehouse. I ain't got boss status. That shit came from over my head."

I shrugged. "Damien's being dealt with as we speak."

Some emotion passed over his face. It was more than confusion, but I couldn't grasp what.

He watched as Jamil brought his friend in. J-Dot surveilled the front of the house. I didn't have much time.

Ab spoke slowly, "Then what the fuck this about then?"

I tossed my chin. "Well, Rory's here, so you know what time it is."

His lips parted as understanding blossomed in his mind. "I told you that shit was over my head. He paid us to rob the joint. I know you ain't here over no ass."

"Ass?"

"My sister's. I know you ain't trippin' 'cause of her. Man, that's some family beef that go way back. Me and you street niggas, Deek. We 'on't trip over no ass. Right? I came home to a empty house and she had to explain for it. I had to wait here with the fuckin' pigs all in my shit till she got here. That shit fucked me up. I been down for six years and couldn't get into my own shit 'cause of her? Plus, I wasn't really gone make her suck Manny dick that day. I was fuckin' with her when I said that shit. Ask him."

With my eyes on Ab, I lifted my finger across the room to "Manny."

"One in the head."

Four seconds later, "Manny" dropped to the floor.

"Nooooo!" the hyper-talker—or beggar—who'd been shitting his pants at the sight of Rory cried.

I leaned over, arms crossed on my knees, gun toward the floor. "You threatened some nigga's dick down my lady's throat," my voice soft, eyes imploring. "You're gonna have to catch me up on the Asad-Yasin family dynamic now."

"The fuck? Like…what you mean?"

"Like why the fuck does she speak of her parents—good and bad—all the damn time, but never mentions much about you? Like why have I been in her life for months and she's never mentioned a call from you—and I've never been around when a call from you came through. My Nalib don't like you, Ab?"

Still next to my leg, the barrel of my gun now facing Ab instead of the floor.

I was just coming out of the employee bathroom, searching for my lotion in my crossbody purse at my hip when Gino called to me.

"Bilan, the Damien guy's out back. Wants to see you!" He turned to the double swinging doors to head to the front.

Amongst the dozen and a half of working bodies, I made my way to the back door. His timing was perfect. Why would he be upset that I quit? Would he continue to keep an eye on the place? I ambled outside, questions flying through my head like a freeway. There was a burgundy van double parked in the lot. A young guy, I recognized from Damien's crew, leaning on the hood. He waved casually before going back to his phone.

Carina called behind me. "Bilan, some big guy named Lamont's looking for you at the counter.

Shoot…

"Tell him I'm out back talking to someone," I replied. "I'll be done soon."

Turning ahead, I made my way over.

"Whadup?" he greeted as I passed by him, his eyes still below on his device.

I murmured a return greeting while making my way to the other side of the van. It had one of those tricked out interiors. Damien sat on a bench facing me. He wore a white t-shirt with sweat shorts and sneakers. Jet black hair shiny with deep waves. The man always looked good.

Oh… "Haven't seen you in a month of Sundays," I joked.

"Yeah," he sighed, rubbing his knees. "And I ain't got a lot of time, so get in." His tone was brisk.

My face folded. "What?"

A sharp blow to my side had me recoiling. "Get the fuck in." *The kid from the hood of the van was pushing a sharp object into my ribs, pain radiating to my back.*

Without thinking, I moved to step into the van, needing the pain to go away. Then I was being pushed inside. Before I landed in a chair, the door was being rolled closed.

"You's a hard girl to track down, Bilan," Damien leered. "Killin' that damn dog of yours pushed you over the edge, I see."

Huhn?

My body jolted hard when the van pulled off.

"What? Dog? You know— You killed my dog?" *I couldn't believe what I was hearing.*

"I thought it was cute you got him in the first place. I sent my goons to your house a few times to fuck with you, so you could cry to your brother about being in danger." *He delivered his blows so casually about the paranoia I'd been feeling when I decided to get Dog…and a gun.* "But either you didn't or that didn't work 'cause Ab ain't flinch."

"Abshir? I don't know what you're talking about."

I noticed two other men in seats behind us moving around. One was mumbling on the phone.

414

With his head cocked to the side, Damien sighed. "I guess you don't. You've been so damn naïve, girl." Damien laughed. "Your big ass head brother stole from me. Well...him and his boy stole from somebody for me, and then he stole some of the shit he was supposed to give to me. The dumb ass did two more things, fuckin' up. He killed three niggas when he did the robbery, then got caught with what he tried jacking me for. That's how he caught that charge. The drugs in the car that night was what he stole from me to make a few dollars from. Dumb muthafucka." He shook his head.

"Anyway, he got locked up still owing me. I had a dilemma at that point." He shrugged as I hung onto each syllable he shared, not able to believe my ears. "I couldn't afford him rattin' me out to the cops. So, I used your mother as collateral while he was on trial. If he ratted, I'd kill her. That worked, because he kept his fuckin' mouth closed and took no pleas. But then I had another dilemma. Care to take a guess what it was?"

My lips trembled from empty words. I shook my head.

"The man I stole from through ya brother and his weak ass friends. That's what I got sending local, low level niggas to do a boss' job. Then I had to hope he wouldn't run his fuckin' mouth in the pen. The nigga I stole from got eyes in there, too. That's where you came in. Ya mom—God bless the dead—died after he got sentenced. So, I told ya brother I was gonna kill you if he talked. He told me to go fuck myself."

He shrugged casually again before continuing. "I tried keeping a eye on you while you worked, thinking that'll make him see how strong and long my arms are. I kept my goons on call for trouble, even though them racist ass dagos at Michelle's used you to serve the niggas. I thought you would tell him I been looking you out, you know?"

My jaw dropped. That's why he'd been around the diner all these years.

"No." I swallowed hard. "I didn't."

"Yeah. That shit ain't work. I don't think y'all really kick it like that. So about a year ago, I sent my goons over to ya crib to fuck with you."

That's when I felt I was being watched...

415

It was when I decided to get Dog.

"But anyway, now that nigga out and owe me money, but the money ain't got shit on my bigger problem."

"What's your problem, and what does it have to do with me?"

My heart banged in my chest. We'd been driving at a speed that made my torso sway uncontrollably. I needed to get out.

Damien laughed again. "A few things, actually. I sent four local niggas to rob a warehouse, ya brother was the lead man. The man I robbed done already caught up to two. The first one, they got right away. Now, that's their style." His index finger pounded the air. "Jamal got clipped right away. That's how they do."

I sucked in a breath, remembering going to Jamal's funeral with my mother. It was sad. He and Abshir had been friends for years. He'd eaten from my mother's table.

Damien continued, "They waited Lenny out. He thought him running is what took so long." He shook his head. "I think they let him think that. I just don't know why."

My face folded again. "Lenny…Lenny?"

Is that why he went missing?

"Yup. Lenny from around the way. His body turned up last week, in the Passaic River by West Broadway. You ain't know?" I shook my head, heart pounding. "Mother had to cremate that lil' nigga."

"Again, what does this have to do with me?" I was on the verge of tears. Something felt awfully wrong about this. It was more than him forcing me in here.

"Apparently, the man I robbed?" I wanted to nod to tell him to get on with the story, but I couldn't buy into the naïve label anymore. He'd just demonstrated with this bag of tales how I had no clue of what had been happening around me. I didn't want to prove him right, though he was. I'd been naïve to my brother's street dealings. Thankfully, Damien didn't hold out for it. "His son like fuckin' you."

My torso recoiled as bile shot from my belly. I swallowed hard—choked to keep it down. Damien laughed in response.

"You ain't know, did you?" The mirth in his voice couldn't be missed. "Awwww… My sweet Bilan had no idea the nigga trickin' her out is the son of the richest Black criminal in the state of New

416

Jersey—and beyond. So rich, the keys I had Ab and his crew rob him for wouldn't have been a big loss to him. That nigga just greedy and egotistical. You know… Possessive. But I get it. I got a little cheddar myself. I flex over lil' shit, too."

I swiped my nose distractingly as Damien peered at me with a gleam of lasciviousness in his eyes. It was the first time he'd given me a clear sign of anything other than ambiguity. All this time, I waited for signs, wondering why he didn't try to date me, and when I experienced the first of his fleshy nature, I was disgusted.

"That's why your pit bull had to go."

"Because you felt possessive over me?"

"I ain't like not knowing you was fuckin' a Ellis under my nose, Bilan. I know I been back and forth, setting up shit in South Jersey, but my sweet, naïve Bilan let that nigga trick her out. Get her to take time off work. Then you quit." His eyes went to my left ring finger. "Oh, shit! I see why now." With his fist to his mouth, Damien belted out a hard laugh.

I didn't get why.

"The Ellis' killed somebody I was 'bout to propose to. Daaaaamn, ain't it funny how life go?"

"What?" My eyes attempted to blink away the confusion. Then I was hit with a jarring thought. "How did you know I'd be here?"

He tossed his chin my way. "Ya brother. I told him to make it happen."

The text. Abshir told me he wanted to talk. He'd lied.

"Yo, we got a trail," the guy driving us notified Damien.

"Who?" Damien asked.

"A black Range."

"That's you?" Damien asked, sparking the realization it could be Lamont.

I didn't answer. I couldn't.

"Lose his ass!" Damien shouted, all humor gone.

"Man, I 'on't know what you want me to tell you," Ab answered honestly, and I understood it.

This kid was a different breed to that of my sweet Nalib. She was well spoken and mannerable, yet strong. This guy wasn't an ounce of the thugs my father employed. I wasn't unfamiliar with his type at all. I could smell the fear on his breath. It was my suit and demeanor. Street niggas thought they'd be killed fast and predictably by niggas who look and dressed like them. So, when a suited man with gentle civility had a gun to them, of course, fear was present. Ab here also had that "recently released" mentality. He wanted to be tough.

"I want you to tell me why she doesn't talk about you. Why would an older brother tell his sister he'd make her suck some nigga's dick? What sick fuck would do that?"

"She ain't innocent, man. Don't let her run game on you." His eyes fell, nostrils flared. "Look, I been knowin' about you and ya family, man. I know you got a sister, too. Y'all gotta fight sometimes."

"Nah. I lead in protection. She follows. We're the same flesh and blood. I would not let a goddamn thug use her as collateral while you're locked away."

"I swear to Allah, I told Damien: my mom dukes died! I ain't give a shit what he did after that. Bilan was on her own. I ain't give a shit

418

no more—don't give a shit. Me and Bilan never been on the same shit. She just different. That fuckin' bookworm shit—"

I stood and pushed the gun into his temple. "Aye! Aye!" he screamed, hands in the air defensively.

"The fuck wrong with reading books?" I asked.

I saw the first tear fall. "It's more than that! She ain't never like me, man. It's just shit between brothers and sisters," he tried to deflect. "I 'on't give a shit how sweet she try to act, she think she better, and my father believed that shit."

I pushed the gun further into his skull. "You better tell me something that makes since, Ab. I got shit to do."

What was I doing? I came here to do one thing. Now, I was defending my girl's honor to her brother.

The tears continued to fall, and breathing grew strained as it became clear to me. This kid was struggling with pure animosity for his sister. My Bilan.

"She tell you our pops was a fuckin' pipe head?"

"Maybe."

"She tell you how when we was mad little, some hustlers ran up on us in the restaurant my family had, trying to get money my pops owed? She tell you that story? How they threatened to kidnap her until he paid up and that nigga cried at their fuckin' Timbo's, begging them to take me instead?"

Ab was choking on the tears he didn't want to break from his throat. His whole damn body vibrated from constraint. He didn't like being forced to tell a story that had been haunting him since he was damn near a baby.

I pulled back on the gun, eyes going into the distance. He hated his sister because he was going to be sacrificed for her. I wondered if Bilan knew this. I'm sure she wouldn't have agreed with her father being reckless with her brother's life. This story was also likely the reason Ab turned to the streets. If his father was this weak—as weak as Bilan tried gently describing him—the streets were an easy lure for this kid.

"Yo, Deek!" Rory barked, voice animated. I turned to her. "Damien got Bilan!"

My entire body went cold at those words. My knees went weak.

"Where?" spilled...strained from my mouth. I couldn't breathe for a moment.

"Lamont on them." She yelled into the phone I didn't hear her on until now. "Stay on them, nigga! Where you at?" She listened in before answering to me, "He said they was headed to the west side, 'bout to turn down that lil' bridge behind the old B-Way Burger till they noticed him. Now, they running around the fourth ward!"

Shit...

I jumped, damn near running out of the living room. "Tell him to stay so far behind, they'll think they lost him. J-Dot, clean the body." I referred to Manny's bloodied mess.

"Wait!" Rory yelled after me. "What about these fucks?"

Ab and his friend.

"Leave them. They won't go far!" I was at the back door, swinging it open and bolting out.

25

I'd never been strung up in my life—before Sadik. I'd also never been faced with my own death. This was some HBO action film type of horror. We zigzagged through the streets of Paterson, nearly hitting people on each block. As awful as it sounds, I was grateful for the chaos, hoping it would call the attention of the cops at some point. I mean, somebody had to be calling about an erratic-moving van somewhere along the way. But that didn't happen. The kid driving told Damien they'd lost the Range. His response was to head over to the spot. The spot ended up being the old B-Way Burger that had been closed down for as long as I could remember.

Now, I sat in the middle of what could have been the dining area. The whole place was stripped of everything resembling a restaurant. Straight ahead, one of the guys was laying out plastic tarp on the floor. Another was pulling out a chainsaw, then another. My eyes flew wide and breathing hiked. I couldn't believe my life was playing out like a movie. Or was it an untold story of a woman's body coming up in the river months later like Lenny's?

So, this type of terror really happens underneath my nose?

When I couldn't stop crying, Damien had one of the guys tape my mouth. Now, I could hardly breathe, no matter how much I willed my mind to calm down so my body could follow. My head was spinning, my stomach nauseous.

Oh, God, my belly…

I tried kicking my feet, wiggling my arms free.

"You gone pass out if you 'on't stop, Bilan."

That had to be Damien warning me. But I couldn't help myself. I was about to die. How could I calm down? How could Damien turn out to be a killer? My chest began to hurt, head whirred, and I couldn't feel my feet.

I was fading...

"I'm not afraid of anything. I've been on my own for so long now, I know how to protect and look out for myself. I don't know what you think you know about me, but I'm just fine."

"You're not," the broad, handsome, eclectic, and mystic man rasped. "But you will be. You do, however, have a turbulent voyage ahead of you similar to Joseph. You see, people focus on the betrayal, then the ultimate overdog nature of his story when I'm always reminded of the journey of his faith. Yes, Joseph was deceived by his siblings and sold into slavery. He was lied on by his boss' wife, accused of attacking her with sexual intent. But Genesis, chapter thirty-nine, verse two tells us, 'The Lord was with Joseph.' Joseph was then imprisoned for, some say, thirteen years.

"It was those years of despair, confusion, and imprisonment that impress me most about Joseph. He was alone and in captivity. And once again, in verse twenty-one, we're reminded, 'But the Lord was with Joseph.' We learn in chapter forty-eight how Joseph may have appeared to have been removed from his birthright, but his birthright remained in him each moment of what turned out to be twenty years of separation from his family. In the end, God not only released him from that prison, but He made him ruler of Egypt under the pharaoh of the time. The second most powerful man of Egypt.

"Joseph became what's called a vizier and decided...what you millennials refer to as 'who got to eat, and eat well.' He went from a slave to a prisoner to a high-ranking official, ruling over the brothers who betrayed him."

"I don't get what you're saying. Why are you telling me all of this?"

"The Holy Spirit revealed to me a similar path you're about to take. You've been in a valley and have more time in it, but the amazing thing about God is no matter your Islamic roots, He covers you. Your upbringing, culture, current knowledge of Him is inconsequential to

His covering and will for your life. He still wants to be in relationship with you."

"Why?"

"In the vision, some of your nights were long. You witnessed things only seen in cinema or between the pages of a novel and/or pamphlet. You were thrust into a world never known to you. You will feel pain, joy, betrayal, bliss, deeper loneliness, and contentment like no other. There will come a time where you will flee—run in fear.. But the Lord will be with you. The stranger you've never known knows each strand of hair on your body and has covered you since your conception, and will continue to during this next phase of your life."

"What phase?"

"The one you would do better in if you remembered He's protecting you every step of the way."

"I declare right now, Satan, you may tempt, but cannot destroy. You may come near, but cannot touch. You may plot, but you will not conquer. In case you did not know, this soul belongs to The God Who Sees. El Roi has already seen into her future, has already lain the trap of her faith..."

My belly fluttered.

Then I heard a strong, zipping sound causing my eyes to fly open. A body dropped. The kid holding the gas canister.

"Shit!" Someone yelped. "You see—"

Another zip and another. I could hear a groan behind me and another collapse.

Then the room went quiet. My pulse roared in my ears and my ankles began to vibrate. I felt someone moving behind me and yelped. A hand covered the tape around my mouth.

"Shhh, baby. It's me, Nalib," was at my ear.

A balm of relief coated my frame. My belly fluttered again, tears fell down my face. The heavy breathing returned when I realized I couldn't talk to or see him. His hands worked around my wrists, untying the knot Jayshon had done. I learned that was the name of the guy who shoved a gun into my ribs.

"I need you to be quiet for me, honey," that velvety alto commanded so gently. Too serene for the occasion. And my body

423

responded to it. My breasts felt heavy, all of a sudden. There was a dead body a few yards in front of us. "I'm going to untie your hands, then your feet. Okay?" Those last two syllables almost melodic, causing my groin to throb.

He worked until my hands were free. Even in my traumatically panicked state, I could have faith in his ability to undo the ropes. Sadik had experience with them.

My hands were free and next, he kneeled by my feet. That's when I learned he was giving commands to someone—people—behind me with the wave of his hand. His thick, bushy brows couldn't hide the darkness in his honeyed irises. He may have carried a cool demeanor, but Sadik was bubbling beneath the surface. His full lips set into a firm line, and there were four wrinkles between those bushy brows. But his deft fingers made quick work at unraveling the rope.

"This is going to hurt. Okay?" he asked gently, moving on autopilot, it seemed. "Don't scream, baby."

My body in a fit of trembles, Sadik glanced behind him and that's when I saw Rory with a gun drawn in her little hands, squatting as she approached a corner like a professional.

"Bilan," Sadik whispered, calling my attention to him.

The moment my eyes hit him, he yanked the tape from my face. It was a horrible ripping, but I don't think my mind could comprehend the pain in the moment.

Damien…

Damien!

I couldn't speak as he stalked behind Sadik, toward us. My hands trembled as I tried pointing. We were going to die. Sadik and me because he came to save me.

And as though coordinated, Sadik turned in perfect sequence, taking me protectively at the hand while en route to Damien. As we drew closer, my body chilled and pulse banged. Sadik lifted and jerked his right arm down, bringing with it a rope. The manila rope I'd just been tied up with. He snapped the rope like a cowboy's whip on cattle. Damien went for his waist. With another yank to bring it up in the air, using blinding speed, Sadik had the other end of the rope wrapped around Damien's neck. On a firm tug, causing a grunt to leave

Sadik's gut, the rope violently wrenched Damien backward, audibly snapping his neck. His eyes bulged from their sockets and tongue protruded as his hand gripped the gun at his waist. His lifeless body dropped, bringing into vision a positioned Rory. She stood with her short legs spread apart and gun pointed our way.

My knees gave out on me. She'd been there in Damien's approach. If Sadik didn't kill him, Rory would have.

"It's okay, baby," Sadik assured so capably, and I almost believed him as he tried to help me to my feet.

I was like a giraffe seconds out of the womb, trying to find my legs. I couldn't rip my eyes from Damien's splayed body. Blood began to pool from his mouth and nose.

"That's right, Bilan," Sadik tried, his strong arms around my waist. "Is it clear?" he asked someone behind me.

"Clear."

"Where's Lamont?" Sadik asked.

"Outside, on foot, circling the building," a man I'd never seen replied.

With me hooked in his arm, Sadik began to move. "Rory, call Lamont and tell him to head to the truck. I need him to take Bilan home." We were closer to the back door of the restaurant where Damien brought me into when Sadik advised. "Baby, I'm going to send you back to the apartment. Lamont is not going to leave your side until I get home. Don't call the police, or anyone for that matter. I'll take care of all of it. Okay?"

That's when I heard a flame. I turned over my shoulder and saw a man light the gasoline Jayshon poured earlier aflame on an adjacent wall. They were going to burn the place up. Still stunned from seeing a man killed by my fiancé, I couldn't speak to react.

Sadik assisted me into the truck outside. He took me at the sides of my face and kissed me long and passionately. Then he leaned his forehead into mine. "I've never been so scared, Nalib," he whispered.

With gingerly care, he pulled the seatbelt over my trembling frame, kissed me again, then closed the door. I watched him go back inside. For a while, I saw no one. No one.

Not a soul.

425

My brain finally kicked into gear. I unbuckled the seatbelt and jumped into the front seat, despite the aches from my wrists, ankles, and side. My hands scrambled at the crossbody at my hip for my set of keys to the truck.

Oh, God, help me…

"Please," I cried in a whisper before the engine cranked.

Without a moment of hesitation, I peeled out of the abandoned lot hidden by overgrown trees and weeds. The thought wasn't lost upon me that I had nowhere to go. Sadik's apartment was not an option. I needed to get away from him. At this point, I couldn't identify him from his father. He killed Damien.

Yes. Damien was going to kill me—

"Oh, God!" I croaked.

I was supposed to be dead, left in that abandoned restaurant.

Inside my purse, my phone vibrated. Quickly, I dug it out, and my eyes went between the road and the device when I saw it was Sadik. I ignored it, sending him straight to voicemail. The sun had set, darkness providing a sense of covering, but I didn't have a destination.

Killers!

Murderers!

Thieves! Every one of them complicit in a crime.

"But in the event you need me, here's all of my information. We have a safe house where women in need can come and…disappear."

My hands tightened at the steering wheel.

Disappear!

That's what I needed. But before I did, there was one thing I needed. Something I left at my parents' home.

The yard was dark as usual, and I could tell someone was home. I didn't need to fight with Abshir tonight and told myself on the way

426

I'd ignore everything he threw my way to get in and out in no time. As I approached the back door, I realized the key to the house was missing from my ring. Panic rang out in my chest. At the top step, I took a deep breath, eyes closing in frustration. I didn't have the key. A key I didn't recall tossing away. My regard slid to the knob. I turned it and felt all the air leave my lungs when it turned enough to open.

I crept inside, finding the lights on in the kitchen and hall. The basement door next to the back door was open and the lights were on. I could hear Abshir down there, though I couldn't make out what he was saying. The volume of his voice increasing by the second, causing me to realize he was on his way upstairs.

Quickly, I darted into the hall for my bedroom. I closed the door behind me and used the light from the face of my cell phone to direct me to the closet. The room felt eerily different being emptied. I opened the door and fell to my knees to reach the back of the closet. I pulled back the carpet, my hand tapping to feel the box. The moment I gripped the box at the side to pull it up, I heard what sounded like a door being kicked in. My body leaped in the air on all fours, then froze when I landed. I heard booms against the floor, shouting in the distance. When I heard what I couldn't deny was a gun shot, I opened the box for the gun. Several more rang out before my limbs went rigid.

Not again…

Abshir! Abshir was shot. I could feel the numbness in my belly. That familiar flurry of loss when you've been told by the doctors your father is gone, or your mother had finally succumbed to the cancer. It was there. Someone killed my brother.

My heart couldn't endure anymore fight or flight trauma. I tried quieting my breathing. Above me was a window I reached up to, to peer between the blinds. There were no movements to call for help, just the usual quiet block.

Why?

Why?

Why?

Why me? Why again? Hadn't I stomached enough in this lifetime?

The crackling sound from the hardwood floors beneath the carpet seized my breath. I tried counting footsteps. I could only sense a cautious one. They were right there. In that small space between the carpet and the bottom of the door my father replaced when I was in high school, but never measured before installation, I was able to see shoes. The moment I heard the knob twist, I cocked the little gun and let off shot after shot. I could hear and feel bullets hitting the walls around in the dark. Someone was shooting at me. Dear Allah, I was about to die in my childhood bedroom. Abruptly, as I continued to fire successively, I heard a man groan before taking off down the hall. It didn't matter: I fired until the gun was empty. Then through the window, I heard fast-paced steps in the front of the house.

"I got shot," a man choked out, not at too high a volume, but alarmed. "I'm coming down the block. Call for clean up now!"

In seconds, I heard a vehicle braking hard over my head as I leaned against the wall, next to the window frame. A door slammed and the vehicle sped off. Whether I was accurate to guess that was the man who tried to shoot me or not, with trembling arms, I gathered the box and rose to my feet. I jetted out of my old bedroom and down the hall. My feet stopped before my body at the sight of my brother's slain body stretched out on our mother's carpet. Just like Damien's body earlier, a pool of blood gathered at his mouth.

My lungs wouldn't move. What had he done? What trouble could he have found this soon after being released? After the story Damien told me earlier, I didn't want to stick around and see. I wanted no parts of the darkness I felt all around me at this point. I needed an escape. Shuffling backward first, I bolted to the front door, and out of the house to the truck I was sure to park a block away. In the dark of the night, I ran like my life depended on it, because it did.

When I made it to the Range Rover, my body shook so violently, I dropped the box at the door. I made quick work of picking it up, along with its contents, including the keys to my destination. Once inside, I pulled out my wallet. In a rarely used compartment in the back was a business card I never thought I'd used and honestly had forgotten I had, until less than an hour ago.

I started the truck and pulled off. As I turned down a new street, I dialed the first number listed on the card, using the light from my phone to see it in the darkness of the interior. The line rang out over the Bluetooth in the truck.

"Hello?"

My lashes fluttered at the sound of a woman's voice on the other end. I was expecting a professional greeting from a hotline, maybe.

"Hello?" a thick New York accent similar to Tasche's demanded. "Lex?"

"Who's asking?" She hadn't lightened in greeting a bit.

I swallowed hard. "Bilan. Ummmmm..." I stopped at a light and dropped my head in my hands. What was I doing? I was not in a movie. I wasn't up for the dramatics of a desperate call to assist with the fact that I needed to get away, and had no money to go far...and I had to be discreet. "I know you don't remember me, but—" My eyes blurred against the red traffic light from tears. "—I saw you when your husband preached at a church in Paterson—"

"I can have a warm, safe bed for you in ten minutes," she didn't skip a beat. "Are you in danger?" her voice was calm. "Do you need transportation."

I shook my head before my brain could think to speak. "No!" I breathed. My salivating mouth stretched wide before I could get words through. "I don't need a bed, either. I just need a few dollars for a bus or train ticket to get out of town discreetly."

"Are you sure that's all you need? I can come to you..."

I needed to disappear, which meant separating from this truck. I could dump it and meet her somewhere.

The light turned green, and I lifted off the brake.

"Okay..."

429

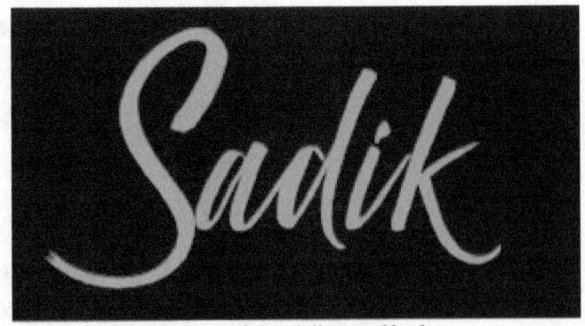

Sadik

"And your dumb ass shot him?" I yelled.

"You wouldn't!" Iban shouted just as loud from the table while his arm was being worked on. "You ain't got the heart for this shit no more, yo."

The doctor stitching him gave warning of staying still.

"Don't seem like your arcade game-shooting ass does either, getting hit in the arm, and not knowing by who or if you killed them." I careened around the doctor, "And you don't know what the fuck I was going to do!"

"Obviously, I fuckin' did when I showed to the nigga's crib and found him still breathing!"

"Muthafucka, I will—" My father, standing in the small room in his warehouse, leaped in front of me, pushing me toward the door.

"I gotta agree with him, Sadik. You're too close to the situation."

That's when it dawned on me. "You two planned this behind my back." When my father didn't deny, I knew. "When I left here, the meeting continued, and you two planned to hit Damien and Ab."

"Duh, muthafucka'," Iban mumbled.

"You and that bullshit with his sister got you blinded, man," my father tried to reason with me. "I know you got your own path in life and don't want no parts of this game shit. So, I told Iban to wait a few hours before confirming you did it."

"Like we knew!" Iban interjected before groaning at the pain of his stitching.

Pain I wanted to intensify.

"Because I was busy thinking ahead of your main target, Damien. How was I able to handle that if I ain't got no heart?"

430

"Nigga, the only heart you had in that Damien shit was that African girl!" Iban groaned.

My father's eyes told me he agreed. It was ironic, the turn of events. We left here hours ago with marching orders, only our targets got switched due to circumstances. I was mentally strained after cleaning the abandoned building of our presence.

A knock at the door before it opened had us turning.

Rory peeked in. My eyes desperate for an answer from her.

She shook her head. "Found the truck downtown Paterson. Just the truck."

My eyes closed in frustration. The last thing I needed was Bilan missing, running because she was afraid of what she saw today. Of me. I couldn't lose her now. I sacrificed too much to finally have her attention mentally, and in my home physically. I fought too fucking hard with my father and brother, all to lose her to the truth of who I was. What I would forever be, whether I liked or not.

An Ellis man.

Three days later...

The seagulls crowed, flying in the salted air, and the wind breezed through my damp hair. The plot of sea oats danced left to right from the night gust. The sun was down and the moon assumed its shift, illuminating the water. The view at night was striking from the master balcony.

My phone chirped on the canopy bed behind me. I wouldn't answer it; I hadn't in days. Nothing would disturb this tranquility. None of the chaos from New Jersey would be brought here. I didn't know how long I'd stay. My next move needed to be settled on soon. But that was hard to do, gazing out at the mesmerizing water.

I was here. The place I felt peace. Mental quieting. Safety.

My belly fluttered and I peered down at it, covered in a cotton slip. My face melted into a contented smile.

"I don't know what our next move is, but let's hope it's near a place with the same vista. You're going to love the beach." My gaze reached the water again. "It may not be this secluded stretch of Macen Beach, but I'll make sure it's just as cool," I whispered, a smile in my heart. "Just me and you, far away from them all."

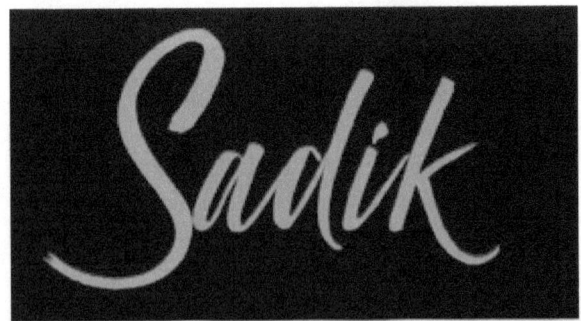

Standing in the swaying sea oats, I browse up to the balcony of the master suite holding some of my most cherished memories in life. I see my world. My future. My Nalib. She's safe. She's happy. Even if it's temporarily without me, I'm thrilled she's found her way to this place. Our place.

It took a couple of days, but she turned up, thanks to the security company notifying me of someone accessing our property for the first time in months. Of course, I told them I was aware. Only one person could accurately use the code needed to get inside the beach house: the woman who created it.

"You're not alone, baby girl," I murmur against the salted night winds to her heart I'd one day conquer. "I'll be back for you."

TBC

~LOVE ACKNOWLEDGES

Visuals: <u>365 Photography</u> – *"Hello, Brooklyn!" Your talent is boundless. Thanks for taking a chance in literature. As you can tell, I'm **still** excited. Teehee! I look forward to more collaborations!* <u>Fierce Faces</u> – *Kaydene, I can't say thanks enough for brokering this deal. As we both learned, what's meant to be will gel seamlessly. Thanks for your artistry and patience (and not cussing me out as you threatened).* <u>KNGQ</u> – *Q. Williams &* <u>Brittney April</u>*, thanks so much for serving as visuals for our Sadik and Bilan. May this be another ideal step in the direction of your promising careers. My best to you in all your endeavors!*

Researcher: Shumethia S. — I know you want to give me the boot. Too bad you can't. With this role, you can't quit no matter how far away you move! Thanks so much for always going the extra mile for me, even when it's inconvenient.

Beta Readers: Sabrina (Triple S.) & Rocita, thanks so much for the time you took to test this baby out and for providing strong feedback. I truly appreciate you! Yorubia, I can't say enough how grateful I am for the way you invest your heart into my career. Thanks for taking the journey with me from conception to publish. Oh, and uggggg yoooooooooou!

LBTR — Afi, Angela J.J., Artemysia, Ash, Ashleigh, Ashley, Ayanna, Ayo, Azaria, Bonita, Brittany, Courtney, Danielle, Dee, Deena, Deidre, Denise, DeVona, Diane, Diva Dee, Doresha, Doris, Erica C., Ericka M., Gail, Grace, Heather, Heidi, Hezie-Ann, Hyacinth, Jasmine, Jessica, Kamashia, Karmen, Katrice, Katrina, Kay, Kendra, Kerry, Keyma, Kim, Kimmiko, Kita, Korei, LaKisha, LaLa, LaSonde, Linda R., Linda W., Lee, LeShonda, Levette, Malaika, Marshall, Michelle M., Michelle R.O., Michelle T., Mocha, Monique H., Monique N., Natoya, Nena, Nikki, Pamela, PJ, Rakia, Quan, Regina, Richell, Rose, Roslyn, Samona, Sharon L., Sharon F.W., Shaun, Sola, Stacey K., Stacy M., Tabatha, Tamara, Tanisha, Tanya, Tara, Té, Teresa, Terri G., Terry H., Tesha, Tia, Tiffany, Tineka, Tonya, Tralaina, Vivian, Wendi, Yolanda P., Yolanda U., Yorubia, and Yvette H., you each are individual gifts to me, wrapped in love.

Thanks for being that core of support. **Jemeka & Rita**: *For the first time, J is in love with our male visual, and Rita-Bita admitted to wanting help with 'smashing' on the fan page. What will the future bring for our union? ROTFL!!!! Love you two intensely.*

Christina C. Jones aka CCJ — *Your friendship grows more valuable by the day. Thanks so much for all you contribute to my life and brand. May God continue to increase everything you touch! And Lord, heal her road rage! Ugh!*

Interior Artist: *Cedeara Ardell McCollum — Thanks, baby girl, for the imagery you've designed for my books! Love you always!*

Proof Reader: *Tina V. Young — I'm so blessed to have you on my team. Thanks for questioning so much. Thanks for that petty eye being on 1,000! P.S. Don't tell people how often I hit you up. It's truly not normal! LOL!*

Editors:

*Zakiya Walden of **I've Got Something to Say!** — I appreciate your hard work and dedication. This process reminds me of our L.I.P. days. LOL! May we have many more!*

*Santisha Taylor of **AccuProse Editing Services** — I appreciate your professionalism and patience!*

MDT: *Thanks for the support and development of the LB brand. Looking forward to another year of growth!*

Master, my **Jireh**, my **Rohi**, *Lamentations 3:22-23 (NKJV) "Because of the Lord's great love we are not consumed, for his compassions never fail. They are new every morning; great is your faithfulness." Great is Thy faithfulness.*

SADIK

See visuals from the series <u>here</u> on my website –
<u>https://www.lovebelvin.com/projects/sadik</u>

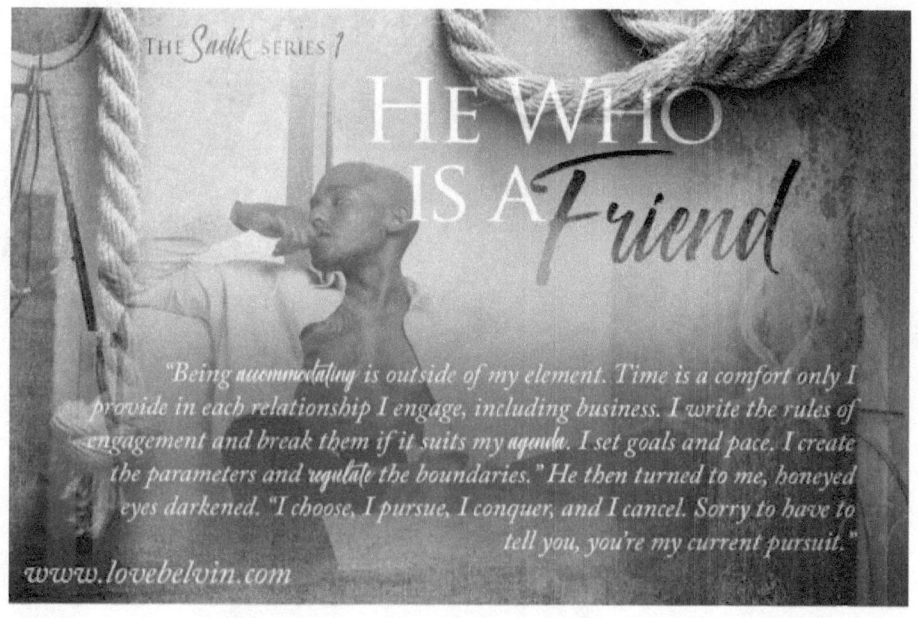

~OTHER BOOKS BY LOVE BELVIN

Love's Improbable Possibility series:

Love Lost, Love UnExpected, Love UnCharted & Love Redeemed

THE LETTER

A LOVE'S IMPROBABLE POSSIBILITY *SHORT STORY*

LOVE BELVIN

<u>*Waiting to Breathe* series</u>:

Love Delayed & Love Delivered

<u>*Love's Inconvenient Truth*</u> (*Standalone*)

The Connecticut Kings series:

*Love in the Red Zone, *Love on the Highlight Reel, *Determining Possession, End Zone Love, Love's Ineligible Receiver, *Pass Interference, Love's Encroachment, & *Offensive Formations (*by Christina C. Jones)*

Wayward Love series:

The Left of Love, The Low of Love & The Right of Love

Love in Rhythm & Blues series

The Rhythm of Blues & The Rhyme of Love

LOVE IN RHYTHM & BLUES series

The Sadik series

He Who Is a Friend, He Who Is a Lover & He Who Is a Protector

The Muted Hopelessness series:

My Muted Love, Our Muted Recklessness, & Our Reckless Hope

the *Muted Hopelessness* series

The Prism series:

Mercy, Grace, & *The Promise*

Low Love, Low Fidelity (Standalone)

~EXTRA

You can find Love Belvin at <u>www.LoveBelvin.com</u>
Facebook @ <u>Author - Love Belvin</u>
Twitter <u>@LoveBelvin</u>
Goodreads: <u>Love Belvin</u>
and on Instagram <u>@LoveBelvin</u>

Join the #TeamLove mailing list on my website to keep up with the happenings!

<u>Click here (with WiFi) to join!</u>

www.ingramcontent.com/pod-product-compliance
Lightning Source LLC
Chambersburg PA
CBHW021213260626
47172CB00002B/405